PRAISE FOR

SHIMMER AND BURN

"Taranta's writing is nearly poetic and casts its own sort of magic. Readers should brace themselves for the last few chapters."
—*Romantic Times*

"Taranta takes all the best lessons from the Hunger Games and the Game of Thrones series and expertly uses them to create a dark, violent fantasy world. This first tale . . . reveres its strong female characters and does not shy from the gritty, gruesome realities of uneasy alliances. . . . Readers will be swept up as the story unfolds. Against a sea of vastly similar offerings, Taranta's story rises above the competition in exciting and unique ways."
—*VOYA*

"In a crowded fantasy field, Taranta's story stands out for its mature writing, inventive and scary creatures (and even scarier humans), and complex and often ruthless characters."
—*Publishers Weekly*

"Taranta's debut opens the door to a magical new world filled with adventure, strong characters, and an intriguing plot. . . . Readers can eagerly anticipate more of Faris's story and adventures."
—*Booklist*

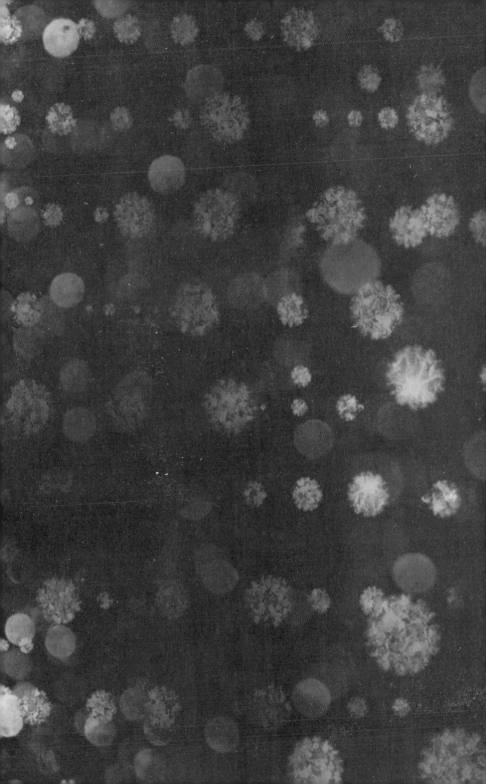

SHIMMER AND BURN

MARY TARANTA

MARGARET K. McELDERRY BOOKS

New York   London   Toronto   Sydney   New Delhi

MARGARET K. McELDERRY BOOKS

1230 Avenue of the Americas, New York, New York 10020

Text copyright © 2017 by Mary Taranta

Cover photo-illustration by Sonia Chaghatzbanian

Cover stock photographs copyright © 2016 by Arcangel Images

MARGARET K. McELDERRY BOOKS is a trademark of Simon & Schuster, Inc.

For information about special discounts for bulk purchases, please contact Simon & Schuster Special Sales at 1-866-506-1949 or business@simonandschuster.com.

The Simon & Schuster Speakers Bureau can bring authors to your live event. For more information or to book an event, contact the Simon & Schuster Speakers Bureau at 1-866-248-3049 or visit our website at www.simonspeakers.com.

Also available in a Margaret K. McElderry Books hardcover edition

Interior design by Irene Metaxatos

Cover design by Sonia Chaghatzbanian

The text for this book was set in Baskerville.

Manufactured in the United States of America

First Margaret K. McElderry Books paperback edition August 2018

10 9 8 7 6 5 4 3 2 1

The Library of Congress has cataloged the hardcover edition as follows:

Names: Taranta, Mary, author.

Title: Shimmer and burn / Mary Taranta.

Description: First edition. | New York : Margaret K. McElderry Books, [2017] | Summary: "To save her sister's life, Faris is tasked with smuggling magic into a plague-ridden neighboring kingdom"—Provided by publisher.

Identifiers: LCCN 2016031758 | ISBN 9781481471992 (hardcover) | ISBN 9781481472005 (pbk) | ISBN 9781481472012 (eBook)

Subjects: | CYAC: Sisters—Fiction. | Magic—Fiction. | Smuggling—Fiction. | Plague—Fiction. | Social classes—Fiction. | Fantasy.

Classification: LCC PZ7.1.T383 Shi 2017 | DDC [Fic]—dc23 LC record available at https://lccn.loc.gov/2016031758

MOM AND DAD, THIS ONE WAS ALWAYS
MEANT FOR YOU.

AND FOR EUGENE: STEADY AS A STAR.

One

MY MOTHER TRIED TO KILL ME THE NIGHT THE GUARDS ARRESTED her.

Only six years old at the time, I remember her earnest face bent over mine, a hand laced through my own. She smelled strange that night, like damp stone and cold earth, and I wondered where she'd been to smell so unfamiliar. "What are you doing?" I finally asked.

"Saying good-bye," she whispered back. "I love you, Faris. Remember that."

What I remember is the look on her face as her blade sank into my chest and my blood darkened her hands. No remorse when I screamed, only fierce determination—as though I were a complicated pattern to be embroidered on the dresses my father sold downstairs.

What I remember is the way it *felt*, to be torn apart, like an imperfect seam.

Within minutes, guards arrived and dragged my mother into the street. Within days, she was dead. And then the guards returned, but this time with torches as they overturned my father's small shop, destroying everything in their search for the gold they claimed she'd stolen from the king.

They never found it. Nobody did. The only thing my mother left behind that night was my broken heart, awoken to the idea that there was gold in this world, that there was *more*.

And she had wanted it more than she wanted me.

Half an inch lower and she could have pinned my heart to my spine. Instead, she only nicked a bone and left a scar threaded with questions. If I press hard enough, I can feel it shifting, like a bad memory trapped beneath the skin. It aches sometimes, when it's cold.

It bites sometimes, when I'm angry.

Tonight it's nothing more than a bump beneath my fingers as I rub absent lines across my collarbone, staring at the Herald Mountains that cradle the sky above us.

"There aren't any stars," Thaelan says, leaning back on his hands beside me, his feet crossed at the ankles. "How can you make a wish if there aren't any stars?"

Dropping my hand, I mimic his stance, a half-empty bottle of barleywine clutched between my knees. We're seated at the edge of the shallows, a series of oval puddles framed by narrow rings of earth meant to hold rainwater for irrigating the farming terraces that stair-step below us. Mist rises from the gorge on the other side of the kingdom's outer wall, cloaking everything with a veil of white and moonlit blue shadow. Candlelight glitters through the gloom behind us, only a few pinpricks here along the Brim where oil and candles cost too dear, but multiplying the higher the kingdom rises and the richer its citizens become until it reaches the brightest lights of all, shining from the castle floating in the clouds.

"Here," I say, pointing toward the castle with my chin, "just use one of those."

"You can't wish on a window," Thaelan says darkly, head rolling toward me.

"It's my birthday. I can do whatever I want."

"It's not your birthday until midnight. *Eight past* midnight, actually, so until then, Faris Locke, you are held to the same rules as always. No wishing on windows."

I grin as he kisses me. "Your lips are cold," he chides, inviting me under his dark wool cloak—sage green trimmed in silver with a clumsy pattern of ivy and stags. It's Queen Robetta's design; it's Queen Robetta's hobby, dictating the fashions of the court and distributing the patterns to the seamstresses of the kingdom to replicate. It's the one thing she's allowed to control; everything else belongs to her husband, King Perrote.

I tug the hem of the cloak over my knee and rub my thumb across the scar of embroidery. My father says her stags look like underfed mountain goats, and I have to agree.

It was my father who sewed me closed that night ten years ago. Nine perfect stitches, the last he'd ever do.

"We should have met somewhere warmer," I say.

"You know I have to be careful."

"You have to be secret." My voice tightens. "Your fiancée might see."

"Hey." He bumps me with his shoulder. "You said you didn't mind coming here."

I duck my head, picking at the grass by my hip. I didn't mind coming here when I was twelve and still believed I would marry Thaelan, back when our inequality was an abstract concept easy to ignore. But there are no excuses to play pretend anymore: The son of nobility does not marry the daughter of a drunkard and a thief.

Music plays in the distance, from the merchant tier of housing known as the Ridge, undercut with warm laughter and the sound of footfalls in a steady tempo of dancing. I try not to listen, to envy. The only dances in the Brim are the kind that end with compromised virtues in dark alleys and dirty rooms.

"What does Ellis's dress look like?" I ask, as if that will alleviate the ache inside me for the life I'll never have.

He groans. "Ellis could be standing naked at the altar and my eyes will still be on you."

No, they won't, because I won't be there. "Don't do that," I say.

"It's your birthday," he says darkly, before taking a drink of wine. "I can't tell you any lies on your birthday."

It's masochism, the way we sit so close I can smell the leather of the doublet he wears and the sweat that salts his skin from an afternoon training. Two years ago, he joined the ranks of the unsworn Guard, a mandatory military commitment demanded by the king from every noble son of Brindaigel. Now almost seventeen, Thaelan's training is complete and he will swear his oaths soon, receiving the king's brand above his heart. With it, a spell woven through his skin with invisible threads of the king's magic tying Thaelan to the crown, ensuring a lifetime of forced loyalty to King

Perrote and his ever-growing list of heirs. We're up to seven now, and between their marriages, another six spares. The Dossel Family line of succession stretches like the wall around our kingdom, built solid and never ending.

Holding back a sigh, I rummage through my bag and emerge with two sallow limes, the rind so thin the bitter flesh shines through. "I brought you something."

Thaelan frowns. "Where'd you get those?"

From a distracted merchant with enough to spare. "I found them."

"Faris."

"It's my birthday," I say with a faltering smile tainted with guilt. I should have stuck to apples. Some guards turn a blind eye if you pocket a few battered windfalls while you work. But it's been days since I've seen Thaelan and I wanted to show off with something exotic. "You can't yell at me on my birthday."

He pulls the limes out of my hand and brandishes them, his disappointment metallic, like blood in my mouth. "One day you're going to get caught and then the king's executioner will cut off your hands. And I need these hands." His accusation softens as he drops the limes to take my hands in his. Kissing my knuckles, he says, "I can't conquer the world without them."

My breath catches in my throat as he turns my palms over and kisses my wrists and each of my fingertips. His hazel eyes tilt toward mine, cloudy beneath the fringe of his lashes. "Promise me you won't steal anymore," he says.

"I promise," I whisper, wanting him so much it feels like a sin.

He draws me closer and kisses me with his own cold lips sweetened by wine: He wants me too. But there are rules to our stolen moments, an unspoken boundary. There are too many unmarried mothers in the Brim left abandoned to fate while their noble lovers never look back. We defy expectation by resisting temptation. It's the way the gods like it: vice balanced by virtue.

"And anyway, I'm supposed to bring *you* gifts." Reaching into his cloak, Thaelan pulls out a scrap of vellum, smoothing it across his leg. "Happy birthday," he says.

Blood hits low at the base of my throat, a sudden frantic dance of adrenaline as I take the paper from him. "You found a new tunnel," I say, already an expert at reading his codes.

He fights to suppress a smile. "Yes."

I trace the path in my imagination, but I'm too eager and skip ahead, losing my place. I have to stop myself and slow down, reading it again.

"Thaelan," I say, eyes lifting to his, my voice rising in question. "This tunnel doesn't end."

"Oh, it ends," he says, "when you reach a staircase carved from stone, leading to a hallway full of marble and columns. And just beyond . . ." His voice drops and he barely breathes the words at my ear though they echo through me like a shout: "Avinea is still out there."

I fumble to press the paper back against his chest as the hairs on my neck stand on end. Despite the dark, despite the cold, I cast a look around us for witnesses, eavesdroppers—maybe one of the king's shadow crows, golems with smoky wings that circle the skies above, trailing embers and drifting ash in their wake. Controlled by scrying members of the king's council, they watch Brindaigel with beady eyes, searching for infraction. And this paper Thaelan holds, this is treason.

Thirty years ago, a civil war divided the neighboring kingdom of Avinea between its rightful king, Merlock, and his younger brother, Corthen. The magic used to fight the war stagnated in the aftermath of Merlock's victory and subsequent disappearance, producing a plague that decimated everything it touched. In an act of self-preservation, King Perrote moved the very mountains around Brindaigel to form a barrier between us and Avinea. It keeps the plague out.

It keeps us in.

Once a year, on the Day of Excision, the king sends his shadow crows over the mountains to survey the world beyond. One by one they return as the kingdom waits for Perrote to emerge with the formal conclusion. Every year it's the same.

Avinea is dead and the plague has destroyed everything.

So with no other choice, Brindaigel hibernates another year, grateful that our king had the foresight to protect us. Of course, Avinea's not the only thing out there. There's a whole world still, separated from the plague by oceans and mountains and continents. But to leave would be to question the king; it would be calling him a liar when he says that we're better off here, crowded in against ourselves, fighting for a broken scrap of sky and a chance to breathe.

Some have tried. Either over the mountains or around them, dropping ladders made of rope into the gorge, following goat paths to the peaks above. Most are young, desperate, eager for a life of their own.

All are dead now, executed where they were caught, their bodies left as warnings: Nobody leaves Brindaigel.

But we will.

Six months ago, Thaelan told me about the tunnels, offshoots of the castle dungeons, buried beneath our feet. He discovered the first by accident, the second by chance, and now, he knows almost all of them by heart. Old supply routes, we guessed, and it became an addiction: Where did they lead? Why weren't they closed, and who uses them now? Every chance he gets, Thaelan risks his life and his family's reputation by sneaking out of the training barracks and making maps, marking the dead ends and the twisty forks, searching for a glimpse of the world we've been told no longer exists. A world where a girl like me could love a boy like him and nobody could stop us.

"There was water," Thaelan says now, tracing the edge of my chin with his knuckles. "And sand, and sky. I could see the stars." He pauses, almost breathless, his fingertips soft against my neck. "I could see the moon."

On instinct, I rock my head back as he steals a kiss against my throat. "You saw the moon?" I ask faintly. Our mountain borders cut off all but a small glimpse of the sky and we only ever see the moon for two weeks out of every four, when it rises far enough east. I've read that it grows fat every month, bloated enough to color the world with a silver light, but not here. Not in Brindaigel. "You saw all that and you still came back?"

Threading his fingers through my hair, Thaelan leans his forehead to mine. "In three weeks, I swear my oath to the king," he says. "He'll bind me to this city, Faris. To him. But I choose you. I choose you and Avinea and whatever we find out there, for better or worse, until death—or the plague—do us part."

It's not the first proposal he's made me, but tonight, it feels more potent—more possible—than any before. "And then what?"

"And then we will have one hundred beautiful babies," he says with a grin, "and all of them will have three heads and five arms."

"It's the plague," I say. "They wouldn't have any arms at all."

His smile turns sad, thumb tracing the curve of my cheek. Exhaling softly, he pulls back, tucking the paper into his doublet. "Look," he says, nodding to the sky. "There's your wish."

A single star emerges from the mist, flickering like the eye of Rook, God Above, whose ambition and courage drew him out of the dark caverns of the earth and into the temples of the sky. We praise him for leaving everything behind, including his sister Tell, the Goddess Below. And we scorn Tell for being too weak—too complacent—to follow his lead.

I accepted my mother's decision to choose gold over me; I accepted the king's orders to destroy my father's shop and my father's life, until the only job he could find for his nimble fingers was in picking rocks from the farming terraces and lifting tankards of ale. Thaelan's betrothal, my life in the Brim, even the mountains that cradle us and keep the rest of the world at bay: I have never argued these facts or this fate.

Is that courage or is that submission?

"There was another raid last night," I say.

"I heard," Thaelan says absently, rubbing dirt from his boots with a frown.

I bite the inside of my cheek; raids are routine to him. A duty to be performed before dinner. "He was our age," I say. The teen-aged son of a man executed for slander over fifteen years ago. Sin begets sin, Perrote had claimed, and bad blood must be cut off at the root to keep it from spreading. But I walk soft through the streets and I hear the whispers that live in the shadows: The kingdom is overcrowded, and so long as there are Brim rats enough to bite back, Perrote will mask his true intentions beneath a banner of overdue justice.

In reality, he's just making room.

Thaelan looks up at my tone, eyebrows furrowed. "Did you know him?"

"No," I say, but I know the warning behind the raid, and the promise it carries for people like me. My mother failed to kill me ten years ago. The king's executioner will have much better aim. "Let's leave."

"Of course," he says, still focused on his boots.

"Right now. Before the tunnels shift again and the path disappears."

"That's only happened once and it was probably just my nerves." He snorts, shaking his head and sitting back. "Those walls are so full of magic, I swear, sometimes I hear them breathing."

"I'm serious," I say.

"Right." He runs a hand through his hair and gives me a sidelong look.

"Thaelan." Shifting, I kneel in front of him, resting my hands on his knees, forcing him to look at me. He does so with familiar resignation: We've played this scene before, and he already knows how it ends.

But I am brave tonight, a true disciple of Rook. "I'm going to marry you," I say, and when I kiss him, it's like drinking too much barleywine: I feel woozy, light headed, completely off balance, and yet, grounded as the mountains themselves with my certainty. "Tonight," I repeat against his mouth, and it thrills down my spine before guilt seizes it mid-shiver. "Cadence," I say suddenly, as I should have said from the beginning. She's only eleven years old and I can't leave her here, not with a father who often forgets to come home, who forgets to bring food, who forgets to say that he loves her.

Who forgets sometimes if he does.

"She's coming with us," Thaelan says without hesitation, and I know he never considered otherwise.

Ignited, I cradle Thaelan's face between my hands and kiss him the way I've never let myself kiss him before: full of hunger and greed and hope, all the virtue in me and all the vice, balanced on my lips.

And he wants both sides of me.

Moments later, we run hand in hand, giddy, laughing our way through the darkened streets of the Brim. When we wake Cadence, her blue eyes flash in the dim gloom of our bedroom, widening as she recognizes the face beside mine.

"Thaelan!" She throws back her blanket and bounds into his arms. "Mother of a sainted virgin, where have you been!?"

"Cadence," I say, alarmed. Embarrassed. She runs wild when I'm working in the fields, and I can't cure her of the vulgarities she learns from the other street rats.

But Thaelan laughs and she shoots me a triumphant smirk. "What do you know about sainted virgins?" he teases.

Her eyes flick to the statue of Charity balanced on the window-sill—a patron saint of virtue, and an apparent virgin like so many have been. It's a cheap reminder to temper the greed that lives inside me, to deny the same vice that sent my mother to her grave.

I stole it, like almost everything else in this room.

"Well, I know they have mothers," she says, and grins when Thaelan laughs again. "Which means I can't ever be one."

"Sweet Saint Cade," Thaelan says, ruffling her hair.

I don't laugh with them, annoyed. Wounded. She was too young to remember anyone but me taking care of her, and I know I don't have soft hands and sweet songs and spools of thread for Cadence to stack in wobbly castles across the floor the way a mother would.

But Cadence doesn't have nine stitches above her heart, either.

"Look," she says, launching herself off the bed, wielding an imaginary sword in one hand, her other fisted behind her back for balance, the way Thaelan taught her.

I sidestep her and begin packing our sparse belongings into a canvas bag. Clothes, a handful of coins, a book that once belonged to my mother—the only thing of hers small enough for me to hide from the guards the night they burnt our house to the ground.

"Lunge, parry, block, and thrust!" She grunts as her arm cuts the motions with a hiss, nightgown stretched wide as her legs shift into place.

"You've been practicing!" Thaelan grins. "Good girl! I hereby promote you to first mate."

"Captain," she corrects, straightening. "First mates are for pirates and I'm going to be a solider. Just like you."

She used to beg me to buy her pirate stories from a peddler who remembered life before the war, when the oceans surrounding our island continent were filled with merchants and mercenaries. But pirates lost their appeal the same time I did, which is just as well. The peddler and his stories disappeared months ago.

"And then," Cadence continues, all seriousness, "I'm going to marry you."

Thaelan arches his eyebrows and meets my eyes over the top of her head.

"Get dressed," I say, turning her toward our bureau. That's another conversation for another day.

"Are we moving again?" Cadence tears off her nightgown after confirming Thaelan can't see her from behind the bedsheet I hold between us—to ensure that I'm not peeking, either. But I do peek as she struggles into her dress, mourning the bones that show through her skin when she bends forward. Like its limes, the Brim grows its children stilted; too much dirt and not enough sunlight.

"Something like that," I say, buttoning the back of her dress as she holds her tangled curls up and out of the way. I've barely finished before she twists out of reach, grabbing Thaelan's hand instead of my own. She's too big but he still swings her on his back, leading the charge downstairs, into the night.

Thaelan boldly marches through the street whereas I resist the urge to stick to the shadows as we head into the sleepier merchant neighborhood of the Ridge, to a narrow alley hidden from any shadow crows by the close-knit corners of the buildings that frame its length. Setting Cadence down, Thaelan casts a glance over his shoulder before he pries open a drainage grate. After waiting a beat to ensure no one heard, he turns to me, hand outstretched and an expectant smile on his face.

All at once, I realize what we're doing. Cadence stands above a sewer drain in the middle of the night while I clutch our entire life in a tattered bag. The giddy haze of Thaelan's kisses fades, replaced with the reality of the guards I can hear patrolling the streets.

Thaelan's smile evaporates. He starts to shake his head even before I speak. Standing, he frames my face in his hands. "Don't you dare change your mind," he says. "Not now, not after you said yes."

"But we have nothing—"

"I have everything I need."

"You need more than me," I whisper, plaintive.

He stares at me, expression dimming into that familiar resignation. Jaw clenched, Thaelan releases me and steps back, rubbing his mouth with one hand.

"Tomorrow," I try, forcing my voice bright. "We'll go tomorrow. You'll have time to pack, to plan—"

"I'll go with you," Cadence says. She steps forward. "I'll go right now."

Thaelan exhales softly and reaches for her, hugging her as tight as he can. "I know," he says.

Candlelight twinkles in the distance and my stomach tightens with sudden longing. The women I work with often joke about what life is like in the streets above us, but we never talk about ourselves. There's no point. Life in the Brim holds no mystery. We'll either die slowly like my father, or all at once, like the boy from the raid the night before.

I can't see the stars from here but it doesn't matter: I don't want to make wishes to the gods or their sainted virtues anymore. I want to be strong enough to survive all on my own, and staying in the Brim will kill me. It will kill Cadence.

Decided, I step around Thaelan, lowering myself into the sewer grate, landing with a soft splash in an inch of brackish water. Craning my head, I meet Thaelan's startled gaze.

"Are you coming?" I ask.

His grin is contagious; I can't help but smile back as he lowers Cadence into my arms and splashes down beside us, stretching to drag the grate back into place. Cadence clings to his side and he dutifully carries her as we hurry uphill, toward the castle and its dungeons. As we reach the mouth of the tunnel, a clock chimes in the streets overhead.

Thaelan stops and I slam into his back.

He swears, mumbling an apology for his language as he turns to face me. "Head count," he says, and my stomach falls. In the adrenaline of committing treason, I had forgotten our first enemy: the barracks curfew. Long before Thaelan mapped the tunnels beneath the castle, he mapped all the alleys back to the barracks, timing each route in order to maximize every last second of our stolen time together.

We forgot to watch the clock.

Swallowing hard, Thaelan surveys the tunnel left and right, debating. "We'll just keep going," he says at last, lowering Cadence to her feet. She resists, clutching his arm. "They'll search the taverns and brothels before they think to look down here. We have a head start."

"But they will come looking for you. No. Make head count," I say, almost relieved. "Grab whatever you can and come back. Weapons. Money. Food. You've snuck out a million times before."

Thaelan nods as he pulls me closer, his arm hooked around my neck. "Keep going," he whispers in my ear. "I won't be far behind. I'll find you, Faris." Then, even quieter, "I love you."

I hug him back, tight as I can, before he pulls away. Handing me the crumpled page of coded directions, he pries Cadence loose and backs away, flashing us another smile, the kind that makes his dimple emerge, before he turns away.

Cadence takes a step after him. "Wait! I want to go with you!"

I hold her back, struggling to read the lines on the vellum in the murky light. "You have to stay with me."

"A captain never abandons her general," Cadence growls, breaking loose, splashing out of reach. War blazes across her face as she glares at me: He loves me but didn't even say good-bye to her.

"Cadence," I warn.

She starts running.

Swearing, I follow, Thaelan's directions balled in one hand. "Slow down! You'll get lost!" We both will.

She doesn't listen, calling after Thaelan, her voice too loud, too obvious; someone will hear us. Fear rolls down my back, icy as the water at my feet. "Cadence, *please*."

She disappears ahead of me. My frantic footsteps drown out the sound of hers and I stop, straining for some indication of which way she went. More drainage grates curve ahead, but the branching tunnels around me are all dark, leading across the city and beneath the castle. I glance to the paper in my fist, useless now, without my sister.

Mother of a sainted virgin.

Biting the inside of my cheek, I force myself to take a deep breath, to calm down, to *listen*. Water splashes ahead of me, but it's steady, pouring in from somewhere else. To my right, an irregular tempo. Footsteps.

Relieved, I turn the corner, bracing my hand to the wall as I peer into a shroud of darkness. "Cadence?"

A match strikes and I flinch away, holding a hand against the light. A face sharpens into view. A young man, with bright blue eyes and dark hair that falls forward, skimming the sharp angle of his cheek.

Alistair Pembrough. The king's executioner.

Fear freezes me in place. Since inheriting the position last winter, Alistair has rarely made an appearance beyond the castle walls, but his reputation permeates every inch of the city. This is the boy who grew up in these tunnels, furtive as a shadow, the boy born to kill. When his eyes lock with mine above the flickering light, something flashes across his face. Recognition.

How can he possibly know who I am?

His match burns out as Cadence finally answers my call. Her voice is muffled but shrill, not far ahead. A lower baritone joins her, low and pleading. Thaelan. He came back for her, which means he's not going to make head count.

We have to run.

Cadence isn't the only one to benefit from Thaelan's training, but temporarily robbed of my night vision, my attack on Alistair is blind, instinctive.

Accurate. I hit something soft and Alistair grunts in surprise.

Emboldened, I strike again, higher than before, connecting to something better. Bone.

His hands skate past my arm and tighten around the strap of my bag. "Wait—"

Abandoning the bag, I run headlong into darkness, ignoring Alistair's shouts behind me. The ground slopes up and light appears ahead, soft and diffusive. The dungeon. Thaelan, Cadence, Avinea— Guards.

I skid to a stop before they notice me. Pressing myself flat to the wall, I backtrack until I reach a tunnel that splits to the left at the level of my knees, pulling myself up and out of sight. Moments later, Alistair sloshes past me, a hand pressed to his nose, my bag around his shoulder.

"There're too many tunnels," one of the guards calls by way of greeting.

"Send the rats," another suggests.

"Whatever you have to do," Alistair snaps in return.

Shadow rats. The alley-dwelling cousins of the king's shadow crows. If they find us, the guards will descend. If they bite us, we'll be marked by magic and the king's provost will sniff us out no matter where we hide.

Either way, I can't stay here.

I double back the way I came, but when I reach the sloping tunnel punctuated with sewer grates, I pause, mind shuffling through Thaelan's maps. Where would he go? Where do *I* go? His directions got lost somewhere in the dark between here and Alistair Pembrough, and wandering into these tunnels without some guidance would be suicide.

Downhill, I think; find an exit. Thaelan has Cadence and he'll know what to do. He'll know where to find me, unless—

Unless it was easier for them to keep going. What if they're already on their way to Avinea?

What if they escape and I don't?

I stop, seized with an envy so sharp it cuts the breath out of me. Turning, I put a hand to the wall, debating the risk of calling for Thaelan and alerting the guards.

But then I hear them coming. The shadow rats.

I run, gaining speed as I slope downhill, stopping beneath the first grate I find, but I'm shorter than Thaelan, and my fingertips barely graze the metal. Not good enough.

I keep moving, dodging debris and floating garbage until there, ahead, a slurry of rubble where the tunnel wall has partially collapsed, forming an unsteady stair-step. From there, I'm able to shoulder a grate open and hoist myself up, not even bothering to look for witnesses before I'm scrambling to my knees on the rough cobblestones above. An instant later, shadow rats flood the tunnel below me, their smoldering bodies hissing steam as they charge through the water, herded by a guard with a torch in one hand, a sword in the other.

Shaking, I find my feet and collect my bearings. Alive. Unharmed. Alone.

Thaelan has Cadence, I tell myself. He'll keep her safe. They'll make it to Avinea and one day, I'll find them again. No matter how long it takes.

It doesn't take long.

Within days, Thaelan hangs from the castle walls, cut open and left as carrion for the birds and a warning for the rest of us. Over the next few weeks, guards bolt down every drainage gate in the kingdom and fit iron bars over every open culvert.

We live in a kingdom carved out of stone, protected from the plague through the mercy of our king. But we are also hostages here.

And nobody leaves Brindaigel.

Two

THE WORKHOUSE SITS BACK FROM THE DUSTY ROAD, BROODING AND unnaturally silent. The iron side gate hangs crooked, shrieking on its rusted hinges as I squeeze it open and slip inside. Grass doesn't grow here, in constant shadow of the mountains, and the ground is rocky, cracked, littered with trash and broken clothespins.

I slink around to the back, avoiding the windows along the first floor. Only one light burns in the growing twilight, near the back: Mistress Ebbidens's office, where she perches stiffly in a velvet armchair, clutching a glass of brandy as she nods in conversation with a man whose back is to me. He fills his own seat with skin to spare hanging over either side, a contrast to Mistress Ebbidens's bony, birdlike figure.

A labyrinth of clotheslines fills the backyard, sagging beneath the weight of damp linens and yellowing shirts. Pale, weary faces dart in between the sheets; the only sound is the clicking of wooden pins being shoved into place and the snapping of linens as they're folded over the lines to dry.

Nobody notices me and yet I step lightly all the same, careful as I wind through the maze, searching faces until I find the one I want. My sister stands in the cave of the three-sided laundry shed, dwarfed by a vat of soapy water that rises to her waist, her features dulled by a veil of steam curling through the chilly twilight. Like the others, she's dressed in a starched gray dress with matching apron, both freckled with bleach. Her blond curls are matted to her head and my fingers flex against my legs, desperate to comb through her hair, to pull it out of her face and braid it down her back. I even have a ribbon for it hidden away—bright green, the color of spring grass.

Her favorite.

Wetting my lips, casting a glance toward the house, I kneel beside my sister. "Cadence," I say.

She plunges both arms into the hot water, fishing for her next garment. Burns shine on the back of her hands; her knuckles have split and healed and split so many times they've formed permanent scabs. Where her skin isn't red, it's leached unnaturally white from exposure to the chemicals they dump in the water, the perfumes they use to hide the smell of lye.

"Number eight-six-three-nine-one," I whisper.

She looks up, blue eyes glassy, darkened by the spell cast across the bridge of her nose and the tops of her cheeks, fading toward her temple. It hides her freckles the way the mud used to after she fought with the Brim boys who challenged her to races and then got angry when they lost.

"Yes?" she parrots.

But there's no fight in her now. There's nothing at all.

My smile wavers as I touch her hair, my fingers catching in her tangles. They'll cut it off before they'll ever bother to comb it, and sell it to a wig maker. I should have brought the ribbon.

Reaching into my bag, I pull out a pear. "Last harvest of the season," I say. "I almost got caught this time."

I force my voice light, breezy: I make it a joke. The truth is, I almost lost my position without wages. The truth is, I almost lost my hands. Luckily, the guard who saw me stealing fruit from the wagons at the end of the day also saw the half-kronet in my palm and vice outweighed his virtue.

Not all the guards are so imbalanced.

You promised me, Thaelan whispers, but I shove his admonishment aside with a jolt of guilt. What good are promises to the dead?

There's no reaction from Cadence. Not a flicker of recognition or pleasure or *life* in her face. The king's spell turns all of the children into mindless golems of skin and bone, stuffed with soap and chemicals. They know nothing but work and aching bones and a room upstairs crammed with twenty-eight other children serving the punishment of their parents.

Or their sisters.

It's my fault she's here. I'm the one who left her behind to be found by an executioner and an army of rats. Every day following Thaelan's death, I haunted the dungeon gates like a ghost, watching. Waiting. Fingers curled around the cold iron bars, knowing that my sister was somewhere beyond those walls, beyond my reach, terrified that her final thoughts would be spent on the same question my mother left me: *Why?* Why didn't I come for her when she called in the sewers?

Fourteen nights spent in prayer to the gods, to the saints, to any virgin willing to barter with me for her safety; fourteen mornings with my heart in my throat as I approached the castle, never knowing if her body would be the next to hang in warning, or if her age—if her *king*—would grant her leniency.

But if I expected mercy for a child from Alistair Pembrough, he soon corrected me.

Cadence wasn't strung from the walls; she was marched on display with all the other liars and thieves and criminals too young for Alistair to murder. He stood by, arrogant and impervious while King Perrote called for family to step forward and claim their fallen children, to spare their innocence by shouldering their guilt and accepting their punishment.

Most of them were orphans already, children of the street who knew nobody would speak for them. They didn't even bother hoping otherwise, their faces set, a fierce and tremulous defiant as they suffered through the aching silence that followed the king's call. But when Cadence was dragged forward, her eyes skated across the crowd, hopeful, expectant, waiting for me to speak. To save her.

And I didn't do it.

I couldn't. I'm sixteen now, old enough to die. And if I died, so would she, eventually, either out on the streets or in somebody's bed. The time Cadence spends in the workhouse is time for me to figure out a way to save us both.

So I didn't say a word, even as the silence stretched into finality, even as her face crumpled with resignation, even as my heart broke, loud enough the whole world could hear.

Even now, I struggle to tame the guilt—the *hate*—that rises like bile in my throat. It's wasted here, in my stolen moment with Cadence, better suited for tonight, when I need the ammunition.

Dropping the pear into the pocket of her apron, I kiss my sister's knuckles before smearing a liniment salve across her chapped skin. We have matching bruises now, but while hers come from working, mine come from fighting, from hitting until I bleed. "I've got a match tonight," I say, like nothing is wrong and everything's perfect. "If I win, maybe tomorrow I'll have enough money to bring you home."

Home. The word hitches, foreign on my tongue.

Cadence stares past me, impassive to my promises. To my lies. The fading sunlight throws shadows across her face, and I push the hair away from her eyes. *Wake up,* I think helplessly, but she needs magic for that, and the king keeps it all locked in his castle.

"I love you," I whisper, and it hurts. I tell myself that it's better this way, that Cadence doesn't remember me, or home, or what she used to be, but it's a coward's truth. It's only better for me that her eyes are dull, devoid of recognition.

Devoid of accusation.

"Go back to work, number eight-six-three-nine-one," I say, and she obeys without question, resuming her scrubbing.

I linger longer than I should, unwilling to leave when I don't know when I'll be back. The last of the harvest means long days stripping the orchards of fruit, and a long queue of hungry people looking for work means short nights to ensure I'm at the head of the pack when the guards hand out positions at dawn.

The back door opens and voices approach—Mistress Ebbidens and her paunchy visitor—and I quickly tuck myself out of sight behind a basket of damp linens. It's not strictly wrong for me to be here—some women come to visit their children, for what good it does—but it is dangerous to risk anyone connecting me to the little girl caught trying to escape through the tunnels. It's the same reason why I still work as a field hand, an anonymous face picked by a guard from the crowd, no interview required. There's no money in the fields, but there are no names, either.

"—choice of candidates," Mistress Ebbidens says, full of phlegm and gravel.

"Someone obedient," the man says, with a watery laugh that turns into a soft cough. "A girl, of course." The top of his head appears over the rise of the linens, thick dark hair slicked back, almost flat. By contrast, Mistress Ebbidens's hair rises like a frothy column of whipped cream.

They stroll the yard and the man simpers over the children, patting their heads or examining their faces by tucking his pudgy hand beneath their chins. They accept his attention like they accept their orders, wordlessly and without a spark of complaint.

When they approach Cadence, the man's eyes sharpen; his smile spreads like oil. "Well, hello," he says, and I pull tighter into the corner, out of sight, fists pressed against my stomach. "What a pretty face."

"Orphaned," Mistress Ebbidens says.

"Excellent," says the man. "Families cause unnecessary interference."

She's not orphaned, I want to scream. She still has me and she has her father, for all he's worth. He wouldn't even come with me that day in the square. "There's no point," he had said, haunted eyes and trembling fingers reaching for his drink. "She's already dead."

Just like him, I had thought as he signaled for another. "You could speak for her," I had said, with a stupid hope that her life meant more than his. "You could save her."

My father had looked at me, gray as the stone walls behind him, a man who had never fought a day in his life. "When have I ever saved anyone?" he'd asked.

"What's this?"

I risk a glance around the linens and see the man examining the pear from Cadence's apron. He cradles it between his fingers and holds it to the light like an exquisite glass of wine. "I'm not her only admirer," he says with a laugh that sends chills down my spine.

Mistress Ebbidens doesn't laugh with him. Her eyes narrow, lips pursed in a frown as she glances around the yard, suspicious: All visitors are supposed to sign in. "She turns twelve on the king's birthday," she says, turning back toward the house with an unspoken command.

The man rolls the pear between his hands. "Worth the wait," he says, before he takes a bite, juice dripping down his chin. "Fruit needs to be ripened."

Rage boils inside me and I dig my fists deeper into my stomach, pinning myself down before I can lunge out and rip his disgusting eyes out of his head to keep him from looking at my sister like she's already his.

Laughing, still eating the pear, the man follows Mistress Ebbidens back to the house. Bending over my knees, I hold my breath until I hear their footsteps recede and the door shuts again, returning the yard to its eerie quiet. Only then do I allow myself to breathe and move out of hiding, to confirm that Cadence is as oblivious to the man's threat as she was to my promises.

I could take Cadence right now and run. At my command, she would wrap her arms around my neck and I would carry her over the crumbling wall that edges the back of the property. We would disappear like shadows into the Brim and share an hour, maybe a night of stolen freedom. But the magic that hides her freckles ties back to the king, same as the loyalty spells on all his soldiers. If she goes missing, all he has to do is twitch a single thread of magic, like a spider sitting fat in his web, and his provost will follow the trail straight to her. To me. No mercy for her age this time; we'd both be carved up like Thaelan, our blood painting a warning to all those below.

Nobody leaves Brindaigel.

I kiss Cadence one last time, hugging a bag of bones that jars against my hip without any warmth, any feeling.

"Avinea is still out there, Cade," I whisper to her. "And I swear to you we'll find it."

Three

BLOOD IN MY MOUTH, SALT IN MY EYES, AND THE SOUND OF encouragement shouted by a ring of featureless men clutching paper bets in their fists. I grin, savoring it all.

My opponent throws a punch but it goes wild, above my shoulder. I duck out of the way and slam her hard in the ribs, knocking her back a step. *Lunge, parry, block, and thrust* echoes in my head, and while I have no sword, I have my hands, and they can be just as lethal.

I manage a sharp strike to her temple before I dart back to catch my breath. The girl lurches forward, teeth bared and eyes wild: All rules forgotten as she attacks for the win.

I welcome the battle.

We're nothing but shoulders and knees and strangled curses as we roll across the floor, scratching, grabbing, hurting. The girl disappears and it's the oil-slick smile of the man who wants to buy

Cadence; it's Alistair Pembrough, King Perrote, the walls around Brindaigel that fall beneath my blows. Hate feeds my adrenaline. Hate and self-loathing and a need for blood, for punishment.

Panting, I pin the girl with a knee to her hip. Blood smears her features and the eyes that stare up at me are swollen, bright with pain and a needling look of fury. She grabs my hair—kept loose, the way the men like it—and I raise my fist for one last strike, inwardly apologizing to her pretty face and her desperate hunger, as familiar as my own. But only one of us can win, and I want it more than she does.

The girl releases my hair and shakes her head, palms flashed toward me. Claiming defeat.

"You're done," a voice barks. Palif, a bartender, hauls me back as another man shoulders the girl to her feet. Men jeer at her loss, throwing wadded up betting slips in disgust. Palif presses coins into the girl's hands—a meager fifth of what I'll earn as the winner, barely worth the bruises in the morning—before she's spun into the waiting arms of a frowning young man who hurries her outside.

Someone offers me an arm up and I accept, touching my nose to find it dripping blood. A handkerchief is shoved in my direction and I rock my head back, staggering toward a table.

Men rattle their own tables with satisfaction as Reed, the organizer, pays out their wins. Pinching my nose, I slump in my seat, heart aching with adrenaline, with fear, with the feeling of absolute power.

And lurking underneath, the feeling of absolute helplessness. With every high comes the inevitable, unavoidable low. Pain layered upon pain; there's no escaping the broken heart inside me.

Someone buys me a beer that I accept with a grunt of acknowledgment, lowering my head just long enough to take a drink. By the time Reed approaches me with my bag and my percentage, a headache's arrived, thick and blistering.

"Am I good?" I ask.

Reed clicks coins together in his palm, expression grim. Wordlessly, he drops the money on the table and I pocket it without looking, as if ashamed. Maybe I am, profiting from my anger, legitimizing my hate.

But not enough to stop.

Leaning my elbows into the table, I curl bloody fingers around the beer glass and roll it along its bottom rim, watching leftover suds slink down the sides. "How is he?" I ask, and despite myself, my eyes scan the crowded bar, searching for my father's back among those that fill the shadows.

"Alive," says Reed.

"And he's good?" I already know the answer: My father's tab comes straight out of my winnings before they ever reach me, and I had coins to spare tonight.

"He's good," Reed says anyway.

I nod, sniffing back a runner of snot and blood. "So is she," I say, standing, dragging the strap of my bag over my shoulder. "In case he asks." My eyes briefly meet Reed's before they dart away. I can't bear the looks he gives me, the pity.

"He never asks," says Reed.

"Tell him anyway."

"Tell him yourself."

I scowl in reply, pulling my hair over my shoulder. He knows my father hasn't spoken to me since I told him that it was my fault Cadence was caught in the tunnels, that it's my fault she's locked away with bleeding fingers and empty eyes and no memory of her own name. I pay his tab to keep him here, drunk, so he doesn't feel the need to ever come home to me, angry.

Wadding up the bloody handkerchief, I shove it in the pocket of my skirt. "What do you have open tomorrow night?"

"Nothing," he says.

I look at him, pressing my bleeding knuckles to my mouth, calmed by the metallic taste. "I saw your lists when I came in. What do you have?"

"Nothing for you," says Reed. "That"—he tips his chin toward the fighting ring—"is not what I pay for."

"That's what your patrons pay for," I say hotly. "Nobody wants a clean fight."

"But they expect a fair one." He shifts his weight, arms folding over his chest. "You're going to kill somebody one of these days. Or you're going to get yourself killed. And it's not going to happen here."

My teeth clench, biting back my rising anger. "I had it under control—"

"Find somewhere else to fight."

"Everywhere else wants sixty percent."

"Nobody else knows why you're doing this," he returns. "Nobody else knows your father."

"You can't stop me," I say. "I barely make a tretka working the fields. I need this money!" I need this *power*, this feeling of being in control of something, even if it's only how much pain I can withstand.

"He's already lost one of his daughters—"

"She's not dead!"

Heads turn toward us and I scowl away the curious stares and whispers. Reed sighs, rocking his head back. He was a fighter too, once, and his body still bears the memory of that strength. The inner anger. "You can't save anyone making ten tretkas a night," he says at last.

The beer sizzles in my head, watery but strong, and I suddenly crave more of it, enough to float down the streets of the Brim and over the wall of the city, out into the gorge.

But beer costs money.

I stare at Reed's chin, the thin lips half hidden beneath his mustache. "Maybe I could make money upstairs," I say, and my stomach turns just considering it. "You only take fifty percent of that."

"Nobody wants a girl who's going to bite."

"I wouldn't—" I stop, cheeks turning hot. Defy expectation, I think. Thaelan would never forgive me if I chose that path. But he's dead and Cadence isn't. "I need this, Reed," I say, an inch away from begging.

"Go home." Reed turns away, dismissing me.

"Where is that?"

Reed stares down at me, unrepentant. "Not here."

Not here, not there, not anywhere. Like Cadence, I'm an orphan with a family.

I take the long way through the Brim, head bowed and arms clutching my bag to my chest, diffusing my anger in the cool autumn air.

I need that money.

Fifty silver kronets is the king's going rate for an unclaimed orphan in the workhouse. A bargain, they tell me, for someone so young, with so many years of service left in her bones. Fifty silver kronets to repay her debt to the crown, and proof that she's my family, that I have the right to buy her back before she turns twelve and is sold to whoever wants her—with or without the spell of obedience still darkening her eyes.

That man today did not want a little girl to do his laundry.

My throat burns, full of acid, and I hug my bag tighter, trying to press the ache out of my chest, but it only rises higher, lodging beneath my scar where it settles with a familiar itch.

Mist from the gorge banks over the kingdom's walls and worms through the streets, shrouding the rot of the Brim with stretching fingers of white. It mutes my footsteps and dims the sparse oil lamps that burn above my head as I press deeper through the darkened alleys, scaling crumbling walls and balconies, emerging onto the rooftops. It's a whole second city up here, full of twists and alleys of its own—even the occasional black market where pawnbrokers buy and sell from blankets easy to roll up and hide if a shadow crow comes scrying, looking for the king's percentage of the deal.

Cadence used to play up here, while I washed our clothes in the water that filled the clogged gutters. She used to practice out here too, living vicariously through Thaelan as he trained for the Guard, filling her hopes with stories of swords and long-ago wars, when Brindaigel and Avinea stood as allies against the rest of the world.

He and I used to meet up here after she'd gone to bed, only we'd climb even higher, to where the buildings spread apart and we could see the stars. There was never more than a sliver of sky we could blot out with our hands held side to side. Never enough to satisfy the hunger in our hearts.

I don't bother looking for stars tonight as I pick my way toward my current residence, a drafty attic abandoned by its former occupants after their young daughter was caught weaving spells with the magic that holds the mountains in around us.

The king tells us that only he can summon magic from the earth, that it's a divine gift from the gods inherited through blood and birthright. But he leaves out the part about the gods demanding balance in all things, especially power among men. While the king alone can summon magic, there are others—even filthy Brim rats—who can manipulate it once it's loose.

In Avinea, King Merlock embraced these magicians, appointing four apiece as provosts to the touchstones he scattered across his kingdom to adjudicate in his stead. A transferent to siphon magic and dispense it as needed, a spellcaster to weave magic into useful spells, an intuit to track the amount of magic remaining; and an amplifier who could thicken a single thread of magic into a rope. At the start of the war, every one of them turned mercenary, draining the touchstones and selling the magic to Prince Corthen to use against his brother. It was this betrayal by Merlock's magicians that sparked his decision to poison his magic and destroy his kingdom before he abandoned both almost twenty years ago.

Which is why in Brindaigel, King Perrote preemptively kills them all.

Magic does not belong to the people, he reminds us every year, after confirming that our borders must remain closed. Look what happens when a king trusts men and treats them as equals. Only Perrote and one provost can be trusted with that power, and they exercise it absolutely against anyone who demonstrates an inkling of ability. Even little girls too innocent to mean harm.

My blistering headache returns as I slide through the broken window of the attic, breathing in the familiar dusty-damp smell of the rotting wood and stale blankets. There's a comfort to it and, exhausted, I clutch my bag to my chest and lean against the wall, wilting across the hardwood floor until my legs are stretched ahead of me. Head rocked back, I hold my breath and exhale slowly as I close my eyes.

The man with the oil-slick smile grins back at me, flecks of pear dotting his chin.

Jolting upright, I dig through my bag, pulling out my change purse and tipping coins across the floor, catching a kronet before it rolls away. Trembling, I add tonight's copper tretkas to the pile and count, recount, sift through them a final time, determined to make more of the little I have.

Nineteen kronets and thirty tretkas and only two months more to double that if I want to save my sister. She turns twelve at the start of the year, but with no one to say so, she'll celebrate her birthday with the king instead, two months too soon.

A desperate sob wrenches loose and I crush it into silence against my arm. Dirty blond tangles fall across my shoulders and I stare at them in accusation. Why haven't I sold my hair yet? That's another kronet in my hand. Am I that selfish, that vain, to cling to my hair while Cadence suffers? Why? Because Thaelan used to spread it across the grass and tell me it was beautiful?

A board creaks ahead of me. In a flash, I'm on my feet, a hand braced to the wall. The air around me shifts, displaced by an unfamiliar smell.

Cigarettes.

"I don't pay my father's debts," I say, drying my cheeks with the sleeve of my dress. The taste of metal fills my mouth as I edge toward my bedroll and the blade I keep beneath it. "Any business with him can be handled at the Stone and Fern Tavern."

"Liar," a man says, amused.

I hesitate, wary. "Who are you?" I demand, squinting through the gloom.

A shadow draws closer, head and shoulders, and then trousers that fit close to the leg, a manner favored by men who don't need to move fast or move often.

A nobleman.

Ghostly fingers lift a cigarette to lips curled in a smirk. Dark hair and blue eyes and a face that haunts my nightmares. "Hello, Faris," he says.

Alistair Pembrough.

The king's executioner.

Four

I'VE DREAMT ABOUT THIS DAY, PRACTICED FOR IT EVERY NIGHT.

The day I kill the boy who killed Thaelan.

Lunging, I barrel Alistair back, both hands locked around his throat. He stumbles before slamming against the opposite wall, cigarette falling to the floor. We're matched for height, an advantage I exploit as I squeeze, furious that he caught me off guard.

That he saw me crying.

Surprise gives way to a half laugh of incredulity as Alistair grabs for my wrists. I easily block him, sliding an arm across his throat and pinning his hand to the wall by his head. His smile fades. "I'm not here to hurt you," he says, "I'm here to help you."

"Like you helped me that night? Like you helped Thaelan and my sister!?"

"Exactly like I helped you that night," he says. "You think that I couldn't have caught you if I wanted to? I gave you an out, Faris; I gave you a chance."

My knuckles strain around his wrist; a quick snap and I could break it, and the temptation is excruciating. "Where was their chance?"

"I'm an executioner, not a god," he says flatly. "Your sister was screaming loud enough even Perrote could have tracked her in the dark. And blessed Saint Thaelan wouldn't"—he chokes as I apply more pressure against his throat—"leave her behind." He arches an eyebrow, arrogant even as color drains from his face. "He lacked the same survival instincts as you. As me."

Rage explodes through me and I press my entire weight against his. "He was a better man than you will ever be!"

"He was a liar," Alistair wheezes. Sweat breaks out above his lip. "He broke his vows to the Guard, he kissed one girl while betrothed to another, and he turned his back on his family, his commanding officers, his *king*. Saint Thaelan—"

I strike him, hard as I can, loosening my stranglehold in the process. Alistair's head rolls away from my blow and he snorts, using his free hand to tentatively touch the side of his mouth. "Not bad," he says, still rasping. "It certainly earns me money every night down at the Stone and Fern."

My blood turns to ice. He goes to the tavern? He watches me? *Bets* on me with the same money the king paid him for killing Thaelan?

I raise a hand to hit him again. With a practiced move, he twists my arm behind my back, wrestling me to my knees. Dark hair hangs over his eyes "I'm not just a pretty face, Faris; I can fight if that's what you want." Swallowing, he adds, "But I'd rather not spill more blood."

"Then why are you here?" I growl. My nose is bleeding again and I wipe at it, humiliated. I was supposed to be iron, unbreakable, reunited with Alistair Pembrough with a blade in one hand, his throat in the other, and nothing between us but his apologies to eulogize his death.

Instead we've barely begun and he's already taken control.

Releasing me, Alistair snaps a handkerchief from the pocket of his coat and offers it, making a face when I refuse. Sighing, he rakes his hair back into place and adjusts his waistcoat, giving the handkerchief a sour look before his eyes fall to the coins spilled across the floor.

"Is this all you have?" he asks, gesturing. "God Above." Laughing, he picks up a copper tretka and bounces it across his palm. "I didn't even know they made them this small."

I hate him. I hate his arrogance, his entitlement; the birthright that gave him inherent power over a Brim rat like me when I know I'm just as strong.

Rising to my feet, I wipe my nose again, edging toward my bedroll.

"It's not there," he says, dropping the tretka before standing, sliding his hands into his pockets.

Frowning, I nudge the bedroll aside with my boot, confirming: My knife is gone. He's been here long enough to have gone through my things. If he was at the fight tonight, he knows what happened between me and Reed, and yet he waited until now to face me, when he knew I'd be powerless.

When he knew he would win.

Blood echoes in my ears, shivering through my veins until I'm shaking with fury. I force my fingers into fists at my sides, taking a position of defense. I'm battered and I'm bruised but I am not broken, not if this is the only chance I'll have.

The glass from the window.

"Thaelan used to talk about you," Alistair says, and I freeze like a rabbit caught in the terraces. "Never by name, of course; he was too selfish to share that, but then, no name was ever needed. You were perfection to him." He scoffs, shaking his head. "I called him a liar. I knew the girl he was going to marry and she did not have gold hair and pale eyes and skin like velvet. No such creature could exist."

My mouth dries; no such creature does exist. After ten years of working the fields like my father, my skin has never been soft, my hair more dross than any gold, and yet, that was Thaelan's gift: brightening everything and turning the ordinary into more.

Despite resenting the temptation of Alistair's words, I crave more of Thaelan the way I crave the sunlight after too many months of winter. I have all my memories; I want more. The Thaelan I never got to see, hidden in the hours while he trained and played dutiful son.

"But then I saw you that night," Alistair says, and he takes a step closer, hands falling out of his pockets. "Standing in the tunnels, terrified. And I understood." The shadows of the room muddy his eyes. "He was smart to protect you, Faris," he says softly. "To keep your name from me. But your name is my weapon now, and I know exactly how to use it."

The threat chills me with its simplicity. This boy could destroy me with one single story told to the king about a third traitor in those tunnels that night. He could destroy Cadence.

So why hasn't he?

"What do you want?" I ask.

"A chance," he says. "An out. The same I gave you. The same I gave *him*—"

Twisting, I knock out a piece of glass from the broken window behind me and lunge, barreling him to the floor. Pinning him beneath my weight, I clutch the glass in my hand, ignoring the way it bites my own skin, angling it against his throat.

He stares up at me, incredulous. "So then kill me," he says. "That's what you want, isn't it? Cut my throat and settle the score."

"Don't tempt me."

"It's not much of a temptation if you're resisting this easily," he says flatly. Dust settles in his hair; his lip has started bleeding. But he's calm, unresisting, blue eyes blazing even as my own hand shakes, the glass skating between his throat and the collar of his overcoat.

Breathe, I tell myself. *Think.* But I'm exhausted from the fight, bruised inside and out. Shadows spin around me, dulling my vision, dulling my nerve.

I shake away my hesitations, dipping the glass against his skin, drawing a line of ruby blood. This is what I wanted, I remind myself: This is how this ends.

"Thaelan was my friend," Alistair says softly.

The sight of his blood is not as satisfying as I needed it to be, and I stare at it in accusation. Tears flood my eyes. "Then that makes you even more of a monster," I say, voice breaking. "If not my sister, you could have at least saved him."

"How?" At last, a spark of anger to match my own. "What power do you think I have, Faris? Only the king grants innocence, and I assure you, his majesty is stingy in his absolutions. Do you know what this is?" Ignoring the glass at his throat, he rakes back the collar of his shirt, exposing a dark symbol on the soft slope of his chest, above his heart.

It's the king's mark, branded with an iron so hot it cauterizes the flesh and leaves a scar. Threads of magic run between the raised lines of the brand, no more than smoke and shadow, like ink diluted in water. A loyalty oath, linking him to the king.

"I mapped those tunnels long before Thaelan did," Alistair says. "I planned my escape long before he even met you. I was going to be a doctor, Faris; I was going to save people. But then my father died with no other heir and I inherited the family business, and with it, the family obligation to the crown."

Disgust fills his voice as he tenses beneath me. "This oath binds me to the king. If Perrote pulls the right string, he could follow me anywhere I went—even beyond this kingdom. If he cuts the right string, I'm no better than your sister, taking his orders without question." He releases his collar. "I told Thaelan where to look. I warned him that the tunnels shifted. Those tunnels were mine and I gave them to *him*. To *you*. You're not the only one who wants out."

Grabbing my wrist, he wrestles me onto my back. The glass slips from my sweaty hand and skids across the floor, out of reach. "You're not in the fighting ring anymore," he says, "and you are going to need more than nineteen silver kronets to save your sister. You're going to need me, the same as he did."

I shake my head, refusing his logic. I know Thaelan and I were not the first to want to leave Brindaigel, but at least we *tried*. Mapping tunnels does not equate to following them, and Alistair had sixteen years to leave before his father died. So why didn't he?

I lash out with my knee, but Alistair anticipates the move and digs his own knee into my upper thigh, applying enough pressure that I cry out in pain.

He swallows hard, eyes half hidden behind his hair. "I envied him," he says bitterly. "Every night, he escaped this city. Every night, he'd sneak back into the barracks, more alive than when he left. And it wasn't even magic, Faris." His eyes meet mine. "It was you."

The fight drains out of me and I stare at him, stricken. Weak street light carves shadows in his face, hollowing his cheeks and thickening his mouth before the light shifts and his sharp edges return, a wolfish boy with eyes that devour.

"I'm a monster because that's what I was bred to be," he says. "I don't expect forgiveness, but I expect you of all people to understand the cost of survival."

Releasing his hold on my arms, Alistair sits back with a soft exhalation, loosening his cravat before lightly touching the cut I made on his neck. He mutters to himself, wiping blood across his trouser leg with open disdain.

I don't move. I can't. When I close my eyes, I'm thrown back to that gray spring morning when I looked up and saw Thaelan's sweet face the color of bruises, the color of stone, the color of never again hearing his voice, seeing his smile, feeling his lips warm against mine.

He told me it was an accident, finding those tunnels. That he mapped them alone. If he was friends with the executioner, why didn't I know?

I turn my head away from Alistair. He was right about that, if nothing else: Thaelan lived a double life, and I was only half of it.

Alistair gives me a wary sidelong glance when I finally sit up, drawing my legs to my chest. "What do you want?" I ask at last, barely more than a mumble.

"I want to offer you a job."

"I have a job."

"There's no fruit to harvest come winter," he says, "and there's no more fights."

I stare at my feet, only inches from his. "I'll find something else."

"Or you can hear me out." Reaching into his coat, he withdraws a fist and offers it toward me. I keep my own hands holding tight to the folds of my skirt and, rolling his eyes, he tips a coin out to the floor. A golden kronet.

"There's forty-nine more of these and a letter with a royal seal that will release your sister into your care, her spell removed, no names or questions asked," he says.

My breath hitches in my throat. Greed unfurls my fingers; temptation draws them to the coin where they hover, debating. Five of these could buy back Cadence. Five seems so few, so deliciously possible, with more than enough leftover for a chance outside Brindaigel. If not in Avinea, then somewhere else, in one of the countries Thaelan used to whisper in my ear.

But then reality returns and I retract my hand, furious at how easily swayed I am by the promise of gold.

"Not interested," I say, a lie that twists in my stomach with a warning that pride begets arrogance, and arrogance is a vice I cannot afford.

Alistair stares at me, a muscle twitching at the back of his jaw, as if he wants to say something but knows he better not. Leaning forward, he retrieves the gold coin and pinches it between his fingers, holding it between us. I shy away from him, eyes tracking to the shard of glass just out of my reach, but his body blocks my path. "If you say no, I leave right now, like this never happened," he says.

"Is that a promise?"

His fingers curl the coin into his palm and he lifts his eyebrows. "I know your name, Faris. I know where you work, I know where you live, I know where to find your sister, and I know where to find your father." He shifts his weight, wetting his lips as he lowers his voice to a dusky whisper, forcing me to lean forward to catch his threats. "Maybe I'll forget who you are," he says. "Maybe I won't. Maybe one night after too many glasses of wine, it'll fall right out of me, that girl that nobody claimed: *Cadence Locke*. And there, hanging on its heels like an annoying burr I can't shake, *Faris* will follow."

So this is how the king's executioner kills. With manipulation and coercion and a smile as black as his soul.

"I want to offer you a job," Alistair repeats.

"It doesn't sound like I have much of a choice."

"There's always a choice," he says. "In this case, it's whether you think I'm more likely to help you or hurt you."

My eyes meet his. "I knew that answer four months ago."

His jaw tightens: I'm testing his patience. His ego. *Good.*

Or bad? This boy could kill me with his words, let alone his hands. I look away, to my own hands balled in bruised fists in my lap. *I need these hands to conquer the world—*

Stop it, I command. Not here, not now, not while Thaelan's murderer watches me for any sign of weakness to exploit. First commandment of the fighting ring: You don't have to be stronger, you just have to last longer.

But agreeing to anything Alistair Pembrough offers me would be treason. How can I even entertain the idea of an alliance with this boy, this *monster—*

Because he knows the tunnels beneath the castle.

I straighten my back and lift my chin. Cheap gestures that offer a small taste of control. "What's the job?" I ask.

He smirks and I hate him for savoring his victory. "Does it matter? You'll be saving your sister. Buying your freedom. Escaping Brindaigel."

"While you stay behind, slave to the crown." I snort, shaking my head. "Right."

"I already told you, I can't leave—"

"Nobody leaves Brindaigel," I say flatly.

Alistair stares at me. "Thaelan did," he says at last. "And he wasn't the first. Take this job, and maybe he won't be the last."

The familiar longing swells through me, but I force it down and shake my head. "Your word is not good enough," I say. "I need guarantees, money upfront, my sister's immediate freedom—"

Alistair laughs and I scowl at him. "I'm not joking," I say.

He palms the kronet, shoving it back in his pocket. "You're not my only choice."

"But I am your first one."

His smile fades and he gives me an appraising look. "You are," he says. "Your mother would have wanted it to be you."

I jolt forward, goose bumps erupting down my back. "What?"

"I made my offer," he says. "Will you take it?"

"What do you know about my mother?"

"Yes or no?"

I tense, prepared to strike, but he shakes his head in warning. "Yes or no," he repeats. "Final chance."

I stare at him, searching his face for any hint he might be lying. But even if he is, what choice do I have? I need that money; I need those tunnels.

I need him.

"Yes," I say.

"Good." Alistair smiles. "This is going to hurt."

He grabs my shoulder, hard. A needle flashes in the light before biting into my neck. I cry out as he depresses the plunger, emptying a syringe of fluid into my veins. My blood slowly hardens into ribbons of ice until I'm frozen, staring at him in accusation before my body turns to stone and I shatter.

And Alistair Pembrough holds out his arms and catches me.

Five

I WAKE WITH A BODY FULL OF LEAD IN A ROOM FULL OF DIAMONDS.

Not diamonds, only firelight reflecting off glass and an assortment of iron instruments, their shapes blurred beyond recognition by the frost clouding my mind. Closing my eyes again, I catch the scent of smoke and charcoal beneath something sweeter, like ladies' perfume, and something darker, like dead things left rotting in the gutter.

The heat of the fire licks at my skin, thawing my body in bits and pieces: eyes, lungs, fingertips, toes. I feel each awakening in turn, wincing at the needling pain that lingers.

This is not my bed; this is not my room.

Where am I?

I'm lying on a table, hard and unforgiving against my spine. To my right, I see Alistair sitting on the floor with his back to a curved wall of gray stone, darkened by age and water. Ignorant to my gaze, he lights a match and watches it burn to the tips of his fingers, grimacing as the flame touches his skin before he flicks it out and lights another. A cigarette dangles unheeded from the corner of his mouth. He's removed his overcoat and his dark waistcoat hangs unbuttoned to the white shirt underneath, sleeves rolled to his elbows. Scars line his forearms like rungs of a ladder, too perfectly even to be accidental. Self-inflicted.

Glancing up, he startles when he sees me, the cigarette nearly falling from his mouth. "She's awake," he says, standing.

Movement rustles on my other side and I struggle to roll my head toward it.

"Mild sedative my ass," a girl says. "Good god, Pem, I thought you killed her."

"An executioner only kills when he intends to," Alistair says darkly.

The girl's face falls into focus and I inhale, flooded with panic. Princess Bryn, the seventh heir to the throne of Brindaigel—and Alistair's future wife. Their engagement was announced the day she turned sixteen, half a year ago, and they celebrated by being paraded through the kingdom in a carriage made of glass, flinging handfuls of copper tretkas into the crowd. We threw back flowers the guards had handed us moments before they arrived, but Cadence had kept hers, carrying it home cradled to her chest, out of view of the boys she often fought with. It had died a day later, the dyed petals faded to the color of ash.

Bryn was beautiful from a distance, even more flawless up close, with golden skin and dark red hair combed high off her forehead, hanging in a knotted rope down her back. She smells warm, a silky blend of perfume and musk that hints at an evening of dancing. Freckles darken her shoulders and the bridge of her nose, half hidden beneath a layer of shimmering powder.

Leaning her palms against the table, she gives me a careful, painted smile. "Hello, Faris," she says.

"Where am I?" My voice comes out dry, cracked.

"The most private room in the castle," she replies, eyebrow arching. "Scream all you'd like; the walls have heard it before."

Blood. That's what I smell beneath her perfume. Blood and fear and gasping final breaths. I'm in the torture chamber.

Jolting upright, I roll off the table, wavering on my feet. Vertigo strikes and I back up to the wall, jostling rows of hanging chains and fraying ropes that dangle from hooks above my head. Twisting away from them, I land on my knees with a crack of bone, palms flat against a clammy floor. It's a gesture of defeat in the fighting ring, and I close my eyes, woozy and disoriented.

"You drugged me," I accuse.

"Necessary precaution," says Alistair. "Some of these tunnels are mine alone, and on the off chance you can run a straight line out of here, I couldn't risk you memorizing the way. Here." He crouches in front of me, a cup of water in one hand. I draw back, but he persists and I finally accept. The water is warm and tastes like smoke, but I swallow it down in one gulp, fingers clutching the wooden cup, estimating its potential damage.

Alistair pries it out of my hand with an apologetic smile.

"I thought you said she could fight," Bryn says, hands on her hips as she frowns down at me.

Fear brines my mouth. Do they expect me to fight the princess?

I've heard enough stories to know the wealthy have unusual appetites and money enough to whet them. A girl fighting royalty wouldn't be the strangest thing they've paid to see.

"Give her a minute," Alistair says, irritated. "I had to guess the dosage based on her size, since you refused to help me——"

"My father will overlook your experiments so long as they only involve you and your prisoners," she interrupts. "You are not allowed to poke holes in his daughter's arms. Nor drug her with homemade poisons in the interest of science."

"Not until we're married," Alistair says with a brittle, humorless smile. He slides an arm around me to help me stand, but I recoil from his touch. Fifty gold kronets, he promised, but at what cost? This is not a place meant for second chances.

I shove him away with a pathetic, open-palmed gesture. He dutifully rocks back, expression inscrutable as his eyes flick from me to Bryn and back again.

"I assume Pem warned you before he dragged you through the streets," says Bryn. "You know why you're here?"

The room shifts and I close my eyes, begging it to stop. "A job," I manage to croak. What drugs did he use? Now that the frost has melted from my blood, I feel like I'm on fire, burning from the inside out. Goose bumps stud my arms like a rash, itchy and tight. Swallowing back the taste of bile, I cut a dark look toward Alistair, laced with unspoken accusation. Gold, he promised. Freedom. My sister—

My mother. "My mother," I say, half question, half lingering surprise.

"Was a thief," says Bryn, pulling the conversation—the attention—back to her.

"There's no proof of that," I say, with a savage twist in my stomach. "No one has ever found any of the gold they claimed she stole."

"On the contrary," says Bryn, blinking at me, bemused. "Gold is exactly what they found, and plenty of it."

I stare back at her. For days after our house was burned, guards sifted through the ashes, and for years after, fortune hunters kicked through the charred brick and charcoal rubble left behind. Nothing of any worth was ever recovered, and there were nights when I would lie awake, convinced the gold had never even existed.

Not that it stopped me from searching the ashes myself not that long ago, so desperate for money to save Cadence I had resorted to believing in legends.

"Your mother was a transferent," Bryn says. "Her crime was not in stealing gold but, rather, stealing magic."

I drag myself to my feet, weight braced against the table. "That's impossible," I say. "My mother was not a magician. Your father's provost would have known."

"Mercer can only sense when someone uses magic," Bryn says. "He can't tell if an ability lies dormant. But whenever you transfer magic, some of it inevitably strays. Like the last drop of water you thought you drank." She picks up the wooden cup Alistair had set on the table and upends it. A drop of water slides out and hits the floor. "Mercer never would have found her and you'd all be living happily ever after in some hovel somewhere, but your mother got greedy and she got caught." She snorts. "They always do."

I shake my head, teeth clenched so tight my jaw aches. I've heard worse said of my mother—often from myself—but it annoys me the way Bryn tells the story as if she knows all the details.

As if she knows more than I do.

"It's not unusual for a magician to have more than one ability," Alistair cuts in. "Your mother was also a spellcaster. For two weeks after her arrest, everything she touched—every*one* she touched—turned into gold."

Now I know they're lying to me. Somebody, some guard or palace servant, would have carried that kind of story out of the palace and into the taverns years ago. Or maybe they did, which is how rumors of her crime began.

"My father is not nearly so talented," says Bryn, beginning to pace. Her skirts hiss across the floor behind her. "He wanted that spell, but removing something so complicated would have frayed its edge; it would have fallen apart in the process. It was your mother's guarantee that he wouldn't touch her. She was too valuable to kill."

I hate the way my stomach somersaults, the way my palms start to sweat; I hate that even now, my mother holds power over me. "Is she alive?"

Uncomfortable silence follows my question, answer enough. Yet Alistair confirms it. "Perrote ordered her execution after discovering she had woven a caveat into her spell. The gold would only last a fortnight before it turned to ash."

Two weeks. The time of respite between my mother's arrest and the time the guards returned with torches. So she sacrificed our family for what? For two weeks of playing wizard?

"What was the point?" I ask darkly.

"The point was that for two weeks," says Bryn, "your mother

had the perfect cover to transfer magic without the king questioning anything that might have spilled in the process."

Reaching into his pocket, Alistair removes a small vial, laying it on the table ahead of me. Ribbons of liquid fire strike against the glass and fragment into narrow threads, suspended in a glossy liquid the color of the winter sky.

Magic.

I stare at it, transfixed. "I don't understand."

"The spell was a distraction," Alistair says. "She intended to steal the magic and run, but when she got caught, she had to change plans."

"Run? Where?"

"Avinea," says Bryn.

My mouth floods with saliva.

"After the war, King Merlock abandoned the capital and went into hiding," Bryn says, tugging at the rings that adorn her slender fingers. "The betrayal of his provosts made him bitter; murdering his brother made him weak. In retaliation, he cut every thread of magic left in the city. Some spells can be recycled, unknotted, and used again and again until the magic fades completely, but to cut a spell apart, it leaves the threads too frayed to do anything but rot. It's—"

"The plague," I say with a chill.

"The plague," she agrees, glancing toward me. "They call it the Burn. It gets into the land and under your skin and . . ."

And you die slowly, poisoned from the inside out, if you die at all. They say that not everyone does, and those who don't become worse than any shadow creature King Perrote could create to scare us into obedience.

They say there are monsters in Avinea.

Bryn flattens her palms on the table, chewing the paint from her lower lip. "The rules of succession are absolute. Only one man may be king and only the king can wield magic. So long as Merlock lives, his son, Prince Corbin, cannot inherit the crown. And without magic, he cannot stop the Burn from spreading."

"Prince Corbin?" I repeat, incredulous. "Merlock had a son? And he survived?"

"*Avinea* survived," she says impatiently. "But not for much longer. As it is, my father supported Corthen during the war. He's not high on Avinea's list of potential allies, nor would he ever willfully offer assistance to Merlock's heir. Why waste the resources or sign any unnecessary treaties? Another twenty years and Avinea will truly be gone and my father can conquer it without opposition. It's the perfect strategy: He declared war on Avinea the minute Merlock abandoned it and he's been winning ever since."

I dig my fingers into the tabletop. "And my mother knew there was something out there?"

The smile that creeps across Bryn's face is infuriating: more secrets that she lords over me. "Someone might have told her as much," she says. "The same someone who told her what tunnels to take when she ran. Who planned to run with her."

My father?

No. The way they look at me, triumph and pity, denies my assumption. Alistair has the decency to look away as he lights another cigarette, and my stomach sinks: It wasn't my father who knew the tunnels out of Brindaigel.

It was *his*.

Bryn plucks the vial from the table, turning it upside down and right side up again. "Clean magic would be worth a fortune to the wife of a tailor out there."

No. My mother embroidered dresses and grew flowers and had two daughters; she did not steal magic and she did not have lovers and she did not abandon us to the Brim in search of money.

But then I remember the strange way she smelled the night she tried to kill me, like damp stone and stilted air. Like the tunnels.

"You're lying," I say weakly. Was that how Alistair recognized me? Not because Thaelan described a girl with pale eyes, but because that girl looked like her mother?

"What can I say, Faris?" Alistair exhales a plume of smoke over his shoulder. His tone is caustic but his expression is troubled. Haunted. "There's just something about broken Lockes in our dungeon that makes our Pembrough blood run faster. He paid for it, if it makes you feel any better." He inhales deeply. "We all did. Perrote guessed your mother had help getting into the castle, and it fueled his paranoia. It was the start of mandatory loyalty spells."

"Brindaigel can't survive another twenty years hidden behind our borders like this," says Bryn, scowling at him for straying off topic. She begins tapping the vial against the table. "We have no land, limited resources, and a swelling population that will need to be culled. My father plans to start in the Brim. Criminals and undesirables first, your sister included, followed by regulated births: only one child per couple. Any more will be thrown in the gorge or drowned in the shallows, parents' choice. No exceptions."

I step back, horrified by how casually she speaks of her father's intentions, as though it were no different than rotating the crops or raising taxes. "He can't do that. He can't just kill people to make room—"

"Who's going to stop him?" Bryn asks, eyes flashing. "He's the king, and anyone with any real combat skill has a loyalty spell burnt above his heart. You think the Brim rats will fight back? Or women and children?" She scoffs. "Your mother was the first to run."

"Shut up."

"The Brim stagnated years ago," Bryn continues. "Fewer mouths to feed would be a blessing to them. More jobs, more space, more—"

"*Shut up!*" I slam my hand against the table. My voice carries to the rafters overhead and lingers as Bryn and Alistair both stare at me. We are not worthless, I want to scream; we are not expendable. No matter what my mother may have thought.

Embarrassed by my outburst, I lower my eyes and temper my anger, tucking my stinging hand under my arm: This is not a fight I have any chance of winning; better to save my strength.

The silence stretches into agony before Bryn finally speaks. "You're going to finish what your mother started," she says. "You're going to be my vessel, Faris. You'll carry that stolen magic to New Prevast as an incentive, a gift to Prince Corbin to ensure an alliance. Avinea needs magic, Brindaigel needs a new king, and you need fifty silver kronets to save your sister's life. Everyone wins."

I stare her down. "I can't carry magic. I'm not a transferent—"

"Not a requirement."

I snap. "Then why do you need me?"

"Because you have something to lose if you don't come back," she says.

I shake my head, backing away from the table, hitting the wall and setting the chains rustling. "There are six heirs ahead of you for the throne—"

"And nothing but good manners prevents a seventh heir from acting before the first one does," she counters with an irritated sigh. "My brother Rowan is as isolationist as my father. I can't risk Brindaigel's future while I wait my turn."

"If you start a war, you're fighting all of Brindaigel. You'll have to kill your entire family to get to that crown."

"Which is why I need an army with no ties to my father," she says. "War requires sacrifice, Faris, but it also brings rewards. If I am crowned queen, I will have the power to sever your sister's enchantment. And I will have the means to offer you a comfortable future. Gold enough for both of you. *Real* gold," she adds with a smirk.

"If," I repeat. "And if we fail, it's my family that suffers. My sister will be sold, my father thrown into prison—"

"And you'll be tortured and killed," she finishes, waving away my concerns with one hand. "Lucky for you, you know the executioner."

"The boy who calls himself a monster," I say darkly.

Alistair's expression hardens as he crushes his cigarette out against the edge of the table. "It's only the truth, Faris," he says. "If you want lies, I can take you down to the shallows and kiss you beneath the stars and tell you everything will be perfect because the world is never cruel."

How dare he mock Thaelan. I lunge toward Alistair but the

drugs are too thick in my blood, making me sluggish, unsteady. I crash into the table instead, and pain blooms across my hip. "I won't do it."

Bryn snorts. "At what point were you ever offered a choice? This"—she gestures to the torture chamber—"is all formality. As far as I'm concerned, you agreed to help me the moment Pem told me your name." Straightening, she looks to Alistair, who looks away, guilty. "Which is why the magic's already inside you."

Six

THIS IS HOW THE KING'S EXECUTIONER KILLS. WITH HOMEMADE sedatives and stolen magic and a princess as twisted as him.

A lifetime of warnings roll through my head with frightening percussion: infection, plague, the king's speech every year on the Day of Excision. Magic was never meant for mortals, and it'll start to clog in my veins until my blood stagnates, turns brackish. Until I die, or worse. Already I feel my blood shuddering, slowing; already I feel the phantom itch of poison spreading through my body.

Ignoring the pain in my hip, I reach a side table lined with instruments, seizing a hook with a sharpened talon at its end. Grabbing Alistair around the neck, I yank him against me, the hook pressed above his heart. "Get it out of me," I demand. "Right now!"

"I can't."

"Liar!"

"He can't," Bryn says, arms folded, expression inscrutable. "He's not a transferent."

"If you put it in me, you can take it out!"

"I used a needle," Alistair says, palms still out. He nods toward the scattered tools across the tabletop, where a silver and glass syringe sits adjacent to an empty vial. "It's not in your blood; it's just under the skin. But only dead magic can poison you, Faris, and this is clean, no spells attached. There's no chance of it fraying or rotting apart inside you. I promise."

"Like I would believe anything you say."

"You don't have to," he says. "It's fact."

Frustrated, I release Alistair, casting a disgusted glance to the hook before I throw it aside. Pressing my hands to my forehead, I back away until I hit the wall. Cold stone bleeds through my dress and I slide down, knees drawn to my chest. It's too much; I can't do this. My palms settle flat on the floor. Defeated.

"Give us a moment," says Bryn, watching me from under half-lidded eyes, her slender fingers tented against the table. Alistair hesitates, glancing to me before dutifully moving for a doorway on the opposite wall, half-hidden beneath a dingy tapestry. He disappears into a sitting room on the other side.

Bryn crouches in front of me. Her skirts kick up, revealing layers of silk and lace petticoats, pale slippers studded with colored beads. Impractical, beautiful shoes that awaken a long-buried hunger for the dances I never had, the possibilities my mother stole from us when she stole from the king. "You can't blame him," she says with a bracing smile. "His mother died when he was young and his father was not the kind of man to teach delicacy."

"Who?"

"Your majesty."

"The king?"

"Your majesty," she repeats, teeth clenched. "When you address me, address me like the daughter of a king, not like a Brim whore you'd leave in the morning. I mean Pem, not my father. Good god." Rolling back her shoulders, she clutches her hands across her knees, spinning one of her rings in restless circles. "You weren't my first choice," she says, "but Pem wanted you to do this. Guilt, I imagine, or some other human frailty he pretends not to have. Given the circumstances, I saw no reason to deny him the request." Her eyes rake over me, taking silent tally. "I feel confident in that decision."

Does she expect me to feel flattered?

Leaning closer in a drift of perfume, Bryn lowers her voice, the words sharp, cut by her perfect teeth: "But I will kill your sister if you do anything to compromise my efforts. Success or failure."

The change in her demeanor is arctic, like snowfall in the spring. Gone is the girl and here stands the future queen. Goose bumps chase down my back and I swallow hard, past the fear lodged in my throat.

"I understand," I say.

Bryn lifts an eyebrow.

"Your majesty," I add softly.

"I don't have to touch you to hurt you, Faris. Remember that." Flashing a smile, Bryn stands, smoothing her skirts and calling for Alistair, who emerges from the other room, a glass of amber alcohol held loose in one hand. Avoiding my eyes, he returns to his tools, straightening the lines I knocked askance before he drains his glass and trades it for a scalpel.

"Oh," I say bitterly, "it gets better?"

Bryn makes a face, resting her forearm against the table. "I trust you as much as my father trusts his council."

"Of course he trusts them," I say. "He branded them all with loyalty spells."

"Exactly." Bryn winces as Alistair dips the blade into the smooth flesh of her wrist. A bead of blood emerges and she hisses through her teeth as it slides down the palm of her hand. "This is disgusting," she says.

Alistair snorts, hair falling over his eyes. "It's only blood."

"But it's my blood," she says.

Uncorking the vial of magic, Alistair holds it to her wrist, catching a fat drop of blood within the glass. It mixes with the liquid already there, fragmenting into ruby beads as small as those sewn on Bryn's shoes. Balancing the vial in one hand, Alistair retrieves an empty syringe and fills it with the viscous mixture before turning to me, eyebrows raised in expectation.

"This spell cannot be given under duress or you'll be no better than your sister," says Bryn. "A mindless slave."

I stare at the syringe with a feeling of dread. This is the spell that Thaelan feared the most as a guard in training, the one that would bind his heart to the king's. "Where did you get that?"

"I stole it," she says, gloating the way I used to after stealing a handful of limes.

"Being betrothed to the executioner has its benefits," Alistair says flatly. "Unquestioned access to the dungeons and all its offices, including Mercer's." He snorts. "It cost him a finger when Perrote found out he was one spell short at the end of the week."

"Can't they trace the spell?"

"Not unless someone casts it," he says. "Hence the needle. An injection avoids any need for transference and ensures the magic doesn't spill." Then, with a humorless smile, "One of my many overlooked experiments."

"My lovely mad scientist," Bryn says, making a face at the track of blood running down her wrist.

Alistair shoves up his sleeve and demonstrates a battlefield of welts and ruby scabs nestled in the crook of his elbow. "I always test my hypotheses," he says. "Neither Perrote nor Mercer will ever know."

"Is that what those are?" I nod toward the ladder of scars on his wrists. "More experiments?"

"No," he says tightly, tugging his sleeve back down. "I consider those more of a control."

Like split knuckles and bruised jaws: We both wear our scars as proof of our strength, defiance of our weakness. My stomach tightens at the thought. I refuse to share anything, even this tiny human grief, with Alistair Pembrough.

"I need your arm," he says. "If you're willing."

Bryn called it a choice but it's just another formality. Even if they let me walk out of here, how long before the Guard storms my desolate attic? Or would they even bother with me? Maybe my father would be taken first, and then Cadence. This is a torture chamber, after all. Nobody leaves this room without suffering.

Scowling, I extend my arm and Alistair cradles it in his hand, threading the needle under my skin with practiced familiarity. He quickly empties the plunger and steps back, tossing the syringe into the fireplace where it shatters against the brick.

At first, I feel nothing. But then, my *gods*.

The magic ignites beneath my skin, drawing bright white lines of heat that braid around my wrist before darkening to the color of charcoal. And like charcoal, the lines begin to smear, forming thorny peaks as the spell anchors itself to my flesh with a dozen tiny knots, no bigger than beads. For one terrifying moment, I feel Bryn's heartbeat echo through my chest before my own heart thunders in reply, screaming to reclaim its territory.

The spell cools, turning to ice, hardening like a bracelet of scars. Across from me, Bryn examines her own wrist, where her meager payment of blood has given way to a smear of ash and silver that unfurls into a crude symbol of a key, a half diamond intersected by a line beneath her skin.

Bryn laughs, bright and delighted, before she sobers, pinching the flesh of her forearm. Pain erupts in my own arm and I clutch at it with a strike of panic. Laughing again, Bryn takes the scalpel and draws it across the pad of her thumb. My thumb bleeds while her skin remains unbroken.

"Pem," she says, "you are incredible."

And now Bryn is invincible.

The dizziness returns and my movements turn slurred, clumsy. The magic begins to spread across my chest, staggering down my spine. I bend forward, hugging myself, pressing my forehead to the slick stone floor.

"Here." Bryn kneels before me, pulling a pin from her hair and pressing the slender iron ornament to my wrist. "A trick I learned from Pem. It won't negate the spell, but it'll mute the pain until your body finds its balance." Forcing a quick smile, she curls my other hand over the iron until I'm holding it in place.

"Thank you," I manage to mumble, surprised by the kindness.

"You're useless to me if you're sick," she adds.

Of course.

"It's nearly dawn," Alistair says, fist propped against the mantel of the fireplace. "Shift change."

Bryn stands and approaches him, kissing him on the cheek. "Thank you, Pem," she says.

He doesn't reply.

She disappears through the doorway behind the tapestry. With a scowl, I toss her hairpin aside before pushing myself to my feet. The pin clatters across the uneven floor before stopping at the lip of a drain stained dark around its rim.

"I wasn't lying to you," Alistair says, speaking into the fire. "You'll get your sister back."

"Alive or dead?"

Alistair ducks his head. "Faris—"

"So do I walk out on my own, or will you drug me again?"

"Look, I'm sorry," he says, turning to face me. "And I have been sorry every day since it happened. I just . . ." He looks away, teeth clenched. "I need you to know that. I need you to hear that. Thaelan—"

"I don't care what you *need*," I spit back. "You followed me, drugged me, and injected me with *magic*! You forfeited any right to forgiveness when you decided you wanted a throne more than you wanted your soul!"

"Yes, envy me, Faris: The stars themselves couldn't have written a more convenient romance. The seventh heir to the throne and the son of an executioner! What a marriage we'll have and what a king I would make!"

"Why else would you do this if not for a crown?"

"Because she chose me," he says, stepping closer, eyes bright, "the same as she has chosen everyone who's ever had something useful to offer her. When Bryndalin is crowned queen, I guarantee you that I will not be standing beside her." He swallows hard, straightening. "Nobody will."

"Well, you chose me," I say, "and I'm warning you that if anything happens to my sister, I hold you responsible."

I move toward the door but he steps ahead of me, blocking my way. "Swear to me you'll come back and I swear to you your sister will be safe. Even if I have to outbid everyone in this kingdom to buy her."

"I'm coming back," I say. "And you won't be the only monster in this dungeon when I do."

His expression shifts, turns sad. "You're not a monster, Faris."

I stare him down, unflinching. "If my sister dies, you have no idea what I'll be."

It's only after I shoulder past him and enter the dark-walled sitting room beyond that I realize my mistake. An entire tray full of weapons, and I left every one of them behind.

Seven

THE DUNGEON SMELLS FOUL, FETID, SWAMPY WITH TRAPPED HEAT and the lingering odor of human excrement. Guards pace the halls with swords slung low on their hips, faces hidden by hooded cowls and hinged metal masks rubbed with oils and spices to hide the smell.

Being down here renews a thousand dreaded memories that shadow my steps. My insatiable heart starts humming through its familiar litany of all the different endings we could have had. I would rather see Thaelan married and forbidden from me than to be reminded that he's dead for memorizing these tunnels—tunnels I commit to memory now, keeping silent record of every move we make, just in case. It's a lesson learned hard, but a lesson learned anyway. *Pay attention, Faris.* Don't let anyone get ahead of you; don't ever lose your way.

"The hellborne are all intuits," Alistair says, keeping a steady pace, his eyes accustomed to the dim light and murky shadows. "They'll be able to smell the magic on you. Most would skin you alive to get to it."

"The hellborne?" I follow his lead without question, stepping where he steps, stopping when he stops, shivering despite the heavy coat he offered as we left. I didn't want to take it, but pride begets arrogance and no god has ever deemed stupidity a virtue.

"The infected," he explains. "Once poisoned magic gets in your blood, it goes straight for your heart. You either die, or you feed it with the same depravities that turned it rotten in the first place. All the vices that make a man a monster." He forces a smile, humorless and brief. "You surrender to those vices, you turn hellborne. Your blood turns to poison and you become addicted to the way it burns through your veins. But like any addiction, you grow immune. Clean blood dilutes the infection; clean magic gives it something to feed on. Either way, it gives them a high."

I shudder, clutching my wrist and the hard-as-scar spell that circles it. Alistair notices the movement, gaze lingering on my hands. "There are also transferents like your mother," he says, lifting his eyes, "looking for any scrap of magic they can sell to the highest bidder. Skin on skin is all it would take for them to steal whatever they want from you—or to try. And a clumsy effort to steal that magic could easily tear it apart."

And magic torn at the edges will start to stagnate and decompose, working its way into my blood, eventually infecting me.

"Trust no one," Alistair says in conclusion. "*Touch* no one. Not until you reach Prince Corbin's palace in New Prevast."

"How do you know all of this?" I ask.

His smile is grim as he glances to Bryn striding ahead of us. Her dark cloak hides the plain riding dress and simple boots she changed into, her dark red hair a loose cascade down her back. "The first man I executed was an old soldier," he says. "He fought in the war, before the borders shifted. There aren't many of them left these days. Do you know what his crime was?"

I shake my head.

The smile fades, replaced with something I can't name. "A good memory," Alistair says. "Knowledge is power, and Perrote doesn't allow anyone he can't trust to have any."

I think of the peddler who sold me pirate stories, there one day and gone the next. "And he trusts you?"

"He trusts her," he says, nodding toward Bryn. "He has to. His family will inherit this kingdom and they can't do that without knowing the truth." He snorts, starting to walk. "Like I said: She chose me, Faris, and it wasn't because she wanted to marry an executioner. She wanted a way out, just like the rest of us. Just like your mother."

I grab his arm, pulling him back. He pauses, almost hopeful. Despite everything, Alistair Pembrough still wants the one thing he can't take from me.

Forgiveness.

"Did you know my mother?" I ask.

He doesn't answer right away, staring instead at my fingers carving divots in the sleeve of his coat. "Yes," he says at last.

I release his arm. Words stall in my throat and I wet my lips, allowing myself a moment of weakness. "Was—was she going to take you with her?"

Footsteps approach in the hall behind us. Silent as stone, Alistair swings me into an empty cell and pins me against the shadowed wall, keeping careful watch over his shoulder. I ball my hands in the baggy sleeves of my coat and stare at the ceiling as two guards pass, joking among themselves before they stop to urinate.

Alistair waits until silence returns to the hall before stepping back. Hair cuts across his cheek and he rubs his mouth with one hand as I hug myself.

"Wrong question," he says at last. "Don't ask what she planned to do. Ask why she changed her mind. Instead of running away, ask why she ran home."

She came home to kiss me good-bye and to drive a dagger into my chest. Nine perfect stitches and one unanswered question: *Why?*

We continue on, passing more turns, more twists, more gloomy halls. Stupid hope rises at each one, as if I expect to see Thaelan around the next bend with a map and a dimpled smile and an explanation for where he's been. It's a cruel game to play, and I suffer the bitter consequences each time I look and nothing looks back but the darkness.

Thaelan is dead, I tell myself. Pay attention, Faris.

The tunnel finally opens into a large antechamber with a barrel-vaulted ceiling and a Rook's Eye oculus open to the world outside, far above our heads. The worn stone floor is dusted with old straw, scraps of fabric, cigarettes turned soggy with rain. An empty wheelbarrow rests against one of the walls, its frame splintered beyond salvage. Bats roost from the wooden beams overhead, chittering with indignation at our arrival.

The floor gently slopes toward an iron grate, hinged on one side, with a handle on the other. A dull roar rises from somewhere underneath, and while the air is still cold, it's balmier. Rust spots spread away from the grate like scabs of old blood; beads of condensation flock the walls.

Bryn arches an eyebrow at our delayed arrival but says nothing, moving out of the way as Alistair bends down, unlocking the grate with a key before opening it with a screech of rusted metal. He cringes and throws a look over his shoulder, toward the half a dozen tunnels that all intersect here. Nervously, I lean forward, but the torchlight barely reaches a foot past the lip of the hole. Anything could be down there.

Avinea is down there.

A soft scrabbling echoes through the hall as Alistair rocks back on his feet. "Shadow rat," he warns.

I spin. A shadow rat lumbers into view, its swollen body dragging along the ground, trailing sparks and leaving a line of fading embers. Wordlessly, Alistair strikes a match and flicks it toward the rat, who turns in our direction, nose lifting to the air a second before the match hits. Its body absorbs the flame before the rat implodes with a flash of light. A tiny stone clatters to the ground.

"I hate these things," Alistair says. "They're worse than the courtiers who lurk in the halls."

"Won't someone know you killed it?" I ask uneasily. "The guard who was scrying—"

Bryn snorts. "You don't actually believe that, do you? Men who spend their days spying through the eyes of rats and birds?" She picks up the stone and tosses it to me. I fumble the catch and it rolls toward the open grate. "We don't have enough men for that. Most of these things are just decoys."

"You can tell by the color of its eyes," Alistair says. "Black means it's just smoke. Red means there's blood running through it. A heartbeat. Those are the ones you hide from."

"It's not real?" I bend for the stone; it's warm in my hand, threaded with tiny striations of silver. Of magic. They bump unevenly beneath my thumb. "I thought all the king's golems—"

"My father won't waste magic when he doesn't have to," Bryn says. She opens her palm and I drop the stone in it. "Or men. Even the king conserves resources these days."

Decoys. The rats that chased me out of the tunnels that night weren't even real. Smoke and a single guard were all that kept me from Cadence—that kept *us* from Avinea.

In that instant, I don't need a spell or stolen magic: I'll find Prince Corbin myself so long as he promises to burn this kingdom to the ground.

A hand falls on my arm, a sliver of clarity that cuts through my fury.

"Here," Alistair says. He offers me a book, bound in twine. *Indigenous Flowering Species of Avinea.* My mother's book, lost in the bag I abandoned to the tunnels four months ago.

"You kept this?" I ask with a frown. I wouldn't have. Books are a commodity these days, and I would have sold it like I've sold everything else of any value.

"I thought you should have it back." His lips twist in a smile. "I thought it might help you to know you're not alone."

My mother is the last person in the world I would choose for company, and yet, six-year-old Faris feels a flicker of yearning for the woman I might have known.

If she hadn't tried to kill me.

My thumb skims the cover and I hesitate. The words taste, sour, salty—like dirty water that stagnates in my mouth. "Thank you," I manage at last, tucking the book into the pocket of my coat.

"Well," Alistair says, "your head didn't burst into flames. I'll consider that a good start." He extends a hand to me, features shadowed. "I'll keep an eye on Cadence."

I sift through his words: Is it a threat or a promise? His earlier apology echoes through me, and for a moment, I'm tempted to believe it. This is not the boy I planned to kill, a monster who lived in the dungeons and deserved to die. This is a boy who was once friends with Thaelan. And while *we* will never be friends, we are something shared nevertheless—prisoners of fate who made the difficult choice to survive.

"I'm coming back," I tell him.

He nods, mouth grim, and retracts his hand. "I'll be waiting."

Turning, he beckons for Bryn and blanches.

A guard stands gaping at the mouth of one of the tunnels with a torch in one hand and a small box under his arm. "Your highness?" he asks, voice hitching in bewildered question.

The answering silence shrinks the room until we all seem to breathe the same gasp of shallow, humid air. "This isn't part of any assigned patrol," Alistair says at length, with an authority that belies his age. "You shouldn't be here."

The guard takes an uneasy step back. "I was sent for the rat," he says, darting a glance to the pile of ashes and dying embers, all that remains of the imploded golem. "Mercer wants the spell stone back, but . . ." A line carves between his brows. "What are you doing here?"

Who attacks, who reacts? Bryn reaches the guard first, but Alistair is close behind and a struggle ensues, arms and legs and rising voices that swell to the rafters and unsettle the bats.

And then, a single gasp. The sound of a knife driven half an inch low enough, pinning a man's heart to his spine.

The guard crumples. Blood begins to pool beneath him, catching along worn tracks in the floor that spread toward the drain. His eyes are still open, glossy and dull, all fight vanished. He could be under the king's spell, the same as Cadence.

But he's not. He's dead, the same as Thaelan.

Is it really that easy? That *fast*?

"Bryndalin," Alistair says, choked.

"He saw us," Bryn says tightly. The knife hangs from her hand. "I had to."

"No—"

"He saw us! He saw *you*!" Her voice rises and she shoves him back, leaving a bloody handprint on Alistair's waistcoat before the knife sings between them, dangerously close to Alistair's face. "I've come too far to turn back now! This is our only chance and I will not waste it for—for *him*." Lowering her voice, she straightens. "It had to be done."

Alistair tangles his hands through his hair, his features caught in the same play of revulsion that skates down my back. "Mercer sent him," he says, pointing to the body—to the *boy*, barely older than any of us. "He's going to notice when he doesn't come back!"

"Just dump the body," says Bryn. She tosses her hair back, lifting her chin. "That's your job, isn't it?"

"How apropos," Alistair growls. "You disappear, a guard ends up dead, and the mad scientist in the dungeons is the one with blood on his clothes!"

Bryn rolls her eyes and crouches, her dark cloak pillowing behind her as she wipes her blade clean on the guard's tunic. "You'll be the last one my father would blame."

"You don't know that, you don't—"

"I know my father," she says, standing, taking a step toward him. "And he knows *you*. The executioner who cried the first time he killed a man." Her voice lowers and she cradles his face in one bloody hand. "My father knows you're too weak to kill without orders."

He stares at her. There is no remorse on her face, no regret for the boy that she killed, and this can't be real, an executioner made of mercy and a princess with a heart as black as sin. What if after all this time, it wasn't the beast in the dungeon I needed to fear, but the beauty who lived in the castle above him?

Blood puddles around my shoes and I move to escape the implicit guilt it carries. My heel wavers over the rusted lip of the open grate behind me, and my breath catches. I don't know the tunnels at my back, but the water that roars below me moves with purpose. The farming terraces, I think. If the current carries me out to the irrigation channels that line the shallows, I could be at the workhouse before they're even out of the dungeon. If I double back, if I run, I could grab my sister and take our chances. If Avinea is still out there, maybe there are magicians too, a transferent who could cut the thread that ties her back to Brindaigel. A king concerned with conserving resources wouldn't chase after the loss of one little girl that no one will miss.

Alistair takes a step forward, eyes wide, expression plaintive. Blood outlines his jaw. "Faris," he says.

"Don't run," Bryn says, the knife still in her hand.

Twisting, I drop through the grate, landing in water cold as snowmelt that rises to my thighs. My legs tangle in my damp skirt and the current pitches me forward, onto my hands and knees. Gagging back mouthfuls of briny water, I struggle to find my feet but I'm being dragged, scraped across the bottom of the channel. There's no light down here and it's disorienting as I grapple for purchase against the slick walls.

Someone lands with a splash behind me, their voice lost to the roar of the water. Rough hands grab the back of my coat and together, we're dragged underwater before the ground gives way.

Bright starbursts of pain flash across my eyelids as I ricochet between narrow walls, landing in a pool of water with enough force I'm flattened on the bottom. Panicked, I begin to thrash, searching for purchase, desperate for air. I can't swim, I can't see, I can't *breathe*—

Bryn yanks me to the surface, bearing my weight against her hip as she paddles us away from the crushing waterfall. "Breathe," she demands. "And stop flailing, you'll drown us both!"

The water's not as deep as I expected, but she doesn't release me until we've reached the edge of the river, framed by soft black sand. Releasing me with a grunt, Bryn lays on her back with her eyes closed and damp hair flattened across her cheek.

She saved my life.

She had no choice, I tell myself: Without me, she has nothing of any value to offer the prince. Even so, it's a debt I don't like hanging over me.

Cadence.

Rolling onto my stomach, I stagger to my feet, spinning a half circle to collect my bearings. The roar of the water screams at my back and I take a hesitant step toward a ribbon of light spilling through the rock ahead of me. But I falter when a staircase catches my attention, sweeping back into the mountain on the opposite side of the river. Broken chunks of rock lie scattered across the risers, but the floor leading away from the stairs is smooth, polished to a shine. Carved columns support overhead arches, almost every one of them broken, or tipped at drunken angles. The rib cage of a forgotten rowboat lies on its side, the iron bands rusted the color of blood.

I know this place.

"Don't you dare run again," Bryn growls, still sprawled on her back.

It hits me, like the ice of the water: a staircase carved from stone, leading to a hallway of marble and columns.

There was water, Thaelan had whispered against my throat. *And sand, and sky.*

Numbly, I turn back to the crevice, to the thread of dawn that bleeds through. My heart slams against my rib cage as my skin tightens in a rash of goose bumps.

I could see the stars.

It's not the farming terraces beyond that crevice. It's Avinea.

Thaelan made it this far. He was here, this close, so close, and then he turned back. For *me*.

Ignoring Bryn's warnings, I take a step, another, hope warring with sorrow, desperate for this one last glimpse of Thaelan. But the cold water has leached into my bones and turned me cumbersome. I trip in the thick sand, over the white stones that litter the shore. Landing hard on my hip, I bite back my profanity and push myself to my knees. My fingers catch against a half-buried rock and I glance down with a scowl of impatience.

Not a rock. Bones. *Bodies*.

This isn't an escape route, it's a graveyard.

This is where the kingdom dumps its dead.

Eight

IT'S BASIC ECONOMICS, SUPPLY AND DEMAND. WE DON'T HAVE CRYPTS enough for all of us, certainly not those of us who die as thieves and criminals. The bodies have to go somewhere, but I never even considered this: savage water and the dark, fifty feet from freedom.

Thaelan is down here somewhere. Discarded. Picked clean by the current and worn smooth with sand. My mother too.

I wilt with the thought as I close my eyes, count to ten. Of course Thaelan never mentioned this part because he always looked up instead of down. Instead of bones, he saw stars.

Bryn approaches, kicking sand, twisting her damp hair over one shoulder. Her cloak snags on a bone and she tears it free with a grunt.

"What's the matter?" she asks, irritable.

I don't look at her, staring instead toward the light. My body is a tangle of bruises, inside and out.

"They're dead," she says, "and we need to reach Nevik before nightfall. Don't linger." Peeling the bag from around her shoulder, she thrusts it at me to carry.

I make no move to take it, staring at the water lapping the edges of the riverbank. "You murdered that man," I say.

"You would have done the same."

"No. I would never—"

"You would never what?" she asks. "You would never make a difficult choice at a pivotal moment? If he stood between you and your sister, what would you do?" Straightening, she wipes her mouth and arches an eyebrow. "Oh, I remember. You would turn around and run. Like a coward. Like your *mother*." Snorting, she says, "If you're not willing to kill for what you want, you don't want it nearly enough. Now get up."

We keep to the shore as far as we can, a princess and her trailing shadow. Rocks block the entrance to the cavern as high as my head, damming the river, creating a pool of water that spreads across the marble floor on the other side. If this was early spring, the snowmelt would make the crevice impassable. But after a dry summer, there's room to spare, footholds to find, space to wiggle through.

After we wade through the water to reach it.

Bones roll beneath my feet, pulling at my skirt, scraping against my legs. Hair ghosts against my skin, and things bob on the surface, hitting the rocks ahead of us with soft clicks and dull echoes. I keep my eyes ahead, the bag clutched to my chest like a talisman before I reach the first rock and pull myself out of the water. Bryn stays a step ahead of me, ducking through the crevice and into the dawn, indifferent to the line she crosses.

Yet I hesitate on the edge of the light, shivering not just from cold but from fear. Here in the shadows, I'm safe, albeit a prisoner of Brindaigel. A step beyond and I'm a traitor, finally in Avinea.

Bryn notices and stops, eyebrow arched. Her skirt clings to her legs, and even bedraggled, she's beautiful. A girl named for a kingdom and born for a crown, determined to inherit both, no matter the cost. "What did you want?" she asks, glancing around her. *"Magic?"* Snorting, she says, "It's the same water, the same sand, the same mountains, the same sky."

But hope had burnished the idea of Avinea into something more, something better. Years of daydreams and wanting had dulled logic beneath an unattainable fantasy and now, disappointment creeps in.

Even I feel exactly the same: Still trapped.

The cavern opens into a steep valley of arching rocks and jagged walls that hide most of the brightening sky. The water sparkles, a deep jewel blue at the center, dulling to wintery gray where it turns shallow and laps against the black sandy banks. Bryn leads an unescorted promenade along the shoals, her cloak trailing behind her. She walks as if it's an empty ballroom floor: chin up, back straight. All she needs is a handful of tretkas to toss to the white-crested birds roosting in the cliffs who cluck in disapproval at our arrival.

An hour passes, then a second. I struggle to keep pace as I absorb Bryn's blisters and cramping muscles on top of my own. Yet she has no patience for me and I refuse to beg her favor. If she doesn't stop, I won't, either.

Finally, the cliffs that frame the river begin to fragment as the landscape opens. Forgoing the thinning, brackish water, we pull ourselves onto a narrow shelf of granite that cuts through a boggy tributary. A thick, sulfurous odor burns my eyes and makes my head throb, and a ribbon of gold flickers to the east, belching up plumes of acrid smoke that turn the sky gray.

The Burn.

Fear shivers through me, despite its distance. A lifetime of warnings race through my head and I stare, both transfixed and repulsed by the way it shimmers and moves.

Something else is moving, closer to us. *People.*

I watch, incredulous, as figures drift through the mud, bending over shallow pools of water as they dig. They're bundled in rags and carrying wide baskets strapped to their backs, communicating less with words and more with barks and hisses as they brandish what they find. Clothing. A fistful of matted hair the color of honey. An arm trailing ribbons of sinew. Like the pawnbrokers on the roofs of the Brim, trash becomes their newfound treasure and they hoard it all. Small, bony children guard several carts, warding off packs of mangy dogs with sticks. Yet other than the mud on their clothes and the strange way they speak, they look normal, not at all twisted or destroyed by the Burn that edges the horizon.

Avinea *has* survived.

A woman slogs toward us, pressing her weight into the edge of the rocky outcropping we stand upon. "Pretty," she coos, gesturing us closer. "Here, pretty, pretty, pretty." Dark veins map her face, full of dead magic and thickened blood.

The plague.

I recoil into Bryn, heart slamming in my chest. Is it airborne? Will it spread through the water, through mud? Am I already infected? The phantom itch of an invisible disease crawls over me and I press the sleeve of my coat to my mouth, terrified.

"Pretty," the woman whispers, stretching for my foot.

"Two lost souls strayed from the herd," a voice says as I sidestep the woman's reach. I spin to see a man flashing a smile, emerging behind a pile of rocks. He's older, with a face full of blisters and scabs that ooze poisoned blood. Mud cakes his boots, up to his knees, and he wears layers of clothes, everything ill-fitting. Like the woman, he carries a woven basket on his back. A pale arm dangles over the edge, the skin loose and bloated, falling off the bone.

"Where did you come from?" The man's eyes are greedy when he looks at Bryn.

"Mine," the woman whispers below us. "Mine, Fanagin, mine-mine-mine. I saw them first."

"Shut up," the man, Fanagin, says, kicking a rock at her. She flinches, ducking her head out of view.

"Mine," she repeats, more sullen than before.

"Yours if you can catch them," Fanagin says.

"Run," I say.

Bryn doesn't even argue. We follow the outcropping as far as it stretches, toward dry land in the distance. But Fanagin's interest has sparked the interest of others and they begin to circle, drawing closer, and I begin to slow, fighting through Bryn's exhaustion as well as my own.

My foot catches in a divot and I trip off the rock, landing knees and elbows deep in the mud below. Bryn throws a look back but continues moving, her red hair flying behind her. Two boys with flaking skin chase after her as I crawl forward, regaining my feet.

But the seventh heir of Brindaigel is not used to running the streets of the Brim or scaling rooftops to see the stars; she's already winded, and I struggle to catch my breath, lungs burning with the labored effort. Fanagin drops into the mud beside me and my fear of the plague outweighs my aim. I swing my fist wild, missing him by inches.

Stumbling back, I ball the sleeves of my coat over my hands and flip the collar up against my throat. Meager protection, but better than nothing.

Fanagin laughs. "I bet you fell from the sky," he says, advancing on me. "A gift from Rook, wrapped up all nice and neat, just for me."

"Don't touch me," I warn. *The knife,* I think, hand straying to the bag around my shoulder. *Did Bryn keep it?*

"But that's the fun part." His smile widens, turns monstrous.

Bryn screams and I gasp as the air is pressed from my lungs. She must have fallen, a suspicion confirmed by the dull ache in my hip that arrives a moment later, shooting pains down my leg.

Fanagin lunges and I take another wild swing, cringing when I hit his throat and a blister erupts, spraying oily blood across my face. Panicked, I scrub it away with the sleeve of my coat, but my weakness costs a chance at defense. Fanagin hits me back before I can block him, a sharp blow across my temple. It knocks me to my knees in a flurry of stars, but before he can strike me again, I lock my hands and slam them down on his knee before scrambling out of the way.

Not fast enough. Fanagin catches me by the back of my coat and pins me face first into the mud. It fills my mouth and nose and I begin choking before he rolls me over, forking a hand around my throat, cutting off all but a trickle of air. Rough, dirty fingers force my lips apart and he scrubs mud against my gums as he assesses my teeth. "Those are worth something, at least," he says, before pulling back the collar of my coat, inspecting my neck, pressing the sore spot where Alistair injected me. "What is this? You ever bleed fire before? Is the meat already spoiled?"

Tears blur my eyes as I begin gasping for air. My lungs ache against my ribs and white spots begin to crowd my vision.

"Keep your collar up and no one will know," he says. "You look clean enough for me and that's clean enough for most." Arching an eyebrow, Fanagin clucks his tongue and shakes his head with mock sympathy before he applies more pressure to my throat. "Didn't Rook warn you there are wolves in this world?"

With one last shuddering heartbeat, darkness swallows me.

Nine

BRIGHT LIGHTS AND FUZZY FIGURES BLUR THE EDGES OF MY VISION. Shapes jostle into focus but are lost again as noises clamor around me, a ceaseless, directionless din of shouting and laughter and the clatter of coins exchanging hands. Slowly, I blink the world into focus. Iron bars, beyond which rises a forest of wooden columns and canvas awnings. Crowded tables bow beneath the weight of the wares for sale, everything from clothing to books to flesh. The people who browse bear marks of magic and poison and the scars of both. Everyone's armed.

I struggle to sit up, wincing. The man from the bog, Fanagin, paces the inside of the cage, beating tempo in his palm with a short length of doubled leather. He's pulled off his outer coat to a fresher one underneath, the sleeves punched up to his forearms. Faded scars of old spells twist up his wrists like pale threads against the dark poison in his veins. He calls for bids and best offers, cajoling the passersby.

Wetting my lips, I try to stretch my hands, testing the give of the rope around my wrists tethering me to a ring on the dusty floor. Only a few feet, and they come painfully, chafing my skin raw.

Beside me, Bryn sits with her chin up and her back straight, legs curled under her as if she's at a palace picnic. She's bound too, but other than a little mud in her hair and the ragged hem of her dress, she looks untouched, thanks to the spell. My body aches in comparison, a medley of pains that are hers and mine and ours combined. Scowling, I tentatively touch my throat and wince at the tender bruising.

"What's the point of running," she says without looking at me, "if you don't follow?"

I lower my hands and stare at her, incredulous. "You'd be dead already if I wasn't carrying your weaknesses!"

Her dark eyes cut toward me before they return to the crowded marketplace. "Strategy is never a weakness."

"And is this strategy?" I ask, lifting my wrists to demonstrate the rope.

She doesn't answer.

A young man dressed in black browses at a table adjacent to the cage, skimming over the odd baubles and trinkets, overlooking a seeping basket of infected body parts. Picking up my mother's book, he thumbs through the pages, watching Fanagin from the corner of his eye.

I touch my pocket on reflex. Empty, of course; skin isn't the only thing worth money. "That's mine," I say hotly.

The man lifts his eyebrows, glancing back at the cover before his eyes return to me with mild interest. Unlike the others who crowd the cage, there's no poison in his face, but he wears a dark coat with the collar flipped against his throat, and leather gloves to hide most of his skin. A weeks' worth of facial hair darkens his jaw and his hair is shaggy, in need of a trim. He carries a crossbow slung over one shoulder, a quiver of bolts on his back.

"Virgin skin, pure as the sainted virtues themselves," Fanagin calls, striking the leather against the bars of the cage. "Begging to be bled or bed at your leisure. Not an inch of infection!"

The man considers me for another moment before his gaze shifts to Fanagin. "I'll give you thirty-five for both," he says, his voice low. Tucking my mother's book under one arm, he retrieves a dark leather book from the pocket of his coat, opening it to where a grease pencil rests in the gutter of the spine. He cradles the pencil in hand, thumb tagging his place.

"Thirty-five each," Fanagin counters.

"Forty for both," the man says with a frown. "You're not going to get much higher around here."

"Fifty," a woman offers from the other side of the cage, leering at the man in black. His frown deepens.

A second man saunters through the crowd, just as young as the first; bony and gaunt, with dark hair pulled back in a ponytail. Loose strands fall forward against his sun-reddened cheeks, half hiding amber-tinted eyes. Curling a hand through the bars above his head, he leans into the cage with a grin, his other hand resting on his jutting hip. "North," he says with a sly glance of acknowledgment to the man in black. "Figured I'd find you sniffing around some virgins."

"Kellig." The man in black, North, stares down at his book, jaw tight.

Kellig wets his lips and glances toward Bryn and I. "What are we buying today?"

"Body bags," says North impassively, eyes briefly meeting mine.

Fanagin turns to Kellig with an eager smile. "Body bags," he repeats. "Perfect, unopened envelopes waiting for the right man to come along and spoil them rotten."

"You never buy body bags," Kellig says, ignoring Fanagin. He tries to read over North's shoulder.

"But you do," North says with an edge of acrimony as he slams his book shut and slides it back in his pocket. "Especially if Baedan's paying."

"She's paying if the price is right and the pieces are all accounted for." Kellig makes a face at the basket of seeping, amputated limbs for sale on the table. "But I admit, it is tempting to make a personal purchase this time. A redhead on one side, a blonde on the other. You don't get faces like that this far south." Straightening, Kellig calls out. "Hey, Fanny. How much for the redhead alone?"

"Fifty," says Fanagin.

"Where is Baedan?" asks North, glancing over his shoulder.

"She gets jealous when I look at other women." Snorting, Kellig releases his hold on the cage and folds his arms across his chest. "She makes a scene, people die, wars are started. Where's your boy at? He can smell out magic thin as a thread. What's he smelling here?"

North doesn't answer him, looking to Fanagin instead. "I'll give you seventy-five for both," he says.

"Gentlemen, *please!*" Fanagin wrenches me up and pulls me

tight against him. A calloused hand stretches over my stomach and clenches the fabric of my dress, hiking the muddy hem toward my knees. "She's rough at the edges but still soft like a woman where it matters. Forty for her, minimum."

"She's already broken," Kellig says, derisive. Blood and mud flock every inch of my dress; my hair hangs in matted tangles. I can only imagine the bruises that cloud my face. "It looks like you already chewed her up and spat her back out."

"Ah," Fanagin says with a grin. "But you know it's what's inside that tastes best."

Growling, I elbow Fanagin in the stomach. It's not a good hit but it surprises him enough to release me, and I use the advantage, grabbing the front of his shirt and slamming my head against his mouth. Bright stars crowd my vision as Fanagin staggers back against the cage, flabbergasted. Shifting my weight, I balance myself, prepared to kick, but he catches my ankle and twists me onto my stomach. Raising his leather band, he strikes me across the shoulders, the back of my neck. I hiss in pain, cowering on the ground at Bryn's knees.

"For gods' sake," she says, "keep your head down!"

She's no better than scrap out here in Avinea, and yet, somehow, she's still somehow *more* than the stink of urine and sweat and rancid flesh around us. Regal and beautiful and untouched by the frustration, the anger that seethes through me. Is she that balanced, to have such control over her own emotions?

Not me. I learned to fight for what I wanted, that it would take more than desire and wishes on stars. My palms are not on the floor and I am far from defeated. After a lifetime of having my choices made for me, I relish this brief moment of power over my own actions. *Control,* I think.

Faces gape at me through the bars, torn between amusement and awe, but it's North whom I challenge with my scowl. His expression isn't hungry like the others, merely curious. Almost concerned. He doesn't belong here any more than we do.

Pressing me down with one knee, Fanagin drops his leather strap and pulls a knife from his belt—Bryn's knife. "I'm not opposed to selling in pieces," he calls to the crowd.

"I'll take her hair," a woman says, her hand stretched through the bars, fingers grasping toward me.

"Twenty tretkas," Fanagin says.

"Fifteen," the woman argues with an offended frown. "It's not that pretty."

"Twenty," a second calls, her own hair brittle, matted against her scabby head in a nest of wisps and blackened stubble.

"Sold," Fanagin says, pointing to the second woman, who claps with delight. Slamming my face into the dirt, Fanagin winds my hair around his wrist, tight and tighter before I feel the blade swing, so close to my neck that the tip draws a narrow line across it.

The crowd roars their approval. Fanagin releases me and I turn in time to see him brandishing my hair like a trophy, spinning it in circles above his head. Anger turns to hate, bitter black and poisonous. Thaelan loved my hair so I loved it, and to see this filthy man trading it for twenty copper tretkas feels like an indignity.

It's worth at least a silver kronet.

Pushing myself back to my knees, I run my tongue over my teeth before I realize Fanagin left the leather strap on the ground ahead of me. Lunging forward, I pull it into my lap, glancing to see if anyone noticed.

North noticed, and he arches an eyebrow. Interested.

"He's going to start pulling your teeth out if you don't stop squirming," Bryn says.

"And he'll sell you to the highest bidder if you don't start acting like you're not worth the trouble," I say. "Nobody wants a girl who might bite."

Standing, I edge closer to the center of the cage, to give my rope tether some slack. When Fanagin turns, I strike the smile off his face, hard as I can.

It feels better than it should.

As he recoils, I slide my arms over his head and pull back, choking him with the rope. The knife hits the ground, just out of reach of my foot.

"Bryn," I say with a thrill of adrenaline. "Bryn, get the knife."

She glances over but doesn't move, eyes locked on something in the distance.

Fanagin twists, yanking the slack of the rope and knocking me off my feet. My skirts hike up as I scramble to reclaim the blade.

He reaches it first, elbowing me hard in the back of the neck. "Who wants her face!?" he roars.

"A hundred for both," says North, "but as is, no blood spilled."

Fanagin hesitates, greed at war with his wounded ego. A harsh welt crosses his face and poison puddles through the furrows, spreading over the bridge of his nose. "A hundred," he agrees at last, spitting in my face before releasing me. Panting, I scramble out of reach, frantically rubbing my face dry against my shoulder.

"A bargain for such a good breed. She bleeds fire, boys."

"She bleeds," Kellig agrees, but his expression narrows, turns calculating, his attention on North instead of on me. He's not here to buy body bags; he's here for North. All of this is superfluous baiting. "One twenty," he says. "At the very least, they'll both carve pretty divots in my sheets."

And bloody divots in your skull, I think.

"Two hundred," says North.

Fanagin straightens with a grin. "That's more like it, my boys!"

Bryn blanches and rises to her feet, earning catcalls of approval and wild shouts from some of the men and women pressing closer. Her fingers sink through my arm in warning. "Loomis," she says with a nod toward the crowd. "Part bloodhound and full idiot."

I tense. A dark figure cuts through the marketplace, face shrouded by a cloak and hidden behind the beaked mask of a councilman. How did he find us?

Fanagin recounts bids as Loomis slinks to the opposite end of the cage, his eyes a bright, vivid blue against the band of dark skin visible above his mask. They flick past Bryn to rest on me, sizing me up, assessing my threat, trying to place my identity before he rattles the door to the cage.

Fanagin slaps the bars. "You haven't won the bid yet," he says. "We're at two twenty. Who goes higher?"

"Two twenty-five," says Kellig.

"Two thirty," says a woman beside him. She cradles a basket to her hip, its contents hidden beneath a ratty blanket. Liquid seeps from the bottom.

"Open this door," Loomis says, his voice coarse and metallic behind the sharp beak of his mask. "In the name of the king and on threat of your death. Any further harm to her highness is an invitation of war."

All heads turn toward him as silence falls, eerie and absolute. The sounds of the marketplace around us seem to dim in comparison, as though we've all been plunged underwater.

Fanagin's grin fades, uncertain. "The king?"

"North, you glorious son of a whore," Kellig breathes, eyes alight. He laughs, bright and barking, rattling the cage. "Body bags my ass! Three hundred for the redhead!"

North draws back, uneasy. His eyes meet mine and my lips part in protest, but no words come out; all I manage is a tight, furtive shake of my head—*no*. Don't stop bidding, please don't go. She might be the daughter of a king but North didn't come for royalty. He came to buy magic.

So I'll sell him magic.

I pinch Bryn as hard as I can. She protests and bats me away, but I rake up the sleeve of my coat, demonstrating the ruby welt that appears on my forearm, not hers.

North straightens, eyebrows lifting. *Yes.* He understands. "Five hundred for both," he says. "Silver paid now, my final offer."

Nobody knows where to look: to Loomis in his cloak and mask, to *her highness* with her impossible grace, or to the man who apparently carries five hundred pieces of silver in his pocket.

Kellig drops his arms, eyes narrowed as they slide from North to me and back again. "What, did she piss magic while I wasn't looking?" he asks.

"Sold," Fanagin sputters at last, torn between disbelief and a gloating grin.

North nods grimly, reaching into his pocket as Fanagin holds out a greedy hand, turning away from Loomis. Dismissing him.

Commandment of the fighting ring: Never, *ever* turn your back on an opponent.

Loomis is efficient, perfunctory: a three-beat murderer. Sword unsheathed, weighted step forward, blade through the back. Fanagin crumples at North's feet, and with deft and certain hands, Loomis reaches through the bars and retrieves the key from where it hangs off Fanagin's belt.

Nobody moves. Not until Loomis unlocks the cage and the sound of falling tumblers shouts an open invitation. A stall keeper from across the aisle darts forward and strips Fanagin of his coat, balling it under his arm before returning to his table, furtive as a rat. A woman takes his boots. It isn't long before his body becomes carrion.

They're not opposed to stealing in pieces.

North steps out of the way, his eyes meeting mine one last time. Apologetic.

No.

I watch, stricken, as he disappears through the crowd, swallowed up by men twice his size and half his relative safety, their bodies poisoned with magic and depravity as they jostle forward, necks craned to see what's happening and if there's any left for them.

Loomis is not the idiot Bryn believes him to be. He seems to recognize the threat he's invited on himself as he hurries to cut Bryn loose, offering an abbreviated bow before lightly touching her shoulder—a gesture of familiarity. "I'm sorry you had to witness that," he says.

"How did you know where to find me?" Bryn asks in amazement, rubbing her wrists.

"I told you once, there are only four corners of the world. It's never far as the crow flies." Only then does he look to me, still tethered to the floor. His eyebrows furrow as he takes in my rumpled coat and mud-stained skirt. "Your name?" he asks with none of the warmth offered Bryn.

I hesitate, looking to Bryn for confirmation: Is this part of her plan? More strategy?

But Bryn offers no answers as Loomis cuts my rope, keeping enough for a lead as he drags me forward. "Who you are doesn't matter," he says. "Your death is already decided."

"Then just leave her for the addicts," Bryn says, flicking her hand, dismissing me. "A prisoner will only slow down our return and I'm eager for a bath."

I stare at her, fear brining my tongue. Is this it, then? One day and I'm dead? Left to rot so there are no witnesses, no stories, no lies to spread?

That wasn't even a chance.

"Your father wants her alive," Loomis says. "The kingdom must see justice."

Bryn shoots me a look, barely there before her eyes lock on Loomis. "I suppose being thrown to the wolves would rob my father of the chance to prove a point."

Gods Above. That's why she didn't go after the knife—so Loomis would imagine her a prisoner, a hostage.

My hostage.

Perrote would never allow his daughter to leave Brindaigel with enough magic to invite a war. But if she was *kidnapped,* if she was coerced and led into enemy territory against her will . . .

My stomach plummets. Will this be the reason he uses to start scouring the Brim? Will my face—my supposed treason—be his justification for culling the population?

Have I just condemned my sister to die?

Kellig watches us, his hands curled through the bars of the cage and forehead pressed against the iron. He flashes his teeth at us when we pass. "Long live the king," he drawls.

Bryn stares him down. "I would have killed you while you slept," she says.

"It would've been one hell of a last night on earth," he replies with a wicked smile.

"Well," says Bryn, pulling her cloak tighter around her. "It's not over yet."

Ten

LOOMIS SHOVES ME THROUGH THE CROWD OF ROTTING BODIES. SOME look newly infected, with only the first ribbons of dark magic threading through their veins. Others are clearly hellborne addicts, their skin colored in shades of smoke, decomposing as they stand. Flies cavort with a restless, incessant hum, inseparable from the din of voices that slide over me like crashing waves.

The decrepit settlement beyond the marketplace is no better. It's a slurry of sights and sounds and sun-bleached color, offset by muddy shadows. Canvas roofs and colored awnings stretch between crooked walls of scrap and wood. Ruins of stone buildings remain like tombstones of another time, when this village might have been beautiful, but they stand rare as the infecteds' teeth now, their exposed innards repurposed as holding pens for sickly goats and listless, dull-eyed people.

The goats roam free; the people are chained. Slaves.

A woman in dark robes stands on a corner, barking brimstone prophecies of the world coming to its inevitable end. Half her face is mapped by burn scars. Her eyes meet mine. "Repent," she says, "for our days are numbered."

I look away, unsettled.

Ash from the nearby Burn drifts like lazy snowflakes, turning the sky smoky and dim; the air tastes scorched and blistered. The only grass is brown, flattened, beaten to dust beneath the feet of so many.

Is this the real Avinea? Not the moon or the stars or the promise of a prince, but pain and blood and human chattel? The Avinea that King Perrote always warned us about, a burning kingdom, ravaged by sin?

Twisting, I sidestep spilled blood and swallow back exhausted tears. This is not what Thaelan promised me all those months ago. Where's the Avinea he imagined?

Where's the Avinea he died for?

The sun fades fast as Loomis steers us to a corral full of withered, miserable beasts. A young man straightens as we approach, swiping a cigarette out of his mouth and crushing it beneath his boot with a look of guilt that dissolves into relief when he sees Bryn.

"Your majesty," he says, dipping into an abbreviated bow before he pulls two horses forward, attention shifting to Loomis. "Took long enough, didn't you? Gods and sinners, the offers I've gotten since you left. They buy skin by the inch out here." A hand absently touches his chest, where Perrote's loyalty spell sits above his heart. "I was tempted to sell."

"You should be so tempted to keep your mouth shut." Loomis thrusts me at the boy. "Did you make the purchase?"

The boy flashes a bundled package before tucking it back in his jacket, wrapping the slack of my tether around his fist.

Loomis helps Bryn onto a horse, far gentler than the boy who drags me to his. As we settle in the saddles, Kellig arrives, lazy and unhurried, hands in his pocket. Two men flank him, built like giants, with arms bared to demonstrate the poison written across their skin. They fall back as Kellig hooks his elbows over the corral fence. He catches my eye and winks.

The night's not over yet.

We ride out of the settlement and into a smoky field. I cling to the horse, trying to watch the landscape rolling past. There's no bog on the other side of the valley we ride out of, no river leading to a hidden stairwell. Instead, the ground opens and we chase the sun's descent, the mountains to our left. They couldn't have brought horses through the river below the dungeon, and I realize with a jolt:

There's more than one way out of Brindaigel.

We don't slow until we reach a forest of silver birch and dense evergreens. With a grunt, Loomis dismounts and pulls his mask off, revealing a face damp with sweat and stamped with the harsh lines of the mask's leather padding. He wipes the sweat against his shoulder. "We'll do it here," he says.

Bryn twists in the saddle, surveying the forest. "Why are we stopping?"

Loomis rummages through the saddlebag. I catch a glimpse of a flintlock inside and my stomach drops. During the war, King

Perrote imported pistols from the Northern Continents to sell to Corthen and his men—brand-new technology to combat Merlock's magic. They're rare now, since loyalty spells limit their necessity, but their purpose is the same.

To guarantee victory.

Sweat breaks out across my back. The last time I saw a councilman with a flintlock, it was to shoot a girl who tried to escape Brindaigel by climbing over the mountains. Even in the middle of the gathering crowd who stood to watch, the reverberation of that shot had echoed through my bones like a drum.

"I apologize, your majesty," Loomis says, exchanging glances with the boy at my back as he withdraws a length of rope. "It's only a momentary detour. King's orders."

Bryn watches him, bemused. The boy dismounts before pulling me down, taking the rope from Loomis and pushing me into the fringe of trees.

"Be careful," says Bryn. "That one bites."

"And what about you, milady?" he asks playfully, a contradiction to the rough way he shoves me to my knees in a cradle of roots. "Do you bite too?"

"Impertinent young man," she says, but it's an absent response, her attention drawn elsewhere. I follow her gaze, to the shadows thickening between the trees. Is there something out there?

The boy grins, humming beneath his breath as he lashes me to the tree. "Do you even remember me?" he asks. "We danced once at the palace."

Bryn regains her composure as she dismounts, shaking out her traveling cloak before twisting her hair over one shoulder. "Did we?"

"She has danced with many men," Loomis says darkly.

"Ah, but this was special," says the boy.

"I'm sure it was magic," Bryn says drily.

Loomis scowls and holds out a hand. Grinning, the boy retrieves the bundled package from his pocket. I strain for a glimpse as it's unwrapped, only to go numb when I recognize the glass and metal flashing in the fading light.

A needle. Another syringe.

God Above.

"What is this?" Bryn asks, plucking the syringe from its wrappings.

"A simple precaution," Loomis says, carefully taking it back before passing it to the boy. "You were spared the effects of the Burn because of your royal blood. But your captor . . ."

All three look at me and I stare back. "You're going to poison me?"

"Avinea is a wasteland," Loomis says. "His majesty keeps his people safe, no matter the cost. A demonstration of that mercy will alleviate the kingdom's fears and prove that the princess was spared by the gods' blessing—"

"Perrote is a liar!"

Bryn slaps me across the face. "That is treason."

I swallow hard, cheek stinging, staring across the trees. She's on my side, I tell myself, but do I really know that? Bryn plays us all so easily, I can't be certain which one of us is the enemy.

Maybe we all are.

Backing up, Bryn holds her hand out. "I want to do it," she says.

Loomis balks. "Your majesty, that would hardly be appropriate."

"I know how to use a needle," Bryn says. "My betrothed taught me, among other things."

"Also not appropriate," Loomis says.

"I do not regret my choice," Bryn says tightly, "nor do I suspect you regret yours. Joyena certainly stands closer to the crown than I ever could."

Loomis looks away, jaw clenched.

The boy's eyebrows arch with interest at Loomis's sudden discomfort, no doubt savoring the story left unsaid to be taken home and embellished in the tavern. But then his attention returns to Bryn and he offers her a lazy grin, rolling the syringe between his fingers. "I'll let you have it if you can remember my name."

Bryn's expression softens, turns beguiling. She approaches the boy, flattening the collar of his tunic, straightening the shoulder of his jacket. He shifts his weight, wetting his lips in anticipation.

"It's right there on the edge of my tongue," she says, folding her hand over his, cupping the syringe between them as if they were about to waltz. She tilts her head and his smile widens, turning devilish as she plucks the needle from his hand.

There's no chance for him to even gasp, to scream. Like a strike of lightning, Bryn drives the needle in the boy's chest and depresses the plunger, releasing the entire vial of poisoned blood into his heart before she unsheathes his dagger and steps back, chin high. His smile turns into a gruesome scream as he claws at the needle, knocking it loose. Dropping to his knees, he stares up at Bryn and she stares him down, unflinching.

"I didn't remember your name," she says softly, "because it was never worth knowing."

Loomis chokes back a strangled gasp of surprise. Bryn rounds on him, holding the boy's dagger to his throat as she unsheathes his sword as well. "I actually liked you, Loomis. You were ambitious in a court full of cowards."

He stares at her, stricken. "Your majesty—"

"But then you chose my sister," she says, gesturing toward me before handing him the dagger, holding the sword to his back. He dutifully drops to his knees and cuts me loose before she reclaims the dagger, crossing it over the blade of the sword in an X at his neck. "Greed always costs."

"Bryndalin," he tries, softer this time, more pleading.

Bryn presses both blades into his skin, drawing twin points of blood. "I should thank you," she says, almost breathless. "You were the first man to show me that human life is its own commodity."

The boy begins convulsing, clawing at his skin. Thin rivers of poison route a map up his throat, across his jaw. How long does it take to turn hellborne?

Bryn scowls at the boy before glancing at me. "Get the pistol," she says, nodding the direction.

I hurry to retrieve it from the saddlebag, holding it for her to take. She doesn't. "Do you know how to use it?"

I push it toward her again. "No," I say, and I don't want to learn.

"I suggest you start by pointing it at his head," Bryn replies darkly. "Pull the trigger when you're ready."

My spine turns to ice. "What?"

"Kill him," says Bryn.

"I—I can't do that."

"Would you rather have the sword?" She pulls back, withdrawing the blade in question.

"No," I say, emphatic. "No, I mean, I can't—" The words tangle in my throat and I shake my head, backing away.

Bryn stares at me, mouth grim. "Once again, you harbor the illusion that you're being given a choice." Tossing the sword aside, she grabs my arm and yanks me forward, pressing the barrel of the gun against Loomis's temple. "Pull the trigger. Shoot. You'd already be done by now."

"This wasn't part of the agreement—"

"The agreement was to start a war," she says. "You chose your side. Now honor your promises or I'll honor mine."

Blood trumpets in my head, a pulsing, beating *no-no-no*. I've fought before, but always against an opponent who accepted the risks of the ring—and who knew a palm on the floor could save them if things went bad. But I can't do this, not to an unarmed man with no chance of intervention. It will unbalance my soul.

"It's either him or Cadence," says Bryn. Her eyes glitter in the twilight, like twin pools of oil. Releasing her hold on the gun, she steps back, out of the way, watching me. Waiting.

Horror rakes down my back: Is she only doing this to prove she has power over me?

Loomis's breath catches, damp and rattling. He wets his lips and shifts his weight across his knees, eyes closed, features contorted with the terror of anticipation.

Loomis or Cadence; Cadence or me. Do I want my sister enough to kill for her?

"His majesty is not a heartless man," Loomis tries weakly. "He would show mercy for your crimes—"

"That is a lie," I say, choking on the words as my throat closes tighter. "Perrote is a murderer."

And now, so am I.

It's almost too easy, it's almost too fast. An instant is all it takes to scar my soul down to the bone as the echo of my choice screams through the trees.

There are monsters in Avinea.

Bryn is there immediately, wiping away the blood, the tears, the goose bumps that tighten my skin. Smoke twines between us as she cradles my face in her hands. "You're all right," she says. Wolves bay in the distance, called by the howl of gunshot, the smell of fresh meat. "Cadence needs you to be stronger than this."

The gun slides out of my hand. I close my eyes, curling my arms over my face, squeezing back the tears and the screams. Pulling away from me, Bryn gathers her skirts to avoid the blood on the ground and crouches, frisking both bodies. The boy grabs her arm, desperation bright in his eyes.

"Please," he wheezes.

"My father would have killed you both as soon as you returned," she says gently, moving his dark curls out of his eyes. "You stupid boy. Nobody leaves Brindaigel."

Standing, she offers me a dagger. "Always aim for the heart," she says. "Be careful of the ribs. Cut the throat if you have to, but use enough force or you're wasting your time."

Growling, I grab her by the wrist; the bones are tiny, fragile, easy to break. Bryn pulls back, but when I don't release her, she stops moving, expression defiant.

I can't breathe. Blood freckles her face; pools of shadow hollow the spaces beneath her eyes. We stare each other down and though I stand several inches taller than her, she towers over me.

"I am not the enemy tonight," she says.

Still holding my gaze, she deliberately pulls out of my grip, proving how powerless I really am.

Staggering back, I bump into a tree and bend over my knees, sucking in harsh gasps of air. Bryn turns for the horses. "We'll ride to Nevik and continue as planned," she says. "Nothing has changed."

A boy lies dying at her feet. Another man is dead at mine. The whole world has shifted an inch to the side; tomorrow, the sun will rise at a different angle than it did before.

I killed a man and nothing will ever be the same.

Turning, I run, graceless and frantic. Spells are woven out of threads, I think; if I run fast enough, far enough, maybe, *maybe* it could snap apart and Bryn couldn't hurt me—

A figure materializes in the darkness and I veer to miss colliding with it, my boots skidding on the cover of dead leaves before I lose my balance and fall. A woman frowns at me as I raise my dagger in delayed defense. The blade shakes in my tremulous grip and she smirks. Amused.

She's the same deadly kind of pretty that Bryn wears so well. Moonlight-colored hair with darkened tips, silver eyes and narrow brows. Spells are woven across her arms and throat, countered by veins of dead magic that trace her face in shades of charcoal.

"Are you the daughter of the king?" she asks in a voice like smoke and screaming.

"That's not her," a voice says, male and familiar. Kellig. He slinks out of the shadows, prowling behind the woman.

Bryn screams in the distance; the woman and I both turn to the sound. "Take what you can and bleed the rest," she says, moving into the trees in search of Bryn. Dismissing me, the useless one.

Kellig waits for her to disappear before he regards me with a grin. "Five hundred pieces of silver," he says, shaking a finger at me. "You see, North knows. He always knows when to buy and when to sell and when to disappear."

I climb to my feet and back into a tree, assessing my escape.

"What's your name?" Kellig asks, still pacing. "Or maybe you'd rather have mine? You can scream it as I kill you."

"Don't touch me."

"I like to start with the teeth," he says. "Those are the first thing to rot, you know? Noble addicts pay good money for good teeth to hide their dirty habits." He bares his own teeth at me, snapping them together. I flinch and he grins. "I'll rip them out one by one," he continues, "while my men fight to drink that virgin blood as it spills down your chin." His dark eyes drop to my chin and lower, to the sagging neckline of my dress. "They bite sometimes," he says. A dark smile carves his lips into something terrible. "You might actually like it."

Another scream, wild and feral, before heat flashes across my calves in warning. *Bryn.* I realize—too late—that she's more of a liability to my safety when I can't see her. If she gets hurt, I get hurt too, and despite everything, she's not my enemy. Not tonight.

"And then I'll peel your skin off," Kellig says. He makes a gruesome squelching noise at the back of his throat as he pantomimes tearing flesh from his face. "Exposing all your secret spells."

"No secrets here," I say, wetting my lips, shifting my weight. I know men like him, the kind who come to the Stone and Fern, their egos outweighing their abilities in the ring. All talk to compensate for little action.

I try to relax into position, fists loose but ready: I'll only have one chance to strike first. Unlike with Loomis, this is self-defense, and I welcome the taste of adrenaline, the familiarity of a fight.

Kellig feints for me but my sidestep is too slow. He grabs a fistful of my hair and twists as my legs buckle and fear clouds my strategy, turning everything muddy. "Let's see what we've got," he says, flattening his palm across my exposed collarbone. Needles of pain slide under my skin and start digging.

Is he a transferent, able to rip the magic out of my skin with just his bare hands?

"Let her go," a voice says, sharp from the shadows behind us.

Kellig spins, swinging me in front of him as a shield, his palm sliding off my skin. Icy relief floods through me, immediately eclipsed with fear: I can't fight more than one at a time.

A man steps forward, slender and ominous, a face framed in all black. North. He aims a crossbow toward Kellig and edges closer, sure-footed, eyes never leaving his quarry. "Let her go," he repeats.

"Make me an offer," says Kellig, hugging me close, grinning as he rests his chin on my shoulder. "Two hundred pieces of silver, North—a bargain considering what you would have paid."

"I'm not bartering with you."

"Where's the fun—?" Kellig starts, as I slam my dagger into his upper thigh. He swears and releases me, doubling over.

I run.

North shouts for me to stop but I ignore him, crashing through the trees, stumbling over roots and sunken gulches. Pine needles slap at my face before I stumble into the same clearing as before. Two horses, one body.

Where'd the other one go?

Three monstrous figures are bent over Loomis, tearing at his flesh in their greed for the magic woven through his skin. The nameless boy is nowhere to be seen, and a detached thrill of fear runs down my back. Am I sure the screams I heard belonged to Bryn? The pain I felt certainly did.

The hellborne pause their eating and look at me with bleary, moony eyes. I stare back, frozen. Every breath aches, and each one is torn from me in short, staccato bursts that threaten to send me to my knees.

And then I *am* on my knees, knocked forward by a blast of heat that scorches the air and thickens it with the smell of blood and brimstone. The hellborne scream in agony, clawing at their chests where tiny striations begin cracking the skin. Boiling poison seeps out, steaming in the cooler night air.

North appears behind me, shaken and gaunt, a bare hand outstretched. With a look of pain, of concentration, he makes a fist and the hellbornes' screams abruptly end as they slump over. Dead.

I scramble away from North, hauling myself to my feet. He turns to me, magic still glowing in his fingertips, casting eerie shadows across his face.

"Wait," he says.

I throw myself back through the trees, shouting for Bryn, voice cracking as I gag on the lingering stench of burnt flesh. The only pain that answers my calls is my own: Wherever she is, she's alive and unharmed.

Even so, when she shouts my name, I pick up speed, angling through the trees before I find her, flat on her back, fighting against a boy pinning her down.

I tackle the boy. He protests, hands flying toward my face, my wrists, holding my dagger away from his skin. "No," he says, panicked. "Wait!"

I draw back, confused. He's not hellborne and he's unarmed; he's a child, barely older than Cadence, with round shoulders and a round face and shaggy hair.

"Kill him," Bryn growls, rolling onto her stomach to see us. Her hair hangs in wild tangles around her shoulders; dirt is smeared across her cheek.

I'm pulled off the boy, momentarily suspended before my feet find purchase. A hand tightens against my shoulder but I wrench free, spinning to find North, crossbow in one hand, the other held open in peace.

"You're all right," he says softly. He reaches for me but I step out of range, holding my blade between us in warning. North dutifully takes a step back as well, widening our distance. "We're not here to hurt you. My name is North and this is my apprentice, Tobek."

The boy, Tobek, scrambles to his feet and falls behind North.

"What do you want?" Bryn asks, as I hold tighter to the dagger, bracing my weight, debating which one to strike first.

North and Tobek exchange glances. "That," says North, "has a complicated answer."

Eleven

NORTH LEADS US THROUGH THE WOODS, CASTING GLANCES BEHIND him every few feet, stopping to cock his head and listen. Tobek trails behind me, penning Bryn and myself between them, and I hold my dagger in an unrelenting grip. It was easier to trust a kind face in a crowd of infected monsters, but out here in the dark, after what I've just seen, I'm second-guessing myself and the faith I've placed in a stranger. A *magician*.

Trust no one, I think.

"We're not far," says North, crossbow half raised to his chest.

"Too far for no explanation," says Bryn, as her cloak snags on a rock.

North watches her from over his shoulder. A branch snaps behind us, jarring as a gunshot. I flinch away from the sound, from the memory, and North's eyes shift back to me, a slight furrow dividing his forehead. "My wagon is warded against the hellborne," he says, turning. "It's not far, and it is far safer than out here."

Bryn scowls and tugs her cloak free.

Before long, the sky opens above me and I stumble through grass as high as my thighs. For an instant, the stars steal my attention before I remember myself. Swallowing hard, I switch the dagger to my opposite hand, looking past North to a wagon parked inside a circle of white stones.

The wagon is old, faded, too long spent in the sun. Dark paint peels in layers, like the necrotic skin of the hellborne. White bleeds into blue and rust bleeds into everything, painting lines from the slanted roof down to the wheels. A stable door is shuttered closed at the top of a small stepladder; two horses graze with utter disinterest at the side. A campfire smolders from a dug-out hole flanked by more stones.

North approaches the wagon, pressing his hand to the door. White threads of magic crawl across the wood and sink into the grain before a lock clicks and the door sags open. Slinging his crossbow over his shoulder, he steps inside and lights an oil lamp hanging from the ceiling. Heat spills out with intoxicating invitation, but I hang back, knocking into Tobek, who stands too close behind me.

North waits, expectant, hands on his hips. "I have tea," he says, gesturing to a tarnished samovar above a fat-bellied stove.

"Your majesty, this is not a good idea," I whisper urgently. "He knows magic."

"But he has tea," Bryn says drily.

North seems to remember the weapon he holds. He pulls off the crossbow and angles it against a chair before demonstrating his hands. "No magic," he says. The fingers are bent, arthritic, the knuckles swollen into painful, reddened knots. My eyes crawl back to a face too young to be suffering such an affliction, barely older than me.

Noticing my gaze, North straightens and tucks his hands across his chest as his face floods with color. Reluctantly, I follow Bryn into the wagon, ready to bolt at the first sign of attack.

It smells sour inside, like sweat and old skin; like two men who live in close quarters and don't often entertain. Dried plants hang in bushels from the beams of the ceiling; an apothecary's chest hugs half a wall, full of drawers and topped with jars filled with rocks, some white, some gray, and some completely black. Books lie scattered across the top of the chest and the small table adjacent, spines and pages haphazardly shoved into place with no apparent system. The stove hisses on the opposite wall, beside a stack of splinted wood and a dresser, while two bunks are built against the back, both framed with carved designs. A single window is set into the wall above the top bunk.

Someone painted stars on the ceiling.

"Who are you?" Bryn asks, nose wrinkled in distaste.

North blinks. "As I said, my name is North, that is my apprentice, Tobek, and this"—a ball of orange and white fur joyfully barrels toward his legs and he scoops it in his arms—"is Darjin."

A cat. It purrs with rusty glee as North cradles it to his chest, scratching beneath its upturned chin. He smiles down at the cat, softening the otherwise fierce lines of his face. Even his eyes are black, I realize, when he looks to me again.

I look away, uncomfortable. Still guilty. Does he know that I pulled a trigger and chose my sister over someone else? Surely murder leaves a mark, some physical note for everyone to see. If he knew, would he have saved my life?

Has he saved my life? After all, he made the first bid in the marketplace, and while I wanted his help at the time, that was before I knew he could stop a hellborne heart with just his hands. What could he do to someone like me?

Tobek stands at the bottom of the stairwell behind me, blocking our escape. Unlike North, he has not relinquished his crossbow, and a low burr of warning raises the hairs on my neck. "Bryn," I whisper, tugging on the edge of her cloak. There are too many walls and not enough doors.

She shakes me off with an irritated scowl. "You weren't looking for guests to invite to tea," she says.

North sets Darjin onto a chair. Cat fur clings to his coat, unnoticed. "You're obviously not safe out there," he says. "Certainly not alone. We're leaving for Corsant in the morning, and I'm happy to take you anywhere along that route—"

"We're on our way to New Prevast," says Bryn. "Either you can help us or you're wasting our time."

"New Prevast is seven days in the opposite direction," says North.

Bryn falls back, flicking her wrist dismissively. "Then you can't help us."

North's hands curl around the back of a chair. He chews his lower lip as his thumb taps an impatient rhythm. "How did you end up at that market?"

"Irrelevant," says Bryn. "Why were you there? And why did you follow us into the woods?"

The complicated answer. North colors slightly, shifting his weight.

Exchanging looks with Tobek, he tilts his head toward one shoulder, considering his words. "For four years," he says slowly, "I've been tracking down rumors of Merlock's whereabouts; any magic cast by the king only lasts so long as he does. If I could kill Merlock, I could potentially stop the plague from spreading any further. All evidence suggests that he's sought refuge within the Burn in the hopes that no one will find him—"

"Your king is a coward," says Bryn.

"But he is still the king," says North with a tight, reflective smile. "And while he lives, Prince Corbin cannot inherit the magic he needs to save Avinea." Drawing a breath, he studies his hands on the back of the chair. "The spell that binds you two together," he says at last, looking up. "I've never seen one that strong before. Tobek smelled the charge of it from the road. Unfortunately, so did every hellborne in the area. Magic like that is worth a fortune, and people are willing to kill for it. As I said, you're safe here, for now. There are wards on the wagon, but out there . . ."

"Is this an offer or a threat?" Bryn straightens.

"It's magic," North repeats, and a flicker of excitement colors his voice, brightening his eyes. He looks more his age now, vibrant in his enthusiasm. "Without a trace of poison in it. That's . . . that's impossible. In four years, I've never found anything more than a thread or a spark or even a—a *candle* leftover from before the war. Yet here you are, brighter than the sun." Sobering, he says, "I want to buy it from you."

"It's not for sale."

"You want a binding spell?" I ask, looking from one to the other, uneasy. "What would you do with it?"

"Unravel it," says North, shifting his attention to me. "I'd proba-bly lose some of the magic in the process, yes, but I could save the rest and—"

My heart sinks. "You're a transferent too?"

North blinks. "Yes."

Despite my dagger, I look around me for something heavier, dead-lier—a contingency plan. North is not a large man but he looks huge, with that kind of power. A single touch could destroy Bryn's mission—and my life.

"If I was going to steal it, I would have done it by now," he says ruefully, noticing my unease. "Look, I can't enter the Burn unpro-tected. I'd be poisoned within hours, either dead or hellborne within days. Clean magic—enough of it—could be used to pave a path, giving me the chance I need to search for Merlock."

He takes a step toward us. Both Bryn and I tense and he freezes, startled by our reaction. "Tea," he explains, eyebrows furrowed, pointing to the samovar.

"Boundary line," Bryn says, drawing an imaginary line through the air before gesturing him back over it.

He straightens with a slight frown. "This is my wagon."

"This is my magic," she counters. "And you were going to pay that man five hundred pieces of silver for it."

Tobek chokes. "Five hun—I told you no more than one! One thirty at the outside! That silver's got to last us another two months!"

North ignores him, frowning at Bryn. "So then name your price."

She smiles, savoring the shift in power. "A man who carries five hundred pieces of silver isn't just *looking* for Merlock and strange spells to buy off girls in the marketplace. You have a patron." She tents her fingers against the table, appearing to study her chipped nails before her eyes cut toward North. "Prince Corbin."

I'm grateful she has experience in negotiations while my experience is more in hitting until it hurts. I wouldn't have even considered wondering where the silver came from, only where he might have hidden it.

North does not look nearly so impressed with her conclusion; he looks annoyed. "Yes," he says, "my search is being funded by New Prevast, but that is not—"

"Here's my offer," Bryn says, flicking a hand to silence him. North closes his mouth, eyes flashing. "Take us to New Prevast, introduce us to your prince, and then, and only then, I will release this spell to anyone his majesty so chooses."

North cocks his head, forcing a tight, humorless smile. "As I said, New Prevast is seven days in the opposite direction. I'm not the only one looking for Merlock, and after tonight, my biggest competition has just become my newest enemy." He points beyond the wagon, back into the woods. "I need more than just a maybe that I made the right decision in burning that bridge by saving your lives."

"It's the strongest spell you've ever seen and your prince is getting desperate," says Bryn.

"*My* prince." North's eyes narrow, a slash of black against his olive face, the distinction simmering between them. "Who are you?"

"Avinea's last chance," says Bryn.

Snorting, North runs a hand through his hair. "Humble as well as cryptic."

"There's no shame in knowing my worth."

"And there's no shame in gratitude," Tobek says, with a flash of indignation. "Baedan and her men would've eaten you alive!"

"You only saved our lives because you wanted something from us," Bryn says. Scorn colors her voice and her expression shifts, so subtle as to be almost imperceptible, and yet, it transforms her from a pretty girl in a muddy dress to a queen without a crown. "I'll kiss your feet when it's actually warranted."

Tobek's features darken like a summer thunderstorm but North shakes his head. "Dinner," he suggests tightly. Scowling, Tobek spins on his heel, slamming his way outside.

North waits a moment, biting his lip before he looks back at Bryn, studying her with a slight frown. "Are you Merlock's daughter?"

"What? Good god, no!" Bryn laughs scornfully. "My father is a king, not a coward."

North's brow furrows. "So a princess wants to go to New Prevast to see a prince," he says slowly. "But the prince doesn't entertain everyone I drag to his door. I need names. Places of origin. Who sent you, and why now?"

"My name is Bryndalin Dossel." Bryn tosses her hair back, chin raised high. "And where I'm from is irrelevant to you, as is my purpose."

"Not good enough, Miss Dossel." He shakes his head. "After twenty years of being ignored by every country within reach, what could you or your father possibly hope to gain in Avinea?"

"I am not here for my father," she says with a warning tone. "And if you can't help us, we'll just find our own way to New Prevast." She turns, sliding her arm through mine and pulling me toward the door. We're halfway down the stairwell before—

"Wait."

Bryn flashes a grin of triumph to me, but immediately sobers before she turns to face him, haughty. "Yes?"

"If I take you to New Prevast, that binding spell is mine," says North, dark eyes blazing. "I won't wait for Prince Corbin's leftovers."

Bryn tips her head back, considering. "Agreed."

He extends a hand. "Will you shake on that?"

"I will not," she says. "And if you ever try to touch me, I will kill you." Releasing me, Bryn pulls a small ring from her finger and drops it on the table. It spins before settling. "It's gold," she says. "Consider that as good as my word. Take us to New Prevast and the spell is yours."

My breath catches. I know that ring. It belonged to Thaelan's grandmother and would, he had confided one night beneath the stars, one day be his wife's. I had held it toward the moon, my insides as green as the stones nestled between the tiny diamonds, wanting the impossible so badly I couldn't breathe. He never mentioned it again and I always believed he'd given it to Ellis, the girl his father chose for him.

"Where did you get that?" I whisper.

Bryn shrugs, indifferent. "From Pem," she says.

My chest cracks along the scar tissue and floods with bile. The only way for Alistair to have gotten that ring is to have taken it from Thaelan. *Stolen* it.

And then he gave it to *her.*

Dropping the dagger, I lurch down the stairwell, out into the field. Tobek looks up from the fire, rotating something on a metal spit. He calls out a warning regarding the stones around camp but I ignore him, breaking into a run.

The ground is hard, unfamiliar beneath feet so long accustomed to cobblestones and the furrows of our farming terraces. Mountains chew the horizon and I run for them, drawn by the only symbol I have of home and Cadence, but the mountains stay just out of reach. Even the Burn is too far away, no more than a ribbon of fire that colors the horizon gold.

Hopelessness overtakes me and I feel the first warning edge of pain reminding me that the last two days have not come easy. Gasping for breath, I fall to my knees, crying for Cadence, for Thaelan, for myself—for believing a girl from the Brim could rise as high as the castle, as far as the stars.

The stars.

There are thousands of them, an entire ocean overhead. Tipping my head back, I raise my hands and frame a span of sky—two hands' worth and no more, the most we ever saw from the roofs of Brindaigel. It settles me with its familiar view.

Footsteps approach behind me. I don't have to look to know it's North; Bryn would never deign to follow me. I lower my hands, my cropped hair falling forward, past my chin.

"What do you want?" I ask.

"You do like running," he says wryly. When I don't respond, he takes another step closer. "I have to ask you to stay within the stone ring for your own safety," he says. "I can't extend a ward beyond its borders and the hellborne are far more active in the night. Especially tonight."

Turning, I see North with his head rocked back to the sky as if to guess what I was looking at. He worries his lower lip beneath his teeth, eyes hooded with shadow when they fall back to me.

"You wanted me to win that bid this afternoon," he says.

"You were the only one who looked like he wouldn't peel my skin off," I say.

"You were right. You're safe."

I snort, casting a derisive look at my wrist. "Maybe. For now."

North edges closer. "Do you need help?"

I need my sister. Answers. Why did my mother steal the king's magic and then waste it on saying good-bye? Why didn't she run, like I would have done? Like I *should* have done, when I had the chance?

Why did I listen to Alistair Pembrough after four months of planning to kill him?

"How much would it cost to remove this?" I ask, brandishing my arm toward North. The spell shifts beneath my skin, dark as the smoke that rises ahead of us.

Remorse clouds his face. "I can't do that."

"You're a transferent, name your price!"

"No, I mean"—he crouches to see me eye to eye—"the spell originates in Miss Dossel. I can't remove it through you."

Frustration floods my veins, edged with despair. I can't run, I can't escape. She'll kill me if I try.

She'll kill Cadence.

Lowering my head, I close my eyes. "So then what did you want from me?"

"I don't understand."

"I don't have any money," I say, looking at him. "I don't have any gold rings, but you came looking for me, not Bryn, back there in the woods."

His expression goes blank. "Happenstance," he says, hands dangling between his knees. "Tobek was just as likely to find you."

"You just said this spell has nothing to do with me. If that's all you really wanted from us, you would've gone after the source."

North ducks his head with a tight, humorless smile as he examines his hands and avoids my accusation. He must know I'm hiding more than just a spell beneath my skin, that there's magic enough for him to steal if he wanted it. He's as mercenary as all the rest of them.

"I just wanted to help," he says.

"I know that trick," I say. "A handsome man offers to help me and the next thing I know, I'm standing in a foreign country chained to a princess."

The edge of his mouth twitches. "A handsome man?"

"You're not a stupid man, either," I mutter with an unwanted rise of heat.

His eyes meet mine. "Would you believe me if I said—"

"No," I interrupt. "I wouldn't."

He tilts his head, eyebrows raised. "You're not even going to give me a chance to lie to you?"

I stare at him.

"Or maybe I might have told you the truth," he says wryly. Brandishing Thaelan's ring, he asks, "Is this yours?"

I look away. Blood echoes in my ears. "No."

"Are you sure?"

"It never belonged to me," I say, teeth clenched. And now it never will. It's like losing Thaelan all over again, and I hate Bryn and Alistair for doing that—for tainting his memory with their own greed.

Standing, I waver on my feet and North rises, offering me a hand. "Don't touch me," I say, stepping out of reach.

"You too, huh?" His lips flatten as he slides his hands in his pockets, rocking back onto his heels. "What's your name?"

"What difference does it make?"

"You asked me what I wanted."

"Don't mock me."

"Names are power," he says. "You underestimate the value of yours."

"I'm a servant," I say. "My only value is in my skin."

North doesn't argue. He doesn't speak at all, he simply watches. Waiting.

I hold back a sigh. I haven't given my name to anyone in months and it feels rusty on my tongue. "Faris Locke."

"Faris Locke," he repeats softly, like it's something special, worth remembering. He offers me his hand for an introduction before remembering himself. No touching. The hand slides through his hair instead, spiking it in dark, unruly peaks that slowly settle back into place on either side of his forehead. "There was an old pistol on the ground back there in the woods," he says.

I flinch, feeling its weight, its power, its finality all over again. Shame warms my skin and yet I hug myself, suddenly cold.

"Where did that come from?"

"It was a gift from the king," I say, staring at the ground.

"Miss Dossel's father the king?"

I nod, and he lifts his chin in acknowledgment, eyebrows drawn in consideration.

"It's probably still out there if you want it," I say, turning for camp.

"It wouldn't do me much good," he says. "Avinea hasn't produced ammunition for almost fifteen years, and our trade routes to the Northern Continents have been closed for more than twenty. Is that where it came from? The Northern Continents?"

I shrug, frustrated: What difference does it make where the gun came from? I used it to kill a man. Why isn't he asking me about that? "I don't know. Yes? Ask Bryn."

"I suspect I'll have to pay for any answers from her in silver and blood," he says, glancing toward the wagon.

"Then maybe I'm offering my answers too freely."

His eyebrows shoot up. Interested. "Name your price."

My price is fifty gold kronets and signed papers releasing my sister from the nightmare of the workhouse. But North can't give me that.

"Just get us to New Prevast," I say, hugging myself even tighter. "As fast as you can." Because if Perrote's councilman was able to find us after only one day, who—*what*—might find us next?

"Seven days," North says, resting his weight on the outsides of his boots. "We'll leave in the morning."

I nod tightly, turning away. "Thank you."

"Miss Locke?"

I pause.

"You're safe now," he says. "I promise."

I glance toward the stars, so many I could drown in them. "I'm sorry," I say. "I still don't believe you."

Twelve

I RETURN TO THE FIRE, TO A PLATE OF FOOD THRUST IN MY HANDS and a seat beside Bryn on a rock. The pheasant Tobek roasted sits in a pool of buttery oil dotted green with herbs I don't recognize. It reminds me of the blisters lanced across the hellborne as they ravaged Loomis's corpse.

I can't eat.

"You and Miss Locke can share the bottom bunk," says North, his own dinner neatly dissected on his plate, fork and knife crossed at the center. "Tobek will sleep on the floor."

The formality in addressing us by titled name seems ridiculous: He's barely older than us and in desperate need of a shave and yet he treats us like we're generations separated.

"Absolutely not," says Bryn. "Faris can sleep on the floor, you and Tobek may share the bottom bunk, and I'll take the top." Arching an eyebrow, she cuts her meat into tidy portions. "I sleep beneath no man."

Tobek snorts into his cup, sobering as both Bryn and North give him withering looks. "Sorry," he mumbles, shoulders hunched over his own plate. Bones litter the side, picked clean of meat.

Bryn shifts with a rustle of skirts. She sits straight where I slouch, prim where I cower. Every time her fork scrapes across the plate, I flinch at the noise.

"I will not allow a woman to sleep on the floor," says North, reaching for a cup cradled at his feet.

"And I do not share a bed with servants."

"Aren't you hungry?" Tobek asks me.

"Are you a transferent too?" I ask to distract him, setting the plate aside.

Tobek looks pleased. "No, only an intuit. Transferents have to touch things before they know whether there's any magic inside, but I can smell it without being anywhere near it. North taught me how to tell clean from dead."

Bryn snorts. "So that's your talent? Smelling magic?"

"Well, I smelled it on you back in Cortheana."

"You and every hellborne addict out there," says Bryn, rolling her eyes.

"I'm not an addict," he says hotly. "And anyway, the hellborne can't read the course your blood will run. Not like me."

"You can tell the future?" She quirks an eyebrow, amused.

He stiffens, turns cagey. "For the right price."

"Of course. You saved my life so you could charge me pennies for my dreams. I suppose you do card tricks as well."

His hand flies to the front of his vest, to a deck of cards that hangs in the pocket.

"I don't mind sleeping on the floor," I say.

"No," says North.

"I don't cheat," Tobek says. "Not anymore."

"I really don't mind," I say.

Bryn's fork scrapes across her plate. "She's fine on the floor."

"I will not argue—"

"My servant," says Bryn, "my magic, my rules. If we are not absolutely clear on the parameters of our agreement, you are more than welcome to leave us here."

"Bryn," I start, embarrassed.

With a slash of silver, her dinner knife cuts across her palm. Crying out, I bend over my knees, biting back tears as I cradle my stinging hand to my chest. North stands, spilling the cup at his feet. His eyes flash with warning, but Bryn clutches her knife, undeterred.

"My servant, my magic, my rules," she repeats. Then, to me, "And you were told how to address me."

Humiliated, I scowl at the fire, cradling my hand. "Yes, your majesty."

"You came looking for us," Bryn says, standing. "Greed costs, gentlemen. Do I make myself clear?"

Nobody speaks.

Straightening, Bryn throws her chin up. "But a good queen knows when to compromise. Faris can have the bottom bunk."

"A good queen doesn't crown herself while her father still breathes," says North.

"A smart man keeps his mouth shut when his opinion is not requested," says Bryn.

North inhales deeply, shoulders rolling back. His hands curl into loose fists at his side, the knuckles whitening. "Tobek," he says, his eyes locked on Bryn; "we'll sleep outside tonight."

"The tent has a hole in it," Tobek protests.

North's expression doesn't flicker. "It's not raining," he says.

Bryn smiles, dropping into an abbreviated curtsy of acknowledgment before she slips her arm through mine and pulls me to my feet. She keeps her knife, and I wish I had thought to do the same, because she's terrifying. Head high, she ascends the stairs into the wagon as though it's already been conquered in the name of Brindaigel.

Once inside, I slide my arm out from hers and put distance between us, balling my sticky hand into the fabric of my skirt.

"There," she says, unclasping her traveling cloak and letting it drape over a chair. "And now we have privacy and a bed apiece."

"You could have just asked."

"That implies equal footing."

"Your majesty, I strongly suggest you don't make an enemy of the transferent. He can pull the spells out of your skin and he can thread poison through you just as easily. I saw what he can do—"

"He won't touch me." She trails a hand over the apothecary's chest, opening drawers at random, sifting through the contents. "I'm too valuable to poison and now he understands that." Finding a roll of bandages, she sets them and her knife on the table. "I'm sorry," she says. "It may seem cruel to you, what I did, but I'm a woman, Faris, and that often requires more sacrifice than a man. I was born as a redundancy but I intend to be a queen. Not a princess or a consort or an ornament. A *queen*. Anything less is a waste of my time."

Bryn surveys the plants above our heads before dragging a chair beneath them, cutting several stalks of comfrey loose.

"What are you doing?" I ask when she jumps down again.

"A little trick Pem taught me," she says. "It's called compassion. Take off your coat."

I hesitate. I've grown accustomed to its weight, the extra layer of protection.

Bryn clucks her tongue and begins tugging on the coat until I shrug it off. She throws it over her own cloak and surveys the bloodied mess I've become. "Pity about your hair," she says, sweeping the blond tangles away from my face.

The door swings open and North staggers inside, a bucket of water sloshing in his hands. With a grimace, he lifts it up, out of the stairwell, splashing a wave of water across the floor.

"I thought you might want to wash the smell of piss off of your skin," he says, his tone acid, eyes on Bryn. "And maybe the blood from under your fingernails."

Bryn turns and brandishes her hands for demonstration. "It's my favorite color," she says.

Nostrils flaring, North slams back outside and Bryn snorts, approaching the bucket. "Come here," she says, beckoning me toward the water. "You need this more than I do."

I wet my lips, eyes on the knife. Would she miss it?

Of course she would.

Protocol dictates that she wash first and I take the dirty water left behind, but Bryn is insistent in this new game of sympathy.

Dipping a wad of cloth into the water, she straightens and begins to dab at my scraped wrists and cut palm with a light, shivery touch, eyebrows pulled in concentration.

"I can do it myself," I say, embarrassed. Uneasy. I reach up to take the cloth from her but she pulls back before I can.

"I don't want your loyalty because a spell demands it, Faris," says Bryn, rinsing the cloth before she swipes it across my cheeks. Pink- and gray-colored water drips down her arms, darkening the sleeves of her dress. "I need to earn it. A good queen honors the people who fight for her. Who kill for her." Rocking her weight back, her expression turns hazy, unfocused. "I know this is hard. But nobody conquered anything without losing something along the way."

What has she lost that she wasn't already willing to leave behind?

Bryn unrolls a clean length of bandage and starts wrapping my hand. "Pem again," she says with an absent smile. The magic beneath my skin skitters away from her touch, dropping out of sight only to resurface again, the braided threads more knotted than before, as if strengthened by her proximity. "I used to watch him conducting his experiments before my father found out." Snorting, she tucks the end of the bandage into place. "I can marry an executioner, but I can't show an interest in his work. Especially the work he's not being paid for."

"Your father thinks I kidnapped you," I say.

Her smile widens, showing her teeth. "Which is good," she says. "I worried he would assume I ran away on my own."

I stare at her, stomach sinking. Everything that's happened, even her insistence that I kill Loomis, has been orchestrated down to the details. Blood on my hands ensures innocence on hers. If her father does find us, he'll find a daughter eager to return home and a girl whose family he first unraveled ten years ago. It's not that she needed a vessel, or even a bodyguard. She needed someone to blame. Just in case.

"My father will send more men when Loomis doesn't return," she continues, "which is why you have to trust the decisions I make for us both. If we don't reach New Prevast before his men reach us, then all that's left is to pray that Pem kills you quickly."

I swallow hard, past the tightening ache in my chest. I doubt mercy will be granted the girl who kidnapped the princess and murdered a councilman. "Why would your father waste the effort to recover a redundancy?"

Bryn eyes me shrewdly. "I'm not the one he's worried about losing," she says.

Her words slide like ice down my back. Of course. Nobody leaves Brindaigel, but I did. And until Perrote knows I'm dead, I'm a liability to the safety of his kingdom.

Bryn cocks her head and studies me, dark red hair curled across her shoulders. "You hesitated in the woods, after I gave you an order. Don't do that again, Faris. An instant can change everything. Do you understand me?"

I press against the table, bone melting into wood as I remember the weight of the pistol, the recoil of its shot, the sound of one last breath and then nothing left. Living with that murder is fear enough; it terrifies me to know that she may ask worse of me before this is done. Seven days to New Prevast, North had said.

Seven days too many.

Swallowing hard, I lower my eyes and take a deep breath to slow my racing heart. "Yes, your majesty."

"Faris." She tips my chin higher and I force myself to hold her gaze even as my fingers clench my skirt against my thighs. If I were home, I could lay my fear on the fighting floor and find solace in the taste of blood down my throat.

But I'm in Avinea now, and the rules are completely different.

"Hate me if you'd like," Bryn says. "Hate keeps people alive when they have nothing else to keep them warm. And I need you still breathing."

Remember this, I tell myself: remember *her*. Pointed teeth and sharpened claws hidden behind soft curves and sweet smiles. I killed a man but she's killed two already. "And how do you stay warm without a heart?"

Bryn smiles, almost sad, and traces the curve of my cheek before she slaps me.

I refuse to touch my face, to give her the satisfaction of knowing that even her pathetic strength has power over me.

"You will never understand what it takes to be queen," says Bryn.

But I do understand what it'll take to get my sister back: the same thing it takes to be a slave.

Complete and utter obedience.

hirteen

I DREAM OF ASH AND BURNING THINGS, BROKEN CITIES AND COWARD kings. Everything is iron turned to gold beneath my touch. Everything is dead. Maybe I am too.

Rough hands shake me awake, pulling me out of my nightmare. "Faris," Bryn hisses with a hint of fear. "We've stopped moving."

I open my eyes to sunset colors seeping across the floor from the window above the bunks. The edge of a dream lingers, gold threads unraveling around me with the feeling of looming inevitability. I frown at Bryn, struggling to place myself in context. Painted stars on the ceiling, a groaning stove beside me, and a striped cat asleep at my hip.

Avinea.

Propping myself up on my elbows, I stare across the empty wagon, confirming Bryn's assessment. The rattling of the wagon, such a constant lullaby since we left at dawn like North had promised, has been replaced with something far less soothing. Voices, muted by distance and thick walls.

My heart plummets. Perrote found us.

I push out of bed, disrupting Darjin, who mewls in protest and jumps to the floor.

Bryn clutches her dinner knife, following me to the door as I brace my weight, hands tightening at my hips, stretching open the scab on my palm. Last night, long after Bryn's soft snores filled the silence, I crawled on my hands and knees across the wagon, searching for the dagger I had dropped, but never found it. Now I scan the room, looking for something to replace it.

Before I do, the door rattles in its frame and swings open. I lunge down the stairwell, knocking into Tobek before he can react. We somersault off the running board and hit the ground hard. Grabbing him by the shoulders, I roll him flat on his back and prepare to strike.

North watches from several yards away, on the other side of a campfire. Stones rattle in his hand. "You are determined to see him dead," he says.

Tobek growls with frustration, rocking his head back in the grass, and I sit against his squirming legs, humiliated by my mistake.

"What's going on?" Bryn demands, still safe in the wagon. Her dinner knife flashes silver in the fading sunlight. "I'm paying you to get us to New Prevast."

"We're making camp for the night," North says, arching an eyebrow before he scrutinizes the stones in his hand. "There's clean water through the trees if it's needed."

Tobek lifts his head off the ground and offers Bryn a wide,

cheeky smile. "Warm enough for a swim."

"That's the second time you've been pinned by my servant," she says.

He deflates a little and I pity him, for believing she might be human beneath that pretty skin. Rocking back to my heels, I stand, offering Tobek a hand up. He refuses it, embarrassed, scrambling to his feet and edging away from me. "Stop doing that," he says, petulant, spitting out a mouthful of dust and casting a sideways glance toward North. Then he notices what I'm wearing and straightens. "Those are my pants."

And his shirt, judging by the size. I found them buried in a drawer last night while looking for the dagger.

"My dress smelled like the marketplace," I say tightly. Like blood and guilt and gunpowder.

"So then wash it."

"Tobek," North warns in a low voice.

I cast him a dark look: I don't need him to defend me. "Look," I say, "fair trade: I can teach you how to throw a punch if you let me wear your pants."

"Why? I can already hit a target at twenty yards." He thrusts out his chest with a swell of pride.

"Because you might not always have your crossbow and it'd be useful to know how to fight with your hands."

Tobek shrugs, glancing toward Bryn to see if she's watching. "Maybe," he says at last.

North snorts and I look over again, annoyed at his uninvited assessment. He crouches, whispering words that sound like non-sense but feel like magic, pressing his fingers to the stones as he completes a circle around our camp. Despite myself, I draw closer, hugging my arms around my chest. When he finishes, he sits back on his heels and looks up, expression unreadable.

"Please don't kill my apprentice," he says.

I shift my weight, eying the rocks. "Were you casting a spell?"

A half smile twists his lips and he stands, brushing his hands off on the seat of his trousers. He still holds several stones and they rattle in his hands. "A barrier ward," he says. "To keep you safe, as promised."

So he's a charmer, just like Thaelan.

"Why don't we just keep moving?" I ask. Basic rule of the ring: A moving target is always harder to hit.

"Because the earth is made of stone," he says, "and stone holds magic better than wood. It's more defensible to stand still than to trust the horses and wagon's walls against the hellborne." He offers me a smile. "Seven days to New Prevast, Miss Locke, but six nights as well."

I hug myself tighter, quelling the nervous energy that comes from standing still after running my whole life. Will Perrote camp for the night too, or are we sacrificing what little lead we may have?

"Is it safe to touch them?" I ask, toeing the edge of a stone.

"Are you a transferent?"

"Are you afraid I'm going to steal your spell?"

His mouth twitches. "Should I be?"

I stare at him, and he shakes his head wryly. "There's only so much clean magic left in Avinea, Miss Locke," he says, tossing a stone through the grass ahead of us. It bounces several times before rolling out of sight. "You saw for yourself the lengths people will go to grab it. I have to protect my investments."

"Are you talking about us or the rocks?"

His smile is a flash of teeth before he pockets the rest of the stones, nudging my foot with his own. "They're safe to touch," he says. "I cast my spells with lots of knots. Makes them harder to steal. Like yours, for example."

My hand circles my wrist on reflex. The hard threads of magic bump beneath my fingertips. "What do you mean?"

"It almost looks like a curse," he says. "Curses are not cast with the intention of being removed. Here. Look." He shrugs half out of his coat and rolls up his shirt sleeve, exposing a slender forearm corded with muscles and veins. A narrow line of magic sits in the crook of his elbow, forked on both ends and weighted by an open circle on the left. "This is a protection spell," he explains, dipping his shoulder toward me so I can see his arm more clearly. "See how the spell has sharp edges? It makes it easier to grab a hold of when it's time to be removed. Miss Dossel has something similar on her arm. But you . . ." He straightens, reaching for me.

I recoil, out of the way, and he lifts his hands. "Sorry," he says. "I forgot. But you can see the difference. Yours is all curves and blurred edges, like spilled ink. There's nothing to hold on to."

I stare at him, cold all over. "But you could still remove it, right?"

"Very carefully," he agrees. "It would take time and a great deal of skill, but yes. I could remove it."

A wolf howls in the distance and I flinch at the sound.

"They're in the hills," he says, pulling his coat back on, shaking out the collar. "They won't come near the camp."

I rub my arms and look away, embarrassed by the way he watches me so closely. "So how do you know if it's a curse?"

"An intuit could tell you. They can trace a spell's lineage all the way back to the king who summoned the magic."

I glance toward Tobek, sulking by the fire. He doesn't look like he'll tell me anything tonight. At least, not without charging me money for it.

"Well, I'm not a transferent," I say, crouching, "although my mother was."

"Really." North rocks back on his heels, eyebrows raised. When I tense beneath his interest, he drops his eyes and quickly adds, "It's probably for the best you didn't inherit the ability. Magicians are worth almost as much as magic these days. The hellborne trade them like animals. Transferents are preferred, but spellcasters aren't bad. And if you're an amplifier with a pack of addicts holding your leash?" He snorts, shaking his head. "You'd be better off dead."

Chilled, I press my fingers to the ward. I don't know what I'm hoping for: a spark, a memory, a miracle; something hidden in the magic that speaks to something hidden inside me. But it's just rock under the press of my fingertips; I'm still just a girl.

Disappointment floods my mouth and I stand, hating myself for falling into that trap of hope, of thinking a girl from the Brim with nothing but a scar above her heart could somehow be special just because her mother was. Or to be special in spite of what her mother tried to do.

But I'm a murderer, I tell myself. I'm the villain now.

"Oh," North says suddenly, with staged surprise that would be endearing in any other circumstance. "I almost forgot." He rummages through his coat pocket and holds out my mother's book.

I struggle to find my voice again. When I do, it wavers, waiting for the trap to spring and his motives to become clear. "What do I owe you?"

"Nothing," he says, "it was already yours." Lowering his voice to a mock whisper, he pulls a guilty face. "I didn't actually pay for it."

How could he, with Fanagin dead on the ground?

Stepping back, I curl the book under my arm, avoiding his eyes. "You mentioned clean water?"

North points to a copse of birch trees beyond the wagon, all skinny, silver things with mottled bark. They cast long shadows in the growing twilight, like iron bars creeping toward camp. "Twenty minutes to dark," he says, as I mumble thanks.

The river is shallow and the water is warm as it twists through the trees. It soothes my fraying nerves, but as I rinse the mud from my hair and the blood from my skin, I awaken the tender bruises on my arms and throat and with them, memories of how I got here. My movements turn frantic and blood begins to drip into the water like loose threads of magic. With a sudden gasp of panic, I crouch and pull my arms over my head.

I killed a man to save my sister, trading virtue for vice, compassion for selfishness. There's no going back from that kind of imbalance, and unless I harden myself into iron, the sacrifice will be for nothing.

My palms are not the floor, I tell myself, and I am not defeated. I am stronger than this.

I have to be.

I whisper the mantra again and again, until my heart slows and the shivers stop. Only then do I open my eyes and confirm that the world still exists, that nothing has changed.

But I have, irrevocably.

Numb—feeling exposed—I climb out of the river and quickly dress, eager for the returning weight of my clothing. My mother's book is knocked aside in the process, and I stare at it with a touch of resignation. Like a rash that never heals, this book keeps finding its way back to me, as inescapable as my scar.

Exhaling softly, I sink cross-legged on the grassy bank and pull the book closer. As I thumb through the worn pages, I almost expect to find some hidden note from Alistair tucked inside and his true intentions laid bare.

Instead, a folded map of Avinea falls into my lap. I slowly smooth it open, biting the inside of my cheek. Thaelan and I spent hours memorizing this map, planning the route we'd take on our way through Avinea, toward the world beyond. We'd lie out on the roofs beneath the stars and imagine how each dot would look, how it would taste and feel and sound.

Like freedom, every single one.

But it's my mother's book, my mother's map, and it's my mother I picture as I trace familiar patterns between the cities, wondering which ones she might have craved. What route would she have taken through Avinea? How far could a vial of clean magic get her?

Why do I even care?

A branch snaps behind me and I twist with a flash of alarm. Darjin bounds out of the growing shadows, tail twitching high, and I exhale with relief. "Hello," I greet as he bumps into my hip and twines around my arm. Throwing himself at my feet, he rocks onto his back and exposes his stomach, paws curling and unfurling, kneading the air with shameless invitation.

I laugh and dangle a leaf for him to bat. We never had any pets of our own—it was hard enough to feed ourselves—but Cadence once came home with someone else's chicken, insisting she could domesticate it and teach it to lay eggs on her command. Only it wasn't eggs it left in our beds and trailed across the floor, and within a week, I sold it for half a kronet. Cadence cried and Thaelan lectured me on the immorality of selling other people's chickens until I cried too, and Thaelan had to bribe us with sugared pastries to get us to stop.

My scar aches with warning at the bittersweet memory. *Don't*, I tell myself.

"He used to be a tiger, once upon a time."

I startle forward, crumpling the map in the process. North appears, barely more than a shadow himself, save the dusky olive of his face above the collar of his coat.

"Were you spying on me?" I demand.

"No," he says, but blushes. "It's dark," he adds with a forced smile. "You weren't back. I promised to keep you safe and I honor my word."

Water drips down my neck and I rub it away. Now that I know there's no threat of attack, my body slowly unfurls. Darjin waits at my feet, purring like a summer thunderstorm. He paws at a leaf, reminding me of the game I abandoned.

"Small tiger," I say, twitching the leaf for him before I stand, grabbing my shoes and cramming the map back into the book.

"Small confession," says North, hands sliding in his pockets as I fall in step with him and we head for camp. "He used to be life size. In truth, Darjin's just a very complicated spell my mother cast almost thirty years ago."

I glance at Darjin as he trots between us, amazed that magic could produce something so real, when all Perrote uses magic for is moving mountains and making shadows. "Was she a transferent too?"

"Only a spellcaster, but a good one." He smiles at the memory, before his face darkens. "King Merlock used to give pretty courtiers a few threads of magic to weave as they pleased if they ever did as he pleased." He holds back a branch while I duck underneath. "After the city of Prevast fell, the court disbanded. My mother wasn't the only one to land on her back. When I was born, she didn't have the means to care for both a tiger and a son."

"So she made him smaller?"

"No," says North, "she sent me to Saint Ergoet's Monastery in the interest of my education."

I look over, nonplussed. "Oh."

We reach the edge of the perimeter ward but pause. North crouches, scratching Darjin's chin. "This cat was her greatest accomplishment and I was the second. In fact, she almost named me Darjin the Second." Dark hair falls forward, framing his forehead. It makes him look younger, more boyish. "Luckily she was persuaded otherwise," he says, eyes flicking up to meet mine.

"North suits you," I say. "Steady as a star."

He smiles in acknowledgment. "She died before I began searching for Merlock," he says, standing, dusting off his hands. Clots of cat fur drift lazily on the soft breeze, clinging to the dark fabric of his pants. "And at the time, I promised to keep him, no matter what. But with Merlock still missing and Avinea dying, I've had to . . . borrow some of her spell for other purposes." Snorting, he drops his chin. "I know it's selfish to keep a cat when the magic could be used for more important things, but the truth is, a magic tiger is all I've ever had of her. Sometimes it doesn't seem enough. Sometimes it seems too much."

I bite the inside of my cheek, eyes dropping to the book clutched in my hands. I don't want to be beholden to North any more than I am to Bryn, and yet, I feel as if he's offered me something too valuable to ignore. "This belonged to my mother," I say, lifting the book. The map falls out, open at our feet, and North bends for it.

"I suspected it was worth more than it looked," he says. "It was the first thing you noticed after you woke up in a cage."

In truth, the book was worthless even to her; she used it for scrap paper, writing client names and measurements along the inside cover. It had no value to me as a child, but my mother's betrayal still felt too raw to be real when I smuggled it from our burning house, in case she might return and needed to work again. In the years that followed, it became its own kind of touchstone, a reminder of my mother's sins and a warning to me on those cold nights with no food and no father and no stories to soothe Cadence's cries. I would never betray my sister, or break her heart the way our mother broke mine, not for all the gold—or magic—in the world.

But I'm my mother's daughter despite it all.

I shiver, fingers brushing the soft bruises along my throat, where Fanagin choked me.

"Going sightseeing?" North quips of the map. "Because you're about thirty years outdated. Here." Gesturing me forward, he spreads the map across the side of the wagon. Pulling a stubby pencil from his trousers pocket, he asks, "May I?"

"May you what?"

"May I continue to prove that you're safe here," he says, "by demonstrating the places that are no longer safe out *there*." His chin tips over his shoulder, and though we're far from any sign of the Burn, smoke clogs the lower horizon, thick and yellowed like old mucus against the inky sky.

I shrug and North hunches forward, rubbing the graphite across entire sections of the kingdom, darkening the paper in shades of gray. "The Burn took Nevik six months ago," he says, eyes on his work as he scratches out entire cities, angling curves around others. Darjin winds between his feet and North edges him away with the side of his shoe. "Corsant has about a year before they fall. The southeast is entirely impassable except by sea. New Prevast used to be called Gorstelt; they changed the name twenty years ago when they moved the capital."

Wordlessly, I watch North reduce Avinea to less than half its size. While the majority of the Burn is focused around the original capital of Prevast in the northwest, there are pockets of it spread in both directions. "How did it get so far away?"

North steps back, pinning the map in place with one hand. "Magic became a commodity after the war. A black market formed. It's how most of the nobles paid their way out of Avinea, selling off spells and talismans they'd earned from the king. And with money to be made, people went into the Burn looking for anything that might have gotten left behind. They went home infected, and when they died, their families buried them, not realizing that the poison would spread through the earth. From the ground to the water supply, the farmland, one city, another." He studies the map and all its dark places with a kind of helplessness. "It spread. And once people figured out that dead magic was still power"—he sighs, lowering his head—"it became an addiction and spread even further."

"Why does it kill some people but not others?"

He considers his reply. "Magic came from the gods," he says, "and the gods gave man a choice: virtue or vice. We"—he gestures between us—"try to live balanced lives between both, but the hellborne surrender their hearts to poison and their souls to sin. They choose vice. It's the difference between turning hellborne or accepting death, Miss Locke."

Of course. Even the damned get a choice, or at least the illusion of one. I'm proof enough of that.

"If it's still magic, can you remove it?" I ask. "Could you survive the plague?"

North makes a face. "Dead magic is a lot like a curse. It's frayed at the edges, which makes it harder to hold. In theory, if you catch it quick enough, you can stop the infection from spreading. In reality, it's a difficult and often painful process. Success is never guaranteed. Anytime you put magic in your blood, it's only a matter of time before it hits your heart." He forces a tight smile. "And the only cure for a hellborne soul is a carved out heart. Prince Corbin's orders. No exceptions."

Rubbing the top of his head, he smiles again, easier than before. "What were you looking for?" he asks.

"Nothing, really," I say. Then, "Why hasn't Prince Corbin ever tried sending a convoy to Brindaigel for magic? I mean, I know we were enemies, but—"

"We're enemies?"

"Our king supported Corthen during the war," I say. "We gave him men and supplies and he gave us a touchstone." And it still stands in the castle courtyard today, a ten-ton granite obelisk that's nothing more than a landmark now, all its magic drained and hidden away so people like my mother can't grab it. "But if you needed magic, why wouldn't you look for it where you knew it would be?"

North makes a face, nonplussed. "Where's Brindaigel?"

I stare at him, skin prickling. "You don't know?"

"Is that one of the new territories in the Northern Continents? I confess my geography has lapsed since I left the monastery, but I thought they traded magic for a republic after they executed their empress."

Is he joking? Anyone who's spent four years searching for magic should know the name of the kingdom that still has it. Anyone who serves the prince should know the history of his enemies—especially when those enemies share his border.

North gives me a sideways look before his eyes fall to the spell around my wrist. "Maybe I know it by another name," he says. "A lot of things changed after the war. Like I said, New Prevast used to be called Gorstelt."

"Maybe," I say with a forced smile to hide my unease.

"I have more maps in the wagon," North says as Darjin stands on his hind quarters, paws on North's thigh, begging for attention.

North begins to rub his back. "Maybe after dinner, we could look them over together."

His arm knocks into mine and I jerk back, alarmed. How did I let him get so close? We're mere inches apart, less than the span of the map North still holds pinned to the wall. He can't remove the spell around my wrist, but if his fingers brushed mine, there's nothing to stop him from taking the stolen magic meant for Prince Corbin.

This is wrong. If I have any chance of saving my sister, it's by keeping North at a distance.

Trust no one.

"Excuse me," I mumble, quickly folding the map and cramming it back in my book. I hurry around the side of the wagon, chased by Darjin and the itchy feel of North's eyes on my back.

Bryn scowls from the doorway of the wagon, her knife laid across her knees. "Where have you been?"

I shake my head in reply, approaching Tobek hunched over the campfire, morosely poking at vegetables with a stick. "Can I help with something?" I ask, eager for movement, some sense of control.

Tobek bumps his shoulder in a halfhearted shrug. "Can you cook?"

"I can poke things with sticks," I say, and he glances over, cracking a smile.

As I supervise potato cakes turning golden over the fire, my mind retraces my conversation with North like Thaelan mapping his tunnels, searching for a path that leads to a logical conclusion. If Thaelan found a way out of Brindaigel, Corbin could have found a way in. Unless he believes us to be dead, the way we were told Avinea was. Is that why Avinea never invaded us before, not because Perrote has kept us safe, but because he's kept us secret?

Can one man be that powerful?

But more than that, if Prince Corbin has no idea that we exist, he has no idea who Bryn or her father is. Will he agree to an alliance based on the strength of a binding spell, a story, and a vial of stolen magic? My life—my *sister's* life—depends on it.

But who would risk their own kingdom by agreeing to fight for one that no one's ever heard of?

Fourteen

OVER THE NEXT TWO DAYS, I LEARN THE RHYTHM OF THE ROAD, THE gestures and nods between travelers that hint at what lies ahead and what was left behind. A tragedy unfolds in between the sweeping fields of crops and the stretches of scorched earth where nothing can grow. We pass villages razed to ash and villages that seem to thrive. The only constant is the wary eyes and forced smiles of the people we pass, weapons cradled in their arms.

I avoid conversation with North and try to displace the constant fear of Perrote's men by spending the interminable days and sleepless nights scrubbing the wagon from top to bottom, or paging through North's mountain of books while Darjin dozes in my lap. But North communicates around my silence, leaving books on the table that he wants me to read, or coins on my pillow so I can buy a new dress from the caravan of merchants who shared our campsite for a night.

I try to ignore his efforts, convinced an inevitable demand is waiting to be made in exchange—nobody is kind without caveat—but he never asks, and I finally realize: He never will.

I don't need a friend, I tell myself after I find a book on plants waiting on the table with enough candles to see me through another night. I need Cadence.

But it's a tempting alliance in a kingdom I don't know, where Bryn is my only other option. What harm could it do, I rationalize after I pour North a cup of tea and he gives me a warm smile that strikes at something buried inside me. In four days, I'll never see him again. And in the interim, it's gratifying to be seen and deemed worthy of someone's attention, to not be immediately discarded as a servant or another rat in the Brim.

We're only a few hours from our halfway point, carefully marked on my mother's map, when the wagon shudders to an unexpected halt. I'm curled on the top bunk, reading a history of Avinea while North studies notes in his leather book at the table below me. He looks up, as if waking from a dream, before his eyes land on me in unspoken question.

I shake my head, nerves firing with adrenaline as I peer out the small window above the bunk. Empty road stretches behind us, but smoke rolls across desolate fields, flecked with ash.

Tobek pushes open the upper portion of the stable door, face full of anticipation and dread. "I—I'm not sure," he says, "but I think . . . I mean, I *feel* like . . . maybe . . . ?"

North closes his book and stands. He reaches for his crossbow, slinging the quiver over his shoulder. "It's worth a look," he says.

Tobek nods, relieved, opening the lower half of the door as North ducks outside.

"Now what?" Bryn growls from the bottom bunk. Unlike me, she sleeps easy every night, and I resent her for it.

"I don't know." I climb down the short ladder of the bunk and lean out the door.

A village lies in ruins ahead of us, all rubble and smoke and shattered glass. Only a simple, two-story farmhouse remains standing in the distance, wilting into the debris around it. Ash streaks the walls; smoke clings to the eaves. Every window is broken, and fat birds drift overhead, looking for lunch. Not shadow crows, I realize with a lurch of relief. Vultures. Even the fields beyond the village have been destroyed, the crops broken beyond salvage.

North and Tobek stand at the head of the road, crossbows cocked and raised into position. There's no movement, no sign of life, and I lean out with a frown. "What's wrong?" I call.

North looks back, holding a hand toward us. "Stay in the wagon."

Bryn snorts, elbowing past me and jumping down. "Wood doesn't hold wards as well as stones do," she says drily. "And I'm not sitting in an unguarded wagon while my escort takes his weapons and goes for a walk."

And I'm not going to be the only one left behind. North and Tobek exchange tight glances but don't bother arguing. "At least stay close to one of us," North says. His eyes meet mine before sliding away. "Doesn't matter who."

I hug myself. Ash drifts lazy through the air, settling on our shoulders, in our hair. "Was it the Burn?"

"Scorchers," he says. "Religious fanatics who feel like the world is better off burnt to the ground, who don't think Merlock is doing it fast enough."

Bile floods my mouth as I survey the spill of houses and barns collapsed into each other. "Were there people in there when they burnt it down?"

"I'm sure they already left," he says with little conviction. "Most people have moved closer to the few cities with any shred of defense. It's not worth the risk to stay behind, not with people like Baedan roaming free."

"Looking for magic?"

"Looking for slaves," he says flatly. "You get someone with clean blood addicted to the Burn and then withhold the next high until they're willing to do whatever they have to for another taste."

A chill skates down my back. "Can't anyone stop them?"

North looks at me, expression inscrutable. "There's nobody left," he says. He takes a deep breath and holds it, chin dipping toward his chest before he releases it softly.

"This way?" Tobek looks to North for confirmation.

"I'll follow you," he says.

"Where are you going?" I drop my arms, alarmed.

North pauses, almost guilty. "There's still some magic buried somewhere."

"But what if the Scorchers are still here?"

"Then we're in luck," he says grimly, hefting his crossbow in hand. "Scorchers are still human. A bolt will suffice."

Openmouthed and reeling, I stare at him. He offers me a tired smile before he turns to follow Tobek's lead into the village, kicking up plumes of ash that veil the sky.

Bryn looks at me, hands on her hips and eyebrows raised.

Wordlessly, we follow.

Our footsteps are swallowed by an eerie silence. Animal pens stand empty, fence posts burned down to the stone foundations. Half walls remain here and there, framed with furniture or peeling wallpaper. I kick a teacup out of the ashes; a broken carriage wheel sits abandoned on the road. My eyes skim past everything but settle on nothing. I don't want to know what I might not be seeing.

Tobek reaches the farmhouse first and steps onto the paint-stripped porch, nudging the front door open with his boot before he settles his weight back and aims his crossbow to the shadows inside. When nothing comes barreling out at him, he lowers his weapon and looks to North for direction. North nods and, face set, Tobek steps inside. After a beat, North waves Bryn and I to follow before he brings up the rear, scanning the road behind us before he too enters the house.

The floors creak in warning as we huddle in the foyer, eyeing our options with some trepidation. A staircase or a parlor.

Swallowing hard, Tobek moves for the stairs, but North hangs back, ducking into the parlor full of broken glass and overturned furniture. A bookcase hugs the far wall, its contents spilled across the floor save a few trinkets and porcelain saints that were spared destruction.

North continues into the next room, a kitchen, but I linger behind, approaching a heavy desk sticky with spilled ink, covered with papers whose edges have curled from heat. A map hangs on the wall above the desk, also warped, and I flatten it back with one hand.

Avinea. Its previous owner marked the places where the Burn has taken the kingdom, much like North marked mine, but where my map lacks specifics, this map lays everything out in minute detail beneath an overlay of grid lines, to include Avinea's proximity to all the lands that converge in the Havascent Sea.

North returns, joining me at the desk, moving papers aside, paging through the books. Books are his weakness, he told me once, because nobody prints them anymore.

When he sees me still staring at the map, he pauses. "Looking for home?"

I don't answer; I can't. My eyes retrace the entire western border of Avinea where Brindaigel should sit.

There's nothing there but water.

North watches me another moment before turning his attention back to the books. "Where did you dock?" he asks lightly.

"What?"

"Your ship. What harbor did it sail into?"

"We didn't come by boat," I say.

"Then how did you get here?"

"We fell from the sky," says Bryn.

I jump, spinning to see her standing in the parlor doorway, arms folded across her chest.

North's smile turns strained. "Like the giants."

"The giants?" I repeat, bemused.

"When the gods went to war, they destroyed everything in their battle for dominance. Nothing survived except"—North reaches into his pocket and retrieves a small rock, pinching it between his fingers for emphasis—"a single seed that a farmer found buried in the ashes. But it couldn't grow without sunlight or water, so he went to the gods and he made them an offer: If he could defeat their strongest warriors, they would call a truce. Tell would rule the earth and Rook would rule the sky, and neither one would be more important than the other. They would be balanced."

"Farodeen the First," I say.

North smiles, pleased that I know his mythology. He wouldn't be so pleased if I told him the rest of the story we're taught, that Farodeen was sacrificed by his more powerful brother, Overen, the king of Brindaigel, and that Avinea was a consolation prize to his heirs. They would be destined to be farmers like their father.

"Farodeen wrestled Rook's giants out of the sky," North continues, "and they damned Tell's volcanoes, ending the war. To reward him, the gods threaded their magic through his veins: starlight from Rook and fire from Tell, so if they ever went to war again, man could fight too."

"Shimmer and burn," I murmur with a chill.

North looks at me, expression unreadable. "But the gift came with a caveat," he says. "Farodeen's heirs would have to kill the gods' greatest warrior to prove themselves worthy to inherit their magic." A wry smile crosses his face. "They would have to kill their father."

That, at least, is shared between our kingdoms: The gods love sacrifice.

Bryn snorts, and North gives her a look of polite exasperation. "Perhaps you know a different version?"

"I know that gods do not make kings," Bryn says, dropping her arms. "Men do."

"Do you not pray, Miss Dossel?"

"I kneel to no one," she says, turning away.

I listen to her footsteps receding, biting my cheek. In Brindaigel, chapels were reserved for the nobles who could afford time to pray. Those of us in the Brim bought totems and statues of saints who embodied our own lacking virtues in the hopes that their grace might transfer to us while we weren't looking.

Here, every night without fail, North prays while Tobek mumbles a self-conscious benediction of his own. Their faith is not so much in Rook and his virtues of ambition and courage and pride, but in Tell and her patience, temperance, and compassion. Perrote would call it the poor man's religion, praying to the dirt rather than aspire to the sky; and yet, the sky and its stars have only ever inspired my vices: greed and the burning desire to be more than I am.

I'm beginning to prefer the earth, grounded and certain and well within reach.

The ceiling creaks as Tobek inspects the second floor, but North doesn't move, fingers tented on the edge of the desk, leaving tracks in the ash that's settled there. He stares at the map, expression grim.

"I need that seedling," he says. "I need something to plant, Miss Locke. Something to grow, or Avinea will never recover."

"I gave you my name so you would actually use it."

"I can't do that."

Annoyance colors my voice: "Because that would cheapen its value?"

"Because it would strengthen its power," he replies, straightening. "You've already threatened to steal my magic and you've admitted your king supported Corthen in the war. As a devout loyalist to Avinea and its current regent, I have no choice but to view you and all your actions as a potential threat to Prince Corbin."

I frown, watching him from the corner of my eye. I can't tell if he's serious. "He can't be too concerned if he trusts his kingdom's defenses to a glorified seamstress like you."

"One of the best." His half smile fades, eyes hazy as they linger on my face, before he clears his throat and drops his gaze.

A splash of warmth fills my stomach and starts to spread. "My father was a tailor," I offer.

"Literally or metaphorically?"

I open my mouth, but pause. "I don't know," I admit, even as I wonder, *what if?* If my mother was a magician, is it possible my father was too? "Magicians aren't nearly so coveted in Brindaigel as they are out here. If he was a spellcaster, he never told anyone."

"Smart man." Bracing the crossbow against the desk, he rests his hands on the butt of the tiller and his chin on top of them. "But what were you, Miss Locke? Before this, I mean."

I hesitate, considering the question. I've been a lot of things, and I'm beginning to realize that most of them distill to one truth. "I was my mother's daughter," I say at last. A liar and a thief, an insatiable heart that always craved more.

North watches me, eyes half lidded, and I shift uneasily, looking away. What does he see when he looks at me? An investment, or something more? I know what I see when I look at him: a boy just like Thaelan, risking everything for a world that no one else believes in.

"I should check on Tobek," North says finally. Straightening, he adjusts his grip on the crossbow and moves past me, angling toward the stairwell.

"North?"

He pauses in the doorway, eyebrows raised.

"Back home, they added ash to the soil every spring, to keep the ground fertile. Maybe . . ." I pause, feeling foolish, but he doesn't laugh and I force myself to finish the thought. "Maybe things will start to grow again."

Only the recycled ash from hearths across Brindaigel is not the same thing as ash from dead magic. But North doesn't say that. "Maybe," he echoes, dark eyes unreadable.

A shout of panic splits the air and he startles.

Bryn.

North runs toward her voice and I'm fast on his heels as Tobek thunders downstairs, nearly falling as he skids on his landing. We find her outside, at the back of the house, framed by a pair of open cellar doors. Bodies are stacked inside, every one of them dead.

They trigger a flash of memory: a man on his knees, begging for mercy; a girl with a gun who didn't listen. Heat floods my face and my skin starts to itch with guilt as Loomis's blood spreads through my mind, coloring everything in shades of red.

"Sainted mothers and their virgin daughters," Tobek murmurs.

I look up, stomach clenching. For a moment, he was almost Cadence, and I have to forcibly remind myself that he's not my sister, that this is not the Brim.

And these bodies are not my fault.

Bryn collects herself, a hand pressed to her chest. She swallows hard and lifts her chin, red hair gleaming in the muddy sunlight. "Scorchers?" she asks flatly, holding out a slat of wood that must have barred the doors shut from the outside.

North doesn't answer. He clutches Tobek's shoulder and gently moves him back before crouching to see deeper into the cellar. He withdraws, swearing softly as he presses an arm to his mouth to escape the smell beginning to rise. The village was small, but so is the Brim, and I know how many people can fit in tight spaces.

Still shaky, North presses his palm to the open door. "There's your spell, Tobek," he says softly. "It must have protected the house from being burned." Magic glows white beneath his hand and he shifts, steadying his weight as his fingers tighten into claws. Silver threads begin unraveling through the charred wood, slim at first, thickening into knots and braided twists. North coaxes the spell loose, thread by thread, winding them around his fingers, where they glow like starlight before dimming.

Sweat beads his face when he finishes, and when he steps back, he's shaking. Tobek darts forward, eager to offer a shoulder and to take the heavy crossbow, and North leans into him with a mumbled thanks. He fumbles through his pockets and retrieves a large stone, reversing the process, wrapping the rock with magic like a bobbin of thread. By the time he finishes, his hands are bent, more crooked than before, as if the act of transference swells his joints.

"Why are you moving it again?" I ask.

"I don't trust myself to hold unspooled spells," he says breathlessly. "There's far too much risk that something snagged in the process and would start to fray inside me." To Tobek, he asks, "Is there anything else?"

Tobek hesitates before nodding once, as if in apology.

North wets his lips, eyebrows furrowed. "We'll bring them out," he says at last. A trembling hand gestures to the bared dirt behind us. "Make rows. Mark the ones with magic and I'll double-back when I'm done and start siphoning."

Tobek tears off his jacket and balls it aside, out of the way. "Yes, sir."

"We don't have time for this," Bryn says.

"We don't have the luxury to waste magic," North counters, cuffing his shirtsleeves. "Your binding spell isn't nearly enough to get me through the Burn in one piece, Miss Dossel, so unless you want to improve your original offer, I'm not leaving an ounce of it behind."

"You agreed to the terms presented," says Bryn. "New Prevast in seven days."

"Then lend a hand and we'll be done faster."

Bryn stares at him, incredulous. "I will not."

"There's still smoke in the air," North says, pointing. His hair falls forward, framing his forehead. "This was a recent attack. We won't be the only ones who feel the magic left behind. The hell-borne will arrive soon, or fortune hunters. You want to leave? Get your hands dirty."

They stare each other down, standing toe to toe in the dirt. Resigned, frustrated—must everything be a competition of power?—I edge past Bryn, hooking the first body under the arms. The chill of death lies dormant beneath the lingering heat trapped in the woman's clothes, and goose bumps shiver down my back as I pull her body over the lip of the cellar and away from the house.

North watches me with a guarded expression as I carefully position the woman, folding her arms across her chest, adjusting her dress to cover her legs. My prayers are rusty, half forgotten, but I manage a mumbled blessing before returning to the cellar.

"Don't touch the skin," North says, falling in line beside me. I nod my understanding and we work without speaking while Bryn prowls an impatient line between the dead, arms folded and skirts flaring at her feet. She throws glances to the sky with increasing agitation, and her nerves spread to me. I move faster, leaving bodies with arms akimbo in favor of speed, eager to return to the wagon and the road north.

Once we've emptied the cellar, Tobek marks several of the bodies with a smeared ash *X* across their foreheads. He then empties their pockets and takes anything of interest, meeting my stare with a bump of his shoulder and a guilty half smile that quickly fades.

"We should burn the bodies," I say, as North follows behind Tobek, deftly unraveling the magic he finds. It's a quick process, the spells barely more than remnants. "The hellborne will turn them into scrap if we don't."

"Why not?" Bryn throws her hands in the darkening air. "Or better yet, why don't we just bury them? That won't take too long."

"No." North misses her sarcasm. "Some of them could be infected. It would poison the ground."

Bryn gives him a withering look.

"There are matches in the wagon," Tobek offers meekly. His pockets bulge.

"I'll get them," I say, already turning.

"Above the stove!" North calls after me.

I break into a run, fleeing the sickly sweet guilt of knowing that burning these bodies does not absolve me from leaving Loomis to be torn apart like an animal.

Hauling myself into the wagon, I brace my hands to either side of the stairwell and force myself to stop, to breathe. I close my eyes and count to ten, but when I open them, my heart crashes.

A black crow feather sits on the table in a hard slant of smoky sunlight, its barbs glowing red and gold with smoldering embers.

Perrote.

I twist with a shock of adrenaline, expecting to see him and his entire council riding up the road, ready to attack and take me prisoner. But there's nothing, not even a bird overhead.

Numbly, I step further into the wagon and stare down at the feather. It spins in the draft I create, leaving a spill of ashes across the table. It's too deliberately placed to be anything but a warning.

He knows where we are.

"What's that?"

I jump, swearing loudly as Tobek pokes his head in the doorway behind me. He frowns at my nerves, craning to look.

I open my mouth but falter. If Bryn knew her father was closing in, she might sacrifice the mission.

She might sacrifice me.

No. I'm too close for a change of heart, too close for cowardice. Three more days is all I need. Somehow we'll convince Prince Corbin that Brindaigel exists, that there's magic enough to save his kingdom. She'll get her alliance and I'll get my freedom, and as much as the idea makes my skin crawl, helping Bryn win is the only chance I have of winning too. I need her to save Cadence and I need North to get us to New Prevast. Neither one of them can know how close Perrote is.

"It's nothing," I say, crushing the feather beneath my palm, guilt aching in my veins.

Tobek lifts his eyebrows. "North said to bring some oil."

I nod, too quickly, before I rummage for the matches on the shelf above the stove. Soot cakes my hand and I resist the temptation of wiping it on my skirt.

"In the box," Tobek says, giving me another frown.

I force a shaky smile and find the small silver tinderbox worn smooth from use. I don't look at the table, grabbing a canister of lamp oil in my other hand before I rejoin Tobek.

Bryn stands by the cellar, a stack of books at her feet. North emerges from the house moments later with even more books in hand, along with the map from above the desk, rolled and tucked in the crook of his arm.

More unspoken conversations.

I can't meet his eyes. He should be warned that Perrote is almost here, but is a binding spell worth being hunted by a king when he has his own king to catch? Or would he simply cut his losses and leave us behind? Can I risk taking that chance?

Tobek douses the bodies with oil before I strike a match and drop it. North murmurs a prayer before all of us but Bryn gather a stack of books and move to a safer distance at the edge of the road. Within seconds, the smoke turns black and acrid; the air thickens with the smell of soured milk.

A bird cries in the distance, spinning overhead, and although it is not a shadow crow, it raises the hairs on my arms all the same. Bryn sees me flinch and lopes her arm through mine.

"Does it remind you of home?" she asks softly, as flames spread to the farmhouse and chew up its walls, hungry for the dry, unprotected wood.

I frown, bemused. "What do you mean?"

"The night my father burned your house down," she says, tipping her head against my shoulder, snuggling closer into my arm. "Did it burn the same way?"

I stare ahead, soot-stained fingers clenched in a fist, and don't answer.

Fifteen

THAT NIGHT, I TEACH TOBEK HOW TO THROW A PUNCH, DESPERATE to keep my mind preoccupied and away from the growing paranoia that Perrote is simply playing with me, waiting for the right moment to strike. When we stopped to make camp, I was the one to protest, arguing both the campfire and our position in open field—under open skies—to no avail.

"We don't travel at night," North had said, with utter finality, and guilt—*greed*—had kept me from telling him the truth.

Three more days, I tell myself, as my eyes track the skies. Tobek exploits my distraction and lands a blow across my shoulder. Grunting with triumph, he backs up and grins, raising his hands to his chin.

"Don't do that," I say, dragging my attention back to him.

"Why not?"

With one short strike, I hit his hand and he hits himself square in the jaw. "That's why not."

North pretends to ignore us, praying with his palms flattened against the earth and his neck exposed to the sky. But his eyes cut toward me from under the fringe of his hair, and I toss my own hair back, out of my face, fully aware of his attention.

"Try again," I say.

"Where'd you learn to fight like this, anyway?" Tobek asks, ducking my next swing.

I fall back and reposition myself with a halfhearted shrug. "Previous life," I say. Bats somersault overhead and I freeze, exhaling softly once they've passed.

"Sounds like a tragedy."

"Give me a kronet and I'll make it a comedy."

"I'm an apprentice," says Tobek. "I don't get paid." An eyebrow arches, mirroring the curve of his mouth. "Play you cards for the story?"

"I'm not playing cards with a boy who admits to cheating."

Tobek dives for my stomach and I barely sidestep a punch to the gut. "That was a previous life," he quips, breathless. His thick hair sticks to his forehead and he rakes it back with dusty fingers. "And anyway, the skill is in cheating."

Snorting, I adjust my coat. "I'll bet."

He lunges again and I easily knock him to his knees. Tobek bows his head, annoyed, touching his forehead to the earth in an eerie mimicry of North.

"Good god," says Bryn, "again?"

Tobek's head snaps up with interest as she emerges from the wagon with a blanket clutched around her shoulders. She looks pale, drowsy; she slept all afternoon, which gave me a chance to search through North's books for any information on Avinea's allies and enemies during the war, but the books were as useless as his maps.

Beyond our own borders, Brindaigel doesn't seem to exist.

She pulls the blanket tighter, eying North with open disdain. "I don't think anyone's listening."

"I don't think it matters," I say.

"Then what's the point?"

Tobek pushes to his feet, brushing grass off his trousers before flexing his hands, itchy for a chance to show off. He begins bouncing on his heels, fists at his chin again. "The point is to thank the gods for another day we didn't die," he says with a tentative half smile: He's serious if she is, but he's joking if she's not.

North kisses the backs of both his flattened hands before sitting back on his heels. "It's an act of gratitude, Miss Dossel."

She scoffs. "For what? You're killing yourself to save the world while Corbin waits for his crown to be handed to him. Do you think he'll thank the gods before he rips out his father's heart? Will he thank *you*?"

Tobek stops bouncing, aghast at her sacrilege.

"Pride breeds arrogance," North warns.

"And a thrifty man becomes parsimonious. Pay your apprentice," she says.

North rocks back onto his feet and stands, dusting off his trousers. "Tobek, do you want a wage?"

Tobek hesitates, torn between the open desire to do whatever Bryn commands, and a deeper loyalty to his master. "I—I don't . . ."

"Stand up for yourself," says Bryn. "He takes advantage of you.

You pitch tents and drive wagons and make dinner. That's not an apprentice, that's a servant. You're no better than Faris, and *that*," she says, eyes cutting toward me, "is a tragedy."

"This afternoon—" Tobek starts.

"And yet you trust your servant with your life," North says.

Bryn smiles. "She was compensated for that trust because I appreciate the value of her skills. As I appreciate anybody for the skills they have that I do not." She steps down from the wagon and joins us by the fire, eyes on Tobek. "Which is why I want you to show me how to shoot a crossbow."

"Oh," Tobek says, relieved. Flattered. "I can do that."

I wipe my mouth, annoyed by her intrusion and by his eager willingness to abandon my lesson to offer her one instead—a lesson I doubt she even needs. "Didn't Pem teach you that too?" I ask darkly, watching North as he heads into the wagon, pausing on the steps to scratch Darjin between the ears. With a storm coming, he and Tobek plan to sleep inside tonight, and the thought of his proximity unsettles me.

"Who's Pem?" Tobek retrieves his crossbow and quiver from the other side of the fire. He makes a show of testing the string, counting his bolts. Preening for attention.

Bryn shrugs, dropping the blanket to her feet. "Nobody," she says, eyes sliding to me in warning a moment before blood fills my mouth as she bites her own tongue.

Tobek groans. "Don't tell me. Previous life, another tragedy?"

"My life is a fairy tale," Bryn says sardonically. "And Faris never actually told you her story."

"Nothing to tell," I say, spitting out a mouthful of blood. "There was a girl who knew a boy and had a sister. One of them was killed, one of them was cursed, and one of them . . ." I swallow hard, picturing the ash and ember feather in the wagon this afternoon. *Three more days*, I tell myself. "One of them is still waiting to be saved."

"Then I win," Tobek says, waving his hand. "You both have been coddled."

"And you haven't?" Bryn gives him a withering look. "North practically tucks you into bed and kisses you goodnight."

Tobek flushes, throwing his shoulders back. *Good*, I think; fight back. Don't give her power over you. "Know what this is?" he asks, pulling his collar away from his neck, revealing three black dots ringed with red.

"Meaningless?" Bryn pulls a bolt from his quiver and drags her fingers through the feathers of the shaft.

"It's the mark of my first master," Tobek says, proud. Defiant.

I lean closer, stomach clenching. "You were a slave."

Bryn looks up sharply. "Are you infected?"

"No! I mean, I was, but"—he wets his lips and glances toward the wagon, tugging his collar back into place—"not anymore." Setting the crossbow down, he pulls out the worn deck of cards he carries in his vest, nervously tilting them in his hands. "A few years ago, I got caught cheating the wrong man," he says. "He got me hooked on poison and wouldn't give me any more unless I kept working. We ran a scam of Crowns." A wan smile flits across his face. "Was pretty good at it too."

I know the game. Requiring no skill to play, it's a game of chance and cheating, and an easy way to trick noblemen out of a handful of tretkas down in the Brim.

"So what happened?" asks Bryn. She picks up his crossbow and sights down the tiller.

"One day he was just gone. Not long after, North found me begging opium in Cortheana." He says it with a shrug, feigning indifference, like the boys who live in the streets who pretend they don't care that there's nothing to eat, nowhere to sleep, no one to hold them and say everything's all right.

But I recognize the worship in his face because I saw it so much in Cadence, in the way she idolized Thaelan. I kept food in her stomach and clothes on her back, but Thaelan carried a sword and taught her how to hold it. I was the sister. He was the hero.

"North removed the infection?" I ask.

Another shrug. "Any transferent could do it if they really wanted, but most won't. It's complicated, and takes time. Anytime you touch dead magic like that, with all its loose edges, you risk spilling some of it into your own blood. But North took a chance." Lowering his head, he toes circles in the dirt. "He saved my life. And my soul. He turned a half-bred monster into something not so bad." He looks to Bryn for approval, even as the fear of condemnation shadows his dark eyes.

Bryn doesn't even look at him. "So how do you shoot this?" she asks.

"Aim and release," he says, sighing, running a hand through his hair.

"Show me," says Bryn.

He smiles.

Excusing myself, I retreat to the safety of the wagon, to where North reads with one knee braced against the table and his chair rocked back on two legs. He chews his lower lip and pretends not to notice me.

I sink into the chair across from him, unnerved. The Brim was rarely ever silent and I feel especially vulnerable tonight, to be so cut off from the world. If Perrote were to attack, we'd have nowhere to run.

North cracks the spine of his book, tilting his head to see me over the cover. "Everything all right?"

"Is it true?"

"It's true," he says. "Tobek is no longer infected. I was there."

"No, I mean Farodeen the First," I say. "Did he actually wrestle giants out of the sky?"

"Of course. That's how Avinea began." North closes the book and tosses it on the table, resting his hands on top of his knee. "Fire and giants and a farmer."

I stare at his fingers, long and narrow but also swollen and trembling, the joints discolored, callused from wear. When he notices my gaze, North slides his hands into his lap, out of sight, a gesture meant to be casual but too deliberate to be anything but habit.

Don't hide them, I want to say. I think they're beautiful. The hands of a boy who knows how to fight. How to survive.

"So how did he get up there?" I ask, leaning forward, my own hands entwined across the table. I pick at the edge of a book. "And how did he get back down?"

"He took a leap of faith and landed in the clouds," says North, deadpan. "After that, he just closed his eyes and fell."

"And he didn't die?"

"Sometimes, falling makes you stronger." North stands, his chair screeching across the floor.

"Did it hurt?" I ask softly. "Saving Tobek's life?"

North tenses. A debate plays across his face before he grabs an atlas from his apothecary chest. "Yes," he says.

He opens the book to the index in the back before angling the book toward me with tented fingers. "I can't find Brindaigel," he says. "Does it have another name, maybe? Or is it a newer territory?"

My stomach tightens. "Why does it matter?"

"Your king was Corthen's ally in the war," he says, scanning the list of countries. "He had to have some stake in Avinea, a possible trade route or resource Corthen promised in return. What did he want badly enough he would send his daughter into enemy territory twenty years later to find, and without an escort?"

"Wrong question," I say with a ripple of nerves. Can Bryn hear us? I cover my wrist, almost unconsciously. "You should be asking what kind of daughter seeks out her father's enemy behind his back."

North stares at me. "So then it is mercenary." He chews his lower lip, expression darkening. "Maybe I should ask what kind of girl agrees to go with her? A binding spell requires mutual agreement, Miss Locke."

"I was compensated," I say, standing to avoid his prying eyes.

"With what?"

I don't answer, sifting through the jars of tea stacked on a shelf above the stove. After unscrewing a lid, I sniff the contents and make a face that doesn't quell the tumult in my chest. "Rosehip,"

I say with a forced smile, turning to offer the jar toward him. "Is that what monks drink in New Prevast?"

North holds my eyes with a half smile before demonstrating his swollen hands. I flush, embarrassed. Of course. Rosehip for its anti-inflammatory properties. It's exactly what monks would drink in New Prevast after years of praying gave them arthritis.

I cradle the jar to my chest and wish I was back outside hitting things, instead of in here, where the conversation feels too delicate—too dangerous—for someone like me. Bryn laughs, bright and sincere, and I look out the door with a strange hitch in my chest.

I didn't know she could laugh.

"Would you like some?" North joins me by the stove, opening the samovar.

Relieved at the change in subject, I slide the jar back on the shelf, aware of how close he stands, within an elbow's reach of me. "I don't drink tea."

"Political or religious opposition?"

"What?"

"Are you socially opposed to the importing of tea from foreign shores, or morally opposed to the rumors of child labor involved in the process? Because I assure you, Miss Locke, I only buy locally grown product. That's all we have anyway."

He's teasing me.

"Traditionally," I say, relaxing even more. "My sister refused to drink tea. It's what old women with bad hats and twelve surnames drink, she said; she wanted coffee. Like soldiers drank."

Like Thaelan did.

"But coffee cost money," I continue. Cheap herbal tea could be grown in the hothouses of the higher stretches of the kingdom, but coffee grew more finicky and couldn't be bought anywhere that gold didn't flow freely. "So to compromise, we drank hot water with sugar."

"You have a sister," says North.

Too close, I think with a mild rise of panic. He's getting too close and I'm getting too sloppy.

"Sangreve," I blurt.

He blinks. "Is that her name?"

"It's a suggestion." I can't look at him. "I used to work in the fields and my fingers would always be swollen by the end of the day. Sangreve helped." Eager to escape his intoxicating closeness, I return to the table, finding my mother's book tucked in between several of North's. Flipping through the pages, I demonstrate the inked illustration and detailed entry on sangreve. "It grows by water," I say.

Taking the book, North skims the entry before his eyes meet mine. "Show me," he says.

"It's dark," I say. And Perrote could be out there, hidden in the shadows.

Leaning forward, he mock whispers, "I know magic, Miss Locke."

"Magic hurts," I say with a half laugh that's half truth, flashing my wrist and the spell shackled around it.

But he's already pulling on his coat, snapping out the collar. "Not always," he says, and there's an invitation in the way his mouth curves, a hint of what it was like those nights when Thaelan snuck out of the barracks to meet me on the rooftops. Familiar places turned new again, transformed by the thrill of stolen freedom. The nights felt crisper, the stars looked brighter, and the kisses tasted sweeter. Defying a king was less a dream and more a possibility.

North watches me, waiting for an answer, his expression cautious. Hopeful.

I miss the girl that Thaelan loved, who wasn't afraid to take chances or make plans for her future. That girl died the night he did, replaced with the girl I am now, full of guilt and grief and only one goal: to get my sister back. It's a risk to leave the safety of the wagon, and to trust this boy with his unsettling curiosity and unwavering kindness.

But it's defeat to let Perrote terrify me into being an obedient Brim rat again.

Like Farodeen the First, I take a leap of faith. I tip my head toward the door in invitation, fighting the hesitant smile that crosses my face.

North smiles in reply.

Sixteen

NORTH WALKS BRISKLY, STEADY AHEAD, AND I HURRY TO KEEP UP EVEN as I slow down, eager to map every labyrinth path between the trees, to touch every shelf of stone that rises from the ground like a mountain made in miniature. Everything is overgrown and green, ringed with flowers smaller than the freckles on Bryn's shoulders. The storm-charged air is damp with smoke and something else, something that seems to radiate from North as he turns to check I'm still behind him. We don't carry a light but I see him clearly, outlined in gray shadow.

"Everything all right?" he asks.

I shake my head. It's dangerous, this wild, this world. Only a few days here and I can taste it melting on my tongue, seeping into my blood, threading through my veins like stolen magic. Closing my eyes, I tip my face to the hidden stars, to the smell of the Burn and the smell of the storm. Slowly, my muscles unfurl and I spread my arms, my fingers, my feet. For too long I've lived cramped, hunched, forced to be small in a kingdom that didn't leave any room to breathe. Now I touch nothing but air.

Is that what my mother understood? She never stole any gold but she stole the idea of it, the luxury of what the world could be like when you were free. Dangerous, yes, but full of choices.

"Miss Locke?"

I open my eyes. North watches me, expression guarded, almost envious. He is the pious and I am the pagan. Raised by monks to be sober, sedate, North thanks the gods for their blessings whereas I was raised by the Brim. I fight and draw blood to get what I want.

A fat bead of rain hits the top of my head and I lower my arms, feeling euphoric, silly. Above all, alive. In an instant, I'm tempted to tell North everything, starting with Thaelan and ending with Perrote and the warning I found in the wagon. But then lightning casts the trees in shades of violet, throwing shadows of doubt back over me.

"I'm fine," I say. "Which way?"

He gestures wordlessly, without pressing, but I catch him stealing glances laced with unasked questions. It's a relief when we finally reach the river and I can direct his attention to the task at hand. Sangreve grows thick and nettled, I tell him, close to water, with serrated leaves and a fat, bristled stem. The sap will cause blisters, I add, so don't touch it. He listens and nods and begins to dig, carefully unearthing a plant, roots and all, before setting it on the ground between us.

Before long, we have a small pile, more than enough for a jar of tea. I sit back on my heels and North wipes his cheek against his shoulder. "Good?" he asks.

When I nod, he smiles. "My turn." Tugging his boots off, he rolls up his pant legs and slides down the riverbank in a spill of stones, splashing into the water. Fog eddies away from him, threading up the bank to creep toward me.

"What are you doing?" I ask, leaning forward to see.

He bends into the river and emerges with a handful of stones. "Resupplying," he says.

"You have jars full of rocks in the wagon."

"These are different." He turns cagey, protective, as if this is a defense he's fought before. I bite back a grin to think of a younger North hoarding stones at the monastery. "The river wears them smooth, see?" He demonstrates one, squinting it into focus. His enthusiasm is endearing, as is the flip of his hair over his forehead. "They hold the magic more uniformly that way. Spells are less likely to fray."

"What about that one?" I point to a dark gray stone, rougher than the others, pockmarked and ugly.

Making a face, he dances the stones across his palm and separates it out. "Pumice," he says, "from when the earth bled fire. It's not really rock, it's just hardened lava. There are whole fields between here and New Prevast made of this stuff. They've all turned green now, but if you dig deep enough, you'll still find it buried underneath."

Intrigued, I hold out my hand and he drops the pumice into it. It's lighter than I expected, and feels brittle, though it doesn't break when I squeeze. "Can't you use these for magic too?" I ask.

"Too porous," he says, clicking his other stones together, discarding several, pocketing the rest. "Magic would slide through it like water."

I curl it in my fist, watching him scavenge. A touch of the giddiness returns, a hint of flirtation. "In Brindaigel, they say anyone who can catch Rook's starlight will be granted a wish from the king," I say.

North's expression is impossible to read. "What would you wish for?"

"Nothing," I say, my giddiness fading as a list of insatiable desires rolls through my mind. "It's a meaningless gesture because it's an impossible task. No one has ever caught starlight before."

"Have you learned nothing from us?" He leans into the riverbank, bracing his weight by my knees. Despite myself, I bend closer, tempted by the secrecy in his demeanor and the mischievous glint in his eye. There's a touch of Thaelan to him, but he's still entirely new. Entirely North. "Hold out your hand," he says.

I do so slowly, and he makes a fist above my cupped palm. Water drips from his hand, forming a small puddle in mine. It shimmers like a mirror before turning deep blue, freckled with twinkling light.

I laugh, incredulous, as North leans even closer.

"The skill is in cheating, Miss Locke," he says softly. And then, "Make your wish."

The temptation is overwhelming; the moment feels like magic, like anything is possible. But all at once I remember myself, pulling back, spilling the water into the ground. I drag my hands across the tops of my thighs, unnerved by how easily I let myself be caught up in his company. "I don't believe in wishes," I say.

He doesn't bother hiding the flicker of irritation as he pulls back. "Not everything has to be hard won, Miss Locke."

It's the same sentiment Alistair offered, made more tempting by a man who has never expected anything in return. But North is not a stupid man. Even if he wanted to help me, he wouldn't risk losing Bryn's potential value as the daughter of a king with magic to spare, not for the small amount of stolen magic that I carry. He needs a seedling to save the world and I'm the annual flower that won't return in the spring.

Clearing my throat, I push to my feet. "I'm going to keep searching."

"Me too," he says, not looking at me.

The thickening fog threads between my feet as I edge away from North and the strange feelings he's awakening, a warring dichotomy of attraction and a deeper, bitter sense of guilt. Thaelan is barely dead, I tell myself, and Cadence needs me to be stronger than this.

But when North approaches me some time later, his pockets weighted with stones that click as he walks, I can't help the smile that flickers across my face.

He sits beside me on a fallen log, stealing an inch closer than I would have ever offered on my own. "Is this in your book?" he asks, holding a small blue flower toward me.

"Phoralis," I say. "It's poisonous."

"So don't eat it," he says.

"They teach you well in that monastery," I say, and smile before catching myself, making my expression serious. Impenetrable.

"Keep it," says North, dipping the flower so it brushes the back of my hand. Maybe it was an accident, maybe it wasn't. "When you go home, you can show your mother all the plants you found in Avinea."

"She's dead," I say.

He blinks.

Maybe I should sit in the river until my rough edges are smoothed out too. Shaking my head in apology, I murmur thanks and accept the flower, twisting it between my fingers.

We listen to the approaching storm, lost in our own thoughts. But when lighting breaks across the sky, I jump at the thunder that follows, close enough it sounds like gunshot.

"We should go back," North says with a sigh, standing.

A gust of wind gutters his hair and snaps his coat behind him, and the first drops of rain slip through the branches. Reluctantly, I follow, hugging myself as the wind rises, howling and growling and—no.

That's not the wind.

Fear slides down my back and pools low in my stomach. "What is that?"

North doesn't answer. He doesn't have to. A beast appears, a shadow figure with its back bent forward, the serrated edges of its spine as pronounced as fresh tilled earth. Withered arms hang limp at its sides, its fingers tapered like tallow candles beaded with wax. Embers flash in the dark; raindrops hit its body as steam releases with a hiss. It turns toward us, blurring its edges out of focus before it redefines itself.

A shadow golem. Another one of Perrote's spies. While it's bigger than his usual shadow rats and crows, I'd recognize the acrid smell of magic anywhere.

North edges ahead of me, in a position of defense. The golem lifts its head with a grunt, beady red eyes scanning left to right, searching for its prey before it locks on us and roars in challenge.

"Run," North orders. He plunges a hand in his pocket and retrieves a stone overlaid with a lacework of magic. "Straight back to camp. Get Tobek and then lock yourself in the wagon."

I hesitate. I ran from Perrote's magic once before and have regretted it every day since.

Not this time.

The golem charges. North stumbles back, slipping on the slick moss, and without thinking, I grab his arm before he falls. He spares me a momentary glance, gratitude framed on his lips, before we break apart as the golem bowls between us, roaring loud enough to silence the thunder overhead.

Sparks scatter across the ground as the golem immediately rounds on North. Mumbling quickly, North unspools the magic around his fingers but there's no time to cast anything complicated. When the golem charges again, North throws out a meager spell, no more than a flicker of light that buys him a scant few meters of time to back away and try again.

Frantic, I pat down my coat, unearthing the tinderbox from that afternoon. Alistair killed a shadow rat in the dungeon with a match, but it was much smaller. What if this doesn't work?

But what if it does?

North is cornered by a brace of fallen trees and underbrush. He searches for a way out, fear on his face. Threads of loose magic roll across his palm, pooling into each of his fingers. He coaxes them into brightened knots, but the golem rears, its tallow-claws curled into meaty fists that glow gold where the knuckles strain beneath the shadow of its skin. It swipes at North and he throws an arm out just in time, sparing his face, singeing the sleeve of his coat. I dart in between them, settling my weight with a wave of terror. I'm close enough I feel the heat of the golem, can smell the charred stink of its skin.

North grabs the back of my coat, trying to wrench me out of the way as the golem raises its arm for another blow. The skin on my face starts to stretch from the heat as my fingers shake, spilling matches to the ground. The rain extinguishes the first one I light and I toss it aside with a curse, striking several more. Throwing them all, I twist into North and flatten him to the ground as a flash of heat and light washes over us, hot enough to turn the rain into steam above our heads; bright enough the world becomes a monotonous field of white before darkness bleeds in from the edges, until finally, the forest returns.

The ground smolders around us, turning raindrops golden, like falling stars that melt when they land. We clutch each other and North stares at me, his breathing hard and irregular. "Miss Locke," he says, "you are terrifying."

And pious North smiles when he says it.

I grin in return from behind the damp hair plastered across my face. There's no reason to hold on to him and yet, I don't let go.

Neither does he.

"Are you all right?" he asks, eyebrows furrowed.

"Yes. You?" I look back, unable to meet his eyes, staring instead at his chin, the divot beneath his mouth, his lips.

Don't do that, I tell myself. His lips are not part of my plan.

"Yes," says North. His forehead creases. "Where did you learn to do that?"

"Previous life," I say with a low burr of warning. This is too close again. Only a foot higher and he could touch my face and devour my secrets.

A foot higher and I could uncover his secrets too. For half a heartbeat, I regret my self-restraint, because that skin is all I want in this leftover moment of adrenaline and triumph.

North smiles again, a disarmingly sweet rise of his mouth. "So you've been a farmer, a royal servant, and a golem hunter," he says. "That doesn't sound like a tragedy, Miss Locke, that sounds like an adventure." Ash settles in his hair and he softens his grip, fingers sliding down my sleeve, skating past my wrist before settling light on my waist.

"Adventure suits you," he says quietly.

My smile fades, guilty. Lying suits me even better, because North has no idea that that golem came from Brindaigel—that there are probably more on their way. He could have died tonight, and I didn't even warn him.

I'm no better than Bryn, manipulating North to get what I want.

I sit up so he's forced to shift out of the way. The cold creeps in and I hug myself, shivering as fog eddies around us. The smell of burnt meat lingers. "We should go before any more come," I say.

"Wait." North rocks onto his knees, grabbing a stick and poking through the ashes. My stomach sinks when he drags something out, a glass vial like the ones Alistair uses, full of shimmering threads. He rolls it across the ground to cool it before hefting it in one hand. The spell that gave the golem life.

"Don't want to waste it," he says with a forced smile, pocketing the vial and standing.

"Will Tobek try to trace the spell to its caster?" I force the question light, but inside, I'm terrified. If Tobek traces the spell back to Perrote, not only will Bryn know her father's nearby, but North can use it to find our kingdom without needing either of us. Why would Corbin sign a treaty if he can simply invade?

But North shakes his head, staring through the trees. "No need. Baedan's the only one with the luxury of golems anymore."

The hellborne woman who found me in the forest outside Cortheana—the one who told Kellig to kill me. "Baedan?" I repeat, surprised. "You think it was her?"

He frowns at me. "And you don't?"

"Our king uses golems as spies," I say slowly, watching him for any reaction. "Rats and birds, mostly, but never men like this. Maybe it was him."

"That's impossible," he says, scanning the trees again. "You need water for a scrying spell, and golems are made of smoke. They're brutes, Miss Locke, built to obey simple commands. Corthen used them in the war as a frontline of attack, to force Merlock's men into wasting magic dismantling them."

"But—" I frown. Shadow crows are the king's eyes in the dark places his guards can't go. "Then why call them spies? Magic soldiers would be more effective."

"Too effective," North says with a quirk of his mouth. "No one goes to war against a spy, but they will rise up against an army. Sounds like he's worried a good transferent would take down his golems and steal his spells."

"There are no transferents in Brindaigel."

"Your mother."

"Was executed for stealing magic," I say drily. "But not from a golem, from the king's treasury."

He looks over, surprised. "Your king stores his magic in a treasury?"

"You store yours in rocks."

"I'm not a king," he says. "Storing magic in any exterior vessel is the easiest way to have it stolen. Merlock made that mistake. Your king should have learned from it."

"Who's going to steal it? You've never even heard of us before and Perrote kills anyone who might be a threat."

He gives me a strange look as rain slides down his nose and drips from his chin. "If your king is looking for you, he wouldn't have sent a golem. This—"

Pain ignites around my wrist, bright enough to make me gasp. The binding spell tightens, nearly a solid bridge of black across my skin that hums all the way into my shoulder.

North reaches for me, his hand wavering in the space between us. "Miss Locke?"

Shouted voices rise above the wind, along with the thickening smell of sulfur. Clutching my wrist to my chest, I straighten with a sense of dread. "It's Bryn," I say, turning for camp. "Something's wrong."

He nods, expression grim. "As I was saying," he says, "golems are usually the first line of an attack."

Seventeen

BY THE TIME WE REACH CAMP, THE GODS ARE BATTLING FOR dominance again, battering us between Rook's icy skies and Tell's rolling earth. The pain in my wrist worsens, inching across my shoulder, into my chest. North unspools magic around his fingers, ready for attack, while I curl the box of matches in my fist, just in case.

I see Bryn first. Standing in the open doorway of the wagon, her red hair looks almost gold in the light behind her. North's crossbow is settled against her shoulder and she sights down the tiller before releasing a bolt into the dark beyond camp. There comes a grunt, a curse, and a sudden flash of movement. Only then do I notice the figures standing in the rain, outlined by the stormy skies. They're too hard, too rough to be anything but hellborne. Two bodies are already laid out on the ground.

Aim for the heart shudders through me as Bryn bends for another bolt from the quiver at her feet, notching it in place with a movement too smooth to be anything but practiced. So she does know how to shoot, just like I suspected.

Only one figure stands within reach of the light from the wagon, crouched by the perimeter, hand hovering above North's stones. Baedan. The rain wilts her hair into scraggly ribbons down bare, muscled shoulders, and Tobek paces her, his crossbow loaded in position. What is he waiting for?

Baedan sees North and grins, white teeth against dark lips. Poison laces her cheek like an old bruise, and her eyes shine silver as she stands. "You killed three of my men the other night," she calls in greeting.

"They got in my way," says North.

Baedan lifts her chin, her smile thinning before her eyes slide toward Bryn. "Name your price."

"Not for sale." Grabbing my arm, North hauls me over the perimeter, into the safety of camp. He holds me behind him, fingers tight through the sleeve of my coat.

Baedan's smile flickers when she sees me, and she casts a dark look over her shoulder toward one of the figures prowling at her back. I can't see his face beneath the hood of his coat, but I can guess the recipient of such disapproval. Kellig, who didn't skin me like he was told to.

"I'll give you two spells for her," Baedan says, turning back to North. "That's more than fair."

"Your spells are sloppy and have too many tangles," North says. "I lose most of the magic unraveling them."

Baedan reaches into her trouser pocket and demonstrates a glass vial, small as the golem's heart, full of liquid fire. "Clean magic, then," she says. "I'll match you ounce for an ounce. I'll even let you cut her open and measure the blood so you know I'm not cheating."

North wets his lips, shifting his weight—an almost unconscious step toward her. Toward the magic.

"No," he finally says, and for such a small word, it takes a lot of effort.

"Then make me an offer, North. You know how this works."

"You're wasting your time," North says. "She's not Merlock's daughter."

"Then you have no reason not to sell." When he doesn't reply, she begins tapping the vial against her upper thigh. "You still have your prince. You don't need a princess, too."

"He already said you're wasting your time," Tobek says, all gruff and bravado.

Baedan doesn't acknowledge him. "I'll overlook three dead men, but I will not overlook greed, North. Don't throw away years of peace on a redundancy."

Bryn tightens at the insult, still sighting down the tiller. Her skirts stick to her legs, outlining her slender frame. "If you want me, come and get me," she says, loosing the bolt. It strikes Baedan and bounces back against her leather vest, useless, no doubt blocked by some protection spell.

Baedan smiles, eyebrows arched. Bending, she picks up the bolt before dropping into a mock curtsy, arms spread wide. "Invitation accepted, your majesty."

With a grunt, she flattens her palms to the earth as poison

bleeds down her arms, fast as lightning, thick as weeds. The grass beneath her smolders and turns black, racing along the edge of the perimeter. The rain hisses into steam as the earth ignites.

The Burn.

Straightening—staggering—Baden tosses her damp hair out of her face, silver eyes cutting toward North. Despite the pain carving lines in her face, her smile sharpens, turns deadly. "This is the moment you lost any hope of saving this kingdom, North," she says. "This is the moment you and I became enemies."

North shifts his weight, still holding me back, and doesn't reply.

"Don't stray too far from your master," Baedan says, finally looking to Tobek. "You fall once, you fall again twice as fast. I know how to tame lost slaves like you."

Tobek doesn't flinch away from her, still holding steady position.

She begins backing away. "Start running," she calls, before turning and barking an order to her men. They fall back, disappearing into the darkness. Kellig lingers, eyes on me, before he too fades away.

"Why isn't she fighting?" Bryn lowers the crossbow, eyes wide, wild with the hunt.

"She can't." Mud streaks North's face and he grimaces with pain, releasing me and pressing a hand to his chest. The unspooled magic he's been holding on to has twisted the knuckles even further out of formation; dark cracks line his skin like dried blood. "Creating the Burn isn't a spell, it's an act of transference. She pulled the poison out of her blood and it'll take time for the blood to regenerate. She's too weak."

"Then why aren't you fighting?" Bryn asks darkly.

North sags, eyeing his ward. "I can't," he says. "I need magic to combat the spells she wears. I don't have enough and it'd be a waste of resources to try."

A draw. The worst possible outcome in the fighting ring, when you're both too weak to take the final blow and the house wins the bet.

Tobek hurries over, shouldering his crossbow. "I'm sorry," he says. "I'm so, so sorry, North. I should have been able to sense them. I should have warned you, but they came up so quickly. The storm must have caused interference—"

"It's all right," North says. "The ward held, that's all that matters." Though he forces a smile, there's a hard edge to his mouth that belies the gesture: He knows it wasn't the storm distracting Tobek from his duties.

Tobek knows it too. He wilts beneath North's disappointment. "I still should have sensed them coming," he protests weakly. His hands curl around his weapon. "That's the only thing I'm good for."

North squeezes his shoulder and I envy Tobek that gesture of kindness. A history is built into that touch. "We need to move before we're cut off completely," he says. "Ready the horses. Miss Dossel," he says. "I may need you. How many bolts do you have left?"

I stare at him, wounded: Her but not me?

Bryn quickly counts. "Half a dozen."

North nods, rubbing his mouth. "Can you watch the rear?"

She stares at him, eyes half lidded, before shrugging with disinterest. "I guess."

SHIMMER AND BURN \ 195

I hover, uncertain, waiting for my own task, but North barely glances at me. "Wait inside," he says.

"I can help. I know how to fight—"

"You can't fight them with fists," he says, in a tone that means no argument. "We need range. Magic. Please." His eyes meet mine, dark and pleading. "Just stay inside."

He doesn't wait for an answer, turning to salvage what he can of the perimeter yet untouched by the spreading Burn. I stare after him, feeling lost. Useless.

Tobek steers the panicked horses into position as Bryn steps down from the wagon. "You're hurt," she says.

Tobek brightens at her attention, touching a thin trickle of blood along his temple. "It's nothing," he says with staged humility. It's everything, if it means she's looking at him.

"This is why you need to be paid," she says, fingers grazing the edge of his temple. "You were as good as a soldier, you know."

Tobek stands straighter, trying to look taller than he is.

Feeling sick, I drag myself inside, picking up Darjin and cradling him to my chest. Sinking onto the bottom bunk, I stare numbly toward the door before shouldering out of my damp coat. Within moments, we're on the move and Bryn and North step inside. Bryn wears the quiver across her chest, holding the crossbow as if it's an extension of herself, and I look away, envious. Still offended.

North doesn't meet my eyes. "I'd like to put protective spells on both of you."

Bryn scoffs. "Absolutely not."

"I don't think you appreciate what just happened. Baedan believes you're Merlock's daughter. *Merlock*," he repeats, when she makes no sign of having heard him. "The king whose heartbeat feeds the Burn—whose heartbeat feeds the dead magic that keeps Baedan and the hellborne alive. Avinea's kings cannot die by their own hand, and only someone with blood tied to the crown can perform the sacrifice. If I find Merlock, Corbin inherits. If Baedan finds Merlock, she'll bury him somewhere I will never find him, and Avinea will be consumed with the Burn until only the hellborne can survive. And now that Baedan believes you're a missing heir—a potential threat to that plan—she won't stop until you're dead."

"Lucky for me, I have Faris to protect me," says Bryn.

"Damn it, listen to me!" North slams his palm against the wall, hard enough to rattle the glass jars above the stove. Darjin wriggles out of my arms, bolting beneath the table. "You're useless to me if you're dead!"

Bryn stares at him, eyes wide. I doubt anyone's ever spoken to her like that. No one would dare.

"I risked everything I had on a hope and a promise," he says, lowering his voice, spitting each word between clenched teeth. "Merlock is my priority. *Avinea* is my priority. And if your kingdom has magic and you're willing to offer that magic to Prince Corbin"—he takes a deep breath, ducking his head—"then you are now my priority. This is about more than just a binding spell, Miss Dossel."

Bryn rolls her shoulders back, recovering. "It always has been," she says.

I look away, prickly beneath my skin. Alistair withheld evidence and exploited my weaknesses to get what he wanted from me, so at the very least, I should be grateful that North tells the truth, that he doesn't pretend I'm anything more than a footnote to his plans. A fail-safe to his priority.

But my priority is my sister, not Bryn and not Avinea. I'm not naive enough to believe a night in the rain and a poisonous flower will trump the desires of a man who sacrificed four years of his life to finding Merlock. North will not risk losing the magic he needs for me. He won't risk losing Bryn.

Supply and demand.

"No protection spells," Bryn says at last. "Not until we reach New Prevast."

Of course not, I think bitterly. If her father finds us, she can't be complicit in her own captivity.

North sighs, raking a hand through his hair. "I'll take a horse in the morning while Baedan's still limping, and ride ahead to Revnik. There's a market there—I can buy the magic I need to get us through the Kettich Pass. We can only hope Baedan won't try to attack until we're closer to her territory by the Burn. Once through the pass, we don't stop until we reach New Prevast."

"Right on schedule," Bryn says.

North stares at her before his eyes shift to me. Guilt briefly darkens his face before wordlessly, he takes his crossbow and quiver from Bryn and ducks back outside, joining Tobek on the running board. He slams the door behind him.

The stove belches in the silence that follows. I shove my coat off the bed and lie down, curled in a ball.

Bryn stares at her fingers tented across the table. "Where were you?"

"Nowhere. I went for a walk."

"What if I thought you'd run away?" she asks, straightening, folding her arms across her chest. "What if I thought you weren't coming back?"

"I'm not going to run," I say. Not at the risk of losing Cadence. Doesn't she know that by now? "I came back as soon as I heard you—"

"Twelve minutes and eighteen seconds," she says. "That's how long it took you to come back. What if they had broken through the ward?"

"I would be the one who died," I say darkly.

"And what do you think happens to me after my safety is dead!? The next time I call for you, I want you here in three minutes. Do you understand me?"

I close my eyes, fingers tightening into knots against my stomach "I went for a walk," I say, teeth clenched.

"Do you know how long three minutes is?"

"Bryn—"

She slams her palm on the table, startling my eyes open. "I have warned you how to address me! Three minutes, Faris! That is how long a soldier is given to report for his summons, and that is how long you are given to report to me! One." She pinches the flesh of her arm and twists; a bruise blossoms on my own arm, dark yellow and cherry red. "Two"—another bruise—*"three."*

Closing my eyes, I grit my teeth and swallow my cry. Every nerve in my body stands on end, rattling with pain as saliva floods my mouth.

Straightening, Bryn tugs down the hem of her bodice. "I thought you were committed to this," she says, softer. "To me. Or if not to me, then to Cadence."

I force myself to look at her. "I killed a man for you. What more do you want?"

Sighing, Bryn sinks onto the edge of my bunk. In the dim stove light, all her hard edges soften. "I'm not your enemy," she says, plaintive. "We have the same end goal, Faris. Fighting won't help either of us."

I sit up, drawing my legs to my chest. "You wanted a fighter," I remind her.

"We could try to be friends."

I bite the inside of my cheek, inwardly snorting. Like Alistair Pembrough, *friend* is the last word I would ever bestow upon Bryn.

"Preparing an army takes time," she says, taking my chin in hand, forcing my eyes to her. "War takes even longer. I threaten Cadence but that doesn't seem to be enough to keep you focused. And I need you to understand how important this is. I need you to understand what your role will be."

"I understand completely," I say. I almost add *your majesty*, but withhold it; an unacknowledged act of defiance.

She smiles, relieved. "Good," she says. Leaning forward, she hugs me, cold in her damp coat. "It's an honor to be the queen's protectorate," she whispers in my ear. "I knew you'd appreciate that."

The room blurs beyond her shoulder as I tighten my fists against my stomach, hard enough to hurt but not hard enough to stop the shock from bleeding through me. I've heard enough of her conversations to know that distinction is everything, and when she said queen, she meant it.

She's never going to let me go. She never intended to.

"Our agreement was that I carry this magic to New Prevast and you released my sister," I say, voice cracking.

"War demands sacrifice."

"Alistair would be better suited to protect you."

"He's bound to my father," says Bryn with a sigh. "Which is why it's so important that I have you."

Goose bumps race down my back as I stare numbly over her shoulder. Will she even release Cadence as a token of good faith? Or will my sister be a constantly dangled reward always hanging just out of reach, tempting me to push one step further and further for her? What kind of monster will she make me?

Pull the trigger when you're ready.

I suffer Bryn's hug, hoping she can feel the hate that burns through my blood, the warning that I will not stop fighting until my sister and I are both free. But I can't fight back yet, not while she holds me in her arms and paints a future that depends on my submission. I sacrificed Cadence for the chance to save her four months ago.

This time I have to sacrifice myself.

I can't sleep.

I sit alone at the table later that night, a book open in front of me, the words blurred into illegible nonsense. All I can think of is Bryn's threat couched in shades of friendship, her arrogance in assuming Corbin will run to her aide on the strength of one spell and a story of a kingdom hidden in the mountains with magic to spare.

Well, I know the same story Bryn does, so what difference would it make if Corbin heard it from her or from me?

The skill is in cheating.

A flutter of hope dances through my stomach. I can't remove the binding spell, but I carry stolen magic—more valuable than a spell North will have to recycle. Maybe Prince Corbin doesn't need a crown to convince him to invade Brindaigel; maybe I could make my own bargain. Cadence is tied to the king, but that doesn't mean someone else couldn't sever the thread.

Someone like North.

The door opens with a rush of cooler air and I start with guilt, as if treason is written across my face. North steps inside, shrugging out of his coat. He hangs it from a hook on the wall before raking back his sleeves, exposing the twin protection spells nestled in the soft skin of his arms. His eyes flick to Bryn, asleep on the top bunk behind me, before they settle on me.

I realize I'm staring and look away, pulling my book closer, propping my head up in one hand. I pretend not to notice him even as I'm aware of every move he makes as he prepares two cups of tea over the stove. Wordlessly, he sets one in front of me and I shake my head—has he already forgotten I don't drink tea?—before I realize what it is.

Hot water.

A moment later, he sets down a jar of sugar cubes before taking one for himself, setting it on his tongue as he drops into the seat across from me. He looks young. Exhausted. Folded into his chair, in need of a shave, with a permanent crease between his brows.

I cradle the mug, heart aching with adrenaline, wondering how

best to broach the subject of taking Bryn hostage until I can lead
Corbin to Brindaigel. Would he listen? Would he agree?

North nudges through the stack of books pushed to the edge
of the table and retrieves my mother's. Pulling a pencil from his
pocket, he takes out the folded map at the back and smoothes it in
front of him. Hunching forward, he shades even more of the continent a soft fuzzy gray to mark where the new Burn has begun.
When he finishes, he drops the pencil and presses the heels of his
hands to his eyes, exhaling softly.

When he lowers his hands to his mouth a moment later, his eyes
land on the three bruises marching from my wrist to my elbow. An
eyebrow arches in unspoken question.

I force a rueful smile and shake my head. Her magic, her servant, her rules.

But not for much longer.

Flipping the map over, North begins sketching across the back,
his hair falling forward on either side of his forehead. A moment
later, he nudges the map toward me.

A flower, crude but still endearing, to replace the one lost in the
woods. Written underneath: *SAFE TO EAT. (NOT PREFERRED
APPLICATION, BUT YOUR CHOICE.)*

My choice. When was the last time anyone offered me a choice
that wasn't a trap?

Rubbing the back of his neck, North gestures for the map again
and I start to pass it back.

"Faris."

I turn to see Bryn watching us from her bunk. Guilt and fear
combine like oil in my stomach: How much did she see?

"Sleep with me tonight," she says, already shifting to make room. She saw enough.

I quickly stand as North sits back and refolds the map, tucking it back in its book. Avoiding his eyes, I climb into bed beside Bryn, holding myself rigid as she drapes an arm around me, the way I used to hold Cadence to keep away the cold, the nightmares, the disappointment that our father didn't come home again that night. But Bryn's arm is not a comfort, it's another warning.

I can't escape if she's holding me down.

Eighteen

NORTH LEAVES AT SUNRISE, RIDING AHEAD TO SOLICIT ASSISTANCE from Lord Inichi, the self-appointed provost of Revnik. Tobek drives the wagon like death is chasing us, white-knuckling the reins and freezing every time another traveler comes into view. On occasion, he touches his crossbow on the running board beside him, his face as pale as the clouds overhead.

Bryn sits at the table, playing a game of cards that get knocked askance every time the wagon hits a divot in the road. I sit in the stairwell, my back to the wall, Darjin at my feet. Maps are spread around me as if desperation will somehow result in finding proof of Brindaigel that both North and I missed before. It's a frustrating endeavor: How can I convince a prince to invade a territory I can't even point to?

I tease out the edge of my mother's map for another glimpse of North's drawing, exposing the list of my mother's clients and their measurements on the inside cover of the book in the process. I glance over them on reflex before shoving the drawing back into hiding.

Wait.

Darjin flicks his tail in annoyance as I sit up, finding the map North took from the farmhouse, breathlessly looking from book to map and back again.

Not measurements, I realize with a lurch, my fingers tracing the grid lines intersecting Avinea.

Coordinates.

Heart pounding, I track each name, the coordinates lining up with a list of villages and cities spread across the continent. Avarin. Nevik. Winchek, Dunck, Stantil—

Gorstelt. *New Prevast.*

I sink back, numb. These aren't clients, they're contacts. People my mother knew, either from Brindaigel, or—

Had she been to Avinea before?

Eagerly, I flip through the book, searching for hints or clues or confessions written in the margins to prove my theory. Alistair gave me this book for a reason, I tell myself. If he knew my mother, maybe he knew what these coordinates meant.

Nothing.

I search again before I toss the book aside, closing my eyes with a growl of frustration. Why is everything about my mother shrouded in so much mystery? Why couldn't she just be my mother, instead of a villain or a hero or whatever she was?

What was she?

My father rarely ever talked about her, and I rarely ever asked.

Only Thaelan heard my wild speculations over who she might have been to do what she did, but it was after a bottle of barley-wine and a bad day, when my anger needed an outlet and she was an easy target. In truth, I know nothing about my mother. She could be anything. Any*one*.

Even a fighter who stole magic from the king and then played him for a fool. Is that someone who would cut her daughter's heart out?

Bryn swears as Tobek hits another dip in the road. I open my eyes as she throws her cards down in disgust. "I hate this place."

I glance through the half-open door. The city of Revnik lies ahead, barely more than a smudge of ink at this distance. "I think it's beautiful," I say, gathering the maps into a pile. Maybe I can track the names in New Prevast after speaking with the prince; maybe someone knows more about my mother than I do.

"It's too big," Bryn says, pushing away from the table with a scowl. "It makes Brindaigel feel small."

"Brindaigel is small."

"Too small." She rocks her head back to the ceiling, pressing her hands to her eyes. "My father is the king of nothing."

So what does that make her?

Sighing, Bryn drops her arms, slumping back in her chair. She looks around the wagon before her eyes settle on Tobek outside.

"Do you think magicians take a vow of chastity?" she asks.

I frown. "Unmarried princesses do."

"It's like he's never seen breasts before." Her fingers tent on the edge of the table. "He stares at them like they're made of gold."

"He's thirteen years old," I say stiffly. "They're better than gold."

"I like that he stares," says Bryn. Her lips curl in a smug, self-satisfied way. "In Brindaigel, men looked because my father had power. But Tobek looks because *I* have power. He gave it to me and I never even asked for it."

I stare at her. "Don't hurt him."

She snorts. "I only hurt people when I have to," she says. "You know that by now. Cruelty is useless when it's applied without mercy." Standing, she steps over me and swings the bottom half of the door open, nudging Tobek aside so she can sit beside him.

"Miss Dossel," he says, surprised. Pleased. He glances from her to the road and back again, drinking her in.

"I want to know my future," she says, tucking her skirts beneath her legs, letting her knee knock into his.

He snorts. "Your future is obvious."

"You think so?"

"And you don't? Fate's so brightly scorched in your veins you practically glow."

Bryn smiles and tosses back her hair. It gleams in the sunlight. "Tell me anyway," she says, leaning forward, both knees against his leg now. "I want to hear it from an expert."

"Costs you a copper," he says with a teasing smile, taking the bait.

Bryn holds her hand toward Tobek, biting back a grin of her own. "I haven't got any copper, but my word is gold, if you trust me to keep it."

"Gold is gold and all else irrelevant." Sobering, he says, "You know it's just a trick, Miss Dossel. It's like cards; the skill is in cheating. Any intuit can see the course your blood will run. Only the good ones can make it sound prophetic."

"So are you a good one?" she asks.

Tobek hesitates, wetting his lips before he weights the reins beneath his boot and takes her hand in his, touching the cup of her wrist with a hesitant reverence. Bryn tips forward even further, lips parted in breathless anticipation as his touch grows bolder, skimming over her palm. When he speaks, his voice is low and husky—a showman with a flair for the dramatic. "You will be queen."

"Good," says Bryn, flashing a triumphant look to me just as a dark figure darts into the road ahead of us. The horse rears, pulling the wagon hard to the right, dangerously close to the edge where the ground begins to slope toward a green-glass lake. Books and rocks fly off the shelves behind me as Tobek swears, correcting the horse. The front wheel hits the berm and slides back to the left. Pulling hard on the reins, he drags the wagon to a halt before standing, turning toward the figure in the road behind us.

"What is wrong with you!?" he shouts, visibly shaken.

A man lurches into view, a little girl cradled to his chest. Fear lines his face; gray colors his otherwise russet beard. "I'm sorry," he croaks, holding a hand out in peace. "I—I'm looking for North. Is this his wagon?"

Tobek exhales, rubbing his forehead. "He's not here."

"But he'll return?"

The little girl shifts, peeking out from the safety of her father's neck. She's tiny, underfed, with big brown eyes and a sad, drooping mouth. Dark lines of poison carve patterns over her face, delicate as lace.

"What happened to her?" I ask softly.

"Berries," the man says, his own eyes glassy with exhaustion. "We didn't know. She ate blackberries from the woods, too close to the river."

"I'm sorry," says Tobek, "we're not for hire. There are transferents who circle the outer cities every month or so—"

"They're thieves. Liars." The man's voice cracks. "Please, we've ridden four days to find North. I've heard rumors that maybe he could . . . ?" He trails off, too hopeful to voice the impossible.

"Why don't you just read her future?" Bryn suggests, straightening her skirts and pushing past me, back into the wagon.

"I'm sorry," says Tobek, strained. "You put your faith in stories and that's all they are. North can't help you and neither can I."

The man blinks back tears. "But if he would just look at her—"

"I'm sorry." Tobek shakes out the reins and settles back in his seat, staring ahead, waiting for the man to move out of the way.

"I have money," the man says.

"Tobek," I whisper. I know this man, I know his story: the people of the Brim who believed money would solve any problem because money was all they lacked.

It's my story too. Fifty gold kronets and here I am.

Sighing, Tobek rubs the top of his head. "Look," he says, "there's a man in Revnik, Gabbistiano. Tell him North's apprentice sent you and he'll see her immediately. I'll bring you the address, just— that's all I can do and even that is a favor I'm not supposed to take on my own."

The man sags back, shriveling like earth without moisture. "Thank you," he manages. Tobek doesn't answer, pushing his way inside.

"Iron," I say in the awkward silence he leaves behind.

The man looks up from stroking his daughter's hair, eyebrows raised in question.

"It might dull the symptoms," I say. "It's supposed to dull the pain, at least until you reach Revnik."

"Iron," the man repeats, brighter than before. "Are you an apprentice as well?"

The idea thrills down my back. After ensuring the road is empty in both directions, I jump down, touching the little girl's forehead with the back of my hand. "What's your name?" I ask.

She mouths it more than speaks. *Sava.*

"Sava," I repeat. "Where does it hurt the most?"

Sava stares up at her father, who gives a slight nod of encouragement, before she touches her arm, above the elbow.

"May I?" I reach for her sleeve.

"Miss, I wouldn't—"

Mother of a sainted virgin.

The scratch is deceptively shallow, no deeper than those I'd incurred on my own as a child, running through the thickets along the edge of the shallows. But the skin around the wound is festering, necrotic layers of blue and gray that have started to peel away to the raw pink tissue underneath. The infection is eating through her body, searching for her heart. She'll turn hellborne if we don't stop it.

Or she'll die.

Tobek returns with the address, leaning over the horse and avoiding the man's eyes. "Here."

"Wait," I say, fingers tightening in Sava's hair.

Tobek shakes his head. "Faris—"

"North could help her," I say, low and urgent. Begging. "The way he helped you."

"Faris," he repeats. This is none of my business, he seems to say; shut up before your broken heart breaks everything. "Go to Revnik," he tells the man. "That's the only chance you have."

"Bring her inside," I say.

The man doesn't hesitate. He practically throws Sava into the wagon and climbs in after her. Bryn groans from where she lays across her bed, covering her face with a pillow, but I clear the table and direct Sava to sit on top, her feet dangling above the floor. My pulse races ahead of me as I rummage through drawers of herbs and stones and birch twigs bundled with thread. Dried yarrow hangs above our heads and I pull it down, dampening it with water from the samovar. Simple, basic steps, executed with far more conviction than I feel because I don't know what I'm doing and Tobek is too busy panicking behind me to offer any help.

"How old are you, Sava?" I ask, pressing dampened yarrow leaves against her arm as she hugs her father's waist for comfort. Reaching for a roll of bandages, I begin wrapping the herbs in place.

"Ten," she says.

"What are you doing?"

I straighten. North fills the doorway, a bag slung over one shoulder. Dust from the road dulls the blue of his ruined coat to the color of winter skies. His eyes are nothing but summer thunderstorms, however, as they flick through the wagon, glancing off me before they settle on Tobek, demanding an answer.

"Sir," Tobek says, but North shakes his head against any apology, dropping his bag.

"You never wrap an infection like this," he says, tugging the bandages loose, undoing my clumsy work. "It'll breed faster beneath pressure. Tobek, you should know this."

Tobek gapes at him. "It wasn't my idea!"

"You should have stopped her! And *you* should not be handling an infected arm," North says, directing his venom at me, scowling at the discolored bruises up my forearm where the blood has broken and pooled beneath the skin—where any infected magic could slide into my blood more easily. "If you're going to read my books, Miss Locke, learn something useful from them!" To the man: "When did you first notice the poison?"

"Ten days ago," he says. "She was scratched two weeks before, but it didn't go sour till then."

"A fortnight for incubation." North draws back, shrugging out of his coat, tossing it across a chair. I swallow hard and step back, feeling stupid, in the way. North begins rolling his sleeves, casting a dismissive look over his shoulder at the rest of us. "Wait outside."

I move for the door but North calls me back. "No, Miss Locke. If you insist on educating yourself, you need to start somewhere. Give me water and stones. Clean ones. Second drawer."

Fresh from the river, I think. Flat to hold magic more evenly.

Tobek hangs in the doorway, wounded that I'm needed and not him. "Sir—" he starts.

North straightens, eyes flashing. "Get out!"

Tobek scurries outside, Bryn on his heels without a single complaint. I don't blame her—North infuriated is terrifying.

"Lie down," North says to Sava. "You"—he looks to the man—"step back."

Sava protests as her father pulls away. North's mouth flattens and I jump forward, clutching Sava's hand in my own. "My sister's name is Cadence," I say, "and whenever she gets scared or has nightmares, we sit on the roof and count the stars."

North scowls. "I can't help her if she doesn't hold still!"

"Her name is Sava," I cut back pointedly. "And she's ten years old."

He draws back, nostrils flaring.

"But we're inside," Sava whispers.

"Look," I say, tilting my head to point to the ceiling and the painted stars nestled between the wooden beams. "Lie down and see how many you can count."

Sava complies, stretching out along the length of the table, a finger tagging the stars as her lips silently mouth the numbers. North pulls back the sleeve of her dress before his eyes drop to the rocks I've arranged in a neat line along the edge of the table. Rolling one between his fingers, he presses it to her arm, at the bottom of her scratch.

"Will it hurt?" Sava asks.

"If it does, just squeeze my hand tight as you can and I'll swallow up all that pain for you."

"You can't do that," North says.

I frown, ready to protest his lack of imagination, but he interrupts me. "Skin is the perfect conductor, Miss Locke. Through it you can transfer heat, cold, pleasure, pain. And magic." Black eyes briefly meet mine. "If I start to extract the poison, I won't be able to tell where her infection ends and where your skin begins. If I try to take more than what's there, if I try to draw something from you through her body, it could collapse her veins."

I release Sava's hand, burning with the embarrassment of my inexperience. "Then why are you using stones? They're conductors too."

"It's a buffer," he says, "to keep the infection from going through me." North exhales softly and dips his chin. "The gloves," he says. "In my coat. Leather doesn't conduct magic. You could wear those and still hold her hand."

I hurry to pull them on as North presses the stone back into position. Closing his eyes, he begins to coax the poison loose. Sweat beads his temple and shadows dance across the planes of his face, like clouds chased across the sun. He bares his teeth, white against the olive of his skin.

Sava whimpers. The poisoned lines across her face begin to unravel, brightening from the color of smoke to the color of freshly turned ash as it works down her throat, into her arm, collecting at the base of the stone. Fat tears roll down her cheeks and pool in her hair.

After a moment, North pulls away with a wrench of breath and I catch a glimpse of the rock, now black as night, and his fingertips, dark as charcoal. He quickly exchanges the stone for a second, knocking the others off the edge of the table with a clumsy sweep of his wrist. He flinches, eyes meeting mine with a flash of humiliation before he presses the new stone to Sava's arm, balancing it with his palm as his fingers have become too swollen to bend. It too turns black within seconds and North recoils, dropping the stone to the table. It misses the edge and hits the floor, not with a rattle as expected, but with a dead weight that sounds leaden.

Pale, North tries to run a hand through his hair but falters, tucking the hand under his arm instead. He's shaking. "She needs rest," he says, not looking at anyone in particular. "Don't take her home by horse, not tonight." He reaches for the cup of water I poured but pain tightens across his face; the cup tips precariously under his fingers.

"We'll just rinse it out and you're all set," I say, jumping in, taking over. After a moment, North nods me once in the right direction, keeping close watch as I quickly rinse the scratch and wipe it dry.

"If the symptoms return," he says, "she'll need to be excised again."

"Will they return?" her father asks.

"It's already in her blood," says North. "Some people can fight a smaller infection. Others can't. If it reaches her heart—"

Sava's father makes a short bark of terror at the back of his throat.

"Siphoning the infection as needed will help," North adds, his voice a bland, hollow monotone, "although you face the risk of the body building an immunity to the process. Each time will be harder than the last. If the infection takes root again, she'll need a full blood transfusion."

"Nobody's ever survived a full transfusion," her father says.

North stares at the floor, still cradling his hand under his arm. Muscles tense beneath his shirt sleeve, tightening along the side of his neck. "Don't eat anything with mold or black spotting," he says in that same hollow voice. "Boil any drinking water within a mile of the Burn."

"Our home is within a mile of the Burn," the man interrupts with a flash of anger. "Our entire village—"

"Leave." North lifts his head. "Take your daughter and go somewhere safe."

The air thickens, like the charge before a thunderstorm. "Where?" the man asks at last. "Merlock didn't leave us anywhere else to go. When is Corbin going to start fighting for his people instead of relying on boys to do it for him!?"

North dips his chin again. Hair falls forward across his forehead, and he looks impossibly young. "One of the cities," he mumbles. "Revnik or New Prevast. Mannon still has some defense left in the south."

Grunting with scorn, the man digs through his pocket and I look away, embarrassed at the telltale click of coins.

"I don't want your money," says North.

"I pay my debts," the man says tightly.

"Up you go," I whisper to Sava, leaving them to argue. She's a familiar weight pressed in my arms and I pretend like she's Cadence even though Cadence hasn't let me hold her like this since she declared herself a soldier—not realizing that even soldiers still needed to be held. Smoothing her hair back with one hand, I surreptitiously drop a kiss on top of her head, blushing when I catch North watching me.

The man offers a final, curt nod of acknowledgment before taking Sava in his arms. She blinks up at North, her eyes not as dim as before, her features not so sallow. A tiny fist reaches toward him, expectant.

North's shoulders sag and he offers his hand. She tilts a glass button in his palm, the color of the lake outside. It's a treasure to her and he stares at it, his entire body rigid. When Sava and her father duck out of the wagon, North follows at a distance and stands, framed in the doorway with his back to me.

Peeling off his gloves, I lay them across the table before running my hands through my hair.

"Please don't do that to me again," he says, back still to me.

"I'm sorry," I say. "I just thought—after what Tobek said, that you healed him, maybe you could—"

"What? Maybe I could heal her!?" He rounds on me, eyes flashing, his features contorted with pain. "I could have! I have the magic, Miss Locke. I have the ability! I could have healed her, but then word would get out that North has clean magic and a weak heart and he'll help whoever comes to his door with a story!" He slams his hand on the wall, rattling the door. "Have you not heard anything I've told you!? Magic doesn't come easy in Avinea and it doesn't come cheap! I don't have the resources, I—I can't save everyone! To pick and choose who lives or dies is cruel!"

"She's only a child."

"That doesn't matter!"

I recoil as a strange, stifling silence falls between us. North rubs his mouth before he growls, hurling Sava's button across the room. It hits the far wall and bounces back on the top bunk, lost in the coverlet. Shaking his head, he sags in the stairwell, pressing the heels of his hands to his eyes. "Saving that little girl doesn't help anyone."

Tears burn the back of my throat and I stare past him, toward the lake through the open doorway. "She ate poisoned berries," I say tightly. "She wasn't an addict, North. She didn't go looking for a high. She was innocent—"

"It is selfish to sacrifice the whole to save a few."

I look away, fingers tented on the edge of the table. Iron, I tell myself. Be strong, impenetrable, callous. *Cadence.* Nothing else matters. No one else matters. I pegged him for a mercenary long before I considered him a friend, and this only proves it.

"I'm sorry," I say, voice cracking. "I assumed you would have wanted to help. I won't make that mistake again."

The floorboards crack as North moves toward me, stopping only inches away. Swallowing hard, he rakes back his sleeve. Charcoal lines seep past the barrier of his protection spell, like tiny breaks of lightning casting shadows beneath his skin. They inch toward his hands, spreading. All at once, the jars of black rocks that line the wagon make sense.

He's infected.

"Skin is a conductor," he says, holding my eyes, his expression fierce, unapologetic, "and the poison inside me wants to spread. I can hold it back with spells, try to bury it, excise it whenever it gets too bad, but any time I transfer magic, even through a buffer, the infection feeds off that power and moves deeper. Using magic is killing me, Miss Locke. And every time it gets harder and harder, and one of these days, the poison is going to reach my heart and I won't be able to stop it."

And I need these hands to conquer the world, I think suddenly, with a twist of guilt. Every night North laid down a perimeter of stone and forced a spell through them even though it had to hurt him to do it, just to keep us safe.

To keep his promise.

Tugging his sleeve back down, North says, "I didn't save Sava and I went to the marketplace that day only intending to buy that spell from Miss Dossel. I will not apologize for being selfish, Miss Locke. That was the decision I made four years ago and nothing—*no one*—will change my course. Merlock is all that matters, and I can't risk saving anyone else while I still have the chance to save Avinea. That doesn't mean—" He falters, features contorted as he looks at me, full of grief. His palm presses against his chest. "These spells only hide it," he says "They don't actually make me heartless."

"North—"

"Nobody will fight for the half-blood prince of a half-dead kingdom," he says. "There's nobody left. Avinea has no money, no military, no defense, no magic, and no hope. I am running out of time and I am running out of options."

Grabbing his bag by the strap, he yanks it to his hip and removes a half-crushed flower from inside. He drops it to the table without looking at me, and my stomach caves in with a sickening twist.

Abbis. From my mother's book.

He lowers his voice to a growl. "I spoke to three different men who fought in the war today, and not a single one of them has ever heard of Brindaigel, or King Perrote, or any other kingdom with the kind of magic that produces spells like that. Like *ours*. Somebody's lying to you or you're lying to me. Either way, I need that binding spell and I have never hidden that from you." Slinging his bag over his shoulder, he straightens. "I told you that you were safe here and I told you that I would help you, but I never told you that I would save you." His voice softens, turns weak. "I can't."

Turning, he slams outside, barking orders for Tobek to hitch the second horse to the wagon. Delayed adrenaline spikes through me and I begin to sway, knees buckling before I hit the floor. Magic presses against my skin, eager for some outlet, some movement. A fight, maybe; dust in the air and blood in my mouth and the fervor of a ring of voices cheering me on.

But there's no one to spar with, no one to hit or hurt but myself. Frustrated, I will myself to be still but my body refuses. It wants action. Movement. Freedom. *More.*

It wants North. Every poisoned inch of him.

A shadow fills the doorway and I lift my head, hopeful, but it's Bryn who approaches, skirts hissing at her heels. She crouches, cradling my face between her hands. No doubt she heard every word between North and I—and all the words—the *weakness*—that fill my silence now.

But my hands are not on the floor, and I am not defeated yet. There's a still a chance to win this game, but it requires playing by her rules for just a little longer.

I lower my head in deference. "I'm committed to this," I whisper.

"Good," she says, and hugs me tight as a viper.

Nineteen

EVEN WITH THE REASSURANCE OF THE MAGIC HE BOUGHT IN Revnik—Tobek looked ill when North told him the cost—North presses the horses as far as possible that night, stopping only when we reach an abandoned trading post on the outskirts of the city. Half a dozen empty storefronts and houses surround a cobblestone square, while a watchtower rises above it all. Scavengers have gutted everything, dismantling all the glass and wood, leaving a majority of the buildings without roofs, windows, or walls.

North casts his ward in the cobblestones themselves as Tobek trails him with a litany of apologies. The spell shimmers like silver cobweb in a frosted sunrise before darkening again, and while North must have excised the infection that broke past his protection spells, his hands are still swollen and cramped. He moves slower than usual.

"Tobek!" he snaps at last. "Please," he says, much kinder, spiking his hair with one hand. "You're distracting me."

Tobek backs away like a wounded dog. North sighs, head bowed for a moment before he resumes his work.

I watch them from the roof of the wagon, the only privacy I could steal from Bryn. She's inside now, and Tobek glances toward the doorway with a familiar look of longing. A restlessness permeates the camp; we're all looking for a distraction.

Rocking my head back, I frame the sky between my hands. A single star emerges through the gray ocher haze of the Burn that rages on the other side of the Kettich Mountains. It sparkles in and out of view, taunting me. *There's your wish.*

Despite lying flat on my back, I feel imbalanced, dizzy, as though I might fall. The edges of the courtyard tilt in, and for a moment, I feel the familiar claustrophobia of home.

I lower my hands. "Tobek," I call, and he jerks back, startled, searching the ground before North finally tells him to look up.

"What?" he asks, surprise giving way to a scowl. I am not forgiven for this afternoon.

"Why doesn't the Burn spread through the mountains? I thought stone was a conductor."

"It would still have to be transferred." It's North who speaks, though he doesn't look at me. He hasn't looked at me all afternoon. "And anyone who tries to pull a thread of poisoned magic through a mountain is going to die long before the mountain will."

So it's not magic that keeps Brindaigel safe from the plague, it's the mountains themselves. But how can a man move an entire mountain and not leave a mark for an intuit to find? A spell that size would draw every hellborne in Avinea to our borders, yet according to Bryn, Perrote is not a talented spellcaster.

So who cast the spell that removed Brindaigel from the map?

I prop myself up on my elbows. "North, what's the biggest spell that's ever been cast?"

Fingers knot at the back his neck, and at first, I don't think he's going to answer. But then he stands, his ward complete. "Thirty years ago, Merlock took an army to defend our Wintirland allies from invasion. Before leaving, he placed a protective spell around Prevast to keep the city safe from outside attack until he returned. Corthen bribed the provosts into unraveling the spell one thread at a time. It took months to dismantle the whole thing."

"Like the touchstones," I say.

He stiffens; I've hit a nerve. "Yes. The provosts who guarded Merlock's magic were mostly addicts and thieves. They are the very souls Merlock meant to punish with the Burn and yet, they were on the first ship that fled Avinea."

"What did Corthen do with it all?" Is it possible that he removed us from the map in exchange for our alliance? Everlasting protection and a possible place to hide from his brother?

"There was a war," Tobek says pointedly.

"Most of it was lost," North agrees, not nearly as sarcastic. "What little he didn't use has been hunted and reclaimed over the last twenty years."

"Was he a spellcaster?"

"No," says North. "Corthen had no magical abilities of his own."

I sink back, disappointed. Even if Corthen had enough magic to hide our kingdom, that doesn't explain how it disappeared from atlases printed before the war. Were we hidden by magic even then? If so, how did Corthen find us when no one else can?

"North," I start.

"Miss Locke, I am more than happy to discuss history or politics, but not while you're perched on the roof like a gargoyle!"

All at once, the anger from earlier returns, needle sharp and venomous. "Then come up here," I say, hoping he'll say yes, that he'll make that first move so I don't have to.

"Humans are meant for the earth, not for the sky."

"Farodeen the First says you're wrong," I say.

North finally looks at me, expression unreadable, and my stomach somersaults before tightening in a cramp. All day, I've retraced our argument, trying to find fault in his anger, to justify my own. But each iteration yields the same result: I was wrong.

I roll my apology across my tongue, softening the sharp edges. Small steps, little words. "North—"

"Don't fall," he says, cutting me off. "We're already half a day behind schedule."

My apology melts back down my throat. "And you're still waiting to get paid."

North's jaw tightens. Giving me one last dark look, he slams his way into the wagon. A moment later, a chair scrapes across the floor and his voice rises, a muted growl in response to Bryn's softer tones.

I scowl at the sky but even the single star is gone, swallowed by storm clouds and smoke. I press at one of the discolored bruises on my arm, forcing my vision to clear and my thoughts to focus. In two days, either Bryn will have a treaty or I'll have my sister. And while Bryn's a master of manipulation and can play the games needed at court, I grew up in the Brim, where the one who wins is the one still standing at the end.

And I intend to win.

Below, North stalks out of the wagon with his crossbow in hand, Darjin at his heels, disappearing into the watchtower. Tobek takes a step after them before faltering. After a moment, he turns for the wagon and Bryn. I wait a beat to ensure she doesn't chase him out before jumping off the roof and following North.

It takes a moment for my eyes to adjust to the dim light pouring in from the missing roof overhead. A spiral staircase hugs the wall, and heavy beams crisscross where a second and third floor would have been. I see North, silhouetted against the crenellated wall at the top of the tower, framed through the torch brackets that once held the fires that would be lit to warn Revnik of approaching danger.

Taking a deep breath, I kick through the thick cover of bracken and debris that litters the floor and make my way upstairs.

North doesn't look at me when I reach the top, although Darjin pads over to sniff my hand. His silence is unnerving and I hang back, second-guessing my decision. "Anything out there?" I ask at last.

He glances over before nodding beyond the wall. A campfire burns in the distance, no bigger than a star. I hug myself, chilled by the icy wind that blows off the lake. "Baedan?"

Another nod. "She'll be relying on her slaves for blood, until she can reach the Burn and refill her veins with poison." He shifts. "We'll leave the wagon in Revnik and take horses through the pass and on to New Prevast."

"You'll abandon the wagon?"

He digs the butt of his tiller into the crumbling cement of the wall, raking chips loose. "If Miss Dossel delivers as promised, I won't need it anymore."

I watch him, wishing I knew what to say to smooth the lines in his face and soften the hard edges of his jaw. "I'm sorry."

He digs even deeper into the cement. "For what?"

"For this afternoon. For everything."

He pauses before glancing toward me. "I shouldn't have lost my temper," he says at last. "It's a weakness I'm working to conquer."

"You had every right to be angry with me. Tobek tried to turn them away but I insisted they come in. I wasn't thinking. It was selfish of me to risk your life like that, and I'm sorry."

Exhaling softly, North gestures to a clutch of broken columns nearby. I dutifully take a seat and he sits across from me, our knees almost touching.

"I used to think saving the world meant saving the people in it," he says, setting his crossbow at his feet. "An effect of my education, no doubt, where I was taught to emulate saints and virtues. Like Farodeen: He saw hope when others saw nothing, and an entire world was created. But even virtue turns to sin when taken to extreme. My ambition became greed and my pride became arrogance. I stupidly thought by some . . . divine right, I would be the exception to the rule. But I failed, like everyone before me."

"What rule?"

"That living or dead, for good or for evil, magic is still a parasite. It was never meant for mortals to wield. That was Merlock's mistake; he offered magic to the people and the people became addicted to easy solutions; guaranteed crops, healthy cattle, ever-lasting love. Pay the right price and a provost could cast any spell you wanted." His expression darkens, turns sour. "When Corbin is king, magic will be viewed as the weapon it is, not as a household commodity. Industry will run this kingdom again."

I search his hands, reddened skin and swollen knuckles, before my eyes stray back to his face. "Do you ever regret the life you chose?"

"Some days yes. Most days no. And every now and then, I wish—" He breaks off, shaking his head with a rueful smile as he remembers: I don't believe in wishes. "There are days when I resent my mother for making the choice for me," he says, expression guarded as he studies my face. "Days when sacrifice starts to feels selfish."

I know how he feels. My mother changed my path irrevocably ten years ago, and I've been stumbling along blindly, resenting her for it ever since.

"But Prince Corbin needs his magic seamstress," I say softly.

"I'd like to think he's not the only one," North says, just as quietly, still watching me. Then he looks away, pulling Darjin to his leg and scrubbing his flank.

I duck my head, hands balled into the pockets of my coat to avoid the temptation of touching him, of offering what comfort I can, proof that he's not alone. I know what it's like, that need to fight until there's nothing left, no matter how stacked the odds may seem.

A rush of adrenaline crashes through me, rubbing every nerve raw. If I'm wrong, North will steal this magic and I'll be worthless to Bryn, to the prince, to my sister, to myself.

But if I'm right . . .

"Prince Corbin's not the only one who needs you," I say.

North looks up, eyebrows drawn.

"Bryn is going to offer an alliance to Prince Corbin," I say. "Our kingdom has clean magic, enough that she plans to trade Corbin what he needs to find his father, if he agrees to help her overthrow her own. She intends to be queen, but that won't come without war."

North continues to pet Darjin, his eyes locked on something beyond our feet.

"I'm the proof," I say. "The peace treaty. Before we left, I was injected with clean magic—"

"Injected? There was no transferent?"

I pause at his surprise. "No. It was done by the king's executioner."

North leans forward with a flash of eager interest. "And it worked?"

"Yes. Can't you feel it?"

"I'm not an intuit," he says. "At least, not the way Tobek is. The infection's diluted my ability to separate the magic in my blood from the magic in someone else. I'd have to touch you to know, and you made your stance on that option quite clear."

"But if you didn't know about the magic," I say slowly, "why did you come after me instead of Bryn that night in the woods?"

The change in his expression is subtle, the difference between an hour before noon and an hour after. "Because I couldn't save you," he says at last. "And you didn't need me to."

My heart slams against my ribs. A man who's spent four years searching for a missing king wouldn't waste time bartering for names from a girl who had any magic to offer instead. It wasn't that he was playing the coy and mercenary magician that night. It was that he didn't know, that Tobek hadn't warned him what I carried hidden beneath my skin.

He came after *me*, not the magic.

North pushes Darjin out of the way and inches even closer. "Miss Locke—"

"I want to make you an offer," I say.

North closes his mouth and sits back. Waiting.

"I made a mistake four months ago and Cadence suffered for it. She became the king's property. A slave. Bryn promised me her freedom for coming with her."

No reply.

Blood aching, I wet my lips and lean forward; our knees collide but neither one of us shifts out of the way. "Take the magic I'm carrying," I say, offering my hand. "And when we get to New Prevast, I'll speak to Prince Corbin before Bryn does. Perrote stores his magic in the mountains like a touchstone; there's nothing to stop anyone from stealing it. We can convince Corbin that we can siphon the magic out of the kingdom without ever starting a war. And then we'll use that magic to find his father and save Avinea."

"We?" No mockery, only question.

I flush, hand falling to my lap. "I don't want any of it, North. All I want is my sister back and this spell"—I touch my wrist—"removed." I bite the inside of my cheek and remember the way he looked at me after I killed that golem. The way it felt to be brave again. "But I would help you," I say. "If you wanted me to."

"I already have an apprentice."

"That's not what I mean."

"I know." North stares at me with a strange expression. "You would sacrifice your own king for mine?"

"I will sacrifice a tyrant. A murderer."

"Be careful, Miss Locke." His voice drops, turns husky. "Magic leaves a mark and love is a magic all its own. As is hate or greed or lust—any feeling that requires any effort. And when left to fester, every single one of those feelings can go sour and destroy you." He examines his opened hands, rubbing at the swollen joints. "Merlock loved his brother and it made him weak. It made him waver. After he killed Corthen, Merlock's guilt and regret infected everything he touched until he finally cut himself loose of Prevast and vanished."

"Loving my sister does not make me weak."

"You've already killed one man to save her."

"And you will kill your king to save your country. To serve your prince—"

"I will kill one man to save thousands," says North. "That's not love, Miss Locke. That's duty. Obligation. Love is a weakness, and a weak heart breaks, a broken heart bleeds, and blood can be poisoned." Sighing, he slides his hands across his knees. "I'm not asking you to be heartless; I'm asking you to be cautious. Your strength could be your greatest weakness if you don't consider the choices you're willing to make and the consequences they bring."

"That's my offer," I say, extending my hand again. It wavers between us. "All the magic you can carry, and in return, you remove this spell and get my sister out of Brindaigel."

North stares at my hand, his fingers tightening across his knees. Remorse colors his voice when he says, "I can't."

"It's three to one," I say in the awkward pause that follows, forcing a smile to combat the sudden weight in my chest. "Tobek and I can hold Bryn down and you unlace the spell."

"I can't." He stands, raking a hand through his hair as he paces away from me. "It's not that simple, Miss Locke. It would take time. More time than we have, and it would take more effort than I can risk with Baedan watching my back."

I sit frozen, staring beyond the half-broken wall around us. "So then when we reach New Prevast, when we have more time—"

He doesn't answer.

"North," I say.

He presses a hand to the wall, his back to me. "I can't make that agreement. If Miss Dossel has access to magic—if she has potential resources she's willing to commit to Avinea, it would be a mistake not to listen."

"I'm offering you the exact same thing," I say. "Only magic without war—"

"No." He turns to face me, expression haunted. "Magic is transferred through the bloodline, Miss Locke. By killing her father, Miss Dossel would inherit. And an ally like that . . ." He trails off, guilty.

He can't sacrifice the whole to save the few.

I stare numbly into nothing before, with a blast of nerves, I stand, moving for the stairs. My skin itches, pulled too taut, and the walls close in, too tight to breathe.

"Miss Locke," he says.

"Nothing has changed," I say sharply. "We go to New Prevast as planned."

"I'll have the spell removed as a stipulation of any agreement—"

"She's using my sister as collateral," I snap. I brandish the bracelet of smoke at him. "I took this oath and I killed that man and you need to know that. You need to know I will do anything—*anything*—to save Cadence. Bryn is not my priority. Avinea is not my priority. Not until Cadence is safe. And if that makes us enemies—"

North reaches out, skimming the sleeve of my coat, timid as a monk, before his fingers skate past my wrist, cradling the back of my hand. Swollen knuckles and sandpaper skin awaken an insatiable greed inside me. It's more than a touch, it's a confirmation: My heart was not buried with Thaelan four months ago and it aches as it comes alive again.

"I am not your enemy," North says softly.

Neither one of us moves. "You have no resources for war," I say at last, pleading with him. "Corbin will need an entire army to invade. Perrote's men all have loyalty spells inked above their hearts, and they will fight—"

I stop, touching my wrist. Bryn stole this spell from the king's provost. It's the same spell given to every soldier in the Guard: forced loyalty to ensure their unquestioned obedience if Perrote ever demanded it. Yet it wasn't loyalty that Bryn wanted from me. Instead I'm bound to bear her wounds, to be a fail-safe against all threats. Including death.

"How do you become a king?" I ask.

"Magic," he says darkly.

"I'm being serious."

"It's a bloodspell," he says. "Corbin will bind his blood to his father's heart and inherit the magic that runs through it."

"But you have to kill the king to inherit the magic?"

"You have to remove his heart, yes. Why?" He pulls back, eyes clearing. "Miss Locke, what's wrong?"

"Perrote can't be killed," I say numbly. Any attempt to hurt him will be transposed over a thousand men; a fatal wound will diffuse, turn harmless. If we return with an army, the entire kingdom will be called to defend its king and everyone but Perrote will die.

Including Cadence.

How will his son Rowan ever inherit the throne? How will Bryn?

The skill is in cheating.

The ground sways beneath me. My legs buckle and I fall to my knees with a crack of pain I feel all the way to my shoulders.

It's like reading Thaelan's secret codes. Turn left, then right, then straight to the answer—a kingdom no one's heard of, a king who fears death and discovery, not just from those beyond our borders, but from anyone who exhibits a magical ability within the city. Like a transferent who could dismantle his golems and steal his magic, or maybe an intuit, who could trace the spells back to their original source. Perrote isn't looking for his daughter; he's looking for me, and not because he's afraid everyone will learn that Avinea exists.

Because he doesn't want anyone to know that Brindaigel does.

North crouches in front of me, concern etched across his face. "Miss Locke?"

All these signs, waiting to be acknowledged.

Pay attention, Faris.

"Do you know how we got to Avinea?" I ask, looking up at him. "We walked beneath a mountain."

He frowns. "I don't understand."

"She's not a princess," I say. "And he's not a king. Which is why Brindaigel isn't on any map and why Perrote hasn't sent any men. He can't risk anyone seeing an army and tracing it back to him." I grab his hand, threading my fingers through his. "You said if you touched me, you could read the magic inside me. Whose magic is this?"

"I can't read the spell through you. It's like I said—"

"Then read the clean magic."

"Miss Locke."

"Please." I tighten my fingers through his.

He swallows hard, staring at our intertwined fingers. Drawing a deep breath, he settles his weight more comfortably, cradling my hand in both of his. A soft, gentle heat bleeds out of his skin, warming mine, but after a moment, his frown deepens.

"What's wrong?"

He shakes his head, bemused. "There's magic there," he says, "but I can't . . ." Shifting, he touches the side of my neck, as if searching for a pulse, before drawing back. "I can't feel anything specific, it's like . . . smoke. Shadow."

"What does that mean?"

"I don't know. Maybe the binding spell is too strong, or maybe . . . Are you sure it worked? The injection, I mean?"

I open my mouth to say yes, only to realize that Alistair injected me while I was drugged. I have no proof he did anything at all except tell me a story so I would have no choice but to accept Bryn's offer.

Ice slides down my spine. Was this all a lie to chain me to the princess to ensure her safety until she reached New Prevast and started a war? But what offer could she make Prince Corbin if not proof of magic?

Bryn doesn't know.

"Miss Locke." North's hand softens in my own.

"I have to warn her," I say, but I don't get the chance.

Shadow crows arrive.

Twenty

THE CROWS STRIKE WITHOUT AIM, HURLING THEMSELVES AGAINST the walls, the stones, our shoulders. North curves his body over mine as sparks rake across the ground, igniting the dried leaves at our feet.

I clutch his arms, terrified. "Perrote," I say, all miserable apology.

Darjin mewls in pain, and North bundles the tiger into his coat as I grab his crossbow, swinging it high. The tiller cuts through a line of crows, useless against the smoke; one of them hits me on the chest and heat blisters through my coat.

North takes my arm and we race downstairs, stumbling, nearly falling. More birds pour into the watchtower, chasing us down until the sky disappears behind a cloud of smoke and feathers and the shrill pitch of a thousand golems with one objective:

Guaranteed victory.

We burst out of the watchtower, to Bryn and Tobek standing in the courtyard outside, gaping at the sky.

"Don't just stand there," North snaps, setting Darjin down. "Get the horses secured!"

Tobek moves to obey but Bryn throws her head back, hands balled into fists. She stands unguarded, unflinching, unafraid.

"How appropriate," she snarls. "He sends magic spells instead of soldiers!"

It's a false bravery as I realize with a sickening lurch: She doesn't know the crows *are* soldiers. She doesn't know they can hurt her, and by extension, *me.*

I call her name in warning as a crow dives, followed fast by the others.

Ignoring me, she throws her arms out wide in challenge. "Do you hear that, Daddy!? Little birds can't bring me home!"

North reaches Bryn before I do, shielding her body as crows slam into his back, shredding his coat before breaking apart. Inky feathers scatter as they wing back to the sky; embers rake across the cobblestones. A few crows fly too close to the campfire and implode, slamming into the walls of the wagon. The faded paint ignites and flames begin to spread.

Tobek notices, pausing in his struggle to lash one of the horses to a column of stone. The horse pulls back, eyes wild as crows nip its flank, leaving shallow scratches through the glossy pelt. It bucks, knocking Tobek flat on his back. He rolls out of the way half a second before the horse lands, narrowly missing his head.

"Take Miss Dossel and get in the wagon!" North orders, loading a bolt in his crossbow.

I pretend I don't hear him, breaking for the campfire where I kick out a stick burning on one end and fall back, keeping close to

Bryn. Months of fighting in the ring taught me patience, but fear edges out all my training and I swing too early, the flame of my torch grazing only a few birds. They burst with pops of light before others batter me in quick succession, forcing me to cower, covering my head. Beside me, Bryn shrieks in pain as a thin scratch appears, running from her chin to her scalp. A moment later, it dissolves and I feel it burning down my face. She stares at me, hand pressed to her cheek, expression incredulous as she finally makes the connection: Her father didn't send spies, he sent monsters.

And they're not here to bring her home.

Shock fades into determination. Falling back a step, Bryn balls her skirt in both hands and hurries to help Tobek with the horses. Only then does Tobek run back to the wagon, recklessly batting at the fire with his arms and hands.

Ahead of me, North abandons his crossbow and crouches, flattening a hand to the cobblestones, leaching magic from his ward. His skin turns a bright and deadly white, and cracks of poison appear almost instantly, still hungry from Sava's transference. I buy him time by fighting off the crows who angle too close, but there's too many, with even more arriving.

North staggers to his feet and casts his spell. Overhead, silver light cuts down the center of the crows; beady black eyes turn dull and polluted. Several begin to fly erratic, favoring one wing over the other, before a series of muted pops fills the night. Their spelled hearts shatter midair and stone fragments clatter to the ground around us, followed by the birds themselves as their bodies hit the cobblestones and implode into half-moons of embers and feathers.

Silence. Jarring and surreal, broken by the hitch of my breath and a soft grunt as North sags to his knees, shaking. Pain tightens his face, and his hands curl across his chest, crammed under his arms. Darjin approaches, sniffing his smoldering coat with caution.

I stare at him as Tobek pushes past me, stamping out smaller fires around us. Bryn stands by the horses with her chin raised to the sky in search of any more sign of her father. Feathers cling to her red hair and spill down her back; thin scratches lace her arms and her face before fading. She looks small in that instant. Fragile.

Adrenaline ebbs and I bend forward with a grimace as Bryn's and my injuries combine. Sticky heat spreads down my back: another dress ruined.

"We should check the stones," North says numbly. "See if there's any left—"

"Forget the goddamn stones!" Bryn spins to face him. "My father just tried to kill me! Once he finds out he failed, he'll try again! If you can't defend me, then get me to the palace like you promised so someone else can!"

"Every intuit and hellborne in the area will start swarming," Tobek cuts in, bloodied and raw. "Sir, we have to move to better ground. You—" He stops and reconsiders, choosing his words with the same delicate care I've learned to speak with Bryn. "The ward is broken," he says. "We can't stay. You don't have enough magic left to recast it and still risk the pass tomorrow."

"There's enough magic," North growls, stumbling to his feet and advancing on Bryn. She backs away from him but he's faster. "A binding spell that strong, and a father with a flock of golems to spare?"

He lunges for her and she throws a wild punch that North easily ducks. "Don't touch me!"

He squints at her, breathless and ragged, his hands splayed across his knees. "New agreement," he says. "Payment upfront or I leave you out here for your father to find."

Her features are wild, framed by tangles of feathers and hair. "If my father finds me, he'll find you too. *All of you.* We adhere to our original agreement—"

North lunges again, catching her off guard. She resists but he pins her to the side of the wagon, angling his tattered sleeve against her throat, careful to keep his bare hand from grazing her skin. "Three to one," he says savagely. "I could just rip that spell out of you and leave your carcass to rot."

Bryn snorts before tipping her head back. "But you won't. You need me."

I stare across the courtyard, into the muddy shadows of the empty buildings that pen us in. "No you don't," I say. My heel grinds through a layer of grit and ash as I turn to face them. "This wasn't a first line of attack, it was a final defense. He's getting desperate." My eyes meet North's, begging him to believe me. "He's not a king, North. There's no magic to inherit."

Bryn stares at me. "What are you talking about?"

North's jaw clenches, his need for an alliance warring with the doubt that I planted. "Tobek," he says at last. "Find out where this binding spell originated."

Tobek hunches forward nervously, tugging on the rumpled waves of his hair. "Sir—"

"Do as I say!"

Tobek flinches and Bryn laughs, eyes narrowed. "So sainted North is too much of a gentleman to touch a lady with his crippled hands. Though I suppose your apprentice comes more in handy on those cold mornings when you can't even dress yourself." She bares her teeth. "All those little buttons."

North looks at Tobek in accusation, and he ducks his head with a flush of guilt. "I already looked," he says. "Earlier today, when I read her blood, I also tried to read the spell, but it—it was scraped clean, North. It's old magic, recycled from somewhere, but I couldn't tell where. Whoever cast that spell did so anonymously. They didn't want credit."

North's nostrils flare; he shifts his weight, arm still pressed tight against Bryn's throat. "Why didn't you tell me?"

"I tried to talk to you, but you wouldn't listen to me! You—" His eyes fall to me in recrimination. He's not the only one who's been distracted lately.

"No king casts a spell anonymously," North says. "Only cowards and thieves do that when they don't want anyone tracing it back to them."

Bryn smiles, but I can see the cracks in it, the second-guesses: She's not as invincible as she thinks she is. "Do you know that for an absolute fact?" she asks. "Are you willing to risk Avinea on the opinion of an unpaid apprentice and the treason of a servant? And you"—her eyes slide to me—"are you willing to risk your sister's life for this? Without my alliance, Prince Corbin has no reason to save anything or any*one* in Brindaigel."

"You can't kill your father, Bryn," I say softly, lifting my hand so she can see the spell she stole from him. "No one can."

Her expression stiffens as my words sink in. Her father didn't spare her his attack; going home an innocent is no longer an option. Despite everything, I feel half a heartbeat of sympathy for her, but beneath that is relief: She doesn't own me anymore. I have control again.

Bryn twists, grabbing North's hand and pressing it against her wrist. I gasp, dropping to my knees, and North looks back, anger dissolving into immediate fear as he realizes what's happened.

He jerks away from Bryn, but it's too late. Tiny ribbons of poison fan across her arm from where it bled out of his skin, drawn by the magic in hers. The ribbons sink out of sight but reappear moments later, twining up my arm like jasmine shooting up the kingdom walls.

At first, euphoric pleasure threads through my veins, unlike anything I've ever felt before. Better than a thousand kisses, a bottle of barleywine, a stolen night beneath the stars with Thaelan's body pressed to mine. Tears of wanting flood my eyes and I hear my heartbeat, erratic and impossible, a whisper-crash that hangs in silence before repeating again, harder, like a pounding fist beneath my skin. The world unravels around me, fallen stitches and hanging threads as the sky melts into a river of silver and smoke.

And then pain.

No, *agony*. Like scissors scraped up my veins, flooding my body with anger and hate and greed, my vices laid bare as the infection marches through my blood like banners of war. The poison burns like a rash now, fiery and getting worse, and I resist the urge to scratch, to look, to confirm what I see reflected in their faces.

It's spreading.

"How can it possibly move that fast?" Tobek asks, incredulous.

North takes a step toward me but falters, looking down at his shaking hands still riddled with poison. If he touches me now, if he tries to withdraw the infection, he could spread it even further—either through me or through him. He stares at Bryn and she stares back, defiant.

"You're an amplifier," he says weakly. "That would explain why the binding spell is strong enough to read a mile out, and why Miss Locke—"

"I warned you not to touch me," she says.

Swearing, North breaks for her but Tobek intervenes, holding him back.

"North," I say. Or maybe I only think it; the world feels diluted, as if I'm sinking underwater.

Tobek looks between us, frantic. "What do we do?"

North stares at me, haunted, before his expression hardens. Throwing back his shoulders, he tears off his coat and begins cuffing the sleeves of his shirt. His arms are peppered with blood and scratches from the crows. "Stones," he says.

"Sir, your blood—"

"Damn it, Tobek!"

Tobek gapes at him, wounded, before he bolts for the wagon. Drawers open and slam from inside as North sinks beside me. "I'm so sorry," he murmurs.

"No!" Bryn darts forward. "My magic, my servant, my rules."

"If we don't extract the poison, it will grow roots and infect her blood." North balls his coat beneath my head. "At best, she'll die, at worst she'll turn hellborne. And if she dies, your binding spell won't protect you anymore, princess." Scorn colors the word. "And it's still a long way to New Prevast. Tobek!"

Tobek flies out of the wagon, dropping rocks that he doubles back to retrieve. When he arrives, his face is flushed and he cowers, terrified of North.

North doesn't even notice. Grabbing a stone, he presses it to my forearm, where the skin has already started to split apart. He hesitates, eyes meeting mine.

I clutch his shoulder before nodding my agreement. *Go.*

Mother of a sainted virgin.

Excision feels like a hundred million of Alistair's needles scraping the underside of my skin. I open my mouth to scream but nothing comes out, only a choked, muted gasp that shimmers like oil in the air above me. My back arches off the ground and every nerve inside me coils tight, ready to snap. Tobek pins me down, but I feel the infection beginning to fray at the edges and sink even deeper, hiding where North can't reach it.

North grunts and pulls harder. Ridges begin to form under my skin, mimicking the mountains around us. Too fast—he's moving too fast; he's tangling the threads and creating knots. My heart races forward, galloping into rhythm like drums of war until there's nothing in me but noise—

I claw at him. "Stop," I cry, as threads of poison snap, recoiling up my arm like lashes.

North growls and rocks back to his feet, twisting away from me and hurling the stone as far as he can. It disappears against the sky before he presses both hands to his forehead, pacing an agitated line between me and the fire.

"You amplified the infection," North says, shaken. "At this rate, it'll reach her heart within a few hours. I can't stop it, not—not while I'm like this. Not while my infection is so close to the surface."

Ash sticks to my lips and I struggle to swallow. He speaks so clinically, impassive, but I know what it means.

I'm dying.

North looks at me, helpless, before his gaze shifts to the wagon. A debate plays across his features as he straightens. Resolved. "I'll take her to Revnik," he says. "There's a transferent there who can draw out the infection. He's clean, there'll be no risk involved."

Tobek shakes his head. "No. We can't split up, not now."

"Continue toward New Prevast," North says, already angling for the horses. "Ride through the night; we'll meet you in the morning."

"I can't fight the hellborne on my own! And if her father attacks again—"

"Take the wagon. I'll recast the remaining ward. It's not ideal but it's sufficient."

"The wagon is too slow! I'm sorry, sir, but she's—" Tobek's eyes meet mine in apology before he looks away. "We're wasting time," he says softly.

"Wood holds magic better than a horse can," North says. "Miss Dossel will be able to make the spell stronger than it would be on its own. And once you reach the pass, Lord Inichi promised an escort." Sucking in a deep breath, he releases it slowly, chin dropping toward his chest.

"Or," says Bryn, and he looks up with a frown. She holds a hand above my chest, her hair hanging above my face. "I amplify that infection again and it goes straight to her heart," she says.

North doesn't move.

"You want this magic," says Bryn. Her hand hovers, trembling, showing her nerves. "You need it to save this pathetic kingdom. But even if she dies, I'm still an amplifier with a binding spell strong enough to make a case for myself with the prince. With someone like me, your prince's supply of magic could last two, three times longer and be that much stronger. I don't need her anymore. So you want to save her life?" Her hand dips above my heart. "Make me an offer for it."

Nobody speaks. I stare at her palm, blackened with ash and dirt, and her face, fierce as the fire behind her. She knows she can't go home now, not without an army, and there's a hint of unfamiliar desperation in her eyes.

North breaks the silence, his voice thin. "What do you want?"

Tobek swears beneath his breath, hands folding behind his neck as he spins away from us.

"My father's throne," says Bryn, triumph spreading across her face. "I win my war, Corbin wins his."

"You have a plan, even with the loyalty spells?"

Bryn lifts her chin and smiles. "I know how to kill my father."

North looks to me and I shake my head, pleading with him. Her throne is worthless.

But her magic isn't.

"Prepare the horse," he says to Tobek.

"Sir. Please don't do this. After all we've done . . ."

"It is not your choice," North says.

Tobek stares at his master, the young man who saved his life by giving him a second chance. It's a look of finality, of farewell, of knowing that tomorrow, the world will have shifted an inch off course and the sun will never rise the same way again.

"Yes, sir," Tobek finally says, all formality. He retrieves his crossbow and stalks toward the horses, shoulders rigid.

North watches him leave with his own sorrow etched in the shadows of his face. Rubbing his mouth, he inhales sharply and lowers his hand. "I agree," he says.

Bryn doesn't lift her hand. "To what?"

"The resources you need to overthrow your father in exchange for the magic and your amplification abilities to find mine. But in return, Miss Locke's life belongs to me. The binding spell will be dissolved in New Prevast, and her sister brought to the city as soon as possible."

My blood runs cold, fire and ice colliding beneath my skin. Beside me, Bryn lifts her hand a fraction of inch. "Your father," she says.

"Yes," says North. He doesn't look at either of us.

Bryn's voice is no more than a hum. "Good god, you're serious."

"Yes."

"But that would mean—"

"Yes," says North, and a rueful smile crosses his lips. "My real name is Corbin Andergott. And I'm the Prince of Avinea."

Twenty-One

THE PRINCE OF AVINEA.

The words burn like the ash that rolls across my skin as North and Bryn retreat to privacy, haggling the price of my rotting body where I can't hear the terms of my worth. Bryn's voice rises with emotion, countered by North's steady hum. He leans closer, emphatic, and she stares at him, silenced. After a beat, North inclines his head and Bryn drops into a mocking curtsy.

They've reached an agreement.

When I sit up, the world rushes at me in a blur and with it, fury. I am not a commodity to be shuffled from one hand to the next. This is how they play their games, with words as their weapons. Not me. I take action, I take aim. I hit until I hurt or until I fall down bleeding.

My palms are not on the floor yet, and there's more than one magician in this kingdom. I'll find someone willing to help me, even if I have to find Baedan and offer my own life as payment.

Determined, I rise to my feet, staggering for the horses. North begins to cast a ward around the wagon, directing Bryn to follow his lead so she can amplify the meager spell. Afterward, he disappears inside but Bryn lingers, alone. She doesn't even look at me. Instead she studies the spell on her wrist with a slight frown, a touch of concern, softly rubbing the smoky signal buried beneath her skin.

I hate her.

It beats in the soles of my feet, echoes in the tips of my fingers; I feel the hate in the way my body burns from the inside out. And that hate fuels my strength as I swing myself onto the horse Tobek prepared and settle uneasy in the saddle.

North emerges from the wagon, eyes downcast as he takes the stairs two at a time, grabbing his coat off the ground. He stops when he sees me, eyes widening. "Wait," he says.

The horse jolts forward beneath the pressure of my heels. It begins to canter and then to run, galloping out of the trading post, back to the road.

Away from the Prince of Avinea and his new ally, the future queen of Brindaigel.

A net of light appears ahead of me, blocking the way. The horse rears back and I lose my tremulous hold on its saddle, tumbling off, hitting the ground hard enough to hear my shoulder crack.

Gentle hands pull me to safety. North's face swims in and out of view and I begin to protest, reaching up to strike him only to falter, panicked, when my arms are too heavy to lift. I'm turning into stone and I can't even stop it.

"Where were you going?" he asks.

"Don't touch me!"

"Miss Locke—"

"We could have destroyed Brindaigel!" Grunting, I try to roll onto my side but I only manage to twist myself between his arms, locked into place. Frustration explodes through me and I summon all of my strength, slamming my hands against his chest. "Get off me!"

"Miss Locke, please. Stop"—he pushes my fist aside again, his expression hardening, turning fierce—"stop for a moment and breathe! This anger, this paranoia, that's what the poison feeds on, and the more you give in to those feelings, the deeper the poison will sink through your body until it's inextricable! You have to be calm or you're going to die!"

My hands clutch at his shirt. He's all bones beneath his clothes, hard angles and slopes that offer no traction as my fingers fall back. I can't catch my breath and my panic cinches my throat even tighter until I'm gasping, head back and neck exposed.

"Slowly," North says, his hand light against my shoulder. "You're all right. Just breathe." And then, quietly, "Please trust me."

No.

I swallow my hiccups. I don't know how to articulate what this feeling inside me is, part bitter, part betrayal, all heartbreak. "You bought me like I was meat in the marketplace," I say.

He looks at me, stricken. "Faris," he whispers.

I close my eyes again, but this pain cuts even deeper than blood, down into my bones. He was right to withhold my name: It sounds too much like magic on his lips.

And magic hurts.

"I can't risk being wrong," he says, almost pleading. "Without being able to trace any magic in you—" He breaks off, looking away. "I would have told who I was," he says quietly. "But you have to understand that Prince Corbin has been a target from the moment his lineage was revealed, and I needed North. I needed freedom to move, to hunt Merlock without being hunted myself." Sighing, he drops his head. "War demands a first casualty. Better it was North than someone like you. Someone who can still fight."

"You bartered with her like she had power. You *gave her* power!"

"I have never infected anyone before," he says. "I allowed my anger to dictate my actions and it would be selfish to make you suffer my consequences."

"It's selfish to sacrifice the whole to save the few," I say savagely.

He sits back, wounded, and I exploit the advantage, rolling out from under his arms, onto my side. The wagon lumbers into motion, Tobek grim-faced at the reins. I watch it pull ahead of us, a washed-out, faded scrap of wood and charred paint. Nothing more than a relic, an illusion.

"I could have taken you to Brindaigel," I say, staring after it. "I could have given you everything you wanted without losing anything."

"You have to trust me," North says. "With Miss Dossel's alliance, with her amplification ability, I could find Merlock in—in weeks. Maybe days. It's an advantage Baedan doesn't have. We'll get your sister back, Faris. I promise."

Doesn't he know better by now?

I shove myself to my knees and then, my feet. North offers me a hand but I shy away from him. "Don't touch me," I say.

"Faris."

"Greed costs," I say. "And she's going to make you pay." She'll make both of us pay.

He straightens, defiant. "You underestimate me."

"You underestimate her," I reply.

In the end, logic prevails and I agree to ride to Revnik. I can't rely on anyone but myself to save Cadence, and I can't save her if I'm dead.

Up close, Revnik is a city of soft-colored stone, of domes and turrets and massive arches. Umber tiles accent everything, from pillars to windows to doors. Oil lights glow in hazy splashes in the darkness, made fuzzy, out of focus by the moisture of the lake that cradles the city with wide arms and narrow fingers.

An enormous wall protects the inner city from invaders, but centuries have spread Revnik beyond its original border, crammed with churches, watchtowers, and hundreds of narrow stone houses and wood-framed shops.

Almost all of it's empty.

For every open window are three boarded or broken. For every bridge standing, another two lie in ruins. Life gathers around the sparse light in clusters: men and women with somber faces and curious eyes that track us as we pass. Rangy dogs nudge through the alleys; a red-tailed fox trots beside us for half a block, a dead rat carried in its mouth.

I see everything but register little, no better than a golem of skin and bone with a deep, dull ache in my chest. Not from the infection, but from the silence that festers between North and I, the conversation we carry on without any words. North's defense in the way his legs tense against mine, the way he strangles the reins in his fists; my accusations in the way I sit bent forward though it hurts my back, to avoid the temptation of his warmth and the beat of his heart and the reminder that he's human.

So am I, but not for much longer. Already the skin of my forearm is peeling back to the raw tissue underneath. Dark cracks web the skin of my hand, oozing bright pearls of blood that look violet in the misty lamplight.

We steer past darkened churches and narrow streets, through alleys choked with garbage and streets wide enough for ten across where we're the only ones in view. Shadows shift along the roofline—hooded men holding crossbows, with swords strapped to their hips.

"Lord Inichi keeps the city watched," North explains, when he sees me looking. "His men are as close to a militia as Revnik has had in almost fifteen years."

Scorn colors my voice. "So why aren't they in New Prevast? Guarding *you*?"

"When you've spent fifteen years making your own rules, it's hard to follow someone else's," North says drily. "His men are better suited to guarding Revnik and the pass."

We finally stop at a high stone wall half hidden behind a barricade of ivy. I catch a glimpse of a beautiful manor house through the iron gate. Built from stone and arches and ornate windows, it sits back from the street, fronted by an overgrown garden. Iron grillwork frames the windows on the first floor and above a double-sided doorway painted a bright and blinding red.

North slides off the horse, lashing it to a ring embedded in the wall. There are none of Inichi's men in sight, but I feel watched all the same.

After helping me down, North shoulders my weight. "Can you walk?"

Barely. He guides me up the stone path, past statues and broken fountains buried in tangles of ivy and brush. When we reach the wide porch, passing through a frame of columns to reach the doorway, he wets his lips and hesitates before lifting the brass knocker and slamming it down Almost unconsciously, his hand strays toward mine, his little finger brushing against me before I pull away, hugging myself with a shiver of pain.

"Who is this man?" I ask.

North doesn't answer as the door opens with a yawn. A young servant in faded red livery bows us into a long hallway of chipped marble and peeling wallpaper. A flickering chandelier hangs overhead, half crystal and half cobweb. A dark staircase sweeps up to the second floor and doorways are open down both sides of the foyer, leading into darkened rooms full of furniture and muddied shadows—arms and legs and lethargic bodies sprawled with little dignity. The smell of opium and something darker thickens the air and stains the edges of the wallpaper the same brown as stagnant water.

I turn to North, accusing, but before I can demand an explanation as to why he brought me to an opium den, an older man thunders down the stairs, stopping halfway. Dressed in an unbuttoned waistcoat and untucked shirttails, he looks wild, interrupted. An owlish look of surprise dissolves into a wicked grin. "Ever North at my door," he says before he laughs and slaps the banister. "Son of a bitch! How are you?"

"Solch," says North with a grim smile, threading his arm through mine.

Solch cocks his head and lifts his shaggy eyebrows above his glasses. "And company?"

"Miss Locke," North says, before I can.

"M'lady," Solch says with a smirk and an exaggerated bow. "Come in, come in!" He beckons us to follow as he turns back upstairs.

He leads us into the right wing of the house, separated from the rest by a dank velvet curtain. Beyond, the air dims with smoke and rattling coughs muted behind doors with numbers chalked across the painted wood. Cheap silk screens hide the peeling wallpaper, shoved in between ratty cushions and discarded pipes. There's vomit on the floor.

Solch unlocks a door at the end of the hall and shoulders it open. A girl looks up from a bed of pillows, counting stacks of coins with stained fingers. She isn't wearing a blouse and her breasts are cracked, blistered; her bare stomach riddled with smears of infected magic and patches of scaling gray skin. She sees North and stands with a crack of bones and a look of tired expectation.

"My client, not yours," Solch says, slapping her hand away.

The girl looks at me in dubious question: Am I the client? She can't be much older than me—maybe even younger, and my stomach tightens with anger, with disgust. This is what Cadence will become if Bryn wins. This is what Tobek used to be, what he might become again if Baedan does. For the first time, I truly understand what North is fighting for.

Solch leads us into another room, larger than the first, a nobleman's bedroom gone to seed like everything else in this house, in this city. There's a wide, rumpled bed against one wall with swaths of dark fabric circling the top. A worktable is pressed against the other wall, littered with strange and wicked medical equipment. Blades of all sizes are intermixed with bottles of all colors, scraps of bones, and a forgotten dinner. Clean needles overlay used ones, cradled by dirty wads of bandages.

And teeth. Dozens of teeth in all colors.

"Are we buying or selling today?" Solch asks.

I look at North, who looks ahead, mouth thin and expression grim. "Buying," he says.

Solch sinks into a tatty velvet armchair by a pair of doors propped open to a small balcony. He bends one leg over the other with an expectant look to me. "The offer?"

My skin crawls and I fold my arms over my chest, away from his prying gaze.

"I pay gold," North says.

"I prefer skin," says Solch, still sizing me up, assessing my value. "Skin makes me more money than gold ever has."

"Gold and poison," says North, "or I find another transferent."

"At this hour? Who can hold their tongue the way I can?" Solch settles back in his chair, fingers tented. "Silence costs, my friend."

"My only offer," says North. "I keep secrets too. Lacing your drugs with dead magic is illegal within city limits. If there's an outbreak, you'll be blamed."

Pressing his fingers to his chin, Solch studies North with narrowed eyes. North shifts his weight, coiled tight like Darjin before he springs after fireflies or field mice.

"My counter," says Solch, lowering his hands with a smile. He enjoys this, haggling. "Gold, poison, and one of your tricky little spells."

"I have no spells on me."

"If there's an outbreak," says Solch, "will the good Lord Inichi blame me or the man who carried the poison into the city looking to sell? Think carefully before you answer that, your majesty."

I look from one to the other, incredulous. North trusts this man with his true identity when that trust is bought and paid for? A man's word is the worst bargain in the world. North's lived too long in a monastery if he doesn't know that simple tenet of survival.

Yet North actually considers the offer. "An ounce of clean magic," he finally says.

Grinning, Solch jumps to his feet and extends his hand. His fingernails are cracked and stained yellow. "Agreed."

North shakes his hand once, brief and perfunctory, not long enough for Solch to send any prying needles of interest into his skin to assess what magic lies beneath, or vice versa.

Glancing toward the bed with a frown of distaste, North pulls his coat off and lays it across the soiled coverlet before guiding me to sit. Solch drags his armchair closer, perched on the edge as he takes my poisoned arm in hand, turning it this way and that. His glasses slide down his nose, eyebrows furrowed.

"There's no entry wound," he says. He frowns up at North. "This is a simple transferred infection. Like hell you can't do this yourself. What else is festering in there that you'd bring her to me?"

"I didn't sell you answers," North says, pacing behind him, arms folded across his chest. "Just take what you can and leave me the rest."

"Performance trouble?" Solch arches an eyebrow with a wink to me. "I've got something that could help with that—"

"I didn't ask for a medical assessment," North cuts in.

Rolling his eyes, Solch pushes the chair back with his heels and crosses the room, picking through his cluttered work space. He hums beneath his breath, and when he returns to me with a piece of bleached bone, his breath washes over my face, sour and fetid.

"Good teeth," he says with a glance at my mouth, wiping the bone against his shirt before he presses it to my arm. "I buy them a silver apiece if you're interested."

Once again, I look at North. Unspoken apology darkens his eyes as he rubs the back of his head, casting a longing look to the door.

Compared to North's earlier efforts, Solch's transference is clumsy, heavy handed. Rather than coax the threads of poison toward his buffer, he grabs them with a fist and tears. Agony shears up my arm and I fold forward in defense, grabbing onto the bed frame as the room spins around me.

Swearing, Solch presses harder, his glasses dangling from his nose, features strained with the effort. "There's something . . . blocking. . . . What the hell is in there!?"

"You feel it too?" North steps forward, expectant. "It's like she's empty. You can't read anything inside her."

"It's not working," I say, jerking back, but Solch grabs my arm and doesn't let go.

"We'll just try harder," he says.

Heat spreads up my neck, across my chest: The poison is spreading, inching toward my heart. The taste of metal floods my mouth, chased by something bitter, something viscous. I cry out and North immediately intervenes, pulling Solch off my arm. "Stop."

Solch tears off his glasses as sweat rolls down the side of his face. The bone in his hand is still bleached white, though. Still clean.

It didn't work.

"There's something wicked hiding in there," he says. "I can't reach around it. Who infected her?"

North doesn't volunteer his name or the story, and neither do I. Still clutching the bedpost, I tip too far forward, sliding to the matted carpet below. North steadies me with one hand and grabs a bowl containing an inch of oily soup with the other. I vomit, more bile and water than anything substantial. Blood and poison flock the rim of the bowl, red and black and undeniable.

The infection's in my blood.

Tipping my head back against the mattress, I press my arm over my mouth and fight another rise of nausea. Flakes of skin peel loose from the motion and the smell is of dead horse in the farming terraces, left to fertilize the rocky soil.

"What did you drag in here?" Solch asks.

North rubs his mouth before dropping his hand. Defeated. "You can't help her."

"Nobody could, not like this, not with that, whatever it is in there. She needs new blood."

"Would the blood take?" Not a question, a demand. Steady North is starting to fray, and any hope I had buried in the secret places of my heart starts to dim. They can't stop it.

"It never has before," says Solch.

I won't become hellborne, I tell myself, stern and unflinching as I stare at the ceiling and fight back my tears. The ceiling is painted pink, with cracked plaster ivy and rosettes along the molding. Beautiful despite the decay, and yet, I crave the stars of North's wagon.

Exhaling, North reaches into his pocket and drops three black stones and a smaller white one onto Solch's worktable, along with several gold kronets. Bending, he hoists me to my feet and I jostle like a sack of bones. "Thank you," he says tightly, always the gentleman.

"She's dead, North," Solch calls after us as North barrels me through the next room, past the ghost girl. "Put a knife through her heart before it goes sour, and then find some new skin to wear to bed."

North's anger darkens the already stilted air in the house. He shoulders my weight down the flight of stairs, wordlessly lifting me into his arms when I stumble and can no longer stand. He slams through the front doors ahead of the mute servant, into the humid air, sticky as a second skin. I curl into his chest, listening to the thunder of his heart as North kicks the gate open and moves into the street, turning both ways in a helpless waltz. His fingers tighten around my hip before his expression breaks and he sags back against the wall, sliding down until he's seated on the ground and I'm cradled in his lap.

"I'm so sorry," he says, staring ahead. "You're going to die and I can't stop it. I've only made it worse."

The truth always hurts.

His legs give slightly across the slick cobblestones as pressure begins to mount in my chest. I feel my heartbeat slow to a crawl as it sucks in the last of my clean blood. Fear floods through me, a desperate need for another day, another hour, another moment to be alive. A tiny, cowardly voice offers my choices: If I die, so does Cadence, and Bryn wins everything. But if I let the poison into my heart and accept my fate, if I turned hellborne, maybe—

No, I think, fierce and absolute.

But, I counter, and it is tantalizing in its possibilities.

Grabbing the front of North's shirt, I force my eyes open. "I'll make you an offer," I say.

He stares down at me. "What?"

"Anything you want in exchange for a spell."

"A spell," he repeats with a frown. "What kind of spell would you—?" Understanding dawns over him and he blanches as he shakes his head. "No. *No!* Absolutely not."

"I saw you do it to the hellborne."

"No."

Taking his hand, I press it against my heart so he can feel the way it shudders in my chest. "The gods love sacrifice," I say.

He stares at his hand beneath my own before his fingers slide more firmly through mine. "There's another option," he says, hoarse and uneven. He wets his lips. "It . . . it would stop your heart instantly. No pain."

"Thank you."

"Faris." There's a story framed in his mouth, a beginning, a middle, but no end, not for me. My fingertips skim the slope of his jaw and I force a smile.

"Ask for something in return," I say.

North touches his forehead to mine and briefly closes his eyes. "An ounce of your strength," he says.

"It's yours," I say, and he returns my smile with a tremulous one of his own.

"Cadence will live in the palace," he says. "She'll grow up, Faris. I promise."

I nod, fighting a spate of tears, an overwhelming sense of envy for the life Cadence will have that I'll never see. The life North will have. "She'll fall in love with you," I say. "But don't give her a sword until she earns it."

He chokes on a laugh before nodding tightly, sliding his hand free of mine. He fumbles through his pockets and retrieves a stone laced with magic before, with shivery softness, he peels back the collar of my dress.

"What is this?" he asks, tracing my scar with his thumb.

"Darjin the Second," I joke, closing my eyes. "My mother's greatest legacy."

North's weight shifts around me; his hand turns steady and his breathing evens out. When he presses harder against the serrated teeth of my scar, the scar bites back, sharp and familiar.

"There's something in there," he says.

I open my eyes just as the door slams open behind us. Solch swings through the gate with a screech, the bowl of soup and vomit clutched in one hand. North twists to see him, expression fraught with unasked questions.

"Iron," says Solch, and he grins.

Twenty-Two

THROUGH THE GARDEN AND BACK INSIDE, INTO PALE LIGHT AND SOUR air. Thirteen steps and through two doors before North lays me on the bed and I finally melt like water. Eyes closed, I press back against the tatty pillow that smells of sweat and darker things. I'm hot, I'm cold, I'm sick, I'm dying.

I'm not dead yet.

"Miss Locke." North presses a hand to my forehead, his thumb rubbing the line of my brow. "Look at me."

It takes me an hour to turn my head, another minute to meet his eyes. My heart beats slow and onerous, overworked; my words come out like graying flower petals on a windowsill. "Miss Locke again?" I ask.

North rolls his shirtsleeves higher, past his elbows and the spells inked there, and kneels beside the bed. At some unspoken order, Solch hands him a scalpel and North hesitates, the tendons in his arms corded like rope. His fingers curl through my hair and he's a whisper at my ear, coarse and uneven. "Faris always," he says.

My mouth dries out, starchy with the taste of fear, of desire. I want him. A greed unlike any I've ever felt before, fringed with dark, sulfurous thoughts: I *need* him. The poison responds with a roar of agreement.

North presses his thumb to the scar above my breast and I feel the pressure of his magic threading through me, tentative and searching.

"If you're wrong," he says over his shoulder.

"She's dead anyway," Solch says, his eyes on me.

Taking a deep breath, North flattens his palm against my shoulder, pinning me to the bed, and I know this moment. The way the light flashes on the blade of the scalpel, the way my heart lurches with fear. The way I lie so powerless beneath the hand of someone I know, someone I trust.

This is how good-bye begins.

I don't know this place.

I stand, a shadow in a sea of light. Masked faces swing and smile past, ball gowns from a different time. Oddly colored hair totters high and higher, frosted pinks and pastel blues. The people who pass are bright and pretty things, dressed in colored fabrics that shine in the flickering light of the chandeliers.

A brooding man sits on a throne, a fist pressed against his mouth as he watches the party with disinterest. Women bow in invitation, but his eyes lock on me, on the poisonous weed in his garden of flowers. Shifting his weight, he lifts his head and his hand unfurls, summoning me closer.

Music eddies around me. When I reach the dais of the throne, I hesitate before I kneel, bowing my head, exposing my neck: a gesture of subservience to my king.

"Your majesty," I say slowly, fighting the words, like wading through the thick bog outside Brindaigel. My words turn to salt and scrape my lips ragged.

"Look at all the liars and thieves," Merlock says.

Frowning, I turn to the hall that stretches like a mausoleum at my back. The colors have bled from the dancers, turning them into vapor, skeletons in ribbons of rotting flesh. Their dancing turns frantic. Tiles crack beneath their feet and the walls rattle loose with the music. Marble falls from the ceiling and the glass roof shatters, while outside a fire blazes brighter than the stars.

I look back to Merlock and realize it's actually North who sits withered and broken, crumbling beneath the weight of his crown. A hole gapes in his chest where his heart should have been, the wound ringed with poison.

"Faris," he says, "I can't save you."

I bolt awake, into North's waiting arms. He cradles my head against his shoulder, fingers digging into my back as he repeats my name like a promise. In the weepy, muddy light, my nightmare clings, sticky and terrifying. Memories begin to return, replacing the fear: Revnik, Solch, *ever North at my door.*

North. Closing my eyes, I strain toward the gentle pressure of his touch, the soft heat of his body, the way he's barely there and yet everywhere, a charge of energy that snaps across my skin like lightning.

"Slowly," North murmurs, holding me tight.

I pull back, in time to see the remorse flicker across his face before his expression turns impassive. "What's wrong?" I ask.

He lowers his head, arms unfurling around me. "The infection got into your blood," he says at last. "I excised as much as I could, but you're still poisoned. I—I can't remove it completely. There's a possibility that your body will fight off what's left, but . . ."

But there's a possibility that I'll always have dead magic hiding in my veins, ready to swell like a rising tide to flood my heart and turn me hellborne.

Guilt colors his voice. "I'm so sorry," he whispers. "I took a vow to serve my kingdom and in a moment of weakness, I—"

I touch his hand and he flinches. "What did you find?"

He stares at my fingers. "Iron," he says, and sighs. "There was iron buried under your skin."

The room spins; metal and light and the taste of blood. "What does that mean?"

"Iron mutes magic," Solch says from the foot of the bed where he sits, glasses pushed high up his forehead. He wipes something clean with a rag before bouncing a tiny chip of metal across his palm for me to inspect. "Magic goes in, none comes out. It means someone was hiding something in you that they didn't want found."

My hand goes to my scar, now buried beneath a thick wad of bandage. "Hiding what?"

Standing, North drags a hand through his hair. My blood freckles his face, stains his fingers, is black against black on his shirt. "The clean magic you promised, for one thing," he says. "The infection sank so fast, it didn't touch it, and there's enough there to convince my council to go to Brindaigel for the rest. With Miss

Dossel—" He stops, catching himself, and I pretend not to notice how easily he's adopted his new alliance. "It's hope," he says at length. "The most we've had in years."

But any future that keeps Bryn in our lives promises nothing but misery.

Avoiding his eyes, I examine my arm, cracked and peeling with dead skin but already starting to heal. Poison lurks in my veins, turning them more black than blue, but when I angle my arm to the light, I catch the first hint of something paler.

Clean magic.

"Here. Drink this." Solch thrusts a glass at me, full of a brown liquid flecked with beads of something black. I accept it with a reluctant thanks.

A bell rings by the doorway, hanging from a coiled rope. Solch glances toward it and stands. "Duty calls," he says wryly, and North nods in tense acknowledgment. He waits for Solch to close the door behind him before he releases a breath and drops into the armchair, fists pressed to his mouth as he stares at me. Wordlessly, he extends a hand and I give him the glass of liquid. He sets it on the ground beside him, out of reach.

"When did your mother give you that scar?" asks North.

"The night she was arrested for stealing magic from the king. Why would she put iron inside me?"

He studies his hands, shoulders hunched. "There's a spell," he says, sitting back. "I can feel the edges of it, but it's buried too deep to read, too long hidden beneath that iron. I can't risk searching for it, not . . . not like this." Not while his hands tremble, swollen from excising too much poison from both of our bodies. "When we reach New Prevast, we can assess the situation in a more controlled environment. But you were right." He stands and begins pacing the room, pausing at the balcony doors. "The magic you carry bears Merlock's mark, Faris. It came from Prevast. From Avinea."

My skin prickles.

"Miss Dossel is not a princess," he says.

I hug myself, relief warring with regret. "I'm sorry," I say softly. "I know you needed that magic."

"Rammesteel," says North, folding his arms over his chest. "It's a fortress, built two hundred years ago by King Tanoseen during the Fire Wars, in case Prevast ever fell from a seaward attack. Only Prevast never fell and Rammesteel was never occupied. It fell into disrepair and then into memory and then into legend." He sighs. "Until you came along."

"I don't understand."

"Corthen wasn't a king," North says. "He couldn't hold on to all that magic he stole; it wouldn't be safe. He had to hide it somewhere. We always assumed he'd expended most of it during the war, but maybe . . ."

"Brindaigel," I whisper.

North smiles thinly. "The Northern Continents cut off our trade routes years before anyone else was scared off by the plague because a shipment of guns and powder went missing off the coast. The entire crew disappeared, but when Corthen showed up on the battlefield with pistols, the Continents blamed Avinea for an act of piracy." He shakes his head. "I'm willing to bet it was an act of mutiny, and the one leading the charge was named Dossel."

Gunpowder, I think with a jolt. That's how you move a mountain without magic.

North returns to the bed and sits on the edge, next to my legs. "There are no rules of succession for the brother of a king," he says. "After Corthen was killed, anyone could have claimed that stolen magic as their own, and only an intuit would know the difference. Especially if that someone had pistols and a trained crew of men to defend their right."

All the lies we've been told—all the death. And for what? So a coward could play king? No. So a coward could *become* king.

"The perfect strategy," I say suddenly. North looks at me, eyebrows raised, and I repeat what Bryn had said the night we met: "Perrote declared war on Avinea the instant Merlock abandoned it and he's been winning ever since. He wants *all* of it, North." I look at him, incredulous. "Brindaigel was only ever meant to be temporary."

North snorts, shaking his head in disbelief. "And he might have won, if not for you." His eyes meet mine, and I flush beneath their intensity.

"What do we do about Bryn?" I ask, dropping my eyes, picking at a loose thread in the coverlet.

"She doesn't have to know any different until this is gone"—he touches my arm—"and we drain every last ounce of my father's magic out of those mountains."

My breath catches. "We?"

"I'll need you," he says.

North's fingers soften against my arm, protected by my sleeve. He half laughs, dry and humorless. "You're glowing," he says.

"Like starlight on water." Swallowing hard, he adds, in barely more than a whisper, "Magic suits you."

My stomach somersaults and I feel the curious press of the infection in my blood, warmed by the sudden heat of desire. Will this be my life now? Tempering my vices, balanced precariously on a narrow edge in which one instant of weakness could send me falling?

How does North resist the temptation?

Pulling a thin cord from around his neck, North snaps it in half and slides an iron ring free, the band simple but heavily worn. "Wear this," he says, standing. "It'll help keep you muted until we reach New Prevast."

I force a smile of thanks. The ring's too big for any finger but my thumb and I roll it into place.

"It was my father's," says North. "Not that he ever meant it for me. He gave it to my mother before she fled the palace in Prevast. It . . . hasn't fit these fingers for many years." He offers me as self-depreciating smile that quickly disappears.

His father. King Merlock.

North's expression mirrors my own. This is a conversation we haven't yet had, that needs to be said. North is the Prince of Avinea and I am a girl from the Brim. When he returns to New Prevast, there will be councils and crowns and guards and Bryn. There's no more freedom after tonight. No more North.

Eager to escape his hungry eyes, I stand and stagger to the worktable, finding the piece of iron North dug out of my skin and cradling it in my hand. Something happened to my mother that night between stealing magic and saying good-bye. Instead of running to Avinea, she ran home and buried this inside me. What kind of spell needed nine stitches to stay hidden? And how could my father not notice *this*?

Unless he's the one who put it there. But was he helping her, or hoping to bury her treason where no one would find it? *When have I ever saved anyone?* I think, with a chill.

"You said the magic in me could be traced to Merlock," I say, bouncing the iron across my palm, turning to lean my weight against the table.

"Yes."

"But Bryn's spell was scraped clean?"

"According to Tobek. Why? What's wrong?"

"Nothing," I say, mind racing. If my mother stole this magic ten years ago while it still bore Merlock's mark, but a spell cast afterward was scraped clean . . .

Did my mother know Perrote wasn't a king? Was that why she planned to leave Avinea? To bring back an army and expose the truth? Perrote must have panicked and scrubbed his magic clean—and ordered every magician in the kingdom executed—to ensure no one else could do the same.

North frowns, concerned. "Faris?"

I shake away my thoughts, dropping the iron. "It's nothing," I say, yet it could be everything if it means my mother never intended to kill me, only to warn me.

The door swings open and Solch returns, humming beneath his breath. Clapping his hands, he rubs the palms together with an eager smile as he looks from me to North.

"So," he says, "I'll be the drunken uncle who makes a scene at dinner by discussing the family fortune."

North straightens. "I thought we agreed—"

"I know." Wincing, Solch offers his hands out in peace. "We did settle up at the start of the tour, but unfortunately, my boy, terms and conditions subject to change without notice."

"What are you talking about?"

"A girl like that glows bright as the sun out here in the dark," says Solch. "Intuits will be at my door for days wanting a taste. Lord Inichi will send his usual dog to sniff around back. That's a lot of hassle. A lot of headache. We have to factor in surgery, she made use of a bed—I'll round down for the hour out of respect—and there's the matter of medical supplies." Solch wets his lips. "I want more than a spell, North. I want half of what's inside."

"Solch."

"Your majesty," says Solch, all joking aside. His hand strays toward his hip, beneath the edge of his unbuttoned waistcoat. "This isn't a negotiation."

"You understand the position you're taking," says North, edging closer to me. His fingertips hang in the air, searching for contact, and I curl my little finger around his with a sudden rush of blood, a sudden twitch of power in my veins. "There's no ever again between us after this."

"You take magic like hers to New Prevast and there's no ever again for me anyway," says Solch. "The days of the transferent are numbered, North. I'll take what I can and hide while I can before the gods come calling my name." He smiles, bittersweet. "You'll make a damn fine king, my boy, but we both know there's no market for a man like me after a man like you finds Merlock. Final offer."

"No," says North.

I catch the flash of glass a second too late. I twist out of the way as North curves his body to protect me.

Solch wasn't aiming for me.

The needle sinks into the slope of North's neck and Solch depresses the plunger halfway before North knocks him aside. Dirty liquid sloshes in the glass tubing as North wrenches the needle out of his neck and hurls it to the floor. It shatters, glass and something thicker that glistens in the light.

I attack without strategy, barreling Solch through the doorway behind him. We stumble and land, arms and legs entwined on the floor. Despite a lingering weakness, I know how to fight, and I strike him across the face, knocking his glasses askew before slamming his head against the floor.

Solch swears, making a halfhearted grab for my hair, but I block his arm, twisting it back until I hear something crack near his shoulder. His sharp cry of agony sends chills down my back, cutting through the fog of primal instinct. It gives me pause, and in that instant of hesitation, I'm dragged off and hauled to my feet, pulled against a hard lanky body that smells of animal and beer. A cold blade touches my throat.

"Fanagin was right," a voice laughs, oily and familiar. "Soft in all the right places. Let's see if he was right about bleeding fire too."

Kellig.

"Don't touch her," North says, already slurring his words. A thin dribble of fluid rolls down his throat into the collar of his shirt, shiny with a watery thread of blood.

"It's not that much of a pleasure," Kellig says with a sickening laugh, casting a derisive glance to the faded poison beneath my skin. "You already spoiled the meat. But Baedan won't want leftovers, your majesty. She'll want you."

North bends over, hands on his knees as he looks to Solch, wounded. "You sold me?"

"I sell everything here," Solch says darkly. Blood drips from his nose. "You're hardly the most exotic item in my catalog."

I test Kellig's hold to find it loose, arrogant—he doesn't believe I'll fight back. I don't know if I can. Blood seeps through the bandage on my chest and my heartbeat is weak, erratic, but I haven't come this far to let someone like Kellig defeat me.

Dropping into a crouch, I slip out from under his arm and twist, kicking his knee. It knocks us both back and I crash into the worktable with enough force to make the ceiling dance. Needles and metal instruments scatter as he grabs my ankle and drags me back. Grinning, he levers his body over mine and presses a sweaty hand to my chest.

"Good girl. Keep that heart rate up," he says. "The magic comes easier when your blood runs hot."

"No," Solch says. "She's mine, he's yours—that was the deal."

"Terms and conditions subject to change without notice," Kellig says, leering down at me. He's as graceless as Solch as he fists threads of magic and snaps them loose, too greedy to be delicate. My skin tightens with goose bumps; tears flood my eyes.

With a grunt, Solch knocks Kellig in the side of the head with a bone awl, knocking him off me, onto the carpet. He then drives the awl through Kellig's shoulder, pinning him in place. Kellig screams as blood immediately pools across the floor.

"You stole from the wrong man," Solch says with a terrifying grin. He grabs a scalpel from the mess on the floor and leans against Kellig, grabbing him by the hair and yanking his head back. "I should carve you up and sell you piecemeal. But I'll settle for a few teeth."

The scalpel scrapes into Kellig's mouth and I roll away with a shock of nausea. Swallowing back the taste of blood, I scramble to my knees and then, with a lurch of vertigo, to my feet. North is slumped against the wall, head hanging low, swollen fingers digging at his neck.

He flinches when I touch him, but then his eyes focus, shifting beyond me to Kellig. Shoving himself off the wall, he pulls Solch back and Solch edges out of the way, hands raised in peace, still holding the scalpel and now, a tooth. Blood runs down his palms. "By all means," he says. "Take whatever you want."

North ignores him. Dropping to one knee, he bends over Kellig, his voice lowered to a gravel whisper. Already his skin is the color of charcoal as poison fills his fingertips, waiting to be transferred. "You have thirty seconds."

Kellig pales even more, one hand wrapped around the hilt of the awl. Blood bubbles out of his mouth. "Baedan's going after the daughter of the king," he rasps at last. "I'm only supposed to delay you; she doesn't know who you are. I—I won't tell her if you don't." He tries to smile, revealing a hole where his left incisor used to be before he begins choking on blood. Turning his head, he spits on the floor.

North shifts to regain his faltering balance. "You expect me to believe you're a loyalist now when you've done nothing but bring her bodies to burn and spells to cast that she would never be able to do on her own?"

"Come on, North." Kellig blinks rapidly. His breath rattles out of him in thinning gasps; the threadbare carpet is soaked. "If she finds Merlock, we'll all be pissing poison and eating our own skin." Desperation inches his voice higher. "A bastard on the throne is better than a bitch."

North stares at him, fingers curling into a fist. "Does she have a lead?"

At last, a more genuine smile, a hint of the man from the marketplace, eager to barter. "I can't tell you if you kill me."

"North." I touch his arm; his eyes jolt toward me and struggle to refocus. "Tobek can't fight Baedan on his own, and if she gets to Bryn . . ." I trail off pointedly. Bryn could persuade an agreement with anyone, and we need Bryn to believe she's on our side as long as possible.

North nods, rubbing the heels of his hands against his eyes. Kellig drops his head back, relived, but then North grabs him by the throat. "You stole from the wrong man," he says, echoing Solch.

Kellig's feet kick out in protest as North takes back the magic Kellig tore out of me. But North doesn't stop, even after the last line of silver dims out of Kellig's skin, and poison begins to spread, rolling down his throat. The skin starts to burn, tiny cracks widening into seeping wounds. The blood at his shoulder darkens and slows to an ooze of thick sludge.

Kellig grabs North's wrist, trying to leach the infection back into him, but it's not enough. His eyes flood black; poison drips from his nose. A moment later, he goes still. Dead? Or is he bartering with the gods now, choosing his vices over his soul?

"North." When I touch his hand again, a shot of pain sparks up my arm with warning. Sweat beads his forehead, rolling down the side of his cheek.

Guilt immediately overtakes anger as he looks to Kellig and back to me. "I—I'm so sorry," he says, stricken. "I didn't—"

"We have to go," I say softly. Even through the cotton of his shirt, I feel his skin burning.

"You have blood on your face," he whispers, and it's heartbreaking, the sorrow in his voice, the shadows in his eyes. He reaches for me only to recoil when he remembers his hands.

"It's probably mine, damn it," Solch growls from the armchair. His glasses hang from one hand; the other hand pinches the bridge of his nose.

Hate needles through me. For a moment, I'm tempted to cut Solch's throat with the scalpel balanced on the arm of the chair next to Kellig's incisor. Is that me or the infection in my blood?

Instead, I grab North's coat off the bed and Kellig's knife from the floor, leveling it in Solch's face. The truth is, he's harmless beyond this city, without North's name to barter, and hurting him would be an act of self-indulgent cruelty. I don't understand North's friendship with this man, but I do understand that poisoned or not, I will never be like Bryn.

But he doesn't have to know that. "If I ever see you again," I warn.

"You won't." He snorts, waving a hand in dismissal. "You don't even have to pay for the room. Consider it a parting gift." His pale eyes settle on me and I hold his gaze.

He looks away first.

On second thought, I pocket the scalpel after all, grabbing North's sleeve before he can step out onto the balcony. "Wrong door," I say, squeezing his arm with a sudden affection.

We're like two drunks defying gravity as we stumble downstairs. Giddy and slow, clumsy and heavy, I miscount the last step and we fall, landing in each other's arms with matching looks of panic. He's losing color fast, but at the very least, he can get on the horse.

Dewy morning humidity turns the cobblestones slick as we ride out of the city, relying on North's failing sense of direction. He clings to my waist, whispering words and nonsense against my back. Promises, prayers, magic spells, or curses, I don't know. I don't care. Only one thing matters.

"Don't let go of me," I say.

He presses his head against my back and holds on all the tighter.

Twenty-Three

NORTH BEGS ME TO STOP JUST BEYOND THE MOUNTAIN PASS, WHEN THE land opens into a sea of hard swells and pitted divots, all grown over green with moss and lacy wildflowers. Lava fields. Water slips in and out of view, running in narrow streams full of stones and silver fish. The road itself has worn a flattened path forward, but the ground on either side is misshapen, uneven, a potential labyrinth of dangerous footing.

Though the sun rises on the southern half of Avinea, storm clouds knot the sky this side of the mountains, and an eerie mist turns the world into something surreal. To our left, the Burn simmers, a ribbon of ash and gold that stretches as far as I can see.

"There," North directs with a grunt, and I steer the horse to a ring of stones too perfectly arranged to be accidental. A forgotten temple, maybe, or a traveler's shrine. Faded wreaths of flowers blanket the ground; scraps of clothing snap in the wind, held in place by totems of various saints. All meager offerings from pilgrims preparing to wind through the mountains, or grateful tokens of thanks to have arrived on the other side still alive.

North dismounts, long legs tangling in the saddle. Once on the ground, he bends into me, breathing hard, irregular, holding his infected hand stiffly away from his body—away from mine. Wrapping an arm around his waist, I brace my legs, struggling to bear his weight against my own, desperate to be useful. *Are you North's apprentice?*

A week ago, all I wanted was my sister. But my insatiable heart has tasted an impossibility and now I want this, I want him, I want *more*, so badly it hurts every bone of my body.

But North doesn't exist anymore.

The Burn is a graveyard beyond the shrine, a battlefield. The remnants of a village lie just beyond its edge, a collection of stone structures and hollow trees worn smooth as glass by years of fire and wind. Nothing could possibly live beyond the gold line on the ground, but the Burn somehow breathes, dunes of scorched earth that drift and eddy and throw plumes of ash into the air. There's an untamed, tragic beauty to the way the world dies.

"My mother knew it was coming," North says softly. "She saw Merlock begin to unravel during the war." A sad, fleeting smile crosses his face. "Dalliances in the court were allowed, but after the Fire Wars, bastards were put to death at birth to prevent diluted blood from ever claiming the throne. So she never told him she was pregnant. She ran from Prevast and took a life that would hide a fatherless son, but she never let me forget who I was. A warning against what happens when ambition turns to greed. When compassion turns to complacency."

Straightening, North steps out of my hold. "Don't—don't follow me," he says.

I watch him go reluctantly, tensed as if to catch him should he fall. But he walks steady, certain, wavering in place before he drops to his knees and faces his father's legacy.

"Avinea," I hear him say, but I don't know if it's a blessing or a curse or maybe a promise of what's still to come.

Bending forward, North flattens both palms to the earth, as though he intends to pray. Then pain ripples through his body and he screams as he excises the poison inside him directly into the ground. I twist away from the heat of it, squinting through my tears to watch the infection sliding out of his skin. The moss beneath his hands turns yellow to brown to brittle to dust as a gold red ribbon curves outward, producing a toxic cloud of yellow smoke.

A new pocket of the Burn.

North tries to stand and almost collapses. Rushing forward, I lead him back to the stones. He leans against them with a breath of relief, sliding down until his legs are spread ahead of him, his hands loose at his sides. Swollen, red, but clean.

Beautiful.

Humid wind ruffles his hair; sunlight leaks through the storm clouds and picks out threads of raven blue and hints of gray in the stubble on his chin.

He's too young to be this old.

"I'll find you some water," I say.

North shakes his head, eyes closed. "Too close to the Burn," he murmurs. "Not safe to drink."

I stare at him, biting the inside of my cheek. We're both already poisoned, I want to say. What difference does it make? Instead, I swallow my complaints; we can't spare the energy to argue. Exhaustion carves lines across his face and there's a hard edge of finality to the set of his jaw. A small bruise, more red than yellow, stains his neck where Solch broke skin with his needle.

He sees me staring and winces, touching the wound. "Bad?"

"I've seen worse," I say, forcing a smile as I demonstrate my own bruised forearm.

"You win," he agrees, closing his eyes again, swallowing hard enough his throat wobbles.

How do I comfort him? Cadence drank hot water with sugar. Thaelan wanted the stars. What does North want? What would he need?

An ounce of your strength.

Anxious, I stand, scanning the horizon. The road curls out of sight, leading northeast; to the south, it cuts back through the mountains. A flash of blue between the green catches my eye, dull against the vibrant hillocks and stones around us, and I stand, straining to see.

The wagon. My breath catches, part relief and part fear: They should have gotten further than that.

Baedan.

Out of habit, I touch the spell around my wrist but there are no new aches, no new wounds, nothing to indicate that Bryn has been harmed in any way.

"I can see the wagon," I say, resisting the urge to sweep a stray hair off North's forehead—the urge to touch him any way I can. "It looks abandoned. Can I trust you alone while I make sure it's safe?"

North cracks one bleary eye open and gives me a weak half smile. "Now you're protecting me."

I squeeze his arm. "I won't be gone long."

He doesn't answer, tipping his head back and closing his eyes.

I jog toward the wagon, slowing on my approach. It sits in a ditch of water, tipped against a rising swell of stone. The front wheel is crushed; the back wheel hangs an inch off the ground.

Holding Kellig's knife in one hand, I edge closer to the open door. Other than the broken wheel and the damage from the shadow crows, there doesn't appear to be any outward sign of attack or forced entry.

Maybe it was just an accident, I tell myself, a rock in the road that Tobek couldn't avoid—that North's magic couldn't prevent. I hold on to that hope as I reach the doorway, squinting through the darkness inside. "Tobek?" I call, soft and cautious. "Bryn?"

Or maybe it's Bryn playing tricks again. Maybe Baedan found them and Bryn exploited the opportunity. But what could Baedan offer her that North didn't already agree to give?

Something shifts, slow and low to the ground. Tensing, I raise the knife as a ball of orange fur hurtles out of the wagon. Darjin. He mewls with pathetic, weak cries of pleasure, winding between my legs before he stretches on his hind quarters, front paws against my leg. Relieved, I crouch to kiss the flat spot between his ears, made braver by his company.

I call for Bryn and Tobek again, wait a beat, then step into the stairwell. My heart breaks at what I see: fallen books and broken glass and everything shattered, every inch of North's home disrupted. Even the stove grate hangs open, spilling ash and charred wood across the tangle of bedsheets from the mattress half torn from the bottom bed.

The first casualty of war.

After coaxing a fire in the stove, I lead North and the horse back to the wagon. He struggles up the stairwell and collapses halfway, too exhausted to go any further. "The wards are still in place," he says breathlessly. "They left on their own accord."

I don't disagree, but he follows my gaze to Darjin, grooming himself in a heap of tea leaves. Tobek would never leave Darjin behind.

I pull the mattress off the bottom bunk and guide North to lie down before filling a bucket with water from the thin stream running along the bottom of the ditch. By the time I return, North has shrugged out of his coat and is on his back, squinting at the stars painted on the ceiling.

"I don't understand what this means," he says, still slurring as he lifts his hands, mimicking the way I often hold mine.

I fill the samovar with water to boil before stretching out a soft pain in my lower back. "It was the view from home," I say. "We could hold the entire sky between our hands."

"We," he repeats, lowering his hands, not looking at me. "There was a girl who knew a boy."

"His name was Thaelan."

"You loved him." Not a question, just a fact. North rubs at his chest, still looking at the ceiling.

"I wanted to marry him," I say softly.

North nods, swallowing hard. "I was never going to love the woman I married," he says. "It would be too much of a liability." He struggles to sit up and I kneel to help, sliding my arm behind him until his back rests against the frame of the bunk. He grunts thanks and winces, adjusting his weight.

"You remind me of him, a little," I say, as the samovar begins to steam. Grateful for the distraction, I pour a cup of hot water and pass it to North.

"Only a little?" he asks, not meeting my eyes.

"More than enough. I wouldn't want you to be the same."

North's ears turn pink as he looks into the cup, tipping it back and forth before his eyes meet mine, dark and shadowed. "No sugar?"

"If you can find any," I say with a forced laugh, gesturing to the mess around us. But there's nothing funny about a life reduced to rubble, and I immediately sober. "Try to sleep," I say, voice cracking. "Baedan and Perrote might still be looking for Bryn, if they haven't already found her. We'll leave as soon as you're able."

"Faris."

"I'll take first watch," I say, ignoring the way he looks at me.

"Faris," he repeats.

"Don't," I warn, but it's too late. He touches the back of my hand, swollen knuckles and sandpaper skin.

Closing my eyes, I curve into his arms and they fold tight around me, pulling me in against the hard edges of his chest and the rattling hum of his breath. I clutch the back of his shirt, inhaling the smoky-sweet-sweat smell of his body, counting the wild beats of his heart. Tears fall, soft and silent, prompted by the simple act of being touched, of being human.

"I have to let you go," North says softly. His voice echoes in his chest.

I squeeze my eyes shut tighter. "Why?"

"I can't—the poison inside me feels the magic inside you and it wants to spread," he says. His fingers thread through my hair; despite what he says, he doesn't let go. "I can't hold it back forever, Faris. Not now, not like this. I'm not strong enough. Or maybe you're too strong and it makes me weak. I don't know. My head hurts."

Forcing a laugh, I release his shirt and pull back, drying my cheeks on my shoulder. Avoiding his eyes, I press a hand to his chest. "Sleep."

"Stay," he says, fingers caught on the sleeve of my coat.

I stare at Darjin, at North's swollen hands, at the way his shirt clings to his body. "I need to keep watch."

"The wards will hold for a little longer. Miss Dossel made them strong."

"North—"

"Please."

I duck my head. "What about these wards?" I ask softly, touching the crook of his elbow.

His eyes are liquid fire. "They'll hold."

I should argue; I should be strong.

Instead, I retrieve North's coat and help him back into it, an extra layer of separation of my skin from his. North shifts his weight to make room and I curl beside him.

"Sometimes falling makes us stronger," North murmurs, half asleep.

But sometimes when you fall, it's because you've been defeated.

When I wake, it's dark outside, later than I expected. I don't move at first, transfixed by the way North traces the back of my hand with the barest tip of his fingers before his little finger curls through mine.

"You let me sleep," I say at last.

"I'm a bastard," he replies. His cheek rests on top of my head but I can hear the smile in his voice. "You can't expect anything better."

I briefly tighten my finger around his, content to sit another moment, locked together like this. But then North sighs and releases me before any damage is done. "The wards have started to fray," he says. "It's time to go."

Reluctantly, I stand, pulling faces. My body feels as craggy as the mountains. "How far to the city?"

"Half a day by horse," he says, picking through the detritus on the floor, scanning the spines of his books as he separates them into piles on the table. When he picks up my mother's, he adds it to the stack closest to him.

Biting the inside of my cheek, I look toward the door, to the glow of the Burn backlighting the landscape. Half a day's ride in the dark is a long time with no perimeter stones. "Can you reuse the wards at all?"

"No. The spell is too loose. I wouldn't risk it."

I don't miss the way his tone shifts, turns guarded. The wards are gone and so is the magic.

I roll a stone in my hands. "You know the magic I carry is meant for Corbin. For you."

"And you know that as I am now, if I tried to take anything from you, the infection in me will likely bleed back into you," says North. He pulls his bag from its hook on the wall and starts shoving books inside. "You haven't had a chance to recover yet, and if I flood your veins with poison again, even if I extract as much as I can afterward, your body will have a much smaller chance of fighting it back on its own. You could be infected for the rest of your life, meaning anytime you come in contact with magic"—his movements turn sharper, more hostile, and I wonder if his thoughts are the same as mine: anytime I come in contact with *him*—"it could be aggravated. You'll need to be excised again and again and again and it is not easy, and it will hurt, and I will not do that unless you fully understand what you're offering me."

"Spoken like a gentleman," I say, forcing a smile to hide the unease his warning brings.

He scrubs his face with one hand before sighing, his own smile incongruent to the shadows darkening his eyes. "A handsome one?"

"A misguided one," I say. "What difference does my blood make if you're dead before we reach New Prevast?" Giving him a withering look, I slide his father's ring off my thumb and set it on top of the table. The magic under my skin brightens immediately, no longer muted by the iron, before sinking back out of sight.

"Make me an offer," I say.

He rests his hip against the edge of the table, fingers tangled around the strap of his bag. "You and Cadence will have the best rooms in the palace."

I shake my head.

"All the books you can read," he offers. "All the maps you can carry. Fresh fish every morning, and blackberry tarts with coffee. And sugar," he adds. "We have sugar in New Prevast."

"Not good enough," I say. "I want more."

"Greed costs, Miss Locke." Arching an eyebrow, North folds his arms across his chest and rocks his weight back on one foot, appraising me. He lifts his chin. "Name your price."

I wait a beat, but I don't wait longer or I'll lose my nerve.

"A kiss," I say. "Just one. Just once."

Surprised, his arms unfold even as my heart stutters. Heat floods my face and I look away, feeling stupid. "Never mind," I say, "I was just—"

He kisses me, cautious and uncertain: He hasn't had much practice. His lips are shy, timid, and the kiss is soft as a whisper, short as a sigh.

"Was that good enough?" he asks, worried as he pulls away.

"Perfect," I say, but not nearly enough for my greedy heart.

I steal the second kiss; the third is mutual. North follows my lead and I lead him through four, five, six, and seven until it doesn't matter anymore, all that matters is the way his hands fold against my hips and the way his lips part beneath my tongue and the way his breath catches when I trace the gaunt lines of his body as it presses eager into mine.

Skin is the perfect conductor and I devour the secrets painted across his, ignoring the warning spread of heat as his poison seeps back into my body at the places where we overlap: fingertips, wrists, his mouth to my throat as he murmurs foreign words against my skin. Fire ignites in my veins and it's perfect, this kiss, this *feeling*, like a satisfied quiet that fills my soul after months of silent screaming.

Beneath our shared desire is the rhythmic trumpet of our hearts. Mine thunders like a roar of water but his is no more than an echo half a beat behind, hollow as footsteps through a mountain. All at once, the taste of blood floods my mouth and North draws back, eyes wide as he presses a hand to his chest. Magic glows silver through the fabric of his shirt—the spell that guards his heart.

But my own heart sinks when I realize what's happening.

The edges have started turning black.

Twenty-Four

EVER THE GENTLEMAN, NORTH USES STONES HE FINDS SCATTERED around the wagon to excise some of the poison now spreading through my body, spreading through his. It hurts, as promised.

I welcome the pain.

North works silently, head bowed, and I bite the inside of my cheek, wondering if I should apologize or if that would only make it worse. His hands shake by the time he's done, and he pockets the poisoned rocks, avoiding my eyes.

You promised me, Thaelan accuses at the back of my head. I want to protest, to defend my honor: I haven't stolen anything.

But I have. I've stolen the Prince of Avinea's only defense, the careful guard he's made of his heart. As someone who's taught herself how to fight, to deflect, to be the last one standing, I recognize the moment the fight turns against you. In kissing me, North allowed his heart to be weak and his desire to become a map for the poison to follow. If it moves any further before he repairs the spell, he could turn hellborne and he won't be able to stop it.

I asked for a kiss and it could kill him.

"It's not your fault," North says at length. His voice is husky, rattled; it startles me. "I swore my heart to a higher purpose a long time ago. And anything—any*one*—who threatened that purpose had to be excised long before they could take root in my blood." He looks at me, through me. "Your strength was my weakness, Miss Locke. The fault is entirely my own."

I don't answer, staring numbly out the door.

North edges around me, rummaging through the spill of drawers from his apothecary's chest. "You've done nothing wrong," he says, sliding supplies and several rocks into his bag. "It didn't get far; the damage is minimal."

"Having a heart is not a weakness," I say softly.

"A weak heart breaks, a broken heart bleeds, and blood can be poisoned." North slams a drawer back into place before exhaling softly. "That is how a king becomes a coward and how a country becomes a graveyard."

I worry the edge of the table with my thumb, but as the silence stretches, I look up to see its source. North watches me, desire warring with self-recrimination, his swollen hand clutching the strap of his bag so tightly the knuckles are white. If I asked, he would kiss me again.

If I asked, he would risk falling.

This is not the North I know, fierce and unflinching with a duty forged by blood. This is the North who would choose me over Merlock.

So I must choose Merlock over him.

I back toward the door. "I'll get the horse," I mumble. Without waiting for a reply, I turn and thunder down the stairwell, grateful for the cold night air to bite color into my cheeks, to jolt me back to my senses. What was I thinking? What was I *doing*? The poison runs through my blood too: Kissing North could just as easily kill me as it could kill him. My life might not be worth much, but there's still Cadence to consider. No one else will fight for her the way I would.

On impulse, I rock my head back to the stars, needing their weight to pin me back into place. Only clouds tonight, but the sky is full of gold colors thrown out by the Burn.

And something closer. Torches.

The hellborne.

They approach on horseback, Baedan in the lead. Her bone white hair streams behind her as she urges her horse faster, teeth bared against the night, flanked by half a dozen brutes dressed in plated armor that covers their chests and exposes their arms. Each one carries a torch or a weapon that looks as if it was pulled from the walls of Alistair's execution room.

Swearing, I unhitch the horse and haul myself onto its back, calling for North. He appears, features shadowed. When he sees Baedan, he grabs Darjin and runs, passing Darjin into my arms before he swings himself up behind me. We're barely settled before he kicks the horse into motion.

Someone shouts behind us and North swears, veering the horse hard to the left to avoid a blast of hot, indigo-colored magic. We move off the road and aim for the swelling foothills, but there are no easy paths and we're not nearly fast enough. Another blast of light knocks the horse off its feet and we hit the ground hard, a tangle of arms and legs and howling tiger. Darjin bolts out of my arms as the horse rights itself with a whinny of protest, disappearing ahead of us.

"Go!" North pushes me away as he staggers to his feet, wincing with pain. White threads of magic begin spooling along his fingertips as he turns toward Baedan.

I grab him by the back of his coat, yanking him behind a rock. "There are a thousand girls like me in the world," I say, "but only one Prince of Avinea. Supply and demand, your majesty! Don't be stupid!"

Still holding his coat, I start pulling him through the labyrinth of channels and valleys, buying us distance.

"We can't run forever," says North.

"But we can reach higher ground," I counter. "And we can make her come to us."

"You have a plan?"

"My plan was to run," I admit, "but since that didn't work, this will have to suffice."

Another crash of magic splinters a rock above us. North pulls me under the protection of his arms until the fragments have settled before we continue, winding further from the road, deeper into the lava fields.

"Your majesty!" Baedan calls in a mocking singsong some distance behind us and far to the left. "Your heritage does not excuse your cowardice. Either fight me or surrender."

Satisfied that she's lost track of us, I pull North into an alcove.

Water seeps through the cracks, dampening our coats. "That spell you used the night we met," I say. "Can you cast that again? That would kill any of them that don't have protection spells. From there, we pick them off one by one until it's only you and her. If you can disarm her . . ." I pull Kellig's knife from my pocket. "The only cure for a hellborne soul is a carved out heart, and I don't need magic for that."

North stares at me in amazement.

"Previous life," I quip to his unspoken question, before I half smile, hoping forced confidence will outweigh my fear.

North pulls me closer and kisses me, fierce and fast and breathless. "If we survive, you owe me that story."

Pulling the bag from around his shoulder, he drops it on the ground and rubs his hands dry down the front of his thighs. "Baedan will have to cut my heart out to kill me; magic won't suffice, not with the spells I wear. I'll have to let her get close. When she does . . ."

"I'll be there," I say.

North hesitates, guilt warring with something else I'm too terrified, too selfish to name—a look he can't afford to give anyone until he's safely crowned king. "If something happens to me," he says, "find Captain Benjamin Chadwick in New Prevast, at the Saint Ergoet's Monastery. Give him this"—he reaches into his coat and retrieves a small stone with a hole worn through the center—"and he'll understand. Do you understand?"

Another nod, a sudden desire to cry. I clutch the front of his shirt, thrown back to that night four months ago, to the last time I saw Thaelan alive.

"Good-bye," I whisper, voice cracking. "Just in case."

North embraces me. "Good-bye," he murmurs.

My fingers find his and I hold on tight. "Take every last thread," I say.

I know what to expect this time, and brace for the discomfort. But North is as gentle with his magic as he is with his kisses; the only pain I feel is entirely my fault as my heart starts to break.

Within an instant, the magic is gone and I'm hollow again as North releases me without looking back. I allow myself a moment of grief before I follow, nearly stumbling with surprise when a bolt of magic splits the sky and webs it like lightning. Cries of pain ring out and I clench my knife tighter, gratified.

He hit his marks.

I scramble higher for a better view. Half a dozen hellborne fight through the lava fields, unsteady on their horses. Baedan has abandoned hers, her fury evident even from here as she spins a circle, searching for North. She casts a spell of colored light, obliterating a rocky outcropping.

"To think," she calls, "all those nights we shared campsites, North. All those mornings we haggled over each other's leads. I could have slit your throat and ended the competition years ago."

"Temperance leads to impotence," North calls from somewhere behind her.

She twists toward his voice, gesturing several of her men to follow. They do so reluctantly, and rightly so: A moment later, they scream as North's spell burns the flesh from their bones.

Only four left.

I use the distraction to dart behind another rock, wetting my lips.

A woman dismounts from her horse a few yards away, clutching a curved spear in one hand. She wears a leather vest that exposes her upper body, and for a moment, I allow myself to doubt my abilities, my conviction. She's huge, built to withstand the Burn. For the first time, I don't think of Loomis's pistol as a nightmare but a blessing. One shot and we'd be down to three.

Guaranteed victory.

Baedan growls, casting another spell that scorches the air with the smell of rotted carrion. "Why waste magic? Face me like a man. Like a prince." She snorts. "Face me like the king your father never was."

Crouching, I grab a pebble from the ground and toss it toward the woman. She twists, eyes narrowing, and takes a step closer. My saliva dries, swelling my tongue, but I tell myself it's no different than a fight back home. As she draws nearer, I brace my weight and steel my nerves: strike first and strike fast.

North appears in the distance, haggard and exhausted. He opens his hands, the palms gray. He can't keep fighting much longer, I realize; the poison is returning, overtaking the magic, making him useless. "Here I am," he says.

The woman reaches my hiding spot and I jerk forward too late. She swings her spear and I scramble backward, losing my footing. Beyond us, Baedan and North face off, casting and deflecting spells until the skies light up with the color of magic.

The woman lunges, her spear striking the stone by my head. I roll out of the way, finding my feet in time to take a swing at her with the knife. She easily sidesteps me, teeth bared in a grimacing laugh.

She's baiting me.

I back away, heart crashing against my ribs. The woman lifts her eyebrows in invitation before her eyes slide past me. She steps back in deference and, heart sinking, I turn.

"This one's mine," Kellig says, grabbing my arm.

North calls my name. He stands over Baedan, pinning her in place with a spell that makes his whole body quiver. His fingers are forced into a painful fist that drips with sweat.

Now. He needs me now, and I can't even move.

Kellig laughs, damp and sticky, his mouth ringed with the brown bruise of dried blood. Poison has eaten through him and his skin is cracking, flaking loose against my coat. He faced death in Revnik and he chose a monster's life instead.

Coward.

"Third time's the charm," I say with faltering bravado.

"Oh, I'm not going to kill you," he says. Locking an arm around my throat, he wrenches me toward North just as North looks back, searching for me. It's only a heartbeat of broken concentration.

It's too much.

Baedan breaks loose of his spell, scrambling back. Her face is discolored now, a mask of shadow and white. One of her silver eyes is black with blood as she spits a mouthful of poison to the ground.

"Let her go," North warns, turning his hands toward Kellig. But he hesitates. He can't risk another spell, not without risking his heart. When his eyes meet mine through the haze of magic that shimmers in the air, there is no accusation, no blame in his gaze, yet I accept it all the same.

He needed me and I wasn't there, and now it's too late.

Baedan notices the way North falters and she lifts an eye-brow. "So stone-hearted North still bleeds," she says, mocking him. "Good." Standing, she reaches for me, and Kellig dutifully releases me into her arms. Holding me by the hair, she pulls my face back so I'm forced to look up at her. Blood leaks from her eye and begins dripping down her cheek, splashing onto my shoulder.

"Do you know how long it takes your body to turn hellborne in the Burn?" she asks. "Five days. And you will feel every second of it. What do you think, North?" She twists me toward him. "I could put a leash on her and give her to Kellig. He's always asking for new pets and I think he's earned this one, don't you?"

Don't, I want to say. Don't single me out, North. Don't make me special. Don't give me power over you.

"Or maybe I'll just take one of her eyes as payment for mine." Baedan pulls a dagger from her belt and dips the blade against my cheek.

"And maybe one of her teeth," Kellig growls.

"Wait," says North.

My heart sinks, but Baedan smiles. Shifting her weight, she tightens her hold on my hair as the blade slides a fraction higher. "Formalities first," she says. "I need your blood to be clean. Or as clean as you can make it."

North cocks his head, confused, and she rolls her eyes. "Come on, North," she says. "We've talked enough history between us that you can guess where this is going."

Horror creeps across his face. "You're not going to kill me."

"And I never intended to kill the princess," she says. "Your blood is useless without a heartbeat behind it." I wince a moment before her icy blade presses against my eyelids. "Your choice, your majesty," she says.

A beat of silence, a moment to consider.

"I need room," says North.

Baedan drags me back, out of the way, lowering her knife in the process. I watch, heart in my throat as North sags to his knees, flattening his palms to the ground. He braces for pain, stifling his cries into his shoulder as he leaches poison into the ground, excising enough of the infection that his protection spells can keep the rest back.

He rises to his feet when he's finished, staggering away from the Burn he's created. He only makes it a few feet before crumpling, too weak to bear his own weight. I struggle against Baedan's hold, but she's stronger than Kellig, and I can't break free.

"Give him a knife," she barks.

North pushes himself to his knees, wavering. His crooked hands rest against his knees as he tips his head back, swallowing hard, watching Kellig approach with half-lidded eyes. "You'll have to do it yourself," says North.

Baedan snorts. "You of all people should appreciate the value of tradition."

"You just need a little help," Kellig says. "I know these fingers don't bend so well on their own." Slamming the knife in North's palm, he begins forcing the fingers into position. North swears profusely as the color drains from his face.

Baedan grins, savoring North's pain as Kellig steps back, leaving North to fumble one-handed with the buttons of his shirt. My heart aches for him, for his frustration, the palpable sense of self-loathing.

Flushed, North finally tears his shirt open before he wipes his mouth against his shoulder, his gaze sliding to Baedan with a spark of defiance. He's bony beneath the black he always wears, gaunt and stretched thin. Faded scars cross his body, and a bold but simple compass rose sits above his heart. A spell. The one I helped weaken by kissing him and allowing his desires to bleed out and the poison to sneak in.

"A bottle," Baedan calls.

Someone tosses a vial toward North. It hits his chest and bounces away, and he has to crawl after it.

Baedan leans forward, eager as North cuts through the soft flesh of his chest, through the heart of his spell—to the cleanest blood in his body. Dropping the blade, he uncorks the glass vial with his teeth and fills it to overflowing.

"Don't spill any," she says in a maddening singsong. "I need every last drop."

North spits the cork out in his palm before thumbing it back into the vial. Eyes locked on Baedan, he tamps it firmly in place with a hard knock on the ground. A woman plucks the vial from North's hands, brandishing it aloft to a round of cheers.

"Like father, like son," Baedan says, catching the vial as it's tossed her way. She slides it in her pocket and releases me. "Bring her," she orders, turning for her horse, and rough hands grab my arm.

"No." North's eyes widen in protest.

I resist, breaking loose, lunging for him. He reaches for me but misses my hand as I'm swept up again, thrown over a woman's broad shoulder.

"Baedan!" North struggles to his feet but falls again almost immediately. Kellig laughs, pressing him down with his foot, and North flattens beneath his weight, his bent hands twining through the soft moss. "Baedan," he croaks. "Please."

She scoffs, watching him from over her shoulder. "Long live the withered king."

I'm thrown onto the back of a horse and steered toward the Burn. My captor walks beside me, holding me in place as we cross the golden boundary, into soft dunes of ash that rise high as the horses' calves. A blanket of heat enfolds me, dry and hard to breathe, smelling of smoke and thunderstorms and the faraway hint of the sea. I struggle to inhale, only to choke, and the woman laughs.

"Breathe it in," she says. "Let your lungs burn."

I fumble in my pocket, grabbing the scalpel I stole from Solch, still dulled with Kellig's blood. Gathering every inch of my strength, I slam the blade into the hollow of the woman's throat and drag it down until it catches on her collarbone. She howls and stops moving, and I roll off the horse, hitting the ground in a plume of ash.

Gasping, I scramble to my feet and start running for North as another man makes a grab for me. I twist out of reach and keep going, but they're on horses and easily outflank me. I fall back, panting, armed with my only my hands but more than willing to use them.

Baedan stares down at me, incredulous, and for a moment I think I've surprised her with my fight. But nobody dismounts to come after me and I realize it isn't me that they're watching. It's what's happening around me—*inside* me.

My mother's spell.

I notice the faint pressure on the underside of my skin, shy as a kiss, before heat spreads across my chest. But it isn't like the Burn; it's far more pleasant, like sunlight on a summer afternoon.

This isn't right. I should be dying.

Instead, the world around me comes alive: The ash dissolves, softening into a patch of moss only wide enough to accommodate my feet. It thickens, dotted now with tiny white wildflowers. As my weight shifts and I stagger to hold balance, more moss appears to cradle my foot. A thin line of magic stretches ahead of me, narrow as a thread. Baedan draws away from it uneasily before it tugs on my heart, urging me forward, demanding I follow.

But where will it go?

Beneath the pull of the magic is the warning of the poison inside me inching closer, greedy and slick. The thread ahead of me wavers, pulls taut.

I fly.

I hurtle over the Burn, over a pockmarked, barren landscape populated by nothing but anger and fear and greed. Dark spires appear, needles on the horizon that thicken, become towers, the corners of a shattered castle nestled by the sea. A forgotten city lies at the base of a broken bridge and I soar over it, landing soft in front of iron gates that rise above me. A man stands on the other side, nothing more than bone wrapped in skin and a bitter heartbeat that echoes in the stones beneath our feet.

Merlock lifts his head and looks at me. His crown sags and he bends beneath its weight, but his features darken, turn ferocious. *"You,"* he growls, accusation laced through his voice.

A shout cracks through the air and the thread snaps, recoiling, throwing my heart against my spine as I gasp, back in the Burn. Baedan stares at me before her eyes shift past me, to a line of guards riding forward on horses. They stop at the edge of the Burn and take aim, armed with crossbows and unfamiliar banners that stand out, vibrant against the sky.

"Grab her," Baedan barks, but I take a step back, then another. I begin to run for the guards, my feet hitting the ground barely long enough for moss to emerge before the ash reclaims its place and hides my steps. Someone tackles me and I land on my stomach, immediately cushioned by more flowers.

North approaches, wasting precious magic and the last of his energy to reach me. The hellborne scatter, but Baedan looks to me one last time, committing my face to memory. I'll see her again, she seems to say. The guarantee is as good as written in blood.

Or poison.

Wordlessly, she turns and rides away, disappearing into the ruins of the nearby village. Staggering to my feet, I race to meet North. We stop just shy of colliding as he takes my arm and we continue to the edge of the Burn, to the safety of the grass on the other side.

"What happened?" he asks, his hands touching my arms, my neck, my face. "Are you all right?"

I clutch his arms. "I saw him," I say, speaking too fast, too urgent, as if the spell is already unraveling "I saw your father, North. He was in the castle in Prevast!"

North stares at me. "What?"

Breath hitching, my eyes drop to the spell across his chest, a compass rose to guide his choices. My mother's spell burns, hidden beneath a thick bandage, but I know what it means now. I am a compass too, and I point to Merlock.

My mother knew Perrote wasn't a king.

"I can help you find him," I say, and it's a relief and a burden both, an excuse to stay close to North in the weeks ahead. "But I don't know how long the spell will last. I don't know if I just wasted it, or if the infection will destroy it, but—but I want to join your Guard. I want to go into the Burn with you, I want to find Merlock, and I want—"

"Faris," he says, and I pause. He touches my face, whisper-soft. "I want everything you do," he says, before embracing me. I melt into his arms, closing my eyes as my chin slides into place against his neck. "Just one," he murmurs, kissing the top of my head. "Just once."

And then never again, not until our blood runs clean and his heart is free from the danger—the temptation—of mine.

When we break apart—who released whom?—I brace myself for what happens next. North does the same, hardening his expression, guarding his thoughts. It's the first stone in the wall we both need to build. Like a buffer of magic, it will have to absorb our heartache before it can infect our blood.

A soldier all in black hangs back, waiting for North to acknowledge him before he bows and strides forward. He holds a silver helmet tucked under one arm, his sandy hair pulled back in a short ponytail, revealing wide features and a narrow scar on his chin where his facial hair doesn't grow. While he faces North, his eyes stray toward me with curiosity.

"We were wrong about Baedan," North says, all business, fumbling to button his shirt closed. "She doesn't mean to hold Merlock hostage; she plans to kill him and inherit the magic herself."

The soldier's eyes widen at North's chest. "She has your blood."

"Which means she can forge the blade to perform the sacrifice," North agrees darkly, shaking out his collar. "That buys us at least a fortnight before she resumes looking for Merlock." He grimaces, still weak, and the soldier takes a step forward, hand out to assist.

North refuses with a tight shake of his head, his eyes cutting toward me. "This is Faris Locke," he says. "She will be vital to our mission to find Merlock, and her safety is priority. Miss Locke"—I flinch at the formality, although I knew to expect it—"this is Captain Benjamin Chadwick, a man with whom I would trust my life. A qualified trust," he adds, with a pained smile at the memory of Solch's betrayal. "If you wish to join the Guard, this is the man who says yes or no."

With a formal invitation to look at me, Chadwick openly stares and I wilt beneath his tactical gaze. I wasn't prepared for an immediate interview: All I want is a bath and clean clothes and a chance to mourn the man who turns his back on me to give orders, take command.

North is gone now, and Prince Corbin takes his place.

More riders approach over the hillocks, a splash of color that doesn't match the black and silver of North's men. My heart quickens in recognition as guards part to allow the new arrivals through.

Bryn cocks her head in acknowledgment of my surprise, her riding dress draped across her horse, her dark red hair a loose bundle of curls over one shoulder. The man who rides beside her is no less familiar, but far more frightening, arrogant beneath a silver circlet that reflects the beginning of the sunrise.

King Perrote.

"Miss Locke," Captain Chadwick says, concerned. "Are you all right?"

"What is he doing here?" I ask in a choked whisper. What is he doing here with *her*, as if she never ran away from Brindaigel, as if she never planned to kill him and he never planned to kill her?

With a frown, Chadwick settles his helmet further beneath his arm. "May I introduce his majesty, King Perrote Dossel, and his daughter, Princess Bryndalin," he says. "They arrived in New Prevast yesterday evening, and are the reason we knew to find you today." His pale eyes slide to North, seeking a reaction. "They come to offer an alliance but they were rather recalcitrant as to the terms. Their incentive, however, is . . ." He trails off, searching for the appropriate term. Only after his eyes land on Bryn does he find what he's looking for. "Tempting."

The ground buckles beneath me. What happened? Did Perrote find her, did he tell her that she wasn't a princess, that there's no throne to inherit? And did she tell him that Brindaigel was compromised, that I was still out there and willing to fight? Killing each other would be useless then, but if they worked together . . .

"Corbin," Perrote says, and the lack of title echoes through the assembled men. "The bastard prince in his charming robes of office." An eyebrow arches as he looks down his nose at North in his bloody shirt and tattered coat. Both his hands hang like useless claws at his side. "Ruling Avinea doesn't suit you any more than it did your father."

Captain Chadwick stands taller, affronted, a hand falling to the pommel of his sword.

"Perrote," North says, shoulders back, spine straight. Tension rolls off him but his voice remains smooth. "I do hope Avinea has treated you well during your brief visit with us. I'm sorry I wasn't there to greet you myself when you arrived. I would have given you a . . . very warm welcome."

"The welcome we received was quite sufficient," Perrote says, sniffing. "I didn't have high expectations."

The silence sparks with growing friction, as charged as the clouds above us.

"Can I presume that Tobek is still alive?" North asks at length, looking to Bryn.

She snorts. "Alive," she agrees, "last I checked, but he did lose a lot of blood on the ride into New Prevast." Her smile turns cold. "Bumpy roads and clumsy horses."

"Well." His voice is tight, controlled, but his nostrils flare and black pulses of poison flit across the back of his hand, fed by his anger. "I look forward to hearing all about Brindaigel and how its resources might best serve its true king. As it is, you find me in a rather inopportune moment—"

"And its queen," says Bryn.

North's muscles tighten even further. "What?"

"My father informs me that I'm further removed from the throne than I originally thought," says Bryn, chin angled high. "And therein lies my problem, your majesty." Her eyes cut toward me. "I was raised to be a queen and anything less is a waste of my time."

A bloody, savage hate fills me with an overwhelming need to hurt her, any way I can, no matter the cost to me. Likewise, the black pulses turn into bold lines as North fights against his own rising fury. "If you think—" he starts.

"You stand on the brink of war," Bryn says, her dark eyes glittering, "and I offer you the weapon you need to win. And I also offer a little advice, your majesty." Snapping back her skirt, Bryn withdraws a small dagger from her boot. She presses it to her wrist and smiles that cold, cruel smile. "Never tell your enemy what your weaknesses are."

North's voice is all warning. "Don't."

I barely flinch, too numb to feel pain. Someone holds me steady, Captain Chadwick, I think. "She's bleeding," he calls as Bryn completes the line down my arm, from my elbow to my wrist.

Settling back in her saddle, Bryn shares a sly, pleased look with her father. "So," she says, tapping the bloody dagger against her darkly painted lips. "Let the negotiations begin."

Twenty-Five

ON NORTH'S ORDERS, I RIDE TO NEW PREVAST WITH CAPTAIN Chadwick, who clears his throat every few minutes and apologizes every time the horse jolts my body into his.

It's a long ride.

North keeps ahead of us, Darjin curled behind him in the saddle, in line with Bryn and her father. They don't speak to him or to each other. Whatever truce they might have called has not forgiven their perceived sins.

"Usually his majesty only brings home jars of rocks," Captain Chadwick jokes at one point.

I humor him and force a smile. He clears his throat and doesn't speak again.

New Prevast is a city cradled by the sea, built from the same granite that forms the Kettich Mountains at its back. Most of the city is arranged around a half-moon harbor, but the palace sits apart, on a spit of land that curves out to sea before angling back at the mouth of the bay. The spit is mostly flat green moss and black sand, but a wave of earth rises along its northeastern side in a natural wall, protecting the palace from the harsh winds and wild waters of the open sea beyond. In contrast, the harbor waters are calm, more placid, filled with a meager handful of fishing boats lashed to a quay and the columns of a covered bridge that connects the palace grounds to the city itself. Everything sparkles in the rising dawn, and I catch North watching my reaction. He quickly looks away when my eyes meet his.

While there are more people here than in Revnik, the city still feels empty, almost haunted, as we ride to Saint Ergoet's, into a courtyard tiled in checkered white and gray stone and surrounded by a two-storied, columned promenade. A bell tower rises at one corner, and vines drip from the moss-covered roof, heavy with blossoms that fill the air with a softly spiced smell. Men in dark robes pause to kiss their fingertips and hold their palms toward North as a younger boy in lighter gray hurries to take his horse.

Dismounting, North faces the rest of us. "You'll forgive the humble accommodations," he says, eyes on Perrote. "We rarely entertain foreign dignitaries."

"Why don't you live in the palace?" asks Bryn with a look of dismay at the unadorned courtyard.

"The palace is meant for the King of Avinea," North says, patting his horse's flank before allowing the stable boy to lead her away. "As yet, I'm merely the regent."

She snorts, derisive, exchanging dark looks with her father. "The sainted North," she says. "We'll make a sinner of you yet."

"The palace costs money to keep," North says flatly. "It is not all virtue, Miss Dossel."

Captain Chadwick helps me down, gentle but steady. Despite his age—only a few years older than North—he commands quiet authority, directing half his men to their barracks and the other half to posts throughout the monastery. Then, with his hand on his sword, he rocks his weight back on his heels to await North's order.

North looks toward me and through me. At some unspoken gesture, Chadwick clears his throat and offers me his arm. "If you please, Miss Locke," he says. "A warm bath and a hot meal are waiting for you upstairs."

I hesitate; no one else is being dismissed.

But North doesn't contradict the offer, and wounded, I accept Chadwick's arm.

He guides me through an arched, open hallway leading to a dining room on one side, a sunken kitchen on the other, before taking a flight of rickety stairs leading to the open promenade on the second floor, past doors marked with slotted windows and numbers hanging on the wall. One of the doors is propped open, a single cot inside, a bloodied face framed against a graying pillow.

Tobek.

His face is swollen with bruises, his throat paler than the sheets pulled to his chest. He sleeps under the watch of two guards—one of North's and one of Perrote's. A girl holds Tobek's hand as she perches on the edge of a hard-backed chair by the bed. Long gold hair falls down her back in softly brushed waves. Iron chains are locked around her feet.

My heart stops. "Cadence?"

She looks up at my voice, but Chadwick ushers me past, toward another set of stairs, before I can see her face.

"Wait," I say, panicked.

"I have orders," he says, holding me back.

Blood beats in my ears, rising to a scream. No. After all that I've done, all I will still do, they cannot keep my sister from me, not when she's right there.

Chadwick hangs back to allow me to go first up another narrow flight of stairs. I feint a step forward before darting around him, bolting back for the door.

"Cadence!" I crash into the door frame and for one breathless moment, my sister's eyes lock on me, bright blue and free of any magic spells, before a man tackles me to the ground, dragging me outside. A second man darts forward and closes the door, standing in the threshold with his hand on the knob, his other hand hovering over the hilt of his undrawn sword. He eyes me in silent assessment before his gaze flickers higher, to the roofline.

Guards. I didn't even see them before. Over a dozen hidden in the shadows, their loaded crossbows aimed for me. A perceived threat.

Fear brines my tongue and I don't resist when the first guard pulls me to my feet. Chadwick gestures to the others and they lower their weapons, but I watch them warily, chilled by how quickly they fade back out of view.

"Why can't I see her?" I ask.

Chadwick takes my arm, more firmly than before. "She is a prisoner," he says. "I have no power to intercede."

"What was her crime?" I twist in his grip, watching the two guards at the door, desperate for another glimpse of Cadence.

Chadwick looks at me, pity splashed across his kind face. "She's your sister," he says simply.

The third floor is shorter than the one below, with only two doors. Jostling a key from his pocket, Chadwick swings open the first and I stumble inside, blood humming, barely noticing the bed or the window or the fireplace. The wooden floors creak as I cross to the window, my shaking reflection thrown across the city. Chadwick watches silently behind me, his hands folded in front of him.

"The water is warm," he says, and I vaguely notice a bathtub in front of the fire. "We've sent for a girl to attend you; I'll send her up as soon as she arrives."

I stare at my reflection, hugging the chill from my bones as I replay that stolen glimpse of Cadence again and again. How did Perrote even know about her?

Alistair.

I'll kill him, I think, and my savageness surprises me even as I welcome its heat through my veins. But my hate is chased with self-reproach: It's my fault for trusting my sister to a boy bred to show no mercy.

Chadwick reaches for the door but hesitates. "Will you be all right, Miss Locke?"

I close my eyes, leaning my forehead to the glass. Despite myself, hot tears roll down my cheeks. "Yes," I say, and it's a beautiful lie—the first of many I'll have to tell if I'm going to survive any future involving Bryn and her father.

Chadwick taps an uneven rhythm against the doorknob. "I'm sorry," he says at length.

I open my eyes and turn toward his words, but the door shuts behind him with a soft but solid click. A moment later, a key turns and footsteps recede.

Locked in, alone.

Only North fills every corner of the room, from the jars of rocks to the spine-cracked books, to the indelible smell of chimney smoke that clings to the walls. Tidy stacks of old lessons fill a desk; more rocks line the windowsill. Reaching into my pocket, I find the rock he gave me earlier, the one that would earn me Chadwick's trust. Rough in places, worn smooth in others, the hole through the center is big enough for my little finger to slide through.

With a growl, I hurl the rock across the room where it clatters beneath the bathtub. I don't want a rock; I want a spell above my heart to protect it from feeling like this, like it's held together by weak stitches and hanging threads.

An instant later, I'm on my hands and knees, retrieving the rock. I *do* have a spell above my heart, and while North removed the iron from beneath my skin, the memory of it remains.

I have to be stronger than this.

The sun is falling by the time a girl knocks and announces herself as Gretik, a dress carried over one arm to replace the filthy one I'd shrugged off before my bath. She's all patience as I fumble through the uneasy act of being dressed by someone else. After bandaging the worst of my wounds, she clicks her tongue against her teeth and smiles like nothing's wrong. "I'll bring you your dinner," she says, and bows her way out the door.

She locks it behind her.

I force myself to eat the heavy stew she returns with, but it sits like lead in my stomach. As she clears away the tray, I finally ask, "Where's North?"

"Prince Corbin retired an hour ago," she says, and I don't miss the light tone she uses to correct my address. "Did you need anything else?"

I shake my head and ignore the ache in my chest, reminding me that this was the choice I made. Even so, I didn't realize how much I craved an acknowledgment from him until I didn't get one.

Gretik returns in the morning, after the bell tower calls the monks to prayer. She escorts me downstairs and I follow like a leashed dog, uncomfortable with so much ceremony. She curtsies and nods me into the dining hall where a single meal has been laid out in a room full of heavy tables and polished bench seats that smell like wax.

I wait for her to disappear down the hall before I enter the room. A figure glances up immediately and I flush, mumbling apologies as I turn to go.

"Faris," a voice says, full of relief.

My heart stops as Alistair Pembrough crushes a cigarette out on the floor. He exhales a cloud of smoke and moves toward me.

The shock of seeing him gives way to rage. I meet him halfway, grabbing him by the front of his coat and slamming him back against a table. It screeches out of alignment beneath our weight. "You were supposed to be watching her! *Protecting* her!"

"I said I would keep her safe and I did," he says hotly, grabbing my wrists. "She's alive and she's here, and that's what matters for now."

"But?" My voice wavers in challenge.

"But you're on dangerous ground," he says. "Brindaigel is in a panic. Perrote opened a bridge across the gorge eight days ago and it's remained there ever since. More than that, he and his men haven't flown to the skies in search of the missing princess. They *walked* into Avinea. And when they return, not one of them will bear any sign of the infection they said could not be avoided. You made them human and you made them liars, and if you think Perrote will forgive you for that, you had better open your eyes and watch your back."

My gaze falls to his exposed scars. *Control*, I think, and release him, dragging my hands through my hair before they curl around my neck.

Alistair sighs, rubbing his mouth with his hand before shrugging helplessly. "What was I supposed to do?" he asks. "Perrote sends his councilmen after you and one of them ends up dead. He sends his shadow crows and none of them return. You were a liability and he was getting desperate. Why else do you think he's here?" He leans closer, lowering his voice to a pointed whisper. "Because if someone was going to uncover his secret, he was going to profit from it too. Cadence was his bartering chip."

All the anger and frustration of the last week burns through my veins, igniting the poison that begins to itch with hunger and a desire to hurt him. "You knew he wasn't a king?"

Alistair fumbles through his coat for his cigarette case. "I've known since the day my father branded me with a thief's coat of arms, injected me with a loyalty spell binding me to a stolen crown, and told me about a promise he made years ago that the daughter of the woman he loved would make it to Avinea so his son could be free. So they both would be free." He meets my eyes, expression searching, begging me to understand.

Pay attention, Faris.

Alistair didn't choose me to carry this magic to New Prevast out of guilt like Bryn suggested, but because that was my mother's plan all along. He had the stolen magic and I had the spell to find Merlock. Together, we could have destroyed Brindaigel. She didn't die because she was sloppy and got caught. She died sacrificing herself to hide what she'd done so we could be free.

I *am* my mother's daughter, I realize with a chill. Even then, she must have known I had an insatiable heart that would always crave more. Only she expected Alistair would fill that hunger.

My fingers dig into the back of my neck and I watch Alistair fumble through his case before sliding a cigarette between his lips. "Why didn't you just tell me the truth?" I ask.

He swipes the cigarette back out of his mouth. "Would you have believed me?"

I stare at him, and Alistair looks away. "I needed an army to tear that castle down, Faris, and I needed to survive that battle. Bryn doesn't want me but I knew she wouldn't kill me when she came back. I'm too valuable as a pet. But if I told you he wasn't a king and you came back with an army, alone . . ."

I swore to kill him four months ago. Would I have spared his life if he became one of Perrote's mindless warriors defending the castle? Or would I see it as justice overdue?

We both know the answer to that.

"So now she's a queen," I say instead. "I'm still a slave, my sister is a hostage, but at least you'll be free."

"Faris—"

"No! I am not your weapon anymore!" I turn away from him, rocking my head back to the wooden arches that frame the plastered ceiling. "Did you tell him about Cadence? Did you make a deal with him!?"

"No." Alistair hesitates. "Your father did. Perrote offered clemency to anyone with information about who could have kidnapped his daughter. Your father knew you were gone, he knew you were angry, and he knew—when he heard about the tunnels, Faris—he knew it was you. He thought he could save Cadence by turning you in."

My heart cracks. My poor father, too drunk—too sad—to know better than to trust Perrote to show mercy. "And?"

Alistair slides his hands in his pockets and stares toward the bank of windows on the far wall. A lock of hair falls over his eye. "And I promise you he didn't suffer," he says, voice thick.

"Oh, but I will," I whisper.

Folding an arm across my stomach, I sink onto the bench seat behind me. Alistair tentatively sits down beside me. "I'm sorry," he says.

I twist away from his sympathy. "Why are you here?"

He tries to light his cigarette but the match dances out of reach and he has to chase it with his other hand. "I came for my bride," he says with a snort of derision, finally succeeding. He tosses the match aside and takes a slow drag. "Who apparently came for a prince. Brindaigel wasn't big enough for her anymore."

"I'm so sorry for your loss," I say flatly.

"Me too." He swallows hard. "Perrote has no reason to humor me and my experiments anymore. I'll be sent back to Brindaigel,

my betrothal dissolved, and resume my court-appointed duties."
The shaking returns, and he barks out a self-deprecatory laugh,
rubbing his forehead with his thumb. "Gods Above, Faris, this is
not how I expected it to happen."

"What was supposed to happen?"

He glances over, expression troubled. "I don't know," he says.

Another mystery gifted by my mother. She left us magic instead
of directions, clues instead of answers. My only hope now is that
her contact still lives in New Prevast and knows more than I do.

Shaking my head, I rub at my forearm, digging at the buried
itch I can't reach. The poison in my blood hums against my skin,
smoky blue and silver, darker than usual, fed by my anger.

"So it's true." Alistair shifts, reaching for my arm. "You're
infected."

I pull away. "Don't touch me."

Rolling his eyes, he rummages through his coat pocket and
brandishes a chalk-colored rock, webbed with holes. He cradles it
between his thumb and fingers. "Do you know what this is?"

"Pumice," I say. "Hardened lava."

"It's a filter," he says, rolling it into his palm. "The entire city's
water supply runs through these rocks before it reaches the cis-
terns. It's cleaner than the water we drink in Brindaigel and we
drink straight from the mountain itself."

"So?"

"So ask me to stay," he says. "Give me a reason to, Faris Locke,
and maybe I can give you a reason to believe that this"—he
touches my arm with the edge of the pumice—"isn't a permanent
parlor trick to show at parties."

Hope is cruel and yet, it rises anyway: Who better than Bryn's mad scientist to perform a miracle? "Are you saying you can clean blood? You can remove the infection? Without a transfusion?"

Alistair arches his eyebrows and reclines against the table with an arrogant smirk that doesn't quite reach his eyes.

I stare at him. "Blood is not water."

"And magic is not science," he says, "and yet a very handsome boy with no magical ability was able to put enough magic inside you to make a not very handsome prince take notice."

"How can I possibly trust you after this?"

"Because Cadence likes me," he says, smirk thinning before disappearing. "We became friends on the ride out of Brindaigel. She's a good girl, Faris."

And Alistair is just the type of boy Cadence would attach herself to: handsome and well read, and with the kind of power she's too innocent to fear. A poor replacement for Thaelan and yet, I can't discount his cleverness or his desire to survive.

Because I recognize the shaking hands, the faltering confidence. He doesn't want to go back to Brindaigel any more than I do. Only this time, Bryn chose *me* and he's the one with something to lose.

Standing, I lean over him, palms braced to the table on either side of his shoulders. "Don't ever threaten me or my sister again," I say softly, savoring the way he shifts beneath my tone. "You help me and I'll help you, or I will leave you behind to rot in that dungeon. Do you understand?"

His arrogance dissipates, exposing the raw desperation underneath. Even so, Alistair cocks his head and forces a smile that frays at the edges. "Is that a promise?"

A man clears his throat and I pull back with a blast of guilt and adrenaline. Chadwick stands in the doorway, eyebrows raised with unspoken judgment of the scene he's interrupted. "His majesty wishes to speak with you," he says to me.

Alistair raises an eyebrow, confidence restored as he takes another drag of his cigarette, but I feel flustered, smoothing my bodice as I hurry for the door.

"I want a room with a window," Alistair calls as I turn into the hall.

I don't look back.

Chadwick leads me outside, across the courtyard and down a set of stairs into a stone cellar full of enormous barrel casks and old brewery equipment. A long table stretches the length of the room and North sits on top of it, feet dangling, hands loose between his knees. He glances up when I enter, eyes sliding down to the dress I wear before they return to my face. Wordlessly, he shoves himself to his feet.

Chadwick bows his departure and leaves.

I hover in the arched doorway as North rubs a hand through his hair. "I've sent for a spellcaster to help us with your mother's spell," he says. "She'll be able to put protective wards on you as well, to keep the infection at bay."

"Thank you."

"If it starts to hurt," he says, "if you start to feel like it's spread-ing . . ."

"I'll tell her," I say.

He nods, looking away, fingers splayed across the edge of the table. "You saw your sister."

"Only for a moment," I say, with a surge of anger. "Not nearly long enough. Your men seemed to think I was a threat."

"I'm sorry," he says, but he doesn't disagree.

I am a threat, at least to him.

North rubs his mouth. "I have a choice," he says, and begins to pace a short line along the length of the table. "I can eradicate the plague and save Avinea."

"At what cost?"

"An alliance," he says bitterly. "I marry Miss Dossel and recognize Brindaigel as a sovereign nation in the heart of my own. Borders are to be drawn, Perrote's to be given the executive power of a king, a seat on my council, and all the legal rights granted therein. And when our bloodlines are joined, it will start a new lineage of magic." He sighs. "One with roots in both families, inheritable by either. We both become legitimized and my children will be raised as experts in the art of assassinating family members who stand in the way of their crowns."

The room sways around me. "And the alternative?"

"I need magic," North says helplessly as he returns toward me, his boots scuffling across the stone. "Withholding it is an act of war, but Perrote won't fight here. Which means a battle in the mountains, in unfamiliar territory, with no army and no money against a man with magic, an amplifier, and a fortress built to withstand attack. Meanwhile," he continues darkly, turning around again, "Baedan now has my blood and a plan to kill Merlock. A war with Brindaigel would guarantee she finds him before I do." Sighing, he pounds the table in frustration before leaning against it, both hands laid flat. "What am I fighting Perrote for if Avinea is to fall anyway?"

The silence squeezes against the walls and the rafters overhead.

"They want an immediate wedding," North says at last. "Perrote will withhold all magic until it's legal and sent to every country with an arm in the Havascent Sea to be recognized." Shoving away from the table, North stalks forward, stopping just out of reach. "Tell me what to do."

"Can you remove this spell?" I demonstrate my wrist.

His expression is answer enough. Of course he can't. Bryn will continue to use me to safeguard her own life and to hurt him in any way she can, even after she has a crown and a kingdom and a child to teach all the ways she knows how to hurt.

"Perrote has agreed to grant your sister's freedom as a wedding present," he says. "But until then . . ." His eyes meet mine. "I'm sorry."

I reach for the table, desperate for balance. There's a long time between now and an immediate wedding, with Bryn and her father holding Cadence in their hands.

North edges closer, gently lifting my chin. "Faris."

I shake my head, pulling away from him. "You'll marry Bryn," I say. "You'll get the magic you need, the weapon you want, and you'll share a corner of Avinea with another king. You don't need me to tell you that. And when you're strong enough, you'll attack and take back what's yours."

"I don't—"

I cut him off, pressing my hand to his chest, feeling the heat of his skin, the soft shiver of the spell beneath it, and then, even deeper, the rhythm of his heart. "This is what will save Avinea," I say. "*You* will. Heal this heart however you can and then guard it with everything you have because she will know whenever it bleeds. She will know the ways to make that poison spread through you until you can't fight it back. She will hurt you in every way possible and I . . . I can't be one of those possibilities."

"I can't marry her," he says softly.

"You have to," I say. "It would be selfish to sacrifice the whole to save the few."

He ducks his head. "Don't say that."

"You don't have to love her," I say. "You just have to marry her." My voice breaks and I wait before continuing. "The skill is in cheating."

North reaches for me but I step back. "The young man who rode in with Perrote," I say.

"Pembrough."

"Yes. Ask him to stay."

North's expression hardens. "Is that your request?"

"Make it yours," I say. "He's worth your time and whatever expense he'll claim he needs."

"Then it's done."

"Thank you." I turn to go, but North intercepts me, curling his little finger through mine. Despite myself, I rest my hand against his chest again, drawn back to his heartbeat. He's dressed in black, as always, and I love that, that Northerly peculiarity of his. And I love this, his breath warm on my cheek and the way he looks at me as if I'm someone worth risking a kingdom for.

"Faris," he says. "I need you."

But I hate this, the truth and how it always hurts.

"You saved my life," I say, "and I can never repay you for that, or for honoring your promises to me and my sister. And I will do whatever I can to help Prince Corbin find his father and save Avinea. And as my king," I continue, my voice wavering, "you owe me nothing for that loyalty. But as my friend—as North—I ask you to remember that not all hearts are protected by magic."

Dropping my hands, I force myself to back away, to put space between us. "You don't need me," I say. "Maybe you want me, but there's a difference, North, and it's the difference between winning a war for Avinea or losing a battle we fight alone. Because we cannot fight it together. Not while Bryn has any power over either of us."

He shakes his head, emphatic, before moving closer again, too close. Why is he doing this when it's cruel to us both? "Wanting is a weakness. It implies a deficit, a desire that is entirely emotional. I want to touch you, for example. I want to kiss you, and to hold you as long as I can even if it hurts." His hands slide through my hair as he cradles my face and kisses my forehead. "But when you need something, it's a requirement for survival. I need air to breathe and food to eat and the occasional hour of sleep. I need magic and I need to kill my father to save Avinea. And, Faris," he says, forehead pressed to mine, "I need you."

"North—"

"This is not a choice I make in haste," he says tightly. "I know the risks, I know the consequences. But I see now how imbalanced I've been, like shadow without light, or faith without hope." Closing his eyes, he whispers against my lips, "Having a heart is not a weakness, Faris. It can only make me stronger. The spell will hold until we find my father, and then . . ."

And then. It is tantalizing in its possibilities.

But I've heard this argument before, the night Thaelan died, when I didn't insist on one more day—one more day that would have saved his life.

I don't resist as North kisses me again, but when I hear the echo of his heart joining mine, I know I must, before the damage is irreparable. I have to be my own iron now. No curses, no wishes, no spells to make it easier.

I wish—

No. I break away from his lips, from the hunger in my blood awakening to the power in his. Avinea needs its king more than I need to feel his skin against mine. I am not the seedling he needs to save this kingdom and I cannot allow this feeling to grow. Don't be selfish, I tell myself, don't be cruel.

Don't be human.

I force myself to meet his eyes. "But I don't need you," I say, and it's almost a relief.

I'm stronger than I thought.

I walk out of the cellar, refusing to look back. I can't, because I *am* human, and I'm weak, and I want him, every last inch of him, and if I look back now, I'll never let go.

By the time I reach the courtyard, I'm running, crashing onto a stone bench half hidden behind a curtain of flowers. North's kisses have drawn out lines of poison beneath my skin and I rub at them, hating them, hating myself because even now the temptation to return overwhelms me. I can't do this, I think; I want more, even if it kills me—even if it kills Avinea.

But slowly, the threads of desire unwind and the infection doesn't spread any further, proving that I *can* do this.

I have no choice.

The sun rises overhead, painting the pale stones of the monastery in shades of gold and shadowed reds. A deeper red catches my eye, made of satin, not of sunlight. Bryn stands on the open second-story promenade, her hands extended across the balustrade. Her eyes meet mine as she arches an eyebrow, a coy, knowing smile carved across her face, as if she overheard every word in the cellar.

I stare up at her, still rubbing my arm. North once told me the difference between being infected and turning hellborne was as simple as a choice, a decision whether you saved your soul through sacrifice, or you let it turn sour with selfishness and greed. The infection might be in me but the poison is all inside her. And Avinea will never be safe until every last line of poison is eradicated.

Bryn shifts, breaking into a smile as two of her father's men approach, a third figure huddled in between them. Blond hair, blue eyes, and a wariness that never existed before.

Cadence.

Fury ignites in my veins as Bryn greets my sister and pulls her close, ducking down to whisper something in her ear. Cadence flinches at her proximity, and I fight the animal instinct that rises up, demanding blood. Bryn can have me, but my sister is mine.

Standing, I turn my back on Bryn's smirk and head into the monastery in search of Captain Chadwick. Avinea is still out there, I tell myself, and I promised Cadence I would find it. My palms are not on the floor yet, and I am far from defeated.

This fight is just beginning.

Acknowledgments

This journey began four years ago, with Quinlan Lee and the phone call that changed my life. Your unwavering enthusiasm always kept me steady, even when it hurt. I'm so grateful for the brief time we worked together. Josh Adams, thank you for stepping in and taking the helm—and for being an unruffled calm in my constant tempest of worries. Calling myself a member of the Adams Literary family still feels surreal.

It is a truth universally acknowledged that a debut author in possession of a manuscript must be in want of an editor. Annie Nybo, you are magic. Faris grew fiercer under your guidance; Avinea more deadly. You knew what questions to ask and what pop culture references to make, and I'm indebted to you for making such a scary-strange process into an absolute dream.

Thank you to Sonia Chaghatzbanian for a beautiful cover that made me cry, and to the entire team at Margaret K. McElderry

Books for their work behind the scenes. Faris might not know where home is, but I have never doubted that it was here with you.

I'm fortunate that my family has never asked if, but only ever when, this day would come. Y'all are too many to name, but I love each one of you. Mom and Dad, while it might not say Bowman on the cover, you know it's in my blood.

Catherine Nieto, Alex Taranta, and Nicole Taranta had to deal with me daily while on deadline, and to them I say: I'm sorry. But also, I'm so grateful you were there to celebrate every milestone.

Audrey Rawlings has handled hundreds of my e-mails, ranging from the panicked to the pleased, with all the patience of a saint. If you're ever magically enslaved by a tyrant king, big sis, you bet your ass I'm coming to save you.

I owe a debt to my critique partner, J. K. Smejkal, who loved Pem before anyone else, and who made this book better, period. And thank you to the ladies of Kick-Butt Kidlit, and to the friends I've made through The Swanky '17s. It's a comfort to know you're not the first, the last, or even the only one to stress out every step of the way.

Finally, this story would be incomplete without its love interest. Eugene Mathew Taranta the II, I adore you. Thank you for all those evening walks, long talks, and color-coded lists written on your marker board. I would be imbalanced without you.

TURN THE PAGE FOR A SNEAK PEEK
AT THE EXCITING CONCLUSION TO FARIS'S STORY,

SPLENDOR AND SPARK

A HUNDRED YEARS AGO THE PALACE OF NEW PREVAST WAS BUILT FOR pleasure: four courtyards, an expansive garden with a hedge maze, two ballrooms, a swimming pool, and more than three hundred windows. It once hosted the royal family, a hundred servants, and a revolving guest list for three months out of every twelve. It was a summer home away from the bustle of the capital. An escape.

Now it's a prison.

A dozen servants, entire halls of empty rooms, shelves to the ceiling with no books or trinkets to fill them, peeling paint and saltwater decay on the wood and metal fixtures.

And a bastard prince who resents every inch of his opulent captivity.

It's suffocating, the way silence and anger ooze through the hallways and fill the ornate cornices of the plastered ceilings. The way they turn every meal into an abrasive symphony of silverware against porcelain, the grating click of teeth against crystal, and the low rumbling interruption of a cleared throat. At least back in the Brim, you could hear music in the dark when you couldn't sleep; you heard some proof that life existed, at least for somebody else.

In the palace all I hear is the ghostly whisper of the sea crashing against the rocks at the mouth of the harbor, haunting and full of loneliness.

Which is why almost every night, I escape to the roof, where I can see the stars and New Prevast and be reassured that someone somewhere is still breathing. Tonight my company is the flickering lights that come from the taverns crowded along the span of the Bridge of Ander, which connects the palace grounds to the city proper across the harbor.

In daylight the wilting buildings are shuttered up tight, while waterbirds sun themselves on the pilings below. At night vice opens its doors for a booming business, and the bridge is flooded with thieves and beggars and drunks. Any waterbirds still roosting become target practice for bottles that shatter against the rocks below. Pieces of colored glass eventually wash up on the black sand beach with the tide, worn smooth by the water. Terrible for holding magic or casting spells, but beautiful for collecting and lining the narrow windowsill of my bedroom on the second floor.

I hug my knees to my chest, balancing my chin on top, staring until my vision blurs and New Prevast loses its shape, becoming a generic smear of light and dark. The chill of the wind masks the briny scent of the sea, and for an instant I could be anywhere: the shallows of the Brim, the open fields of Avinea, the abandoned wagon of a traveling magician trying to save the world.

But then the window shutters open behind me and I hear the sigh that anchors me here.

"Locke," Captain Chadwick says, frustration warring with relief. I wonder how long he's been looking for me, or if I've become predictable. "You promised."

My fingers dig into the soft folds of my skirt. "I lied."

Another sigh, and I know the expression that accompanies it, the disappointment. A sliver of guilt worms through the chill, and I close my eyes. Poor Chadwick. As the captain of the Guard, his talents far exceed the role of unwilling babysitter, and yet, as the captain of the Guard, he follows orders from his prince.

"His majesty explicitly forbade you from the roof," Chadwick says, reciting the memorized spiel. "The tiles are slick—"

"And the courtyard is unforgiving of bodies and bones," I finish sourly, because it still hurts that his majesty told Chadwick to tell me, as if I were a servant unworthy of direct address. I open my eyes, biting the inside of my cheek, numb fingers circling the spell around my wrist.

I *am* a servant, I tell myself as I stare across the placid harbor, and his majesty hasn't spoken to me in weeks.

A third sigh, softer than those before it. "Faris, please," Chadwick says. "Not tonight."

Tears sting my eyes at the unexpected familiarity, and I fight them back with a savage fury. *Not tonight*, I repeat, but it's an impossible request. Tonight of all nights, promises have been broken.

Pulling himself out the window, Chadwick edges closer and sinks down beside me, adjusting the hilt of his sword out of the way. He's dressed in the ceremonial black and silver of Avinea: tunic, vest, and coat; too many layers for practicality but just enough for formality. He looks nice with his sandy hair pulled back and his beard trimmed to a mere shadow across his chin. He looks solid.

"The ceremony is over," he says softly. "It's done."

"And I survived," I say.

"As expected." He shifts his weight and cradles his hands between his knees. Glancing over, he says, "You did the right thing, Locke."

"Come on, Captain," I whisper with a forced, wavering smile, fighting around the dull ache in my chest. "Grant me a moment of self-pity."

He gives me a withering look, and I turn away, toward the glittering sea. I know what he's thinking and I know that he's right: I've had three weeks to wallow in my decision, three weeks to acclimate myself to its conclusion. When I walked away from the Prince of Avinea, I truly believed my feelings for him would fade, that our brief relationship had been nothing more than two lonely people clinging to each other in a moment of panic. He needed to focus on saving his kingdom; I needed to focus on saving my sister.

But for a moment we had needed each other.

I told Chadwick nothing of what had happened that morning in the monastery cellar when North offered me his heart and I refused it, yet Chadwick knows every detail anyway. There can be no secrets between a prince and his captain, and Chadwick knows everything that has happened from the moment I met North to the moment I turned my back on him.

I don't regret my decision. I can't afford to. But it still hurts sometimes, like a scab I keep picking off before it can heal.

Especially tonight, when I know Bryn—North's *wife*, I force myself to acknowledge—is being escorted to his bedroom in the eastern wing of the palace, where they will be supervised by members of the council. North's infected blood and Bryn's amplification ability prevent them from physically consummating the marriage, but sharing a bed and binding themselves through blood magic will suffice to prove the point until a true heir can be produced. Proclamations are already written, waiting to be sent to the few remaining strongholds left untouched by the Burn, and even beyond, to the nearest countries and potential allies scattered across the Havascent Sea. The Prince of Avinea has taken a bride and now has the means of finding Merlock, his missing father. Please send money and, if possible, men. While they won't arrive in time to help find Merlock, they'll be needed to clean up the mess he's made.

After twenty years of dying, Avinea is ready to live again.

I savor the way my envy burns through my blood at the thought of Bryn in North's bed, fueled by the traces of dead magic that still linger in my veins from an infection that nearly killed me. Allowing my vices such free reign is a dangerous, intoxicating game, and the court magician, Sofreya, will have my head for it when she sees I've been testing the limits of her protection spells again. Nestled in the crooks of my arms, the spells keep the infection pinned in place, away from my heart. But magic only runs skin deep; if I really wanted to succumb to my vices, the poison could easily be coaxed past the spells.

"So that's it, then," I say, and the ache in my chest sharpens, cutting the last threads of impossible hope I had buried inside me.

Chadwick squints toward the city. "*Wife* is only a title. No different from *prince* or *captain* or *king*." Looking at me, he says, "Respect the office, Locke. But don't assign it any more sentimentality than it warrants."

I bite back a snort of derision. It's more than a title; it's a guarantee that Bryn will always have power over North. Over me. And power to keep us apart.

"At least now we can leave," I say, my voice thick. Now that the wedding is official, Perrote, Bryn's father, will make good his promise to deliver clean magic to the palace, and North will be free to search the Burn for his father. Killing him is the only way North can inherit control of his dying country and its magic—thereby stopping the Burn at last.

"Locke."

I shake my head, petulant as a child, and Chadwick takes my chin in hand, forcing my face toward his. I avoid his eyes, staring instead at the thick scar on his chin, where the facial hair doesn't grow. He earned it years ago, he told me, playing swords with North when they were both boys being raised at the Saint Ergoet's Monastery. It was the first—and only, Chadwick was always quick to add—time North got the better of him in a fight.

"She's going to destroy him," I say, daring him to contradict me.

"No." Chadwick shakes his head, lips flat. "You and I will never let that happen. But if I have to defend him alone, I will do it."

"I don't—"

"You will be left behind if your only interest is in being a liability. Do you understand me? You have had two weeks' worth of training at best, when you actually put in the effort. You're not exactly an asset to the expedition."